NICOLA CORNICK

"A rising star of the Regency arena."
—*Publishers Weekly*

"Nicola Cornick creates a glittering, sensual world of
historical romance that I never want to leave."
—Anna Campbell, author of *Untouched*

"A wonderfully original, sinfully amusing
and sexy Regency historical by the
always entertaining Cornick."
—*Booklist* on *The Confessions of a Duchess*

"Fast-paced, enchanting and wildly romantic!"
—*SingleTitles.com* on *The Scandals of an Innocent*

"Witty banter, lively action and sizzling passion."
—*Library Journal* on *The Undoing of a Lady*

"RITA® Award–nominated Cornick deftly steeps
her latest intriguingly complex Regency historical
in a beguiling blend of danger and desire."
—*Booklist* on *Unmasked*

"Cornick masterfully blends misconceptions,
vengeance, powerful emotions and the realization of
great love into a touching story."
—*RT Book Reviews*, 4 ½ stars, on *Deceived*

Don't miss other titles in the
Scandalous Women of the Ton series, available now!

Desired
Notorious
Mistress By Midnight
Whisper of Scandal
One Wicked Sin

**Also available from
Nicola Cornick
and Harlequin HQN**

Deceived
Christmas Keepsakes
"A Season for Suitors"
Lord of Scandal
Unmasked
The Confessions of a Duchess
The Scandals of an Innocent
The Undoing of a Lady

Browse www.Harlequin.com
for Nicola's full backlist.

NICOLA CORNICK

Forbidden

HARLEQUIN®
entertain, enrich, inspire™

Recycling programs
for this product may
not exist in your area.

4967 4897
9/12

ISBN-13: 978-0-373-77667-2

FORBIDDEN

Copyright © 2012 by Nicola Cornick

All rights reserved. Except for use in any review, the reproduction or
utilization of this work in whole or in part in any form by any electronic,
mechanical or other means, now known or hereafter invented, including
xerography, photocopying and recording, or in any information storage
or retrieval system, is forbidden without the written permission of the
publisher, Harlequin HQN, 225 Duncan Mill Road, Don Mills, Ontario
M3B 3K9, Canada.

This is a work of fiction. Names, characters, places and incidents are
either the product of the author's imagination or are used fictitiously,
and any resemblance to actual persons, living or dead, business
establishments, events or locales is entirely coincidental.

This edition published by arrangement with Harlequin Books S.A.

For questions and comments about the quality of this book,
please contact us at CustomerService@Harlequin.com.

® and TM are trademarks of Harlequin Enterprises Limited or its
corporate affiliates. Trademarks indicated with ® are registered in the
United States Patent and Trademark Office, the Canadian Trade Marks
Office and in other countries.

www.Harlequin.com

Printed in U.S.A.

To Bellbridge Montagu, Monty,
the most loyal animal companion and best friend
a writer could have, with love and happy memories.

Dear Reader,

Welcome to *Forbidden,* the sixth and final book in the Scandalous Women of the Ton series! *Forbidden* is a rags-to-riches story featuring Margery Mallon, maidservant to so many of the previous scandalous women.

When Margery discovers that she is heiress to the richest earldom in England, she is swept from her drab existence into a world of unimaginable luxury with beautiful clothes, glittering jewels and the most handsome men in the country begging to marry her. But the one man she wants is Henry, Lord Wardeaux, the man whose inheritance she has stolen and whom she can never trust. Margery and Henry's passionate love story unfurls against a backdrop of elegant country houses and fashionable Ton balls. But can the Cinderella from the backstreets of London ever find true happiness? Featuring all the previous characters from the Scandalous Women series, *Forbidden* is a fairy tale I had such great pleasure in writing and I hope you enjoy it, too!

Best wishes,

Nicola

Forbidden

Author's Note

In the Peerage of Great Britain, there are a dozen titles that can be inherited in the female as well as the male line. The earldom that Margery will inherit is one of these.

Tarot cards are used to foretell the future and the fortunes of the characters in *Forbidden*. The Tarot has been used for hundreds of years to predict the future.

PROLOGUE

The Wheel of Fortune: Fate turns its wheel
London, April 1817

THE MAN SITTING BEFORE HIM had a certain reputation.

Ruthless. Intelligent. Controlled. *Dangerous.*

Mr. Churchward knew a little of his history. Baron Henry Wardeaux had been a soldier. The way he spoke still bore the trace of command, clipped and direct. He had fought with Wellesley in the Peninsular War where he had been known as The Engineer for his skill in military fortifications. He had done other work, too, spoken of in whispers, secret work behind enemy lines. Mr. Churchward was a lawyer, a man given to dealing in facts and figures, but he believed the stories told of Henry Wardeaux.

"So, Mr. Churchward," Wardeaux said, sitting back in the high-backed armchair and crossing one elegantly booted leg over the other. "Have you discovered proof that Miss Mallon is Lord Templemore's granddaughter?"

No pleasantries about the weather, which had been mild and wet of late. No enquiries into Mr. Churchward's health, which was good but for a few twinges of gout. Lord Wardeaux never wasted words.

Mr. Churchward shuffled his papers a little nervously. He cleared his throat. "We have found no definite proof, as yet, my lord," he admitted. "It has only been two days," he said, trying not to sound defensive.

Two days since a man had come to Mr. Churchward with information that the Earl of Templemore's granddaughter, who had been missing for twenty years, was alive and well, and working as a lady's maid in London. Two days of frantic activity to try to discover if the information could possibly be correct.

It had been astonishing news, news that had revived the health and hopes of the old earl. He had sent his godson and heir, Henry Wardeaux, to London immediately. If the report was true, Henry Wardeaux would no longer be the heir. Templemore was one of only a handful of titles in the country that could descend through the female line.

Churchward wondered how Lord Wardeaux would feel about losing the huge Templemore inheritance. He would never know. Henry Wardeaux would never reveal his emotions on that or any other subject.

"If you have not yet found proof, what have you found?" Wardeaux asked.

Mr. Churchward gave a sharp sigh. "We have discovered a great deal about Miss Mallon's adoptive family, my lord. None of it is good."

Wardeaux's firm lips almost twitched into a smile. "Indeed?"

"Her elder brother owns a business buying and selling secondhand items. It is a cover for the sale of stolen goods," Churchward said. "Her middle brother works in a tavern and her youngest brother..." The lawyer shook his head sadly. "There is no criminal activity he has not dabbled in. Highway robbery, fraud, larceny..."

"Why is he not locked up?"

"Because he is good at getting away with it," Mr. Churchward said.

This time, Henry Wardeaux did laugh. "And from this den of thieves comes Lord Templemore's granddaughter and heiress," he said.

"Perhaps," Mr. Churchward admitted. The circumstantial evidence that Margery Mallon was really Lady Marguerite Saint-Pierre was very strong, but he disliked circumstantial evidence. It was irregular, lacking firm verification. He wanted facts, witnesses, written testimony, not the faded miniature portrait and the garnet brooch that his informant had provided.

He fidgeted with the quill pen that lay on his desk. Never, in his long and distinguished career serving the nobility, had he been involved in such a case as this. When the earl's daughter had been murdered twenty years before and her four-year-old child stolen, no one had ever expected to see little Marguerite again. No one, neither Bow Street nor the private investigators the earl had hired, had been able to trace her. The earl had mourned for years.

Wardeaux shifted slightly in his chair. "If you cannot prove one way or the other whether Miss Mallon is Lord Templemore's granddaughter, Mr. Churchward, I shall have to do so myself."

"If you gave me more time, my lord—" Churchward began, but Wardeaux lifted one hand in so authoritative a gesture that he fell silent.

"We don't have time," Wardeaux said. There was an edge of steel beneath the quiet words. "The earl is anxious to be reunited with his granddaughter."

Mr. Churchward understood the urgency. The earl

was dying. Even so, he hesitated. He knew Margery Mallon, and in turning over the case to Henry Wardeaux he felt as though he was throwing her to the wolves.

"My lord…" he said.

Wardeaux waited. Churchward sensed his impatience. He was a hard man, a cold man whose life had driven all gentleness out of him.

"The girl has no notion of her parentage," he warned. "According to my enquiries she is quite…" He groped to find the appropriate word. "Innocent."

Wardeaux looked at him. Mr. Churchward found it disconcerting. The darkness in his eyes suggested he had long ago forgotten what true innocence was.

"I see," Wardeaux said slowly. He stood up. "Where do I find her?"

CHAPTER ONE

The Moon: Take care, for all is not as it seems

THE CLOCK ON ST. PAUL'S CHURCH was chiming the hour of ten as Margery went down the servants' steps into the basement of Mrs. Tong's brothel. She had not intended to arrive so late. Normally, she called at the Temple of Venus during the day when there were no customers and the courtesans were resting in their rooms in anticipation of a busy night ahead. Mrs. Tong's girls were generous, which was more than could be said for Mrs. Tong herself. They let Margery into their rooms and let her take away their discarded gowns, hats, gloves, anything they had finished with, in return for the fresh pastries and sweetmeats that Margery made herself.

Tonight Margery had brought candied pineapple and marzipan treats, sugar cakes and tiny Naples biscuits made of sponge and jam.

She made her way up the back stairs to the boudoir on the first floor. The room was a riot of color, silk cushions in purple and gold, red velvet curtains drawn against the night. The air was thick with chatter and the scent of perfume and candle wax. The girls were ready for their night's work but they almost swooned with greed and delight when they saw Margery with her marketing basket. They ran to fetch scarves and gloves to trade for the cakes.

"Girls, girls!" Mrs. Tong bustled in with the air of a circus trainer rounding up her performing animals. "The gentlemen are arriving!" The madam clapped her hands sharply. "Miss Kitty, Lord Carver is asking for you. Miss Martha, try to charm Lord Wilton this time. Miss Harriet—" she permitted a small, chilly smile to touch her lips "—the Duke of Tyne is very pleased with you."

Mrs. Tong tweaked a neckline lower here and a hemline upward there, then sent her girls down to the salon. They left in a chatter of conversation and a cloud of perfume, waving farewell to Margery, licking the sugar from their fingers. Margery watched them flutter down the main staircase like a flock of brightly colored birds of paradise. Accustomed to coming and going via the servants' passage, she had only once glimpsed the brothel's reception rooms; they had seemed lush and mysterious, a dangerous and different world, draped with bright silks and rich velvets, adorned with the prettiest and most skillful courtesans in London.

The room emptied, the chatter died away. Mrs. Tong's dark, beady gaze passed over Margery dismissively, as if she was a trader who knew the price of everything and could see nothing worth her time. Margery knew what Mrs. Tong was thinking. She had seen that thought reflected in people's eyes for years. She was small and plain, a mouse of a creature, all shades of brown. No one ever wasted a second look on her. She was used to it and she did not care. Good looks, Margery had often observed in her career in service, so often led to trouble.

"You'd best be on your way." Mrs. Tong popped one of Margery's marzipan treats into her mouth and blinked in ecstasy as the sugar melted on her tongue. "Make sure you take the back stairs," she added, sharply. The sugar had not sweetened her mood. "I don't want any of the customers thinking you work for me." She caught the corner of a golden gown that was trailing from Margery's basket. "Is that wasteful strumpet Kitty throwing this away? There's plenty more wear in it." She tugged and the gown fell to the floor in a waterfall of silk and lace. "Go on, be off with you. And leave those pineapple candies."

"No gown, no pineapple," Margery said firmly.

Mrs. Tong rolled her eyes. She bundled the gown up and threw it at Margery, who caught it neatly. Mrs. Tong pounced on the packet of candies.

"I'll take the marzipan, as well," she said, snatching it from the basket.

Margery's last glimpse of Mrs. Tong, as she closed the door and slipped out onto the landing, was of the bawd slumped in a wing chair, wig askew, legs akimbo, stuffing sweetmeats into her painted face as though she were a starving woman.

The landing was quiet and shadowed. The girls were downstairs now, plying their customers with wine and flirtatious conversation. No doubt Mrs. Tong would be joining them as soon as she had recovered from her excesses. Margery could hear snatches of music and laughter from the open doors of the salon. She trod softly toward the servants' stair, her steps muffled by the thick carpet. Even had she lost the golden gown through Mrs. Tong's miserliness, she would still have had a good haul tonight. There were three pairs

of gloves, two hats—one of which was squashed flat,
rolled upon in an amorous encounter, perhaps—two
more gowns, one ominously ripped, a beautiful silk
scarf that was a little stained with wine, and an assort-
ment of undergarments. These had surprised Margery;
the girls had told her they wore none.

Billy would be pleased with her. There was a great
deal of material that could be reused and clothing that
could be resold. Margery's brother and his wife ran a
shop in Giltspur Street that traded in secondhand clothes
and various other things. Margery never enquired too
closely into the nature of Billy's business interests—
she suspected he was a fence for stolen goods—but he
was fair to her and gave her a cut of the profits on the
materials she brought in.

Tomorrow, on her day off, she would deliver the
clothes and join Billy, Alison and their brood of infants
for tea. Tonight, though, she had to get back to Bedford
Square. Lady Grant was the kindest of employers but
even she might be taken aback to learn that her lady's
maid visited the London brothels on a regular basis.

Margery was halfway along the landing when her
foot caught in the Turkey carpet and she stumbled. The
basket lurched from her hand. The golden gown, which
she had quickly stuffed on top, unrolled like a balloon
canopy, tumbled through the gaps in the wrought-iron
banister and floated slowly and elegantly down to land
in a heap on the marble floor of the hall below.

Margery stood transfixed. She did not want to lose
the expensive silk gown, and she had traded three pack-
ets of sweetmeats for it.

On the other hand, she did not want to get caught
venturing into those parts of the brothel that were for-

bidden to her. Mrs. Tong was quite capable of refusing her entry ever again if she broke the rules, and then a very lucrative source of income would be lost to her.

Very slowly, very carefully, Margery started to tiptoe down the broad main stair, all senses alert to discovery. She was halfway down the steps when there was a sound from above and she froze, pressing back into a shadowy alcove among erotic statues of naked frolicking nymphs and shepherds. Something long and hard prodded her in the ribs—a phallus belonging to a marble satyr with a particularly dreamy expression on his face. There was no wonder he looked so happy. Margery looked critically at his physique. She had no firsthand knowledge of such matters but common sense told her that it simply could not be life-size. Perhaps all Mrs. Tong's statues were overendowed. Margery hoped they did not make the customers feel too inadequate.

Margery took another cautious step down, then another. Only three more to go and then she would be standing on the black-and-white-checkered floor of the brothel's hall and the beautiful golden gown would be within her grasp. She would grab it, stuff it back in the basket and scoot through the green baize door that led to the servants' quarters below stairs.

It was a simple plan and it almost worked.

She'd almost reached the entrance to the servants' quarters when she saw that someone was blocking her way. It was not Mrs. Tong, full of righteous indignation, but a man, lounging in the shadows. He did not move. Nor did he speak.

The candlelight skipped across his face, emphasizing some features, concealing others. Margery could see that he had black hair but not the precise shade. It

needed a cut. His face was thin and brown with high
cheekbones that reminded her of the carved stone statues she had seen in churches. He had a groove down
each cheek where he smiled and a groove in his chin,
as well. An odd shiver rippled through her, for this was
a man with a saint's face but with sinner's eyes, dark,
wicked eyes, hiding secrets. His brows were strong and
dark, too, and his mouth neither too thin nor too wide.
When he smiled, Margery realized that she was staring at him, staring in fact at his mouth, which looked
tantalizingly firm.

A bolt of heat streaked through her, fierce and unfamiliar, like the burn of spirits. It made her tingle and
set her head spinning. She took a step back, trying to
steady herself. It was very hot in the brothel. Perhaps
that was why she felt so faint all of a sudden, or perhaps
she was sickening for something, as her grandmother
would have said.

Still the gentleman did not move. He looked at Margery. She looked back at him. He *was* a gentleman; there
was no doubt about that. He was beautifully dressed,
something Margery, with her eye for style and color,
was quick to appreciate. His cravat was tied in a complicated arrangement she did not even recognize, and held
by a diamond pin. A jacket of elegant proportions fit his
shoulders without a wrinkle, in much the same way that
his tight buckskins clung to his thighs. A dandy, Margery thought. She had a servant's finely honed instinct
for recognizing various qualities in men and women.
This was a man of fashion, but she sensed that there
was more to him than that, something dark, deep, dangerous perhaps, in a way she could not begin to understand. She shivered.

He was blocking her escape.

"May I help you, sir?" she asked, wanting to bite back the words as soon as they were spoken, for she realized that they were perhaps not the most felicitous choice in a brothel.

Something flared in his eyes like the shimmer of heat from the candles. He straightened and took a step closer to her. Margery involuntarily tightened her grip on the handle of her basket. The wooden struts creaked.

"I am sure that you can." His voice was very mellow. He sounded amused. His mouth had curled into another slow smile. It crept into those dark eyes and lit them with warmth that made Margery's face burn. The strange awareness drummed more persistently in her blood.

This is a rake. Take care....

"I don't work here," she said quickly.

He paused. His gaze slid over her in a slow, thorough appraisal. Oh, yes, this was a rake. He knew how to look at a woman. There was an expression in his eyes that Margery had seen before. She had seen it in the eyes of many men looking upon the beautiful scandalous ladies for whom she had worked. She had also seen it in the gaze of people looking at her homemade sweetmeats. It was a mixture of greed and speculation and desire.

No one had ever looked at her in that way. No one had looked at *her* as though they wanted to eat her up, sample her, taste her and savor that pleasure. Such an idea was absurd, impossible.

Except that it was not, for this man was looking at her with acute interest and—she gulped, her throat suddenly dry—definite desire.

There had to be some mistake. He was confusing her with someone else.

"You don't work here," he repeated softly. He took a step closer to her, put out a hand and touched her cheek lightly with the back of his fingers. He wore no gloves and his hand was warm. Margery's skin felt even hotter now.

"I'm only visiting," she said in a rush.

His eyes widened. That smile, like sunshine on water, deepened. "There's nothing wrong in that," he said.

"No! I mean—" Margery floundered. "I'm not here to—" She stopped, wondering how on earth to describe the many and varied sexual practices that Mrs. Tong's customers indulged in and she did not.

"I'm a lady's maid," she blurted out.

"Of course, you wish to be incognito." The stranger shrugged. "Don't worry. Mrs. Tong caters to all tastes. Many ladies enjoy dressing up as maids. Marie Antoinette, for example." He smiled. "The marketing basket is a nice touch."

"I'm not dressing up," Margery said. She whispered it because he was now so close that she seemed to have lost the power of speech. "I really am a lady's maid."

The stranger laughed. "Then it is enterprising of you to supplement your income like this."

Oh, lord. Now he thought she worked part-time as a lightskirt. It was not unheard of. Margery knew plenty of maidservants who sold their favors. It was more lucrative than scrubbing floors. It was whispered about Town that Lord Osborne had once visited his favorite brothel only to be confronted with his housemaid, who was working as a courtesan on the side. Margery had never considered supplementing her income that way. When she had left Berkshire for London it had been with her grandmother's warnings ringing in her ears.

"London is a cesspool of vice," Granny Mallon had said. "You take my word for it—I've been there once. Keep yourself nice for your husband, my girl."

Margery had not cared much about finding a husband but she did care about keeping herself nice. It was important to her.

Besides, no one had asked her to give up her virtue anyway. Lady Grant's twin footmen were too pretty and too much in love with themselves to notice anyone else, and the rest of the male staff were too young, or too old or too unattractive. And they were her friends. Margery had not felt a single amorous flutter toward any of them.

She did have a servant follower, Humphrey, who was the second gardener at the house next door. He brought her flowers and moped about the kitchen inarticulately, staring at her and reddening if she spoke to him. Humphrey reminded Margery of a stray animal. She felt pity for him and a kind of impatient affection. He did not make her tremble, or cause her knees to weaken, as they were weakening now. He did not make the breath catch in her throat or her heart beat like a drum, as it was beating now.

But Margery had also been warned about handsome gentlemen, men who preyed on naive country girls. Granny Mallon had not been wrong. London was indeed a home to every vice beneath the sun, and Margery was fairly certain that this man was intimately acquainted with quite a number of them. There was something downright wicked about him.

"We are at cross-purposes," she said. She had to force the words out and her voice sounded husky and high-pitched at the same time. "I am not a lightskirt, nor am I here to sample any of the pleasures of the brothel—"

"Are you sure?"

Had he heard the note of wistfulness in her voice? Margery gulped.

"Not even—" his mouth was dangerously close to hers "—one kiss?"

"I'm a virgin!" Margery squeaked.

She saw him smile. "It takes more than one kiss to change that, sweetheart."

There was a long, long moment in which Margery could feel the warmth of his body and hear the thunder of her pulse in her ears. She did want to kiss him. Her stomach dropped with shock as she realized it. Fierce curiosity licked through her, laced with wickedness. She could barely believe how she was feeling. Things like this did not happen to her; she was far too sensible to want to kiss strange gentlemen in brothels. Or so she had thought. Yet something of the sumptuous, bawdy atmosphere seemed to have infected her like too much wine in the blood, and here she was with this man who was temptation personified....

His lips brushed hers, so light a touch she thought she had imagined it. He captured her gasp of shock in another kiss, hot and sweet, that took her completely by surprise. It was her first kiss. Occasionally, she had wondered what it might feel like and now, all of a sudden, she knew. It felt as though there were too many sensations for her to grasp. She was aware only of the strength of his arms about her and the touch of his mouth on hers. It was all sparks and flame, fiery desire and the ache of wanting. It was enough to set her trembling in a way she had never felt before.

His lips very gently nudged hers apart, his tongue touched hers and everything became dizzying and molten and shocking in a perfectly delicious way. Now she knew why people liked kissing so much. She never wanted to stop. Her body felt soft and yielding against the strength and hardness of his. The pit of her stomach felt hollow with a peculiar longing. She was lost in a dangerous new world and did not want to be found.

A door shut sharply, away to their right, and Margery jumped and awoke, stepping back out of the circle of his arms. The sweetness fled and she felt cold and shocked. She was no Cinderella. Nor was she the heroine of one of the Gothic romances she read in secret. She was a servant girl and he was a gentleman. She wondered what on earth she had been thinking. No, she knew what she had been thinking. She had been thinking that kissing was the most delightful occupation she had yet discovered. More accurately she had been thinking that kissing this particular man was the most delicious thing imaginable. But that did not make it the right thing to do.

"No." She pressed her fingers to her lips in a brief, betraying gesture and saw his gaze follow the movement and his eyes darken.

"No," she said again. "This is quite wrong."

"You!" Mrs. Tong was swooping toward Margery like a vengeful harpy, scarves flying, bangles clashing. "I told you—" She broke off as the man moved protectively close to Margery's side. A smile of ludicrous brightness transformed her sharp features. "I beg your pardon, sir," she said. "I did not see you there. Was this girl importuning you? She does not work here." Mrs. Tong shot Margery another vicious vengeful look. "My girls are a great deal more professional—"

"I don't doubt it, ma'am." The gentleman cut in, so smoothly it did not sound like an interruption. "But you have the matter quite mistaken. I was lost—" a hint of amusement in his tone "—and Miss Mallon was doing no more than giving me directions, for which I am most grateful."

"Since she is in the wrong place herself," Mrs. Tong said sharply, "it amazes me that she could direct anybody." She softened her tone and placed a hand on the man's arm. "If you would care to come with me, sir, I can help you with whatever you require. You." She jerked her head at Margery. "Out."

"Goodnight, ma'am." Margery did not spare Mrs. Tong more than a brief nod of the head. She could feel the madam's eyes boring into her. She knew that Mrs. Tong suspected her of trying to tout for business. This would be the last time she was permitted in the Temple of Venus.

"Sir…" She dropped the gentleman a curtsy. "I hope you find your way."

That provocative smile lit his eyes again and made her shiver. "You sound like a Methodist preacher, Miss Mallon."

Margery turned away. She did not want to see him accompany Mrs. Tong into the brothel's salon to be pounced upon by all those twittering courtesans. The thought set up an odd sort of ache in her heart. It was foolish to care, when all he had done was flirt with her. He will have forgotten her in less than a day, or very likely in less than an hour. The door of the salon opened, and light and music spilled out across the tiled floor of the hall. The real business of the evening was about to start. Margery tucked the basket beneath her arm and hurried through the door to the servants' quarters, past the kitchens where the steam was rising and the cooks were sweating to prepare delicacies for Mrs. Tong's guests. No one looked at her as she passed. Once again she had become invisible.

Out in the street the evening was bright and starlit but Margery's feet suddenly felt like lead. It was no more than tiredness, she told herself. It had nothing to do with the gentleman she had met in the brothel and the contrary disappointment she felt because the encounter was over. She was tired because she had risen early to launder Lady Grant's silk underclothes, for they were of such exquisite quality that they could not be trusted to anyone else. She had worked a whole day and here she was working a long evening as well, and once she was back in Bedford Street she would need to stay up into the early hours to await Lady Grant's return from the theater. Those people who thought that lady's maids had an easy life had absolutely no notion.

"Moll!"

Margery jumped and spun around. Her brother Jem was the only one who called her Moll. She waited as his tall figure detached itself from the shadows of the street corner and strolled forward.

"Thought it was you," he said, as he caught up with her. He grinned. "What the devil were you doing in a bawdy house, Moll?"

"Minding my own business," Margery said sharply. Jem lifted the cover on the basket and took out the last of the honey cakes. Margery slapped his hand but he ate them anyway.

"They'll spoil if they don't get eaten," Jem said. "They taste good," he added with his mouth full, scattering crumbs on the cobbles. "You should have been a cook rather than a maid."

"I don't want to be a cook," Margery said. "I only want to make sweets and pastries." Her ideal was to be a confectioner and sell her beautiful cakes and sweetmeats for a living, but to set up in a shop was too expensive, so in the meantime she earned use of the oven at Bedford Street by helping Lady Grant's cook with the more complicated French desserts and pastries.

"When I make a fortune," Jem said, wiping the back of his hand across his mouth, "I'll set you up in your own shop. I promise."

Margery laughed. "I'll die waiting for that day," she said without rancor. She knew Jem spent every penny of his rather dubious earnings on gambling, drinking and women.

Although she would never admit it, Jem was her favorite brother. He had always been there for her, even though he was ten years her senior. She knew she should not favor him over the others because Billy worked hard to support his wife and growing family, and Jed, back in Berkshire, was a pot man in a respectable hotel. Jem was a scamp who never seemed to do an honest day's work. But Jem was merry where Billy was serious. There was something about him that made it impossible to be angry with him even when he was helping himself to the rest of her stock. It was charm, Margery thought, as she fastened the cloth down firmly over the remaining cakes. Jem could charm the birds from the trees.

"I'll walk you back," Jem said.

"You'll get no more cakes for your trouble," Margery warned him.

Jem laughed. "You're a hard woman, Moll."

"And if you weren't my brother," Margery said, "I wouldn't give you the time of day."

Covent Garden piazza was full of evening crowds. An elegant lady, passing on the arm of a very smug-looking elderly gentleman, turned her head to stare at them. Margery sighed. It was always the same; ladies seemed quite unable to resist Jem. His golden hair and blue eyes, his smile and air of raffish charm worked on them like magic. They shed their clothes, their inhibitions and their husbands to fill his bed.

Jem sketched the lady an exaggerated bow and grinned with unabashed arrogance.

"For pity's sake," Margery said, pulling on her brother's arm to draw him away. "Why don't you just charge by the hour?"

Jem laughed again. "Now there's a thought."

"I'm sure Mrs. Tong would give you a job," Margery said. "She likes pretty boys."

"She's not the only one," Jem said complacently. He patted her hand. "Come along then, Miss Mallon. You had better lend me some of your respectability."

Margery stopped dead again on the pavement, causing another couple to cannon off them in a volley of exclamations and apologies.

"What the devil?" Jem enquired mildly.

Margery did not hear him. She was clutching the handle of the basket a little more tightly as a frisson of disquiet rippled through her. She was back again in the hallway of the brothel, feeling the stranger's hands on her, tasting his kiss and hearing his voice, smooth, mellow, charming the bawd out of her anger.

Miss Mallon was doing no more than giving me directions....

For the first time, Margery realized that he had known her name.

CHAPTER TWO

The Magician Reversed: Trickery and deception

MARGERY WAS SITTING on the top step of the sweeping staircase in Lady Grant's house in Bedford Street. Next to her sat Betty, the second housemaid. They were hidden by the curve of the stair and the soaring marble pillar at the top. None of the guests thronging the hall below could see them, but they had the most marvelous view. Tonight, Lord and Lady Grant were hosting a dinner and a ball—one of the first major events of the new London Season—and word was that the ton were begging, buying and bartering for tickets. Lady Grant's events were always frightfully fashionable. To fail to secure an invitation was social death.

"Oh, Miss Mallon," Betty said, her big brown eyes as huge as dinner plates as she stared down on the scene below. "Look at the clothes! Look at the jewels!" She dug Margery slyly in the ribs with her elbow. "Look at the gentlemen! They are so handsome!"

"I'm studying the gowns, Betty, not the gentlemen," Margery reproved, "and so should you if you wish one day to be a lady's maid."

She made a quick pencil sketch of one of the gowns in her notebook. Lady Grant was modish to a fault, a leader of fashion, and as her personal maid it was Mar-

gery's responsibility to keep her at the forefront of style.
She watched the ladies as they strolled out of the dining room, making notes of the dresses and the jewels,
the combination of colors, materials and styles. She
could spot the work of individual modistes and guess to
within a guinea or two the price of each gown. She was
good at her job and on evenings like this, she enjoyed it.

Margery paused in her sketches, chewing the end of
her pencil. Betty was correct. There were some very
handsome men present tonight. She could hardly pretend otherwise. For a moment she saw another face, a
man with a wicked smile and laughing dark eyes, and
she remembered a kiss that was hot and tender and
promised so much. She felt a tingling warmth sweep
through her, as though her entire body was slowly catching alight.

Margery had thought about the gentleman from the
brothel in the week since they had met, and it was starting to annoy her that she could not banish him from her
mind. She had thought about his voice, smooth but with
that note of command, she had remembered the tilt of
his head, the light in his eyes, his smile. Oh, yes, she
had remembered his smile. She had seen nothing else
when she went about her work, whether she was dressing Lady Grant for a drive in the park, or re-dressing
her for an evening at the theater or undressing her afterward. She had been so distracted that she had over-
starched the lace, mended Lady Grant's hem with a
most uneven stitch and added the wrong color of feather
to her French bonnet. She had mislaid Lady Grant's
jewel box and had folded her favorite pelisse away in
the wrong clothes press.

Then there was the kiss. It had haunted her dreams as

well as her waking moments. She had lain in her narrow bed under the eaves and dreamed of kissing him, and she had woken flushed and confused, her heart racing, her body quivering with a delicious foretaste of passion. She was not quite sure what it was she wanted, only that her body ached and trembled for him, and that the more she tried to ignore it the more those illicit, demanding sensations rose up in her to beg for fulfillment. She felt on edge and inflamed, angry with herself that she could not conquer it. She was not a girl normally given to fantasies and it was odd and disquieting to be dreaming of a man, especially one she had met only once.

"How red your face is, Miss Mallon." Betty was looking at her curiously.

"It's very hot in here," Margery said. She pushed the memory of the kiss from her mind and concentrated sharply on the crowd of guests now thronging the hall. Lady Rothbury, Lady Grant's sister, was looking particularly stunning in a gown of *eau de nil* that shimmered with gold thread. Her gaze moved on, over the welter of colors and styles, the flash of diamonds and the flutter of fans. The air was scented now with a mixture of hothouse flowers and perfume. The chatter of the guests rang in her ears. Margery craned forward for a closer look at a tall, thin woman in a striped gown that shrieked *Parisian design*. The movement caught the eye of the gentleman by her side. He looked up and their eyes met.

All the air left Margery's body in a rush. The candles spun in the chandeliers like a wheel of light.

It was the gentleman from the brothel.

For one very long moment they stared at each other while the sound beat in Margery's ears, and the light

dazzled her eyes and she could neither move nor breathe.
Then the gentleman inclined his head in the slightest of
bows, and a mocking smile curled his mouth, and Margery knew he had recognized her. Movement returned
to her body, and with it an intensification of the hot
blush that spread through her so fast she felt as though
she were burning up. The pencil slid from her fingers.
The book tumbled off her lap as she jumped to her feet,
smoothing her skirts with clumsy hands. She drew back
behind the shelter of the pillar. Her heart was hammering underneath her bodice and her palms felt damp.

*Who was he? What was he doing here? Would he
give her away?*

If he should mention to Lady Grant that one of her
maids had been in Mrs. Tong's brothel, that would be
the end of her. She would be thrown out in the street
without a reference and with no prospect of another respectable job. Her heated body turned cold. She would
be forced to beg her brother Billy for work. She could
not be a tavern wench or even a courtesan because she
was not pretty enough, and anyway, that was no way
to think....

"Miss Mallon!"

Margery's frightened thoughts were scuttling around
and it was a moment before she realized that she was
being addressed. Mrs. Biddle, the housekeeper, was
standing a foot away, glaring at them. Betty gave a little gasp and leapt up, pressing her hands to her reddening cheeks, horror in her eyes at being caught. Margery
retrieved her pencil and notebook, trying to regain a
little composure.

"Run along, Betty," Mrs. Biddle said sharply. "You
have work to do."

Betty scrambled a curtsy and scurried away.

"I'm sorry," Margery said. "It was my fault. Betty would like to be lady's maid one day and I was teaching her a little about the job."

"Lady Grant is asking for her silver gauze scarf," Mrs. Biddle said, her tone softening. She was always respectful of Margery's position as a senior servant. In other ways, she mothered her. "If you could take it down to the parlor, Miss Mallon, Mr. Soames will deliver it to the ballroom for her ladyship."

"Of course, Mrs. Biddle," Margery said. It would be unheard-of for her to take the scarf to Lady Grant herself. No one but the butler and the footmen could be seen at an evening function. The rest of the servants had to be invisible.

She hurried to Lady Grant's bedchamber and found the silver gauze scarf that perfectly complemented Lady Grant's evening gown. It was impossibly sheer and silky, embroidered with tiny silver stars and crescent moons. For a moment Margery raised it to her cheek, enjoying the soft caress of the material against her skin. She had never owned so luxurious an item in her entire life.

With an envious little sigh, she tucked the scarf under her arm and went out along the corridor and down the servants' stair. She hesitated before pushing open the green baize door that separated the servants' quarters from the hall. She was not quite sure why. Her mysterious gentlemen, whoever he was, would be in the ballroom by now with the skinny woman in the elegant gown. There was no chance of meeting him.

Sure enough the hall was empty. She felt a slight pang of regret.

Mr. Soames was waiting for her in the parlor. She handed over the shawl and he took it as reverently as though it were a holy relic. Margery tried not to laugh. Mr. Soames was always so serious about everything, but then a butler's job was a serious business, the very pinnacle of a male servant's ambition. He had told her that, if she was lucky and worked hard, she might reach the top of her profession, too, and become a house-keeper one day.

Mr. Soames went out carrying his precious burden, closing the door softly behind him. Margery waited for a moment in the warm, silent confines of the parlor.

Margery had a hundred and one tasks waiting for her. Lady Grant's dressing room needed to be tidied. Her nightclothes needed to be laid out for the moment, several hours ahead, when she finally retired from the ball. In the meantime, there was a pile of mending to be done, invisible work that required Margery's keen eyes and nimble fingers. Her head ached to think of peering over tiny stitches in the pale candlelight.

On impulse she released the catch on the parlor door instead and stepped out onto the terrace. The mending could wait for a few more minutes.

It was cool outside, so early in the year. The air was fresh, the sky blurred with mist and scented with the smoke of all London's chimneys. Beneath that was the sweeter smell of flowers mingled with perfume and candle wax. Margery drew in a deep breath. She could hear the music from the ballroom. The orchestra was playing the opening bars of a country-dance. She could picture the scene, the candlelight, the jewels, the vivid rainbow colors of the gowns. It was a world so close and yet so far out of reach.

The music called to something long lost inside her. In her memory, she could hear an orchestra playing and see an enormous ballroom stretching as far as the eye could see. Light sparkled from huge mirrors. The swish of silken gowns was all around her.

Her feet started to move to the music. She had not danced in years. She usually sat out the servants' balls that employers insisted on holding each Christmas. She had no desire for her feet to be crushed by a clumsy coachman who fancied himself a dancer.

She twirled along the terrace, feeling lighter than air. It was ridiculous; she smiled to herself as she imagined quite how ridiculous she must look. It was also the sort of thing she never did. She was too serious, too sensible, to indulge in such a frivolous activity as dancing alone on a misty moonlit terrace.

The music changed, slid into a waltz, and Margery spun up against a very hard, masculine chest. Arms closed about her, steadying her. Her palms flattened against the smooth material of a particularly expensive and well-made evening jacket. Her legs pressed against a pair of very hard, masculine thighs encased in particularly well-made and expensive trousers. Margery noticed these things and told herself it was because she was a lady's maid and trained to assess fashion, male or female, at a glance and a touch.

"Dance with me," her dark gentleman said. He was smiling at her in exactly the way he had smiled in the hall of the brothel before he kissed her, that wicked, provocative smile. "You were meant to dance with me."

Margery faltered. He was holding her in the way a man held his partner in the waltz, but suddenly she wanted to twist out of his grip and run away. She felt breathless and trapped and excited all at once.

"I cannot waltz," she protested. It was a modern dance, new and more than a little scandalous. At least, it was the way that he was holding her. She could feel the heat of his body and smell his lime cologne. It made her head spin, which was a curious sensation.

Once she had drunk too much ale at the fair. This was similar, but a great deal more pleasant and a great deal more stimulating. The brush of his thigh against hers made her skin tingle, even through the ugly black wool of her gown. Oddly, it also made her feel very aware of the latent power in him, a strength and masculinity kept banked down under absolute control.

"You waltz beautifully," he said. They were already moving, catching the beat of the music. "Where did you learn to dance like this?" His breath feathered across Margery's cheek, raising delicious shivers deep within her.

"I learned to dance as a child," Margery said. She frowned, reaching for the memories. It seemed ridiculous to think that in the rough-and-tumble of the Mallon household she had learned something as refined as dancing. She could not place the memory precisely. Yet she knew it had happened. Dancing was instinctive to her.

"This is very improper," she said uncertainly.

"And completely delightful," he said.

"You should be in the ballroom."

"I prefer to be here with you."

It was, indeed, delightful. Margery was forced to agree. His body was pressed against hers at breast, hip and thigh. His hand rested low in the small of her back in a gesture that felt astonishingly intimate. Heat flared through her, the sort of heat one simply should not be feeling on a cool April evening.

"Good gracious," she said involuntarily. "Is this not illegal in public?"

She saw amusement glint in his eyes. "On the contrary," he said. "It is positively encouraged."

He drew her closer. His cheek grazed hers. His scent filled her senses. The warmth of his hand seared her back through the woolen gown and the cotton chemise beneath. Another shiver chased over her skin at the thought of his hands on her. She felt feverish, aware of every little sensation that racked her body. She felt as voluptuous as the nudes she had seen in the paintings in great houses, languid and heavy with wanting, her body as open and ripe as a fruit begging to be plucked and devoured.

It was shocking, it was delicious and it was wanton. She was tumbling down a helter-skelter of forbidden pleasure.

"You make me want to be—" She just managed to stop herself before the scandalous words came tumbling out.

You make me want to be very, very wicked....

He laughed, as though he knew exactly what she had been going to say and exactly how wicked she wanted to be. His lips touched the hollow at the base of her throat and she felt her pulse jump. Then they dipped into the tender skin beneath her ear, and this time her entire body twitched and shivered. She could not prevent it. She was helpless beneath the sure touch of his lips and his hands.

His shoulder brushed a spray of cherry blossom and

the petals fell, the scent enveloping them. Somewhere
deep in the gardens a nightingale sang.

A stray beam of candlelight from the parlor fell
across them and in its light Margery saw that he was
studying her face intently, almost as though he was
committing it to memory. She felt disturbed. The mood
was broken. She slipped from his arms and felt cold and
a little bereft to have lost his touch. The music continued but he stood still now, his face in shadow.

"I should go," she said, but she did not move. Suddenly she was scared; she wanted to beg him not to
tell Lady Grant what had happened at the brothel but
she was too proud to beg for anything. She always had
been. Her brothers often said that pride and stubbornness were her besetting sins.

"Wait," he said. "I wanted to ask you—" He broke
off. It was too late. Some of Lady Grant's guests spilled
out onto the terrace, chattering and laughing. Margery
knew that in a moment they would see her; see her with
a gentleman, a maidservant caught in a guilty tryst.

"I must go," she whispered.

He caught her hand. His was warm. He pressed a kiss
to her palm, a feather-light caress. It made her tremble.
The light in his eyes made her stomach swoop down to
her toes in a giddy glide.

"Thank you," he said, "for the dance."

She had been seen. She heard the voices and spun
around, pulling her hand from his. Her fingers closed
over her palm as though to trap the kiss and hold it
there.

"Who is that?" A woman in a filmy flame-red gown
was peering at Margery through the darkness. Margery

shrank back into the shadows as a couple of ladies giggled and pointed.

"It's no one. A maidservant."

Someone tittered. "How encroaching of her to be out here spying on her betters in the ballroom!"

Margery's cheeks burned. At least they had not seen her dancing. And the terrace was empty. Her mysterious gentleman had gone.

Something glittered at her feet. She bent to pick it up. It was a cravat pin, slender, with a diamond head and a couple of initials entwined around the gold stick. She turned it over between her fingers and watched the diamond catch the light.

For a moment temptation caught her in its spell. The pin was valuable. If she gave it to Jem, he would give her money for it with no questions asked. There had been times in the past when he had asked her if Lady Grant had any jewelry or clothing or other possessions that she might not miss. Margery had given him a fine telling off and he had not mentioned it again, but now, staring at the glittering diamond, she thought longingly of the money she could put toward a little confectionery shop.

She gave herself a shake. No and no and no. Thieves and criminals had surrounded her since childhood. Billy was bad enough, a chancer and a con man, and Jem was worse. There was something very dangerous about Jem. Growing up among thieves was no good reason to become one. She would hand over the cravat pin to Lady Grant and tell her that she had found it. She would imply that one of the guests had dropped it and she had come across it by chance. She slipped it into the pocket of her gown.

"You, there! The little maidservant." One of the women on the terrace was calling to Margery. "Fetch me a glass of champagne." Her voice was haughty. The light from the colored lanterns skipped over a gown of striped silk. Margery recognized the thin, disdainful woman she had seen in the hall.

"I'll ask one of the footmen to serve you, ma'am," she said politely.

"Fetch it yourself," the woman said. "I don't want to wait."

Someone else laughed. They were all looking at Margery, sharp and predatory as the bullies she remembered from the streets of her childhood. Jem had fought those children for her. Now she was on her own.

"I'll ask the footman, ma'am," she repeated, and saw the woman's eyes narrow with dislike.

"What a singularly unhelpful creature you are," she said contemptuously. "I will be sure to mention your insolence to Lady Grant."

"Ma'am." Margery dropped the slightest curtsy, enough to fulfill convention, but so slight as to be almost an insult.

She walked slowly, head held high, to the terrace doors. Once inside the parlor she shut the doors against the laughter and chatter on the terrace, then locked them for good measure and drew the curtains closed. Her hands were trembling and she felt tears pricking her eyes. She knew that it was foolish. Spiteful comments from people like the lady on the terrace were common in a servant's life. She tried to disregard them. Most of the time the aristocracy ignored those who waited on them. Margery was accustomed to being considered a part of the furniture but it did not make cruelty or rudeness any more tolerable.

She slid a hand into her pocket and felt the prick of the cravat pin against her fingers. Already the waltz on the terrace felt like a dream. She had stepped out of time, forgotten her place as lady's maid, forgotten her black woolen gown and practical boots, and had stolen a moment of pleasure in the arms of the most handsome man at the ball.

She took the cravat pin from her pocket and ran her fingertips over the entwined initials, *H* and *W.* She wondered who he was.

She knew she would not see him again.

CHAPTER THREE

The Hanged Man: Reversal and sacrifice

"COME CLOSER, HENRY, so that I can see you." The voice was dry as tinder but the tone was still commanding, bearing overtones of the man the Earl of Templemore had been before illness ravaged his body. He sat in a chair before the fire, a fire that roared despite the high sun of an April day. The bright morning light made the red-flocked wallpaper look faded and dull, and struck blindingly across the rococo mirrors, reflecting back endless images of the earl hunched in his chair, a blanket shrouding his knees.

Henry Wardeaux came forward and formally shook the old man's hand, just as he had greeted him for the past twenty-nine years. They had never been on more intimate terms, even though the earl was also Henry's godfather. Lord Templemore was not a man given to displays of affection.

"How are you, sir?" Henry asked. It was a courtesy question only. He knew that the earl was dying; the earl also knew that he was dying and never pretended otherwise.

A dry rattle of laughter was his reply.

"I survive." One white-knuckled hand grasped an ivory-headed cane as the earl sat forward in his chair.

"If you have good news for me I might yet feel quite well. Did you meet my granddaughter?"

For a man who showed little emotion there was a wealth of longing in his voice. Henry felt a simultaneous jolt of pity and exasperation, pity that the old man was so desperate to find his daughter's lost child that he would grasp after every straw, and exasperation that this very desperation made a shrewd man weak.

Mr. Churchward was still working to establish whether Margery Mallon was definitely the earl's grandchild. Churchward was not the sort of man who liked to make mistakes, particularly not over something as important as the lost heir to one of the most ancient and prestigious earldoms in the country. Lord Templemore, however, had been certain of it from the start because he had wanted it to be true.

Henry took the seat that the earl indicated. "I have met Miss Mallon twice in the past ten days," he said, taking care not to commit himself over whether the girl was the earl's granddaughter or not. "In point of fact, I first met her in a brothel."

The earl's gaze came up sharply. Gray eyes, so bright, so cool, a mirror image of Margery Mallon's clear gray gaze, pinned Henry to the seat.

"Did you?" The earl said expressionlessly. "Mr. Churchward indicated that Miss Mallon was a lady's maid, not a courtesan."

Henry wondered if it would have made any difference to the earl if Margery Mallon had been the most notorious whore in all of London. He thought it would probably not. The earl had waited twenty years to find his heir and he was not going to be dissuaded from his quest now.

"That is correct, sir," Henry said. A smile twitched his lips as he remembered the small, bustling but efficient figure that was Margery Mallon. There was a no-nonsense practicality about her that was strangely seductive. "Miss Mallon does indeed work as a lady's maid for Lady Grant in Bedford Street," he said. "But she also makes sweetmeats and sells them to the whores in the bawdy houses of Covent Garden."

The earl's brows shot up. "How enterprising," he said. "I assume Mr. Churchward warned you not to disclose that piece of information to me?"

"He counseled against it, sir." Henry's smile grew. "He thought that the shock of learning that your granddaughter frequented such a place might kill you."

"And you said?"

"That you had frequented many such places yourself in the past, sir," Henry said politely, "and that you would consider it far preferable that your granddaughter sold sweetmeats to whores rather than selling herself."

The earl gave a bark of laughter. "How well you know me, Henry."

Henry inclined his head. "Sir."

The earl glanced at the array of family portraits that marched across the drawing room walls. "Perhaps Miss Mallon is the first Templemore in two hundred years to possess some of the mercantile spirit of our Tudor forebears."

Henry followed the earl's gaze to the portrait of Sir Thomas Templemore, founder of the dynasty, pompous in cloth of gold, the chain of office around his neck commemorating the peak of his success as Lord Mayor of London. Sir Thomas had been a self-made man who had risen to enormous wealth and power in the cloth trade, and greater riches still lending money to the feck-less courtiers of Queen Elizabeth I. He had been the first and last of the Templemores to demonstrate any business acumen.

Henry's mouth turned down at the corners. More recent generations of the family had maintained their wealth through spectacularly rich marriages. Temple-more was costly to run and each earl had possessed a range of expensive vices from gambling on fast horses to the keeping of fast women. The present earl's late wife had been the daughter of a nabob and he had married her solely for her fortune.

"I am prepared for Miss Mallon to have had a… checkered past." The earl's words drew Henry's attention back. His gaze was shrewd, searching Henry's face. "In some ways it would be surprising if she had not, given her upbringing. You may tell me the truth, Henry. It will not kill me."

Henry sat back. He examined the high polish on his boots. His mother, whom he suspected was currently standing with her ear pressed to the other side of the drawing room door, would be silently urging him to take this God-given opportunity. She would be willing him to blacken Margery Mallon's name in the hope that the earl might forget these notions of reclaiming his granddaughter and return to the accepted order, the one in which Henry inherited everything, estate, title and fortune.

But there could be no going back. And Henry was, if nothing else, a gentleman, and he was not going to lie.

"As far as I could ascertain," Henry said, "Miss Mallon is a woman of unimpeachable virtue."

The earl raised a brow. He had read into Henry's

words everything that Henry had not said. "Did you test that virtue?" He was blunt.

"I tried." Henry was equally blunt. "We were, after all, in a brothel."

Seducing Margery Mallon had been very far from his original intention. His purpose was to get to know Margery a little and see if he could determine whether she was the earl's heir or not. Yet, when he had come face-to-face with her in the hall at the Temple of Venus, he had been presented with an opportunity he could not resist.

Or, more truthfully, an opportunity he had not wanted to resist. There had been something about Margery's combination of innocence and steely practicality that had intrigued him. He had wanted to kiss her in order to put that innocence to the test, because the cynic in him told him that such virtue could only be pretense. Surely no woman of her age and station in life could be as inexperienced as she had claimed to be.

He had wanted to kiss her from sheer self-indulgence, too. She had smelled of marzipan and sugar cakes, and he had wanted to find out if she tasted as sweet as honey. He had been fascinated by her pale, fine-boned delicacy, by the vulnerable line of her cheek and jaw. Her mouth in particular had transfixed him; it was full, willful and sensual, a complete contradiction to the neat respectability of her appearance and enough to make a man dream of kissing her until she begged for more. The fact that she seemed to have no idea of the effect she had on him had only sharpened his hunger for her.

He had kissed her and discovered that she did indeed taste of honey, so he had kissed her some more and been floored by the desire that had roared through him. It had prompted him to carry her into the nearest room and strip off her disfiguring servant's clothes and make love to her. If Mrs. Tong had not come upon them he was not sure how far his wayward impulses would have led him.

It had been as bad—worse—when he had seen Margery at the ball. He had forgotten all the questions he had prepared to ask and had lost himself in the pleasure of holding her in his arms. There had been an element of need in his fierce attraction to her. She was all sweetness and innocence and she washed the world clean of the violence and darkness he had seen in it. He wanted that sweetness in his life. He wanted to lose himself in her.

Arousal stirred in him again. Henry dismissed it ruthlessly. It was no more than an aberration. It had to be. He had never been attracted to ingenues and even if he had been, he had no business finding Margery Mallon sensually appealing. If Churchward discovered that she was not the Earl of Templemore's granddaughter, she would continue her life as a lady's maid none the wiser. If she was the lost heiress, then she would one day become Countess of Templemore. Either way, she was utterly forbidden to him, and the only thing that surprised him was that he had considered seducing her at all.

He had a beautiful opera singer in keeping who was sophisticated and experienced and everything that Margery was not. He thought of Celia, silken, skillful, obliging, and felt nothing more than vague boredom. He was jaded. No matter. He had long-ago stopped expecting to feel otherwise. Besides, Celia would leave him now that he was no longer heir to Templemore and could not afford her. He thought about it and found he did not greatly care. Mistresses came and mistresses went.

"And after you tried to seduce Miss Mallon," the earl said, recalling him abruptly to the room and the business in hand. "What happened then?"

"Miss Mallon refused me," Henry said. "She has no time for rakes."

The earl's smile was bitter. "A pity her mama did not display the same good sense." He shifted in his chair as though his bones hurt him. "I'd scarcely call you a rake, though, Henry. You have far too much self-control to indulge in any excess. You do not have the temperament for it, unlike your papa."

Unlike you, Henry thought. He studied the earl's face, the tightly drawn lines about his mouth and chin that indicated both pain and grief. Guilt and remorse were his godfather's constant companions these days. The Earl of Templemore would never admit to anything as weak as regret and yet Henry knew he must feel it; regret for the quarrel that had driven his daughter from the house twenty years before and led to her murder and the disappearance of her child, regret for the years of unbridled dissolution when he had tried to drown his loss in worldly pleasures, regret even for the difficult relationship that he had endured with his godson because Henry was not the heir that the earl had wanted and he had never been able to forgive him that fact.

Enough. If the earl had regrets about the past, that was his concern. Henry had no intention of emulating him.

"I have been remiss." The earl's dry voice cut into his preoccupation. "Will you join me in a glass of port wine, Henry?"

Henry did not trouble to ring the bell. He was perfectly capable of pouring two glasses of port. Besides, he would have to become accustomed to managing without servants if Margery Mallon inherited the Templemore title. His own estate was poor; everything that was unentailed had been sold off to pay for his father's profligacy. He had been building it back up for years but the estate was small and would never be wealthy.

He could deal with hardship and struggle. He had seen plenty of it, in the Peninsular Wars. His mother, on the other hand, was too sheltered a flower to relish so drastic a change in circumstances. She had been living on the expectation of his future for years and had been in an intolerably bad mood ever since she had heard the news of Margery Mallon's existence.

"Thank you." The earl took the glass from his hand and took an appreciative sip. The cellar at Templemore was as fine as the late-seventeenth-century house itself. The collection of wines alone was worth thousands of pounds. Henry wondered if Margery Mallon had the palate to appreciate it.

"I want you to bring her to me." The earl placed his delicate crystal glass on the Pembroke table and sat forward again, urgency in every line of his body. "I want to meet her, Henry."

Henry stifled another burst of impatience. "My lord," he said. "It is too soon. There may be some mistake. Churchward has not yet finished his enquiries and I have not been able to prove Miss Mallon's identity beyond doubt."

The earl cut him short with an imperious wave. "There is no mistake," he said fiercely. "I want to see my granddaughter."

Henry bit back the response that sprang to his lips. The earl's face was ashen, his hand shaking on the head of the cane. Henry felt his unspoken words: *if we delay I may not live to see her....*

"Take Churchward," the earl said, his gaze pinning Henry with all the fierce power his body lacked. "Go directly to Bedford Street to acquaint Miss Mallon with the details of her parentage and her inheritance. Then bring her here to me."

It was an order, a series of orders. The earl never asked, Henry thought wryly. He was steeped in autocracy. There could be no argument.

Henry thought about Margery Mallon's brothers. Unlike Margery, who had promptly returned the diamond pin he had deliberately let fall on the terrace, the Mallon men were dishonest through and through. He and Churchward had been at great pains to protect the earl from their exploitation. For all his fierceness, Lord Templemore was a sick and vulnerable old man whose life had been devastated by tragedy once before. Henry would not permit Margery's adoptive siblings to manipulate the situation to their advantage.

There was also the danger to Margery herself. Twenty years before, someone had killed the earl's daughter. The only witness to that murder had been her four-year-old child. If the murderer or murderers were still alive, the news that the earl's granddaughter had been found could put her in the gravest peril. Henry had to protect Margery from that danger.

Which was why he had to find out the truth about Margery's identity as swiftly as possible.

Henry forced himself to relax. "Very well, my lord," he said easily. "It will be as you wish." He checked the gilt clock on the mantel. He could be back in London before nightfall if he rode hard.

He would seek out Margery Mallon, but not to bring her directly to Templemore. He would learn as much as he could about her in this one night and then he would decide if she was truly Lady Marguerite de Saint-Pierre, heiress to the Templemore title and a huge fortune. He felt a pang of guilt at his deception but quashed it as quickly as he had dismissed the flare of lust. He could not afford either emotion. The future of Templemore was too important.

The earl sat back against the embroidered cushions, closing his eyes, suddenly exhausted. His skin was stretched thin across his high cheekbones. He groped for the wine and drank a greedy mouthful, sitting back with a sigh.

Henry stood abruptly, leaving his glass of wine untouched.

"Excuse me, sir," he said. "I will go and fulfill your commission at once."

"You're a good boy, Henry." The earl had opened his eyes again. They were weary, shadowed by all the unhappiness he had experienced. "I will see that you do not lose out when my granddaughter inherits."

Henry felt a violent wave of antipathy. "I want nothing from you, sir. I have my own estate and my engineering projects—"

The earl dismissed them with a lordly wave. "Such matters are not work for a gentleman."

"They are work for a penniless gentleman," Henry corrected.

The earl laughed, that dry rattle again. "Marry an

heiress and all your difficulties will be solved. Lady
Antonia Gristwood—"

"Will not wish to throw herself away on me, my
lord," Henry said matter-of-factly.

"Perhaps a cit's daughter would not be so choosy.
You still have the title."

How flattering. But it did rather sum up Henry's
prospects now. "I've no desire to wed, sir," Henry said.
The heiresses would melt away swiftly enough when
they heard of his reversal of fortune. In their own way
they were as fickle as his mistress.

The earl seemed not to have heard. His chin had
sunk to his chest and he looked as though he was lost
in thought. Henry wondered whether his godfather was
still lost in the past. The earl, Henry thought, had a re-
markable talent for alienating members of his family:
first his wife, whom he had married for her money and
betrayed before the ink was dry on the marriage lines,
then his daughter, then his godson. He hoped to high
heaven that if Margery Mallon was indeed the earl's
granddaughter he would not devastate her life, as well.

He swallowed the bitter taste in his mouth, bowed
stiffly to the earl and went out. The hall was empty
although the air trembled and the door of the Red
Saloon was still swinging closed, a sure sign that Lady
Wardeaux had indeed been eavesdropping. Henry did
not want to have to confront his mother and her ruined
hopes yet again.

Nor did he wish to see Lord Templemore's younger
sister, Lady Emily, endlessly reading the tarot cards
and reassuring him that his fortunes would turn again.

They would turn because Henry would make them turn.

He had grown up at Templemore. He had been told

from childhood that he would inherit the title and land and that he had to learn to be a good master. He had done more than that. He had taken the estate to his heart and he loved every last brick and blade of grass there. It would hurt to give them up, but he had suffered reversals in his life before. He had overcome them all.

The tap of his boots echoed on the black marble floor of the hall. He paused by the door of the library to study the John Hoppner portrait of four-year-old Marguerite Catherine Rose Saint-Pierre, painted just before she had vanished from her grandfather's life.

The window in the dome far above his head scattered light like jewels on the tiles of the floor and illuminated the painting with a soft glow. Marguerite had been a pretty child, small, delicate, with golden-brown hair. She gazed solemnly out at him from her gilt frame, watching him with Margery Mallon's clear gray eyes.

The earl had summoned him with such haste that he had not had time to change out of his riding clothes. He strode out to the stable, calling for a fresh horse to take him back to London.

CHAPTER FOUR

The Knight of Swords: A tall dark-haired man with a great deal of charm and wit

IT WAS SEVEN O'CLOCK on a beautiful spring evening. Warmth still shimmered in the air, and the sky over London was turning a deep indigo-blue. The sun was dipping behind the elegant facades of the houses in Bedford Street and the shadows lengthened among the trees in the square.

It was Margery's evening off. She came up the area steps, tying her bonnet beneath her chin as she walked. She stopped dead when she found the gentleman she had danced with at the ball the previous night loitering at the top. He gave every appearance of waiting for her.

"What are you doing here?" she asked, her tone deliberately sharp. She had come down to earth since her encounter with him and had been berating herself for being a silly little fool whose head was stuffed with romantic nonsense. She was a lady's maid, not Cinderella.

Even so, her heart tripped a beat, because his smile—the *wicked* smile that curled his firm mouth and slipped into his dark eyes—was so much more potent in real life than it had been in her dreams and memories.

"Good evening to you, too," he said. "Are you pleased to see me?"

"Of course not," Margery said. She put as much disdain into her tone as she could muster, knowing even as she did so that she was betrayed by the shaking of her fingers on the ribbons of her bonnet and the hot color that burned in her cheeks.

Damnation. Surely she had learned enough over the years to know how to deal with a rake. She had acted as maid to any number of scandalous women who had perfected the art of flirtation. She should meet this insolent gentleman's arrogance with a pert confidence of her own. Yet she could not. She was tongue-tied.

She started to walk. "Why would I be pleased to see you?" she asked over her shoulder. "I barely know you."

"Henry Ward, at your service." He sketched a bow. It had an edge of mockery. "Now you know me."

"I know your name," Margery corrected. "I have no ambition to learn more."

He laughed. It was a laugh that said he knew she was lying. He was right, of course, though she was damned if she was going to admit it. She quickened her pace. He matched it with minimum effort.

"Wait," he said. "I'd like to speak with you." He hesitated. "Please."

It was the *please* that stopped her. She was not accustomed to courtesy from the aristocracy but by the time she had realized her mistake she was standing still and he was holding her hand. She had no idea how either of these things had occurred, only that his charm was clearly very dangerous to her.

"Miss Mallon—"

Margery snatched her hand back. "That reminds me. When we met in the brothel you addressed me as Miss Mallon. How did you know my name?"

She saw a flash of expression in his eyes that she could not read. Then it was gone; he shrugged lightly.

"I forget," he said. "Perhaps Mrs. Tong mentioned your name."

Margery shook her head. She knew that was not true. "No," she said, refusing to be deflected. "She did not."

Henry looked at her. His gaze was clear and open, yet she sensed something hidden. Instinct warned her that there was something he was not telling her.

"Then I do not know," he said. "Someone must have told me your name. The brothel servants, perhaps, or one of the girls…"

Margery turned a shoulder and started walking again. A sharp pain had lodged itself in her chest, like a combination of indigestion and disappointment. She did not want to think about Henry spending time with Mrs. Tong's girls, taking his pleasure with them, lying with one of them or perhaps more than one.

The images jostled in her head, bright, vivid, intolerably lustful and licentious. Jealousy, sudden and vicious, scored her with deep claws. It disturbed her because she had no right to feel it. She did not want to feel it. She had no claim on him. She might as well be jealous of the horribly disdainful lady in the striped gown, the one who had been clinging to Henry's arm at the ball.

She paused. Now she thought about it, she *was* jealous of the snobbish aristocrat in the striped gown.

"I didn't stay at the brothel." He put one hand on her sleeve. She stopped again. "There is no need to be jealous," he said softly.

Margery shook him off. "Why would I be jealous?" She did not want him reading her mind. It was too disconcerting.

"You are jealous because you like me." He smiled at her. It was arrogant. It was irresistible. Something heated and unfurled within her like a flower opening in the sun.

"I like you, too," he said gently. "I like you very much."

He touched her cheek and Margery could not help herself; she felt her whole body sweeten and sing at his words. It was impossible for her to withstand his charm. Her defenses felt like straw in the wind.

"Why did you come to find me?" She could hear that her tone had lost its sharpness.

"I wanted to thank you for returning the cravat pin," Henry said. "I hope it did not cause any difficulties for you with Lady Grant. I would not have wanted you to get into trouble."

Margery smiled. His concern for her made her feel warm and cherished. It was a new sensation. Jem was a protective brother but he did not make her feel as special as she did now.

"Thank you," she said. "That is kind of you." She smiled. "There was no difficulty. Lady Grant was only grateful that your lost property had been found. She is the best of employers. All the ladies I have worked for have been so kind—"

She stopped, aware of the smile in Henry's eyes, wondering why she was telling him so much. She was not usually so open. Disquiet stirred in her as she realized the extent of her danger. Henry was too charming and too easy to talk to, and she was too inexperienced to deal with him. She should run now, while she still had the chance.

"Thank you for your thoughtfulness," she said quickly, "and for not giving me away to Lady Grant."

Henry shook his head. "I'd never do that." There was warmth and sincerity in his tone. Margery's pulse fluttered.

"You could have sent a note," she said. "There was no need—" She stopped abruptly as Henry took her hand again. Her breath caught in her throat. Her heart seemed to skip a beat.

"No need to see you again?" His thumb brushed her gloved palm and she shivered. She felt hot and melting, trembling on the edge of something sweet and dangerous. "But perhaps," he said, "I am here by choice. Perhaps I am here because I wanted to see you."

Margery closed her eyes against the seduction of his words. She wondered if she had run mad. Maybe there would be a full moon tonight to account for her foolishness. For she knew she was being very, very foolish. There was nothing more imprudent than a maidservant who succumbed to wicked temptation and a rake's charm.

Her sensible soul told her to dismiss him and go straight home again.

Her wicked side, the part of her she had not even known existed until Henry had kissed her, told her that this was just a small adventure and it could do no harm.

She took the arm that he offered and they started to walk again, more slowly this time, her hand tucked confidingly into the crook of his elbow. She had thought it would feel like walking with Jem or another of her brothers. She could not have been more wrong. Even through the barrier of her glove, she could feel the hardness of muscle beneath his sleeve. The sensation distracted her; she realized that Henry had asked her a question and she had failed to answer.

"I beg your pardon?"

"I asked where we were going." Henry sounded amused, as though he had guessed the cause of her disturbance. She blushed to imagine that he knew the effect he had on her.

"*I* am going for a walk," Margery said. "I like to get some fresh air and see the people passing by." She hesitated and cast a shy glance at him from beneath her lashes. "I suppose you may accompany me if you wish."

Henry slanted a smile down at her and her wayward heart did another little skip. "That," he said, "would be entirely delightful. Do you go walking often?"

"As often as I have an evening free and good weather," Margery said.

"Alone?"

"Of course I go alone," Margery said. "I am not going to sit inside on a beautiful evening because I lack a suitable escort."

His lips twitched. "How very practical of you," he murmured. "I hope that you are not troubled by importunate men when you are out alone."

Margery looked at him. "Only tonight," she said dryly.

His smile was rueful. "Touché."

"It is not a problem because I do nothing to draw attention to myself," Margery said. "A maidservant is nothing more than a fool if she does. Besides—" She stopped on the edge of further confession. It seemed fatally easy to confide in Mr. Henry Ward.

Henry looked down at her. "What is it?"

Margery blushed. "Oh, it is nothing."

"You were going to say that no one notices you," Henry said. "But I do. I see you."

They had stopped walking. "How did you know?" she demanded. "How did you know I was going to say that?"

Henry smiled. He put his fingers beneath her chin and tilted her face up to his. Margery met his eyes and felt fear as well as excitement shimmer down her spine. There was something in his expression that was bright and hot and searing; it matched the expression he had worn that night in the brothel. She shivered.

"You are always trying to hide," Henry said quietly, "but you cannot hide from me. I noticed you from the very first."

Margery tried, she really tried this time, not to let his words go to her head. But it was hopeless. She was already half seduced. She felt her lips form a tiny "oh" sound that was a mixture of disbelief and pure longing. She felt her stomach clench with the echo of that desire. She saw Henry's gaze slide along the curve of her cheek to her mouth. He brushed his thumb over the line of her jaw and her heart jumped almost out of her chest as she heard herself give a little gasp.

Are you mad, my girl? The man is a rake. You will be in his bed before you can say strumpet.

Once more, Granny Mallon's acerbic words slid into Margery's mind, wrenching her back to reality. It was impossible to lose her head over a handsome gentleman with Granny Mallon metaphorically sitting on her shoulder all the time, the voice of her virtue.

"I was not fishing for compliments," she said. "And I am not looking for carte blanche, Mr. Ward."

He stepped back, his hand falling slowly to his side.

There was rueful amusement in his eyes. "I beg your pardon. I never imagined that you were, Miss Mallon, and I am sorry if I offended you." He smiled at her and Margery felt her tension ease. Soon, she knew, they would have to turn back to Bedford Street. Darkness was falling and it would be beyond foolish for her to stay out with him at night. Her small adventure would end very soon.

Henry offered her his arm again and after a moment they resumed their walk, silently now as the sun sank behind the roofs of the town houses and the sunset turned red and gold.

There was a flower seller on the street corner with a cart that was empty but for a few bunches of delicate pink rosebuds. Margery looked at them and her heart ached. She loved flowers, from the huge hothouse arrangements that overflowed in Lady Grant's ballroom to the tiny wild harebells that grew in profusion on the chalk lands where she had grown up.

Perhaps her longing was in her eyes, because Henry had turned to the flower girl. "I'd like to buy the rest of your stock, please," he said, and the girl's tired face lifted as she handed him the bouquets and took his coins. He presented them to Margery who buried her nose in the sweet-scented sprays.

"How lovely," she said. She was trying to guard her heart against him but it was no good. She was so touched and happy. "No one has ever bought me flowers before."

Henry smiled at her. "It is my pleasure."

"My mother said I was named after two flowers," Margery said. She was inhaling the scent of the roses with her eyes closed. When she opened them she saw that Henry was watching her.

"Marguerite and Rose," she said. "Those are my names."

She saw some expression cloud Henry's eyes. Doubt clutched at her. Something was wrong but she had no idea what it was.

"It's quite a mouthful, isn't it," she said uncertainly.

"Is that why you changed it to Margery?" Henry said.

"It seemed more practical," Margery said. "For a lady's maid."

Henry nodded and smiled at her. "I would like to take you for supper," he said. He took her hand. "Please. Allow me."

Margery hesitated, hanging back, wary of him again. A walk in the evening was one thing, supper with its suggestion of intimacy and seduction, quite another.

"Why would you do that?" she asked cautiously.

"Because you look as though you are hungry," Henry said.

Margery could not help her peal of laughter. "That was not what I meant."

"I know," Henry said. He was laughing, too. "But you do."

"I had no dinner today." Margery was surprised to realize it. "Lady Grant is attending a ball tonight so I dressed her and then came straight out."

"Then you need to eat," Henry said. He gave her hand a little tug. Still, she hesitated.

It can do no harm....

Not Granny Mallon's voice this time, but the voice of her own desires, dangerously persuasive.

She felt her heart sing with pleasure and anticipation

that the evening was not to end yet and that she would always have something sweet to remember in the future.

"Thank you," she said. "I should like that very much."

From the broad, elegant spaces of Bedford Square, they turned southward toward the higgledy-piggledy jumble of cobbled streets that crowded near the Thames. The evening was cool and bright, the roads busy and noisy, but Margery did not notice the crowds. Her entire attention was wrapped up in Henry, in the brush of his body against hers as they walked, in his smile and in his touch. She wanted no more than this. She held the pink rosebuds carefully and breathed in their heady scent. She was very happy.

LADY EMILY TEMPLEMORE sat at the cherrywood table in the Red Saloon at Templemore House, her tarot cards spread out in a horseshoe shape before her. She had been in her teens when she first started to use the ancient wisdom of the tarot to foretell the future and to guide her. People had laughed at her for her credulity and her interest in the occult. She had been labeled an eccentric and a bluestocking but there had been a hint of fear in those who mocked her. She did not really care. No one understood her; they never had and they never would.

Tonight she had asked the cards a direct question and, as always, they had answered her. She had asked if Margery Mallon was the lost grandchild of her half brother the earl, and if so, what she should do. That was two questions, really, but the one went with the other. If the child had been found, then Lady Emily knew she could not keep quiet and wait for fate to catch up with her. She would need to take action.

Card one in the spread represented the past. It was Temperance, but it was reversed, speaking of quarrels and strife. A shiver shook Lady Emily's narrow frame as the cruelty and guilt of the past reached out to touch her again. There certainly had been quarrels aplenty at Templemore.

Card two, representing the present, was the Eight of Swords. The card summed up her current emotions very accurately. She felt trapped and powerless and very afraid. She reached for her glass of ratafia and swallowed three quarters of the sweet liqueur in one gulp. A flush lit her sallow cheeks. She felt a little warmer. The neck of the bottle rattled against the glass as she topped it up. The fire hissed as a log settled deeper in the grate.

Card three was very important, because it gave an insight into the hidden influences at work. It was the Knight of Swords. She thought this was probably Henry. Henry was ruthless and determined and driven by duty. He would do his utmost to bring Lady Marguerite home, even though he would be the one who would lose the most by it. Lady Emily shrugged her thin shoulders. She knew Henry was dangerous, her most dangerous enemy.

Matters did not improve with the fourth card, which represented the obstacles in her path. It was the Seven of Cups. The card spoke of important choices to be made. The problem was that there were so many different options that she felt quite overwhelmed. The card held a warning, as well: take care in your decision, for all is not as it seems.

Frowning, Lady Emily turned her attention to the final three cards. Card five showed the attitudes of other people. There was help here, though not in very reliable form. The Page of Pentacles was a wastrel, dissolute and impatient. He was not a good ally, but at the moment he was all she had. Lady Emily's gaze strayed toward the writing desk. Later she would write, secretly and swiftly, to put him on his guard and to ask for his aid.

There were two cards remaining. They told her what she should do and the final outcome. The first was Strength, but it was reversed. She had to overcome her fears. If she did so then the final card promised her reward. It was the Six of Wands. Victory. Already she felt flushed with success and achievement. If she was patient, if she was brave, she would triumph.

In the depths of the house a clock struck eight. It was the only sound. Templemore House felt as though it was waiting, waiting to awaken, waiting for the lost heir to return. Lady Emily's gaze went to the portrait over the fireplace. Her father. It was a great pity that, having lost his first wife in childbirth when his heir was born, he had failed to marry his mistress, Emily's mother, until after her birth. For the first two years of her life Emily had been illegitimate. She glared at the fierce-looking man in his Georgian finery. He had been no more than a smug, licentious, arrogant scoundrel. How she hated him for the sexual excesses that had led to her being branded a bastard. Legitimizing her through eventual marriage to her mother had been too little, too late. It had barred her from the succession and turned her into an oddity, scorned by society as the daughter of a whore, laughed at behind her back.

The old fury rose in her. Her silver bracelets clashed as she sent the tarot pack tumbling with one flick of her wrist. The card showing the Fool fluttered into the fire, its edges curling in the flame. Damn her father and damn her half brother and damn his spoiled daughter who had deserved to die. Emily stood up. Lady Rose had been destroyed but now her daughter was coming home. The Wheel of Fortune was turning once again.

CHAPTER FIVE

The Seven of Swords: Do not give your trust too easily

MARGERY HAD SUGGESTED taking Henry to the Hoop and Grapes Inn for dinner. It was, as Henry pointed out, the haunt of footpads, highwaymen and any number of criminals. Margery had chosen it for the good food and because they knew her there.

"You do not strike me as the sort of female to frequent a place like this, Miss Mallon," Henry said as they stopped in front of an ancient black-beamed and white-plastered building that boasted a battered wooden signboard above the door. "You seem far too respectable for such a flash house."

"I'm far too respectable to frequent a bawdy house," Margery said, "but you found me in one."

"So I did," Henry said. Amusement glinted in his eyes. "What an unusual woman you are, Miss Mallon."

He opened the door to usher her inside. The air was so thick with the smell of pipe smoke it almost made Margery choke. Her eyes watered, and the smell of strong ale and warm bodies caught in her throat.

The taproom was packed with men and a few women. Total silence fell as they walked in. Margery saw the amusement deepen in Henry's eyes. His lips twitched into a smile. "I've had warmer welcomes behind the French lines," he murmured.

"They think you might be from Bow Street," Margery said.

Henry looked offended. "They think I'm a Runner when I dress as well as this?"

Margery giggled. She took his hand and led him through to an inner parlor flickering with golden candlelight. There was a rickety wooden table in the corner by the fire. Henry held a chair for her before taking the one opposite.

"So you were a soldier," Margery said, resting her elbows on the table and studying him thoughtfully. He looked entirely relaxed as though the unfriendly atmosphere of the Grapes had completely failed to intimidate him. "No wonder you're not afraid," she said slowly.

Henry raised a dark brow. "Were you trying to scare me by bringing me here?"

"Not scare you, precisely," Margery said. She dropped her gaze and traced a circle on the top of the table with her fingertip. She had to admit that she had been testing him. She was curious; he gave away so little of himself. There was something watchful and closed about him, as though he held himself under the tightest control. A little shiver edged down her spine.

"My brothers drink here," Margery said.

"Ah. You wish to introduce me to your family." Henry sat back in his chair, stretching out his long legs. "Our acquaintance proceeds quickly, Miss Mallon."

Margery laughed. "No, indeed. You need have no fear of that. I am simply being careful."

"Very wise," Henry said. "In case I fail to act as a gentleman should." He was smiling but there was something challenging in his eyes that made Margery's stomach curl and the heat rise through her blood. She tore her gaze away from his. At this rate she would not be able to eat a mouthful.

"I am relying on you to behave properly," she said.

Henry gave her an ironic bow. "Not a cast-iron way of ensuring success," he drawled.

"Do your best," Margery said tartly and saw him grin.

"So, your brothers are criminals." He slid his hand over hers where it rested on the table. His touch was warm and sent quivers of awareness trembling through her. "How stimulating."

"Are you sure you are not a Runner?" Margery asked sweetly. She drew her hand gently from under his, not because she wanted to but because she knew she had to, if she was going to stick to the straight and narrow.

"Of course they are not criminals," she said. Then honesty prompted her to qualify the statement. "That is, Jed is certainly not a criminal. He is a pot man at the Bear Hotel in Wantage. Billy runs his own business buying and selling cloth." She ignored the other, less respectable things she knew Billy bought and sold. "And Jem…" She paused. "Well, I have to admit that Jem does sail a little close to the wind."

Henry was laughing at her but she did not mind. There was warmth and admiration in his eyes that made her feel very happy inside.

"I like that you defend them," he murmured. "You see the best in everyone."

The Grapes's three maidservants now converged upon them, squabbling for the privilege of serving them. Margery knew exactly why the girls were competing for Henry's attention. It seemed that he rated even more highly than Jem, for he was not only good-looking but he looked rich, as well. All three girls were eyeing him with fascinated speculation and more than a little anticipation. Margery felt jealousy stir in her, the same jealousy that had beset her earlier.

"What would you like to eat and drink?" Henry asked her, while the tavern wench who had won the tussle for their order eyed Margery with ill-concealed dislike.

"I will take the mutton pie and a glass of ale, if you please," Margery said.

The girl turned her attention back to Henry. "My lord?" she asked.

"I will have the same, please," Henry said. He passed over a guinea and the maidservant pocketed it faster than a rat moved up a drainpipe. She dropped him a curtsy. "That would buy you plenty more than food and drink, my lord," she said, opening her eyes very wide to make her meaning explicitly clear.

Henry raised his brows and smiled at her with such charm that even Margery blinked. "Thank you," he murmured. "If I require more I will be sure to let you know." He turned to Margery as the girl strolled away with a suggestive swing of the hips.

"She thinks me a nobleman and you are not even sure that you rate me a gentleman," he said.

"She thinks you ripe for fleecing," Margery said crushingly. "She is judging the guinea, not you." She put up a hand and untied the ribbons on her bonnet, laying it aside. Looking up, she saw that Henry's gaze was on her hair. Her first thought was that it must have got squashed beneath the hat, but when his eyes met hers she saw a spark of something hot that made her heart jerk. Her hair was a golden-brown, fine and entirely without curl, completely ordinary, yet Henry looked as though he wanted to reach out and touch it. She saw him swallow hard. It was extraordinary. She felt hot and bewildered, but excitement tingled in the pit of her stomach as she thought of his fingers slipping through the strands.

She was glad when the ale came. It broke the rather odd silence between them. Henry poured for them both from the pitcher. Margery took a mouthful, looked up and saw Henry's eyes on her, a gleam of humor in them.

"It tastes rougher than a badger's pelt," he murmured.

"I prefer it to wine," Margery said. She could feel the ale loosening her tongue already. It was indeed rough, with a kick like a mule. "Mrs. Biddle tells me I should cultivate a taste for sherry if I am to be a housekeeper in my turn," she said, "but I find it too genteel a drink."

"Do you want to be a housekeeper?" Henry enquired. "Is that not the pinnacle of achievement for an upper servant?" He topped up her glass.

"Mrs. Biddle says that I could do it if I wished, for I am already the youngest lady's maid she has ever known." She sighed. "Truth is, I do not want to be a servant."

Henry's lips twitched into that irresistible smile that always led her into indiscretion. "What do you want to be, Miss Mallon?"

"I want to be a confectioner," Margery said in a rush. "I want to have a shop and make comfits and marzipan cakes and sweetmeats. I want to own my own business and sell my cakes to all the lords and ladies of the ton."

Once again Henry's eyes gleamed with that secret

amusement. "It is good to have ambition," he murmured.

"But I need money to set myself up in business." Margery drooped. "I save all that I can from my wages—and the money that Billy pays me for collecting old clothes for him—but it will never be enough to buy a shop."

Henry's eyes met hers over the rim of his glass. "You had not thought to…ah…raise funds another way?"

The spark in his eyes captured and held her. She saw speculation there and desire that burned her and set her heart racing. She also saw exactly, explicitly, what he was suggesting.

She took another gulp of the ale. "Certainly not. I told you I was not a lightskirt! Besides—" even in her indignation she could not quite escape the force of logic "—I am not certain that I would be in any way successful enough to make the necessary capital."

A corner of Henry's mouth twitched upward into that dangerous smile. "I am sure you could learn."

Their gazes tangled, his dark, direct with an undercurrent that made Margery's toes curl. Then his smile broadened.

"Actually," he said lightly, "I only wondered whether there was someone who might give you a loan."

Margery almost choked on her ale. "You were teasing me," she accused.

"Yes. Although…" Henry paused. "If the other idea appeals to you—"

"It does not. I told you I was not looking for carte blanche!"

She had spoken too quickly, intent only on denying the quiver of desire in the pit of her stomach. It was illuminating to discover that her morals were nowhere near as stalwart as she had believed them to be. She thought of Henry's hands on her body, his lips against her skin, and she felt the tide of warmth rush into her face. Oh, how she wanted him. How seductive it was and how much trouble she could get herself into with the slightest of missteps. She was completely out of her depth.

Henry was watching her. He *knew*.

Margery sought to hide her mortification in her glass of ale and took several long swallows, which only served to make her head spin all the more.

The pies arrived, fragrant with mutton and dark gravy. Henry refilled her glass. They talked as they ate, which Margery knew was not refined, but suddenly there seemed so much to say. Henry asked her about her childhood in Wantage, and her work there and her family. She told him about Granny Mallon and her dire warnings about London gentlemen and Henry laughed and told her that her grandmother had been in the right of it.

Margery laughed, too, and drank until her head was fuzzy and the candlelight blurred to a golden haze and her elbow slid off the table, which made Henry laugh some more. A fiddler struck up in the other room, and the scrape of tables being pushed back was followed by a wild jig, the notes rising to the rafters.

But in their corner of the parlor, it was warm and intimate and felt as though it was theirs alone.

"Tell me," Henry said, leaning forward, the candlelight reflected in his dark eyes. "What is the earliest thing that you remember?"

Margery wrinkled up her nose. It seemed an odd, fanciful question, but then she supposed they had been discussing their childhoods. Or rather they had been discussing her childhood. She could not recall a single thing that Henry had told her in answer to her questions. She knew she was a little cast away, so perhaps she was not remembering. Henry was drinking brandy now and she had a glass of cherry brandy, sweet and strong.

"I recollect a huge room," she said slowly, "with a checkered floor of black and white and a dome high above my head that scattered colored light all around me." She looked up to meet an odd expression in Henry's eyes. It was gone before she could place it.

"I have no idea where it was. I have been in many great houses since, but have never seen anything like it. Perhaps I imagined it."

There had been other memories, too; people whose faces she could see only in shadow, scents, voices. She thought she remembered a carriage, a flight through the night, raised voices, cold and tears, but the memories were overlaid with others of her childhood in the tenement house in Wantage and the rough-and-tumble of life with her brothers.

Henry was watching her and the expression in his eyes was intent and secret.

"Sometimes," she said slowly, knowing that the drink was prompting her to be indiscreet, "I do think my imagination plays tricks on me. It disturbs me because I remember things that seem quite fanciful—silks and perfumes and such soft beds, yet I am not a fanciful person."

"And yet you do have a romantic streak, do you not, Miss Mallon?" Henry said. "I know, for example, that you read Gothic romances."

Margery jumped. "How could you possibly know

that?" It was unnerving the way in which he appeared to know so much about her. No one, not even those people who had known her for twenty years or more, realized that she loved those stories of beautiful heroines and handsome heroes and haunted castles.

Henry raised his brows. "I saw that you had a copy of Mrs. Radcliffe's book *The Romance of the Forest* in your reticule. I assumed that it was yours, unless you are taking it home for the admirable Mrs. Biddle."

Margery was betrayed into a giggle. "Mrs. Biddle reads nothing other than books on household management," she said. "She thinks fiction is frivolous."

"We won't tell her your secret, then," Henry said with his slow smile. "For fear of damaging your future prospects."

The music was becoming wilder still, the customers more raucous and amorous. One of the tavern wenches was enthusiastically kissing a tall fair man who had her pressed up against the plaster wall and looked as though he was about to ravish her there and then, in full view of the customers.

"He's a scamp," Margery said. "A highwayman. Jem says he works the Great West Road."

Two men at the next table were coming to blows over a game of shove ha'penny. One planted a punch on the other; the table rocked and overturned and then they were locked in grunting combat. A knife flashed.

"Time to go, I think," Henry said. He stood up, drawing Margery to her feet, one arm about her waist as she stumbled a little. "You may have a taste for dangerous company," he said, "but I have more care for self-preservation."

"I'll protect you," Margery said, smiling up into his

eyes. She felt happy and a little dizzy and more than a little drunk. Fortunately, Henry's arm felt exceedingly strong and reliable about her. It felt perilously *right,* as though she belonged in his arms, a foolish, whimsical notion that nevertheless she could not dislodge.

She turned toward the door—and found herself face-to-face with her brother Jem.

"Moll!" Jem's voice snapped like a whip and the sweet, heady atmosphere that had held Margery in its spell died like a flame doused with water.

"Hello, Jem," she said, disentangling herself from Henry, who seemed inordinately and provocatively slow to release her.

"Who's the swell?" Jem said, cocking his head at Henry. There was an edge to his voice and an ugly look in his eyes.

"Henry Ward," Henry said, stepping between them. He offered his hand. Jem studiously ignored it. Henry looked amused.

"Jem," Margery said reproachfully.

Her brother flicked her look. "You should be careful, Moll," he said. His gaze returned to Henry. "You can pick up all sorts of riffraff in here."

"And you should mind your own business," Margery said, furious now. She felt Henry shift beside her. She could sense the sudden tension in him, an antagonism that matched Jem's except that Henry was watchful and controlled, appraising her brother with coolly assessing eyes. She remembered that Henry had been in the war and felt a shiver of alarm. Jem was hotheaded, a street fighter, but he was no match for a trained soldier.

The atmosphere was as thick as smoke now. The music had died away; everyone was watching, apart from the highwayman who was fumbling with the barmaid's bodice, his face buried in her cleavage. Even the men from the next table had abandoned their fight in anticipation of one that promised to be more deadly.

Jem put his hand on Margery's arm. "I'll take you home," he said. "Come on." He nodded toward the door. "I'll not have my sister treated like a fancy piece."

"No," Margery said stubbornly. "I'm not going with you." She shook him off. She felt humiliated and upset; she wanted to cry because Jem had taken all the fun and excitement from her evening and torn it to shreds. Everything looked tawdry now and Jem was making her feel like naive fool and worse, like a whore whose favors were up for sale for the price of a mutton pie.

"Don't confuse me with the sort of women you consort with, Jem Mallon," she said sharply. "I'm no lightskirt." She bit her lip against the sting of tears. "You've spoiled my evening," she said. "I was having such a nice time." She felt forlorn, like the little girl she had once been, stamping her foot with anger and hurt when Jem or Jed or Billy had broken one of her precious toys.

"For God's sake, Moll," Jem said contemptuously. "Can't you see all he wants is a quick fumble down a dark alley and he's just loosening you up for it?"

Henry stepped between them then with so much intent that Margery grabbed his sleeve in urgent fingers. The atmosphere had changed now. It was deadly.

"No," Margery said. "Please."

Her eyes met Henry's. There was such protective fury in his that she was awed to see it. Something sweet and warm settled inside her. Here was a man who cared about her good name and would do all he could to defend it and her against the world. She had never felt so cherished before.

"Your sister does not want me to hit you," Henry said, his voice lethally soft. "Out of respect for her, I will not. Don't insult her again."

There was an ugly look on Jem's face. He would not back down. "I don't trust you," he said. "If you touch her I will kill you." He turned on his heel and stalked out of the inn, sending a glass tankard spinning to smash on the floor and pushing a drunk out of his way.

There was a long, heavy pause and then the music struck up again, raucous as before. The sound of voices rose above the din, and everyone moved, resumed whatever they had been doing and pretended that they had not been watching and hoping for a mill.

"I'm sorry," Margery said. She was shaking. She felt Henry take her hands in his. His touch was very comforting.

"He only wanted to protect you," Henry said. "I would have done the same."

Margery gave a little hiccup halfway between a sob and a laugh. "I doubt you would have threatened to kill anyone," she said.

"I might have expressed myself slightly differently, but the sentiment would have been the same." His lips grazed her cheek in the lightest and most fleeting caress. "I'll take you back," he said. "Completely untouched, so that your brother does not come looking for me to slide a knife between my ribs."

He took her bonnet and tied the ribbons beneath her chin with quick efficiency. His fingers brushed her throat. Margery repressed a shiver. She felt shaken and upset but beneath that was a deeper emotion, something so precious and tender she trembled to feel it.

The street was silent and dark, the leaning houses pressing together, their windows blind, their shutters closed. High above the sloping roofs, Margery could see a sky spangled with stars. She felt tired all of a sudden, as though the pleasure she had taken in the evening and in Henry's company had drained away, leaving her empty. She sighed. "I did not want the evening to end like this."

Henry stopped walking and turned to her. "How did you want it to end?"

The quiet words made her heart skip a beat. She glanced up at him but in the dark his expression was unreadable.

"I wanted to go to Bedford Square Gardens," Margery said, in a rush. "I wanted to look at the stars and feel the breeze on my face and hear the sounds of the city at night…."

"We can still do that," Henry said. "Since that is what you would like to do."

Margery paused. They were alone and the night pressed in about them, silent and secret. Somewhere, streets away, a clock chimed the quarter hour. She could hear Henry's quiet breathing and feel the heat of his body where it brushed against hers. He said nothing more. He was waiting for her to decide what she wanted.

A strange feeling swept through Margery, part excited, part fearful. Jem had been right; she had taken a risk tonight, but she trusted Henry. She knew that in all the drab repetition of her daily life this one evening would always sparkle as bright and exciting as a jewel. She did not expect it to happen again, but she wanted it to end well, not on the sourness of Jem's intervention, spoiling the magic.

"Yes," she said. Her voice was husky. "Yes, please."

Henry smiled but said nothing and took her hand in his. They walked back through the quiet streets, the brim of her bonnet brushing his shoulder. Neither of them spoke. It did not feel necessary. When they reached the gate at the corner of the gardens, Margery opened her reticule. Her fingers shook a little as she took out the key and turned it in the lock. The gate swung open on well-oiled hinges and they stepped inside.

"Lady Grant gave me a key when she realized that I like to take the air here of an evening," Margery said. "The gardens are private to the residents."

On this evening it was like a secret garden, belonging to them alone. The gravel of the paths crunched softly under their feet as they made their way beneath the spreading boughs of poplar and oak. Margery ran down the path to the place where a pool was sheltered by the overhanging branches of a willow. She trailed her fingers in the cool water and watched the ripples shatter the reflection of the stars. Somewhere, distantly, in one of the grand town houses that bordered the square, an orchestra was playing a slow, dreamy waltz. It reminded Margery of the previous night, when she had danced with Henry on the terrace.

With a sigh, she straightened and turned back to look for Henry. He was standing still and straight in the shadows of a plane tree. His silhouette was dark, his shoulders broad and strong. The moonlight glinted on his glossy black hair. Margery went up to him and put her hands against his chest.

"Thank you," she said simply.

He smiled. "My pleasure, Miss Mallon."

Spontaneously, Margery stood on tiptoe to kiss him on the cheek, as she would have kissed one of her brothers if they had given her a present. Henry's cheek was smooth beneath her lips—evidently he had shaved before coming to meet her—and warm. Margery was suddenly vividly aware of the scent of his cologne mingled with the smell of crisp linen and sweet scented grass. The combination went straight to her head and she felt a soaring dizziness that was far more dangerous than the light-headedness induced by the ale.

She drew back, made clumsy by shock and awareness, and in the same moment Henry turned his head and her lips brushed the corner of his mouth. Margery felt him go very still. The moment turned from something sweet to something profoundly awkward. Heat suffused her. She felt inept and mortified. She was ready to curl up with embarrassment.

"I'm sorry," she said. "I didn't mean... It was a mistake—"

"Does this feel like a mistake?" Henry said. His arms went around her, pulling her against him, and then he was kissing her properly. Margery's head spun, and the ground shifted beneath her sensible half boots and she realized that the kiss in the brothel had been nothing at all compared to this.

Henry's lips moved over hers, his tongue touching hers, tasting her, searching, exploring. It was astonishing. It was bewitching. Little ripples of pleasure shimmered through her, down to her toes. She was shocked and intrigued all at once. It lit her blood with fire, making her shiver with heat and cold simultaneously as though she suffered a fever.

She had wanted this. She realized now how very much she had wanted Henry to kiss her. She had wanted it all evening and now it was happening. Her whole body tingled with surprised delight and a sudden fierce triumph.

With one hand Henry pulled the ribbons on her bonnet and cast it aside on the grass, and then his arm was across her back and his fingers were tangled in her hair, sending the neat pins flying, tilting her face up so that he could kiss her more deeply and more urgently still. Margery felt sweet lassitude seep through her body, weakening her knees, filling her with the most agreeable sensation of pleasure that she had ever known. She wanted more of it; suddenly she felt starved and greedy for it, her senses waking into life.

She drew closer to Henry, sliding her arms about his neck and opening her lips beneath his, kissing him back. He tasted of brandy and fresh air and something she had never known before, something that was elemental and special only to him. Her breasts were pressed against his chest as he held her close. There was a lovely, painful ache in the pit of her stomach. She had never known anything to compare with this combination of driving need and wanton weakness.

Henry's mouth left hers, but only to press kisses against the tender line of her neck and to linger in the hollow at the base of her throat. She trembled now, alive to his touch, as he slid the striped spencer from her shoulders and dropped it to join the discarded bonnet on the grass. His hand cupped the curve of her breast through her gown, his thumb insistent as it rubbed over her nipple. The friction of rough cotton against her skin was exquisite and Margery stopped thinking abruptly, her mind swamped instead by pure, hot desire. She gave a keening little cry and Henry's lips returned to hers in a ruthless kiss that swallowed her cry and drew her tighter still into a spiral of need.

If she had thought his touch through the material of her gown incendiary, it was nothing to the experience when he slid his hand inside her bodice and she felt his palm, warm and firm, against the side of her breast. The heat and the longing exploded inside her.

It felt as though the very stars were spinning in their courses. She had long ago forgotten to think. She was consumed by sensation only, her whole body clenched in such desperate wanting that she thought she would scream with it.

Her back was against one of the trees now. She could feel the bark snagging against the thin cotton of her gown. She tilted her head back to allow Henry greater access to the bare skin of her throat and shoulders, delighting in the nip of his teeth and the caress of his tongue. There was no shame or hesitation in her. This was a part of her nature that she had not suspected for a moment, but now it drove her.

When Henry tugged down the neck of her gown and she felt his mouth at her breast, she was shot through with such intense pleasure that she would have crumpled to the ground had he not held her pinned against the tree.

A moment later she realized that he was lifting her. The bark scored her bare back but the roughness of it was no more than additional and delightful stimulation against her nakedness. His hands were beneath her thighs, somehow her legs were wrapped about his waist, and her palms were flat against the solid hardness of the tree trunk. She could feel the kiss of the night air against her breasts.

She was filled with a ravenous greed to take Henry completely. She did not want to give herself to him. That felt too passive for the need within her, which was hungry and concentrated. She wanted to take. She was learning so much about herself and so fast. Her mind could not grapple with it, but her body knew what it wanted. It knew it with a knowledge that was deep and primitive. Henry's mouth was at her breast again, his tongue licked, his teeth tugged on her nipple and she arched back against the hard trunk of the tree, bending like a strung bow.

"Henry, please." Her words came out a whisper.

Taken by such pleasure she had meant to urge him on to more, but her words had the opposite effect.

She felt the loss of his touch first as he let her slide gently to the ground. She stumbled, disoriented and confused, and he steadied her. She could see his face in the moonlight now, see the vivid shock in it before a frightening blankness replaced it.

"I'm sorry," he said. He was breathing hard and his tone was rough. There was a note of furious anger in it but Margery instinctively knew it was at himself, not her. "I'm very sorry. That should never have happened."

The pleasure vanished. Margery felt cold all of a sudden, shivering in the summer breeze, shamefully exposed in the silver moonlight. She pulled up her bodice, tidying it with fingers that shook.

It felt as though her mind was trembling, too, at the enormity of what she had almost done. The thoughts, the images rushed in on her; she could see herself abandoned to all modesty and sense, pinioned against the broad oak, half-naked in Henry's arms, begging him to ravish her.

Icy shame seeped through her, yet at the same time the blazing demand of her body could not be denied. It felt as though she were split in half, part shamed, part wanting. She could neither make sense of it nor put back those sensations that had almost devoured her. She could not go back to the way she had been before.

She reached for her spencer, struggling to slip it on, making a small noise of distress as it slid from her grasp. Henry helped to arrange it about her shoulders and she felt profoundly grateful for the scant cover it gave her. His hands lingered against her bare skin for one long, aching moment and she shook. Even now, full of shock and mortification, she could feel the flutter of desire echo through her body. She did not know how she could have behaved so badly. It seemed impossible. And yet her body was awakened now and it possessed a dark and disturbing set of desires that were quite beyond the control of reason.

She wanted to run but Henry was too quick for her and caught her arm.

"I'll take you back." His voice was his own now, cool again, distant, while she still felt lost and utterly adrift.

"No." She could not bear to be with him another moment. She was so embarrassed she thought that she would melt with it. Those wicked, delicious sensations of his mouth tugging at her breast…the mere memory of it turned her hot. She did not know how she could have permitted it but she wanted to permit it all over again. She was a wanton and worse still, she actually *wanted* to be wanton. She was bad through and through. And how lovely that felt. No wonder the church deplored such licentiousness. No wonder everyone warned about the dangers of lust.

"I'm not leaving you here." Henry's tone brooked no argument. He walked beside her to the gate and waited patiently as she tried to turn the key in the lock. She was all fingers and thumbs. Eventually he sighed, took the key from her and locked the gate behind them, quickly and efficiently.

They walked back to Bedford Street an impeccably respectable two feet apart. They did not speak. The five minutes it took felt like an hour, but at least it gave the heat in Margery's blood time to cool. She could see what had happened now and mostly it made her feel like a fool. She had met a handsome gentleman and she had liked him rather too much for her own good. She had been in some danger of tumbling foolishly into love with a man she did not really know. As if that were not bad enough, she had discovered that far from being indifferent to carnal pleasures, she rather liked them. In fact she liked them a lot. And between liking and loving she had almost been undone.

"Goodnight, Mr. Ward." Once she was within sight of the area steps Margery was itching to be gone. She knew she would not see Henry again. Her silly Cinderella dream was over and she had almost been fatally burned by it. There was a reason why maidservants were warned to steer clear of handsome gentlemen. It was all too easy to tumble from virtue. She knew that now.

Henry put out a hand and touched her wrist, a light

touch that seemed to sear like a flame. "Margery," he said. "There is something you should know."

He's married, Margery thought. She felt another thud of disappointment and grief. Of course he was. Well, she had learned her lesson good and proper tonight.

"Best not," she said. She pressed her fingers to his lips to silence him and smiled even though there was a prickle of tears in her throat. Better to pretend that she had not been hurt. She did not want him knowing that, as well.

"Goodbye, Mr. Ward," she said.

She hurried down the steps without looking back and closed the door behind her.

Before tonight she had been an innocent but she had not been naive. She had possessed no sexual experience herself but she knew full well what happened between a man and a woman. She had witnessed plenty of passion in the lives of her scandalous ladies. The mistake she had made was to assume that such passion would never touch her, that she, plain Margery Mallon, was an observer in love, not a participant.

Henry's kisses, Henry's touch, had changed all that.

CHAPTER SIX

The King of Pentacles: A man who holds consider-
able responsibility, wealthy and shrewd

HENRY WALKED TO ST. JAMES, the cool night air helping to
clear his head. On the way, he repeated every creative
curse he had learned in a long and active army career.
There was a sharp edge of anger in him and something
that felt disturbingly like guilt. It was not an emotion
that generally troubled him but tonight he felt plagued
by it, guilty for deceiving Margery when she had been
so candid with him and guilty for coming so close to
seducing her. And he had been so close. He had been
within a whisper of dishonoring her. He did not know
what had possessed him. It was the first time in his
entire adult life that he could remember being at the
mercy of his passions. Really, it was quite inexplicable.

Henry raked a hand through his hair. He wondered
if the fact that Margery was denied to him had acted
as some sort of perverse incentive to make her fatally
attractive to him.

Damn it all to hell and back.

He liked Margery. He had not expected to like her.
He had not wanted to like her. It was unnecessary; all
he had to do was fulfill his duty in reuniting her with
her grandfather, and that did not require any emotion

at all. He mistrusted emotion. Too often it was a sign of weakness.

Truth was, he liked Margery very much and that was most definitely a weakness. She possessed candor and sweetness and he found her very appealing. She had almost made him believe that in this harsh world such generous qualities still existed. Almost he was persuaded that Margery could make the world a sweet and sane place for him once again.

He shook his head sharply. He had lost those illusions in his youth. The world was not a sweet, sane place and his impulse to take Margery and lose himself in her was foolish and misplaced. It had almost led him to do something unforgivable.

He straightened his shoulders. Tomorrow he would go to Bedford Street and acquaint Margery with her inheritance. He would escort her to Templemore and then he would be gone from her life. It was the best way. It was the only way. He would forget the beguiling softness of her body and the scent of her hair and the generosity of her nature that had worked on his parched soul like dew falling on dry ground. He would forget it because there was no alternative. In fact, tonight after he had spoken to his cousin, he would go directly to Celia's bed and forget Margery in the most fundamental ways possible.

The cold lack of response in his body told him that it was not Celia he wanted, no matter how willing, no matter how skillful. He swore under his breath. The sooner he had done his duty in delivering Margery to her grandfather the better. He would return to his home at Wardeaux, immerse himself in his latest project and forget her.

The quiet opulence of White's welcomed him. Henry felt a little odd, as though he were an impostor. Once, he had taken all the discreet luxury for granted, the deep armchairs, the excellent brandy, the smell of money, privilege and power. After tomorrow, his title and a handful of land was all that would be left to him. His lost inheritance would be the talk of the ton, at least until the next scandal came along. He did not particularly mind; society's gossip had always been a matter of supreme indifference to him. What he did mind was losing Templemore, not from pride but because he loved it.

"Henry!" His cousin Garrick Farne was waiting for him. Garrick was eight years his senior, his cousin on his mother's side. He pushed out a chair with one lazy foot, gesturing to Henry to join him at a table scattered with the day's newspapers and adorned with a half-full bottle of brandy and two glasses. "I had almost given up on you," Garrick said. "Not that I am complaining. Our appointment saved me the tedium of Lady Dewhurst's rout."

"My apologies for keeping you waiting," Henry said. He shook his cousin's hand.

Garrick made a dismissive gesture. "Always a pleasure, Henry, late or not." His dark eyes appraised him. "We see far too little of you, but I know that you dislike Town."

Henry settled in the chair and accepted the glass of brandy Garrick proffered. "I hope that Merryn is well?" he said. He liked Garrick's wife. She was a bluestocking with an intelligence as sharp as Garrick's own.

Garrick smiled. "Merryn is very well, thank you," he said. "She is *enceinte*."

"Congratulations," Henry said. He knew how much

Merryn wanted a child. She and Garrick had been wed several years and there had been much speculation on when they might set up their nursery.

"Thank you." Garrick inclined his head. "Merryn is very relieved. I think she was afraid we might never have an heir for Farne."

One of Garrick's sisters had died in childbirth. The provision of an heir for a grand estate was often a dangerous affair and the pressure to provide one was huge.

"I imagine that you would rather have Merryn than any number of heirs," Henry said.

It was a well-known fact in the ton that Garrick's second marriage had been a love match. Many people thought Garrick odd for it. Some pitied him. Garrick did not give a damn and Henry admired him for that.

Garrick shrugged. There was a ghost of a smile about his lips. "How perceptive of you, Henry," he said lightly. "As long as Merryn is in good health I am sure all will be well."

The silence settled between them, comfortable as it often was between old friends. There was no sound but for the tick of the clock on the mantel and the hiss of a log falling in the grate. A servant passed by, soft-footed.

"I have news for you, too," Henry said, after a moment.

Garrick raised a brow. "You're getting married. I heard the rumors."

"Not anymore," Henry said. "Your rumors lag behind the times."

"Thank God," Garrick said. "Better to embrace holy orders than Lady Antonia Gristwood."

"Don't preach," Henry begged. "It is not given to us all to marry for love."

"You made one mistake," Garrick said mildly.

"A colossal one," Henry said, "given that my father was one of many men enjoying my wife."

He took a mouthful of the brandy. It did not wash away the taste of betrayal. Drink had not helped at the time, although he had tried to lose himself in it. It did not help now.

"Your father was a first-class cad," Garrick said with unimpaired calm. "And Isobel was somewhat indiscriminate in her affections."

Henry laughed. *Indiscriminate* did not even start to cover the licentious abandon with which his wife had indulged herself. Which was why he had been determined that the second time he married it would be to a cold-blooded aristocrat who understood the meaning of duty. The emotional chaos of his first choice would never be repeated.

He moved his shoulders uncomfortably against the high velvet back of the chair. He seldom thought about Isobel these days. Revisiting the mistakes of his youth was a pointless exercise. Regretting the past achieved nothing.

Suddenly restless, he got up and moved to the window, pulling back the thick red velvet curtains that shut out the London night. He looked out into the dark. Shadows pressed against the window. Above the city he could see the stars hard and bright as diamonds, as they had been a half hour ago when he had almost taken Margery beneath that ridiculously romantic sky.

He sighed. Perhaps there was something dangerously seductive about nights like this. Not that he should be susceptible. Yet, it was at a ball on such a night ten years before that he had first met Isobel Cunningham, the daughter of an impoverished country gentleman, beautiful, sweet-natured, charming, all the things he had thought he had wanted in a wife.

He had been nineteen, a year into his studies at Oxford, romantic by inclination despite—or possibly because—he had witnessed the miserable hash his parents had made of their arranged marriage. He winced now to think of all the bad poetry he had written for Isobel. He had actually composed a love song as well, with harpsichord accompaniment. He shuddered at the memory.

In the end, his wife's sexual indulgence had become so notorious that his godfather had paid her to go away. The Earl of Templemore had bribed her lavishly, dismissively, like a rich man throwing some coins to a beggar in the street. Isobel had taken the money. She had gone abroad with her new fortune and become the mistress of a German prince with an enormous castle on the Rhine. She had died a year later in a carriage accident when she was running away with the prince's groom. Her death had been as lurid a scandal as her life, and Henry's name was a laughing stock, his romantic dreams shredded.

Henry had promptly enlisted in the army to fight Napoleon, much to his godfather's fury. For a while he had wanted to get himself killed, but the passionate anger soon wore off, leaving nothing but cold indifference in its wake.

A cynical smile twisted Henry's lips now. He had been a fool. Marriage, as the Earl of Templemore had said to him, had nothing to do with love. Love was nothing but a weakness.

Garrick was watching him speculatively. "So, if you are not to wed, what is your news?"

Henry resumed his seat and reached for the brandy.

He looked up and met Garrick's perceptive dark gaze. "Lord Templemore has found his lost heir," he said. "His granddaughter is alive and well."

Garrick put down his glass with a snap that spilled the brandy. His eyes narrowed with incredulity. "I had no notion that Lord Templemore was still searching for his granddaughter."

"He never gave up looking for her," Henry said.

"And now he has found her." Garrick shook his head. "Good God, how extraordinary. This will set the ton by the ears." He checked himself. "Good God," he said again, more quietly. "Well, thank you for giving me due warning before the news hits the scandal sheets, Henry. Who is the fortunate lady who will inherit the richest title in the country?"

"Her name is Margery Mallon," Henry said. "She is currently Lady Grant's personal maid. Apparently she was found as a child and adopted by a family in Berkshire."

Once again Garrick looked winded. "A *maidservant?* Wait—" He leaned forward in his chair. "I know Miss Mallon. I met her several years ago." He smiled. "In those days she was maid to Lottie St. Severin."

"If Templemore hears that, he will be reassessing his granddaughter's respectability," Henry said. Garrick's half brother Ethan Ryder, Baron St. Severin, was a notorious rake who had scandalously set Lottie up as his mistress before marrying her. "It would probably be best keep that quiet," he added. "There will be enough gossip without a rehearsal of Miss Mallon's checkered employment history."

"Miss Mallon was also maid to Lady Devlin and

Lady Rothbury," Garrick said dryly, "so I think that any attempts to keep quiet are doomed to failure."

Henry almost choked on his brandy. Even he was starting to reconsider Margery's apparent chastity. It was hard to see how she could have worked for so many scandalous ladies and preserve her innocence. Yet she had been innocent, radiantly so. He knew that. She had been untutored and sweet and eager in his arms. Henry shifted uncomfortably, aware of his growing arousal. He could not get an erection in White's. There were some things that were simply unacceptable, frightfully bad form, and that would be one of them.

"Are you feeling quite well, Henry?" Garrick was looking at him closely.

"I am perfectly well, thank you," Henry said. He took a reckless swig of the brandy, saw Garrick's brows shoot up and hoped his cousin would assume he was drowning his sorrows.

"I feel sorry for Miss Mallon," Garrick said unexpectedly. "What an inheritance. A tyrannical grandfather, a fortune that will be more of a curse than blessing and a family history riddled with tragedy." He sat back in his chair, cradling his brandy glass in his hands. "I assume that you—and Churchward—are absolutely certain she is the rightful heir?"

"We are." Henry spoke a little shortly and saw amused comprehension spill into his cousin's eyes. He had wanted to warn Garrick of the impending scandal. He did not want to talk about the detail. He might move on from the loss of Templemore but there was no need to rub salt into his own wounds.

"I remember the murder of Lady Rose and the loss of her child," Garrick said somberly. "I was only in my teens but a tragedy so great makes an impression on everyone it touches."

Henry remembered the tragedy, as well. Templemore had been enveloped in a terrifying dead calm. There had been no outbursts of emotion, of course; the earl and his relatives were too well bred to show grief. Henry, eleven years old, had tiptoed around everything and everyone, aware of something terrible that was never mentioned.

"They said it was a highway robbery that went wrong," Garrick said, "but I sometimes wondered."

Henry frowned. "You think it was deliberate murder?"

Garrick shrugged slightly. His face was in shadow. "I don't believe in random coincidence as a general rule," he said. "Who benefited from Lady Rose's death?"

"I did," Henry said dryly, "since I became Templemore's heir."

Amusement lit Garrick's eyes. "I acquit you. You would have been a most precocious murderer." He stretched. "What will you do now that Miss Mallon will inherit Templemore?"

"Work," Henry said tersely. "Wellington suggests that I work for the Board of Ordnance."

"Explosives?" Garrick asked.

"Mapping and coastal fortifications," Henry said.

"I thought you might restore your fortunes through marriage." Garrick reached lazily for the brandy bottle, refilling his glass. He offered it to Henry, who shook his head.

"You sound like my mother," Henry said. "She has already proposed that I should wed Miss Mallon, but then I imagine she would probably advocate a match with an elephant if it were heir to Templemore."

"Probably," Garrick agreed. "But she has a point." He leaned forward. "What is Miss Mallon like?"

Henry closed his eyes to ward off the memory of the vivid sweetness of Margery's kiss, to push away the recollection of her warmth and silken softness beneath his hands.

She is exquisite. Seductive. Delicious.

She is forbidden.

He opened his eyes to see Garrick studying him with intense interest.

"Good try, Garrick," he said.

His cousin laughed. "Why not marry her if you want her, Henry?"

Not for the first time in his life, Henry wondered how Garrick always knew everything. It was uncanny.

"Why not go to hell?" he replied.

"Indulge me," Garrick said. "Explain."

"Because Miss Mallon deserves better than me," Henry said shortly. "I'm too cynical. I'd make the devil of a bad husband." He sighed, his gaze on the brandy glass as he turned it round and around in his hand. "Miss Mallon would wish to marry for love," he said, "and that is something that I can never give her."

"Ah, the influence of the lovely Isobel," Garrick said ironically.

Henry shrugged. "Call it what you will. Truth is, there are a hundred reasons why I cannot marry Miss Mallon. I'd be the biggest fortune hunter in London if I did and I'll not live off my wife's money."

"You have too much pride," Garrick said, with the ghost of a smile.

"Perhaps," Henry said. Pride, duty, honor and service were the virtues that had held his life together through all that had happened to him since childhood. They were the principles he would never abandon.

"How did you know?" he was unable to resist asking. "How did you know I had been with Miss Mallon this evening?"

Garrick looked so smug he wanted to punch him.

"You looked as though you had spent the past few hours in Celia Walter's bed," Garrick said. "However, if you had, you would not be in such a bad mood." He shifted. "Then there was the fact that you were quite open about your loss of Templemore but very reluctant to discuss Miss Mallon herself. At first, I thought this was because you disliked her for taking Templemore away from you. Then—" he steepled his fingers "—I thought the reverse was probably true. You were reticent because you like her very much and you didn't want me to guess."

"Bloody hell," Henry growled. "Have you finished?"

"Almost," Garrick said. "Finally, there is the fact that you smell of rose perfume and that you have a hairpin stuck to your jacket." He grinned. "I rest my case."

"Hell," Henry said again. He stared blankly into the fire. "I had no idea I was so easy to read."

"You're not," Garrick said dryly. He rested his chin in one hand. Henry felt his narrowed gaze on his face. "I have to ask, though. What were you thinking?"

"I wasn't thinking," Henry said through his teeth. He felt a sudden and unexpected pang of tenderness for Margery, as though he had failed somehow to protect her. "At least not with my head."

He thought of Margery, with her passion for Gothic romances and her sweet starry-eyed generosity. He felt an utter cad for the way he had behaved, deceiving her, damn near seducing her. It was unforgivable. He was unforgivable.

He pushed back his chair and stood up. "Tomorrow I will tell Miss Mallon about her inheritance, take her to Templemore and get back to my work for Wellington—" He stopped, arrested by the expression on Garrick's face.

"Henry," Garrick said slowly. "Did Miss Mallon know who you were when you met tonight?"

"I—" Henry stopped. "Damnation," he said, after a moment. He could see all too clearly the point that Garrick was making. He wondered that he had not thought of it before. He had felt guilt at deceiving Margery when she had been so open with him. He had deplored his raging lust and his lack of self-control.

He had not thought how Margery might react when she discovered his real identity and that he had been heir to Templemore before her.

"Hell," he said.

"That," his cousin said dryly, "is exactly what will break loose tomorrow when Miss Mallon finds out who you really are."

CHAPTER SEVEN

The Ace of Swords: Change. There are battles
to be fought

"MISS MALLON! MISS MALLON!"

Margery swam up through layers of sleep to find the face of Jessie, the third housemaid, hanging over her. Even though Margery was now awake, the girl continued to shake her shoulder as though she could not stop. "Wake up!"

"I am awake." Margery sat up and reached for her wrap. The room was already bright with sunlight even though the battered little clock on the shelf over the fire registered only eight o'clock. Margery's head ached. Normally she was up at six. She had overslept. "What on earth is the matter?" She took in, for the first time, the pinched expression on Jessie's face and the fear in her eyes.

"Lady Grant is asking for you." Jessie sat down heavily on Margery's little narrow bed, which sagged in glum protest. "There's trouble. I don't know what, but it's bad. Something terrible has happened."

Trouble.

Margery felt a clutch of fear. Lady Grant seldom rose before ten and only then in the direst emergency. Surely—her stomach did a dizzy swoop and she felt sick—surely Lady Grant could not know what had happened last night, could not know that her maid had behaved like a wanton, drinking ale in an inn of ill repute, dining with a gentleman and then kissing him to within an inch of her life. More than mere kissing, if she were truthful....

Her body heated to a burning blush as she remembered all the liberties she had allowed Henry to take and the way in which she had responded to him. For a second when she had awoken she had hoped that it was all a dream. It was not.

But perhaps Lady Grant *did* know. Perhaps someone had seen her with Henry in Bedford Square Gardens and reported her for lewd behavior. Her mind spun and the ache in her head stabbed at her viciously. She could imagine the outcry. She could even see in her mind's eye the constable coming to take her away. They would put her in the stocks and brand her a whore. She grabbed the wooden rail at the end of the bed to steady herself.

"Are you quite well, Miss Mallon?" Jessie was looking at her with sharp curiosity. Margery knew that some of the housemaids resented the fact that she had achieved the rank of lady's maid so young. Some of them would not be sorry to see her fall from grace.

"I am very well, thank you," she said briskly. "Pray tell Lady Grant that I shall be down directly."

It took her only a few minutes to slip on her gown—thank goodness she had one freshly pressed—and to braid her hair into a neat plait. Those few minutes also enabled her to persuade herself that Lady Grant's early rising and the trouble that Jessie had referred to were in no way connected to her. Of course they were not. It was both fanciful and presumptuous of her to imagine it.

As she hurried down the stairs to Lady Grant's bed-chamber she was aware of a strange atmosphere in the house. It was silent and yet it felt tense, waiting. Margery shivered. Her hand shook a little as she knocked on the oaken panels of Lady Grant's door and turned the handle.

Lady Grant was in her nightgown in the dressing room, rummaging through her chest of drawers, leaving all of Margery's carefully arranged piles of clothing in complete disarray. Her rich red-gold hair tumbled in artistic profusion over her bare shoulders above the lace embroidery of her neckline. She looked at once harassed and fragile, and when Margery came in she swooped on her with a cry of gladness.

"Margery! Oh, thank goodness! You have no idea…. Mr. Churchward is here—the lawyer—at seven-thirty in the morning! I sent Alex to deal with him but he insists that I join them and I have no notion what to wear. I simply *cannot* be expected to decide such matters before I have had my morning chocolate…."

The door opened and Lord Grant strode in. "Joanna," he said. "I left you twenty minutes ago and you are no further forward now than you were then."

"Ten more minutes, my lord," Margery said, pushing Lady Grant gently but firmly away from the chest and selecting a range of undergarments at the same time. "I promise."

Lord Grant's incisive gaze swept Margery from head to foot. "Miss…Mallon, is it not? I think that you had better attend the drawing room with my wife when she is ready." He nodded to her, smiled at Lady Grant and went out closing the door with a decisive click.

Margery's heart gave a great, sickening lurch. Lady

Grant was staring at her as though she had suddenly grown a second head. "Well! What can that be about?"

"I have no notion, ma'am," Margery said woodenly. "Here are your stockings, ma'am. And may I suggest the pink day gown and matching slippers?"

She managed to get Lady Grant into her clothes with great difficulty. It was like trying to dress a slippery fish, because her ladyship was forever changing her mind about what she would wear, kept wriggling out of one outfit and into another, and rushed to the mirror to check which colors were most flattering to her morning complexion. Finally, a half hour later than promised, they were both ready.

The challenge of getting Lady Grant dressed had distracted Margery for a while, but as she trailed her employer down the broad sweeping stair her anxiety returned, the feeling of sick dread intensifying with every step she took.

She had no notion how she would defend herself against the charge that she had behaved with lewd abandon the previous night. She could not bear to see the disgust and shock in Lady Grant's eyes when she heard what had happened. For all Joanna Grant's maddening butterfly mind, she was the kindest and most thoughtful of employers. They respected each other, they liked each other, and Margery could not bear to disappoint Lady Grant. Her throat felt dry. Her tongue seemed to be sticking to the roof of her mouth. She swallowed hard as the footman opened the drawing room door and she followed her employer inside.

Immediately matters became a whole lot worse.

There was a man standing beside the long windows that looked out across the terrace and the garden beyond. He was tall and broad and the sunlight fell on his hair giving it a blue-black sheen. He was dressed immaculately in a coat of green superfine and skintight breeches that emphasized his muscular thighs. His boots had a high polish. His linen was starched, his cravat a masterpiece of mathematical complication.

Margery could not see his face clearly; the sun slanted across the room hiding the expression in his eyes. He turned to look at her as she walked in and she thought that she was going to faint. She barely noticed Mr. Churchward, who had stood up and was bowing over Lady Grant's hand with old-fashioned courtesy.

"I do apologize for disturbing you at this shockingly uncivilized hour, Lady Grant," the lawyer was saying. "Only the urgency of my business can excuse it." He gestured to his companion. "I believe you are already acquainted with Lord Wardeaux?"

Lord Wardeaux.

Margery's heart jumped. Not the gentleman Henry Ward, then, but the nobleman Lord Wardeaux, whom she was already sure was no gentleman at all.

"Of course," Lady Grant said. "Henry is practically a member of the family, since my sister Merryn is married to his cousin." She was masking her curiosity and her puzzlement behind her exquisite manners. "How do you do?" She gave Henry her hand and Margery watched as he bent to kiss her cheek.

"My lady," he murmured. "I hope you are well?"

Margery was far from well herself. She felt sick. She tried to reverse out of the room but the door had been closed and her hot palms met nothing but the cool wood. From a distance she could hear Mr. Churchward's

voice and she realized that all four of the others were
looking at her.

"I believe," the lawyer was saying with careful lack
of emphasis, "that you, too, have already met Lord
Wardeaux, Miss Mallon?"

Margery straightened. She was not going down without a fight.

"Indeed I have," she said coldly. "Although he was
calling himself something different at the time."

A flicker of a smile touched Henry Wardeaux's handsome mouth. He bowed. "Miss Mallon."

"My lord." Margery was damned if she was going to
curtsy to him. She inclined her head the slightest inch
and saw his smile deepen.

There was an odd silence. "Perhaps, Mr. Churchward," Joanna Grant interposed, "you might explain
your urgent business? In simple terms, if you please. I
fear I do not function well without my morning chocolate." She reached for the bell pull. "In fact, let us order
some more coffee—"

"Brandy," Lord Grant said, his eyes on Margery's
face, "might be more useful."

His wife's eyebrows shot up. "At this time of the
day?"

"And *sal volatile*," Alex said. "Just in case Miss Mallon requires it. Won't you take a seat, Miss Mallon? I
believe you are going to need one."

Margery's pulse was pounding so hard she could feel
the tremor of it through her entire body. Bonelessly, she
slid into the chair that Henry held for her. Mr. Churchward was fumbling with the fastenings on his battered
document case.

"I realize that this will come as a shock to all of you."

He looked up, directly at Margery. "But most particularly to Miss Mallon." He hesitated.

"Out with it, Mr. Churchward," Alex Grant said, "before my wife and Miss Mallon expire with the anticipation."

Mr. Churchward shuffled his papers. "Very well, my lord. Miss Mallon…" He cleared his throat. "I have to tell you that you are, in point of fact, not Margery Mallon at all but Lady Marguerite Catherine Rose Saint-Pierre, granddaughter of the Earl of Templemore and heir to the Earldom of Templemore in the county of Berkshire. You were lost when you were a child and the earl has been trying to trace you ever since."

Having finished his announcement, Churchward sat back in his seat.

Margery had not really heard him. She had been braced for some lurid revelation about her conduct the previous night, and looking up she saw that Henry had read her mind and knew exactly what she was thinking. For a moment she saw the secret amusement leap into his eyes before his expression closed down again. Then Churchward's announcement penetrated her preoccupation and she looked at him in complete confusion.

"I… No… What? Lady Marguerite Saint-Pierre? I beg your pardon?" It was scarcely coherent and glancing around she saw that Lady Grant was looking almost as shocked as she felt. Lord Grant, who had obviously heard the tale already, was not.

"You are heir to the Earl of Templemore," he repeated. "Congratulations, Miss Mallon." He glanced at Lady Grant. "I do believe you have achieved the singular attainment of silencing my wife, Churchward. Unheard-of."

"My lord," Churchward said reproachfully. He mopped his brow on a surprisingly frivolous spotted handkerchief.

"This is a joke," Margery said. "A trick." Her voice came out louder than she intended and seemed to bounce off the walls of the drawing room.

She looked at Henry. "You," she said. "This is all your doing. Who are you anyway, and why are you here? No, thank you—" She pushed away the coffee cup he was proffering. "I do not want your coffee. I do not want anything from you, you…you snake! You deceived me—"

Her voice broke and she could feel the tears pressing on her throat. It was foolish, so very foolish, to want to cry now. Half her mind was wrestling with the lawyer's startling and impossible news while the other half was grappling with the extent of Henry Wardeaux's perfidy. The latter, extraordinarily, seemed more important to her. All the previous evening, when Henry had plied her with ale and questions abut her childhood, he had known the truth. When he had held her in his arms and kissed her with such skill and passion he had known he was kissing Lady Marguerite Saint-Pierre, not little Margery Mallon. When he had so nearly made love to her, he had exposed her, body and soul, but given nothing of his true self. He had deliberately withheld the information from her. He had not told her who he was.

He had been lying to her from the first.

She felt sick and angry and betrayed.

Henry put the cup down gently on the table beside her. "Pull yourself together, Lady Marguerite," he said, with no discernible sympathy. "You are made of stronger stuff than this."

Margery wiped away a furious tear with the back of her hand. So now she was expected to act like some bloodless aristocrat simply because they had told her she was one. She glared up at him.

"Pig," she said distinctly. "Snake in the grass."

"Oh, dear, oh, dear," Mr. Churchward was saying. "I knew this would all come out the wrong way."

"I am not sure," Lady Grant said, "that there could have been a better way, Mr. Churchward." There was a rustle of silk as she moved to kneel by Margery's chair and took her hands in a comforting grip. "Margery," she said. "My dear, I know it is a shock."

"It's a trick," Margery said again, faintly this time. "A hoax. It cannot possibly be true."

"Mr. Churchward does not play tricks," Lady Grant said. "It is not in his nature. Especially not over something as important as this."

"Indeed not," the lawyer said, heartfelt. "Jokes? I do not think so." He rooted around in the document case and withdrew a couple of items. "You recognize these, I believe," he said, laying two battered velvet cases on the table in front of her.

Margery picked them up. The first case contained a big locket in gold, engraved with a swirl of letters, *MSP,* and a family crest. It was dull with dirt and age but Margery still recognized it. She gave a little gasp.

"I remember this from my childhood," she said uncertainly. "My brother Billy found the locket in my mother's effects when she died last year. She had told me it was mine."

They had argued about it, she remembered. Billy had said he would have the locket and accompanying brooch valued for her. Margery had accused him of stealing them from her. She knew he would sell them. It was a small inheritance to lose but she had been hurt and angry.

She opened the catch and stared at the painted figures inside. One was a lady with golden hair, the other a dark man in a blue velvet coat. The paintings were yellowed and cracked. "I used to make up stories about them when I was a child," she said, frowning a little. "There was a golden brooch, as well...."

Silently, Mr. Churchward laid a brooch on the table beside the locket. It also had the letters *MSP* spelled out in precious stones. One of the jewels was missing. The others had lost their luster and were dull and dark.

"Your brother William brought these to me a month ago," Mr. Churchward said. "He told me that he had taken them to a reputable jeweler who had recognized them as being of great value. The design matched that of some other pieces that the man had seen. He recognized the crest as being that of the Earl of Templemore."

A cold shiver ran down Margery's spine. Something shifted in her memory. There were images and thoughts that were still a confused blur but were trying to tell her something, something she felt very deeply and insistently, like a memory that had been lost. She could picture the gold jewelry and a little blue silk and lace gown, torn and dirty....

"The blue silk..." she said. "Silk and lace. The dress..."

"Blue silk was what you were wearing when you disappeared," Mr. Churchward said.

Margery gave a gasp and pressed a hand to her mouth. Immediately, Henry offered her a glass of brandy, and this time Margery did not refuse it. The spirit burned her throat and almost made her choke but it did steady her.

"It cannot possibly be true," she said. "It's nonsense." She could hear the beseeching note in her own voice, begging for someone to tell her that it was all a ruse. She tilted the glass to her lips again. The fiery spirit streaked through her, making her feel reckless and unguarded.

She felt as though she had stumbled into some nightmarish fantasy. Lady Marguerite? If she was a lady then pigs might fly. She was Margery Mallon, daughter of a Wantage blacksmith, a lady's maid with ambitions to be a confectioner. She liked being Margery Mallon. She did not know how to be anyone else. She felt a clutch of fear. This had to be a mistake. She drained the glass.

"Don't have too much," Henry instructed. "We cannot do with you being three sheets to the wind at a time like this."

Margery fixed him with a withering look. "You have changed your tune from last night! Plying me with ale in order to gain information from me—and worse...."

Mr. Churchward cleared his throat very loudly. He looked as though he was blushing. He shuffled his papers back into his document case. "Lady Marguerite," he said. "Such recriminations must wait." He shot Henry a reproachful look. "Lord Wardeaux is the Earl of Templemore's godson and I assure you that he has been acting out of the purest motives."

"Nonsense," Margery said coldly. "Pure? Lord Wardeaux? He is a blackguard and I do not believe a word he says. Nor do I do believe I am Lady Marguerite whatever her name is. The idea is absurd. There must be some mistake."

"You can certainly make no claim to behaving like

a lady at present," Henry said grimly. He grabbed her by the upper arms, ignoring Joanna Grant's murmured protest. His eyes blazed into hers. "Lady Marguerite," he said, "entertaining as this is, we do not have the time right now. Mr. Churchward will explain everything on the way to Berkshire. We will leave immediately."

"No, we will not," Margery said stubbornly. "I am not going anywhere before Mr. Churchward explains. In full."

She thought for a moment that Henry was going to shake her—or kiss her. Something fierce burned in his eyes, reminding her of the previous night and the passion that had flared so hot and so fast between them. His hands tightened on her shoulders before he released her as quickly as he had grabbed her, dropping her back in her seat and turning away.

"You have your grandfather's stubbornness." He bit out the words. "That is for sure."

Margery knew she was behaving badly but shock and disappointment together had knocked her off balance. All she could think of was the ache of betrayal deep inside, the knowledge that Henry had only sought her out because he was asked to do so, and everything that had followed had been a lie. It hurt.

It should not matter, but it did. She had liked him far too much and now she could see he was not the man she had thought he was. He had charmed her completely and for his own ends. He had ruthlessly pursued his own agenda out of no more than duty and she, naive little fool that she was, had been utterly taken in.

"Mr. Churchward," Henry said. "As briefly as possible, if you please." He had evidently accepted that she would be going nowhere without an explanation. Mar-

gery felt a flash of triumph that, in this one small thing
at least, she could make him do her will.

"As you wish, my lord." Mr. Churchward looked
pained, as though to be brief was an abdication of responsibility. "Your mama," he said to Margery, "was
Lady Rose Saint-Pierre, the Earl of Templemore's only
child. When she was one and twenty she eloped with a
French émigré, Comte Antoine de Saint-Pierre, against
the wishes of her father." Mr. Churchward fidgeted with
the clasp of his briefcase, avoiding Margery's eyes.

"The marriage was a fiasco," Henry intervened bru-
tally. Margery flinched but he did not soften his words.

"Saint-Pierre was a fortune hunter and a French spy
who after a few years left Lady Rose and their daughter—" He paused, his gaze resting on Margery's face.
"You, Lady Marguerite, in the country while he pursued the life of a bachelor here in London. Drinking,
gambling, whoring—"

"Ladies present!" Mr. Churchward protested faintly.

Henry bowed ironically. "Ladies, my apology. In
brief, after a year or so of this humiliation, Lady Rose
set out for London with her child, intent on pleading
with her husband to take them back. According to the
servants at his rooms, Saint-Pierre turned her away.
He told her that he had no further use for her and never
wanted to see her again. On the way back to Berkshire,
Lady Rose's coach was ambushed and she was killed."

Margery pressed her hands together. They were cold
and trembling. She felt chilled all over. There was a
buzzing in her ears.

"It was a terrible, terrible business." Mr. Churchward's face was pinched with old memories. "When

the rescuers came upon the carriage they found Lady Rose dead and the child vanished."

Gooseflesh breathed along Margery's skin again. The carriage, she thought. The flight through the night, the tears…the memories that had haunted her, that had lived at the back of her mind, were suddenly garish and vivid in their horror.

"My parents quarreled that night," she said very slowly. "I remember now. There were raised voices. I think they were throwing things at each other. A mirror broke." She could see the shattered reflection and the slivers of glass on the carpet. She could see herself cowering in a corner of the room.

"My mama was crying," she said. "She picked me up and ran out and bundled me back into the coach and we set off for home—" She broke off, shivering. On the edges of her memory she could feel the jagged horror of that night. She had known that something was dreadfully wrong and that her world had broken into a thousand pieces, but she had been too young to understand. "What happened to him? What happened to my father?"

Mr. Churchward's hands shook; his coffee cup rattled in its saucer. It was Henry who answered.

"After your mama died and you disappeared, Saint-Pierre went back to France," he said. "There were those who thought he had arranged his wife's death and taken you away, but he always swore he was innocent of it."

"I never saw him again." Margery frowned. "I cannot even really remember what he looked like." She gave a violent shudder and covered her face with her hands. Instantly, Lady Grant was by her side again, holding her close in a comforting hug.

"Margery," she said. "My dear child. Don't think about it anymore."

"I don't remember anything else," Margery said. She put a hand up to her head as though to soothe the jagged memories. "I don't recall what happened."

"Good," Lady Grant said robustly. "You must have been very young. Of course you will not remember and it is better that you do not."

Henry was looking at her quizzically. "You remember nothing of how you came to be living in Wantage with the Mallon family?"

Margery shook her head. There were disconnected snatches of pictures in her mind but nothing that made any sense. "I remember nothing else," she repeated.

She sat up straighter and ran her palms down her skirts, fidgeting nervously, trying to gather some composure. She felt shocked and distressed. The bottom had fallen out of her world and she had no certainties anymore. She did not even know who she really was. Everything she thought was true had been built on sand.

She looked up to see Henry's steady, dark gaze on her. She wished she could trust him and look to him for support and strength. She felt a powerful impulse to turn to him. The intensity of her need shocked her. But hot on the heels of it came disillusion and bitterness. Henry had deceived her. He had done so callously, ruthlessly. She had to remember that his first loyalty was to her grandfather, not to her. He was a man driven by duty, not by compassion, a dangerous man to her.

"So it was Billy who went to you," she said to Mr. Churchward. "I wish he had spoken to me first." She shook her head. Suddenly she wished—oh, how she wished—that Granny Mallon were here with her sound good sense. She longed suddenly for her parents; she wondered why they had never told her about her true identity. Her past suddenly felt like a puzzle with the pieces broken and reforming into new shapes. There were gaps and sharp edges and she was alone in dealing with them.

"Jem!" She exclaimed. "I must speak to Jem. Surely he will remember something of what happened?"

She did not miss the look that flashed between Henry and Mr. Churchward.

"You may, of course, speak with your brother just as soon as it can be arranged," Henry said smoothly. "But in the meantime—" he glanced at the pretty little china clock on the mantel "—it is a matter of urgency that we leave for Berkshire as soon as we can."

Margery felt as though everything was happening too quickly, reality sliding away from her. She grasped for something familiar. "I want to see Jem," she insisted. "It cannot be so urgent that we have to go at once. We could send for him—"

"You are seeking to delay the inevitable, Miss Mallon," Henry said, with brutal directness. "It is urgent we leave, because your grandfather is dying. If we do not go at once, it may be too late."

Margery's gaze instinctively sought out Mr. Churchward. He nodded. "Lord Wardeaux is correct. The Earl of Templemore is a very sick man. I am sorry, my lady."

My lady, Margery thought. *Help.*

"I think," Lord Grant said, effortlessly taking charge, "that it might be a good idea to slow matters down a little. We shall send immediately to Lord Templemore to tell him that his granddaughter is now apprised of her situation and will be setting out for Berkshire later this morning. I am sure that the good news will give him heart and lift his spirits. Then—" he smiled at Margery "—Miss…um…Lady Marguerite will have a little time to prepare for her journey, send a message to her brother to join her in Berkshire and do whatever else is necessary."

"An excellent idea, Alex, darling." Lady Grant leapt in to second her husband. "A lady has so many matters to consider at a time like this. I shall advise Lady Marguerite on what to pack, though I scarcely know where to start."

"Please," Margery said. "No more of this 'Lady Marguerite.' My name has been Margery for twenty years and I cannot adjust to another now."

Henry looked doubtful and Lady Grant seemed most put out. "But Margery, darling," she said plaintively, "that is a name fit only for servants whereas you are going to be a countess."

Margery blinked. She looked at Churchward again. "Am I?" she said faintly.

"The Templemore title and estate is one of only a handful in the country that may devolve down the female line," Mr. Churchward confirmed. "Until you were found, Lord Wardeaux was the Earl of Templemore's heir—" He stopped abruptly, his face the picture of guilt. There was a long, heavy silence. Margery looked at Henry. His expression was completely blank.

"I see," she said slowly. "Thank you, Mr. Churchward." She looked at the array of faces looking back at her. "I should like to speak to Lord Wardeaux now," she said. "Alone, if you please."

"It would be most improper," Lady Grant pointed out. "You are a young, unmarried heiress."

Margery laughed. "And I have been a young unmarried maidservant for the last twelve years," she said. "I assure you, ma'am, that my life has been most improper by the standards of society and nothing will be able to rectify that. Now, please, I would like to speak with Lord Wardeaux."

And because she was now Lady Marguerite and heir to Templemore, no one argued with her.

THE DOOR CLOSED BEHIND Lord and Lady Grant and Mr. Churchward. Through the thick walnut panels Henry could still hear Lady Grant's voice. "This will set the town by the ears, Alex! How are we to make Margery respectable enough to be a lady?"

Henry also heard Lord Grant's laconic reply. "My love, Lady Marguerite's immense fortune will make her the most respectable heiress in London without any help from you."

"Lord Wardeaux," Margery said, claiming his attention. She spoke very precisely, as though she had been raised with a silver spoon in her mouth rather than gaining one five minutes before. Everything about her, the determined jut of her chin, the challenge in her steady gray eyes and the indignant grace with which she held herself, spoke of character and strength.

This morning she looked neat and buttoned up, a far cry from the passionate woman Henry had held in his arms the previous night. The silken gold-brown of her hair was fastened up in a bun beneath a ridiculously frumpy lace cap. Not a single strand escaped the pins. The plain black gown she wore as befitting her status as a lady's maid was unflattering, draining the color from her face and obscuring her figure, making her almost invisible. None of this seemed to influence the potent physical desire Henry discovered he still had for her. In fact, it made it worse. The prim uniform was already driving him to distraction. He wanted to peel it off her. He had never had a fixation about servants or uniforms. This was something new and, he suspected, an attraction confined solely to Margery.

"Lord Wardeaux." Margery sounded impatient and Henry realized that she had already addressed him once. "You are not concentrating."

Oh, he was concentrating, all right. Though not on the right things.

"Lady Marguerite," Henry said, sketching a bow.

Her direct gray gaze made no secret of her dislike for him. "You were not so formal last night," she said, her chin at a very haughty angle.

"Nor," Henry said, "were you."

He saw the anger in her eyes increase a notch at the reminder of just how informal they had been with each other. "I was under a misapprehension," Margery said coolly. "For a start, I thought you were a gentleman."

Touché.

"I am sorry—" Henry started to say, but she cut him off.

"I beg leave to doubt that." Her voice was laced with contempt. "I doubt that you regret anything that you did last night." She paused as though struck by a sudden and unwelcome thought. "We are not *related,* are we?"

"Nothing to signify," Henry said. "Seventh cousins, perhaps. We are close enough for you to call me Henry if you wish."

Margery's eyes narrowed. "There are many things I wish to call you," she said, "but Lord Wardeaux will suffice for now." She turned and walked away from him as though she could not bear to look at him.

"Mr. Churchward said that my grandfather was also your godfather," she said.

"That is correct," Henry said.

She spun around. "And that before I was found, you were the heir to…Templemore, is it?"

"That is also correct," Henry said. He could see very clearly where this was leading. "But—"

"And now I have taken all that from you," Margery said, with devastating frankness. "The title, the estate and a fortune."

"Yes," Henry said. "You have. You are the richest heiress in the country."

For a moment she looked shocked but she recovered herself quickly, partly, he suspected, because she had no idea quite how rich the richest heiress in the country would be. That would only become clear to her when she saw Templemore. And when the ton started toadying to her.

"How gratifying it is to be so rich," she said dryly. "The point I was intending to make, however, was that I know that your behavior last night—your low, scheming, *despicable* behavior toward me—" she enunciated very carefully with searing scorn "—was intended to lose me my inheritance."

Henry was entertained despite himself. "You know more than I do then," he said politely.

Her gaze narrowed on him. "You deny it?" she demanded. "When you were going to seduce me." Her voice rose sharply with anger. "And then tell my grandfather I was no more than a strumpet so that he disinherited me in your favor?"

Having delivered this broadside she stood, hands on hips, regarding Henry with disdain. There was something slightly comical about her tiny, dignified, infuriated figure. Henry tried to repress a smile but he was not quick enough. She saw his expression and glared at him.

"Would that it were so easy," Henry said. "Alas, Lady Marguerite, the laws of inheritance cannot be bent to my will. You could be the most notorious courtesan in London and it would not change the fact that you are heiress to Templemore."

He caught her wrist and pulled her close, moving so suddenly that she jumped even though he held her lightly. "Your logic is also at fault," he said softly. "If I had intended to seduce you I would not have stopped."

So close to her now, he could smell the honey scent of her skin and feel the flutter of her pulse beneath his fingers. He allowed his gaze to travel over her. His gaze lingered on her lips and she blushed. Her own gaze fell, her lashes lowered against the curve of her cheek. The awareness flared between them as quick and hot as it had done the previous night. Arousal stung her cheeks pink and gave a slumberous glitter to her eyes. Her lips parted and all of a sudden he was within an ace of kissing her. He bent his head.

"Do that and I shall plant my knee in your groin," Margery said wrathfully. "You treacherous *bastard*."

Well, he had deserved that. Henry grinned and released her wrist. The ton, he thought, had never seen anything quite like Lady Marguerite Saint-Pierre. The dowagers would be fainting in the ballrooms.

Margery's color was still high and she was rubbing her wrist where he had held her.

"Even if you did not intend to ruin me," she said, "you certainly meant to compromise me sufficiently that I would be obliged to marry you so you would regain your inheritance. You are a manipulative scoundrel."

"Acquit me of those motives," Henry said. "I have no desire to marry you."

Now he had really annoyed her, which was hardly surprising since he had been less than flattering. She was upset, too. He saw hurt behind the anger in her eyes, though she tried quickly to hide it, turning away.

"You do not trouble to charm me any longer, Lord Wardeaux," she said. "Now that there is nothing to gain."

"I had to do it," Henry said, exasperated by the distress he could see in her face. "My first loyalty was to the earl and to establishing the truth. I needed to know if you really were Marguerite Saint-Pierre."

"And you think that justifies your behaving like a *snake* and deceiving me?" Margery demanded. "You could simply have told me what you were about."

"I could not confide in you," Henry said. He ran a hand abruptly through his hair. He felt frustrated and angry. It was impossible to tell her all the reasons behind his actions. This was not the time to warn her that as sole witness to her mother's murder she might be in danger; already she had had to accept so much and frightening her further would achieve nothing. "Your family might have exploited the situation," he said truthfully. "What if you had been an adventuress, set on preying upon the weakness of an old man? How easy it would be to convince Lord Templemore that you genuinely were his granddaughter—" He broke off, but not quickly enough. Margery's eyes had widened with shock and for a moment he saw vivid pain reflected there.

"I see," she said. "Not only do you think my family are a bunch of criminals—and these are the people who took me in and cared for me out of no more than kindness—but you also suspected that I might have an eye to the main chance." She turned her face away. "So that is your opinion of me." The contempt in her voice was cutting. "I thought that we knew each other better than that—but of course I had not realized it was all a pretense."

Henry interrupted her, his voice hard and angry. "It was not all pretense—"

Margery placed her hands over her ears. "Stop it! I do not want to hear any more of your justifications."

"You will hear me," Henry said. It was terrifying how quickly she could cut through the cold logic that normally governed his actions and make him feel. He did not like losing control, yet he could feel it slipping from him. He stalked across the room and Margery retreated before him until she backed into a rosewood table. Henry placed one hand on each side of her, trapping her against the solid wood, his body only inches from hers. Immediately she went rigid.

"Let me go," she said through her teeth.

"You will hear me out," Henry said.

Their gazes locked, turbulent, dark and stormy. Henry raised a hand and traced a line along her jaw. Her skin warmed beneath his touch. She tried to turn her face away from him.

"You have all the Templemore pride, Lady Marguerite," he said softly, mockingly.

She jerked her chin away from his hand. "And you are every inch the arrogant nobleman." Her eyes met his defiantly. "Very well, say your piece, but do not expect me to believe you."

"My motives were of the purest, I assure you," Henry said. "I did what I had to do for the sake of your grandfather and for Templemore."

Clearly he had failed to convince her. "Is that the best you can do?" she asked contemptuously. "It would not convince a child. You did not need to kiss me to establish my ancestry. You did not need to make love to me."

Their eyes met. Awareness, sweet and hot, shimmered between them again. Antagonism gave it a sharp, dangerous edge.

"No, I did not," Henry said. "But how hypocritical you are being if you pretend that you did not enjoy it, too."

He heard her gasp of outrage a second before his mouth took hers in a tumultuous kiss. He felt her instant response and how hard she struggled to resist it. But she was as lost as he; where attraction flared there was no withstanding it. He held her still against the table and he bit down gently on her full lower lip, and when she opened for him he slid his tongue into her mouth. He kissed her with hunger and demand and felt her melt for him. It was delicious, and he most certainly should not be doing it, but he let his good intentions go to hell. Perhaps he had more of his late, unlamented, rakish father in him than he had previously realized.

"Admit it," he said, as his lips left hers. "You like me."

She gave an infuriated squeak, pushing ineffectually

against his chest. "Are you trying to prove something? You know I *detest* you."

"All right," Henry said. "I accept that. But you are still attracted to me." He stepped back an inch and Margery slid past him in an angry rustle of her black bombazine skirts.

"Coxcomb," she said, turning on him. "I do not find you remotely attractive." She gave her head an impatient little shake. "You are insufferable. I want you to know that you were not the first to kiss me and you were certainly not the *best*."

Henry laughed. "I do not believe you on either score," he said. "No one had kissed you before I did."

Margery looked infuriated. "They most certainly had!"

"You lie badly," Henry said. He smiled at her. "Most honest people do."

"You did not seem to have much trouble last night," Margery said cuttingly. She made a dismissive gesture. "No matter. I am hopeful that, now you have informed me of my inheritance, I need not see you again."

"A vain hope, I fear," Henry said. "I am escorting you to Templemore."

"You are mistaken," Margery said. She was drumming her fingers on the top of the desk in anger and impatience. "I have no desire to be Lady Marguerite. I like being Margery Mallon. I don't want the title or the estate. You were the heir. You wanted it." Her gaze defied him. "You take it."

Henry could feel his impatience rising. "Once again, you misunderstand the laws of inheritance," he said. "You cannot refuse your title. It is who you are."

"I'm not going," Margery said. She crossed her arms, small but decidedly immovable.

Damnation but she was stubborn. She had all the obstinacy of her grandfather and more. Henry toyed with the idea of simply picking her up and carrying her out to the waiting carriage.

"Your grandfather…" He stopped. He had promised the old man that he would deliver his granddaughter to him and he was going to do precisely that. "He deserves better than this," he said. "Templemore deserves better than this."

"They are nothing to me," Margery said. "I am Margery Mallon, a lady's maid. I want nothing more than that. Bring me the papers—" She snapped her fingers. "I will sign away my claim."

With a monumental effort of will, Henry held on to his temper. The one thing he cared for, the only thing he loved, was Templemore, every brick, every blade of grass. He wanted the place with a passion. Margery was rejecting it sight unseen.

It had not once occurred to him that Margery might repudiate her inheritance. What person in their right mind would give up the estate, the title, the position, the money? No servant, brought up in poverty, would turn down such advancement. It was absurd.

"Your wits are gone begging if you think that Lady Grant would continue to employ you as her maid," he said coldly. "Nor would your grandfather stand for it. You do not have a choice in this. If you refuse to go to Templemore I shall pick you up and put you in the carriage myself."

Margery had turned away. She pressed her hands together. "I'm not going," she repeated, but this time there was a wobble in her voice and Henry heard it.

"You're afraid," he said slowly.

"No!" She rejected his comfort instantly. "Of course I am not." Her shoulders were hunched, her entire body taut with tension. "I…I simply do not want to be Lady Marguerite."

Henry heard it again, the betraying tremble in her voice. She was trying so hard to conceal her fear but her body betrayed her. He came over to her. He put both hands on her shoulders, gently this time. He could feel her shaking; she was racked with tiny shivers. She would not meet his eyes.

"It will be all right," he said. He stroked her shoulders, feeling the slenderness of her beneath his hands. She was so taut it felt as though she might snap. He had no idea how to console her, how to help her. He wanted to pull her close and comfort her and the realization shocked him. He was no good at intimacy. He had no use for it.

"What is he like?" she asked. "My grandfather?" She raised her gaze to Henry's at last and he saw all the apprehension and bewilderment in her eyes. It was the look of someone whose life had been turned inside out in the space of a few short moments.

It would not help to tell her that her grandfather was a terrifying autocrat who, once he had set his mind to something, would not be gainsaid.

"He is a lonely old man," Henry said, "and he will be extraordinarily happy to know you."

It was the right thing to say. The spontaneous smile that he remembered from the previous night broke across Margery's face and Henry was taken aback to feel another stab of tenderness for her, this one more piercing, more compulsive than the last. He almost drew her into his arms but she stepped back, deliberately putting space between them.

Her trust in him was gone. Henry told himself that it was better that way.

All he had to do now was take her to Templemore. And then he would be gone from her life.

CHAPTER EIGHT

The Nine of Pentacles: Comfort and prosperity

IT WAS THREE HOURS before they were ready to depart, by which time Margery was pleased to observe that Henry was in a very bad mood indeed. It was not that she had been deliberately slow, more that there suddenly seemed to be so much to do.

First, Margery wrote to all her brothers to tell them what had happened and to ask them to visit her at Templemore. She suspected that Jem would be the only one to come. Billy never left London and Jed would be unable to read her news since he had never learned his letters.

She had also sent a hastily scrawled note to Lady Grant's cousin by marriage, Francesca Alton. Lady Alton was a widow whose husband had died the previous year when he was run over by a carriage while reeling blind drunk across the road. Everyone had agreed that Fitzwilliam Alton's death was no loss, but his family had cut Chessie out completely, consigning her to live off the generosity of her relatives. Joanna Grant had pointed out that Chessie would make Margery the most perfect companion. She was young, pretty and fun and she knew how to go on in society. Margery had agreed. She liked Chessie Alton and she desperately needed a friend.

Then there had been the packing.

"You need not take any portmanteaux," Henry said. He was striding impatiently back and forth across the checkered marble floor of the entrance hall while he waited for her. "I am sure Lord Grant will be kind enough to send on your belongings. and once we reach Templemore you may purchase anything else you need."

"That sounds frightfully extravagant," Margery said. "I do not know the sort of ladies you are familiar with, Lord Wardeaux, but my packing will take all of ten minutes and fill no more than one small box."

Lady Grant had other ideas, however. "You are Lady Marguerite now," she said firmly. "Come with me."

Margery followed her former employer up the stairs to her bedchamber. There was no question this time about her using the servants' stair. Those days, she realized with a pang, were gone forever. Already her former colleagues were treating her differently.

Not everyone was pleased for her. In fact, it felt as though no one was pleased for her. Lady Grant's matching handsome footmen were positively seething with annoyance that someone so plain could turn out to be an heiress. Jessie, the third housemaid, was so overcome with jealousy that she had hysterics and Mrs. Biddle had to slap her.

"I am afraid we are all at sixes and sevens with your news," Lady Grant said, as she ushered Margery into her dressing room and shut the door on Jessie's loud sobs.

"Dearest Margery." She clasped Margery's hands

tightly. "I am so very happy for you, but where shall I find another maid? It really is most unfortunate."

"Lady Durward's personal maid is looking to move, ma'am," Margery said. "She is extremely accomplished and has studied hairdressing in Paris."

"Has she?" Lady Grant brightened. "Then I will most certainly try to tempt her to come here. Thank you!" She released Margery's hands and hurried over to the chest of drawers by the window. "Now, my love, you need underwear and gowns and accessories and a hundred other things that a lady requires."

She threw open the drawers, swiftly disordering all the tidy piles that Margery had stacked the previous night. "You are very welcome to some of mine—"

"Ma'am," Margery said, placing a soothing hand on Lady Grant's arm. "You are five inches taller than I am."

"And five inches wider, as well." Lady Grant sighed. "You are right, Margery. It will not serve." She sat down heavily on the embroidered stool before the gilt peer glass.

"My Sunday best will do very well for now," Margery said. "You heard Lord Wardeaux, ma'am. I may purchase anything I need."

"Ten times over, I should think," Lady Grant said.

"Am I really so rich?" Margery said. She stared at her reflection in the pier glass. The richest heiress in the country, Henry had said. A shiver that was part excitement, part apprehension tickled its way down her spine.

There she was in the mirror, Margery Mallon, pale, small, brown hair, gray eyes and cheap blue cotton gown, four shillings a yard.

She was the richest heiress in the ton.

It was almost enough to make her faint with shock, except that she never had the vapors and she was certainly not going to start now she was a lady.

She was Lady Marguerite Saint-Pierre, daughter of a French count and granddaughter and heir to an earl.

No, it was no use. She could repeat the words as much and as often as she wanted but she still could not quite believe them.

"You have two-hundred-and-fifty-thousand pounds," Lady Grant said, "and seven country estates and a London town house." She frowned. "Or is it two hundred thousand, and eight houses? I forget."

Once again Margery felt quite faint. "Oh, my goodness. I cannot possibly be that rich," she protested. "And no one needs eight houses. There is only one of me so why would I require more than one house?"

Henry had known, she thought. Henry had known everything about her inheritance. She felt misery and anger knot in her stomach again just as they had when she had confronted him earlier in the drawing room. She should be glad that he did not want to marry her, because she would only marry for love and not to a man she could not trust.

She thought about the way Henry had kissed her in the drawing room. Slowly, unconsciously, her fingers came up to press against her lips. It was odd that Henry could kiss her with such tenderness and passion so that she came apart in his arms and yet at the same time she really did not like him at all. She wondered if that was the effect that kissing had on her rather than the effect that Henry had on her.

Since she had not kissed anyone else she had no basis for comparison, but she suspected that when it came to

kissing, when it came to making love, not all men were
equally adept. She had a suspicion that it was something at which Henry excelled. But that was a direction that she was never going to take again. She would
go to Templemore and Henry would go away and she
would not see him again. Hell would freeze before she
allowed him even to touch her again.

Lady Grant had started to collect up a few pots from
the dressing table top. "I am giving you my bluebell
scent from Floris of Jermyn Street," she said. "Nonsense—" She held up a hand as Margery started to
protest. "A lady needs some elegant perfume. And you
need an attractive bonnet, too. My emerald plumes—"

"I beg you, ma'am, no," Margery said, thinking how
ridiculously out of place the plumed bonnet would look
with her plain gown. "The straw hat with the pink ribbon, if you insist…"

"I do!" Lady Grant was flying about the room now,
placing items into a disturbingly large portmanteau.
"Oh, this is such fun! The pink spencer and the beaded
reticule to match…" There was more rummaging. A
waterfall of gowns tumbled from the chest in multi-
colored profusion. Margery automatically picked them
up and started to refold them.

"Margery, you should not!" Lady Grant looked horrified.

"I know," Margery said. "I am Lady Marguerite now.
I assure you it does not affect my ability to fold clothes,
ma'am." She thought of what Granny Mallon would
have said about idle ladies who needed to be waited
upon and had to stifle a smile.

By the time that Lady Grant had selected what she

referred to as "a few small items" for Margery, the long case clock in the hall was chiming the hour of eleven.

"Lord Wardeaux is waiting in the library, my lady," Soames imparted as they came back down the stair, followed by a footman panting beneath the weight of the portmanteau. "He asks if there is any likelihood of you being ready to depart before midnight, ma'am."

"How odiously sarcastic of him," said a voice behind them. "A gentleman can have no idea of the number of matters a lady has to deal with at a time like this."

Margery spun around to see Chessie Alton hurrying in at the door. "I came as quickly as I could," she said, folding Margery in a warm hug. "I am so pleased you sent for me, Margery, though I am not sure that I am the dowagers' idea of a respectable companion."

"I need a friend," Margery said, "someone who knows society's rules."

"Well, I can help you there, Margery," Chessie agreed, "since I have broken every one of society's rules at one time or another." Her big blue eyes sparkled with amusement. "As for friends, you will be overwhelmed by them once word of your inheritance gets out."

"That's why I want a real friend," Margery said.

"I can imagine," Chessie said. She checked herself. "Actually, no, I cannot imagine it at all. It must feel like a dream."

"A nightmare," Margery said, with feeling. She saw Chessie frown and tried to explain. "Everyone thinks that I should be happy to be rich and titled, but I liked being Margery Mallon. Now I don't know who I am."

Chessie nodded slowly. "Give it time. When your life changes in such a dramatic manner you cannot expect it to feel anything other than strange. And don't let Henry tell you what to do," she added, giving Margery's arm a squeeze. "He can be dreadfully autocratic."

"Do you know him?" Margery said.

"We're distant cousins," Chessie said. "Everyone is in the ton. Ah, Henry!" Her eyes lit with mischief as Henry came striding bad-temperedly from the library. "We were just talking about you. Are you ready to go?" She arched her brows. "It is very poor of you to keep Lady Marguerite waiting like this."

"Francesca." Henry sounded exasperated. Margery stifled a giggle. "I was quite delighted to hear you would be accompanying us."

"I am sure you were," Chessie said, smiling demurely.

Henry turned to Margery. "I hope that you have had sufficient time to prepare for the journey," he said. "You were so long that I thought you had run off."

"Not yet," Margery said sweetly. "Give me time."

Their eyes locked. The tension rippled between them, fierce and hot. Henry was the first to break it, turning away.

"We're leaving in ten minutes," he said abruptly. "As it is, we shall be fortunate to reach Templemore before nightfall."

"Will you ride?" Margery enquired. The prospect of sitting in a closed carriage with Henry for hour after hour, even with the soothing presence of Chessie and Mr. Churchward, was not an appealing one. The atmosphere between them felt scratchy with conflict and underscored by a disturbing thread of awareness.

"Certainly not," Henry said. "I am not risking you climbing out of the carriage and running off when my back is turned."

"I am surprised you do not handcuff me to your side," Margery said shortly.

Something flared in Henry's eyes. Margery felt suddenly hot. Then he smiled and she felt even hotter.

"Don't tempt me," he said softly, leaning close, speaking for her ears alone. "You have no idea how much the idea of restraining you appeals to me."

Suffering from an uncomfortable combination of irritation and acute awareness, Margery stalked out to the carriage. Her sore heart was aching again. She had made a terrible mistake with Henry. Not only had she been led astray by her attraction to him but she had liked him.

And he had used that against her with cold calculation. Every time she looked at him, she remembered the way that she had trembled in his arms with emotion and passion. She wanted to curl in on herself, to shrivel and hide, except that she had too much pride. So she would travel with him to Templemore, and she would pretend absolute indifference, because the only thing worse than being vulnerable to him would be for Henry to know it.

IT WAS LATE BY THE TIME they approached Templemore, and the sun was setting across the hills to the west. Henry was watching Margery and saw her sit forward as they passed the edge of Templemore land on the left of the road and the long estate wall started to unroll beside them.

As mile passed after mile and the wall did not end he saw Margery's expression change and her whole body tighten with tension. She had been told that the estate was huge; she had known it in her mind but now she was seeing for herself just how vast was her inheritance. Henry saw her clasp her hands together tightly in her lap. She gave a little shiver. He could feel her nervousness but he knew better than to mention it. Margery had made it plain during the long journey that she was only tolerating him out of courtesy to Mr. Churchward. She had reluctantly accepted his hand in and out of the carriage during the snatched stops to change the horses and take refreshment. She had eaten little and conversed less. The rest of the time she had ignored him.

The carriage finally turned through the entrance with its huge iron gates emblazoned with griffins, and set off up the lime tree drive. A lake flashed past on the right, illuminated by the last rays of the setting sun.

"That is known as the Little Lake," Henry said. "There is a larger one to the west of the house."

The carriage rattled over a narrow, elegant bridge and veered to the left, through an archway and onto a gravel sweep at the front of the house. There was a range of fifteen stone steps up to the wide frontage. Henry suddenly saw the house through Margery's eyes, a dark, daunting edifice full of the unknown. He wondered if the earl had decreed that the entire servants' hall should be drawn up to welcome the lost heir home. Margery, he thought, would absolutely hate that.

He offered Margery his hand to help her down. Her fingers trembled in his and he gave them a tiny squeeze of reassurance. Her eyes met his then, troubled and dark. For a second he thought she was going to smile at him but then she withdrew her hand smartly from his and started off up the steps like a small but determined ship on a choppy sea. Nothing could have made it plainer that she did not need his assistance and did not want him at her side.

The butler bowed them inside where no fewer than four footmen were waiting to take their outdoor clothes away. Henry saw Margery hesitate for a second as though she could not quite believe her eyes. Her gaze swept around to encompass the black-and-white stone floor and the soaring marble pillars. Her lips parted on a gasp and Henry knew she had recognized the house from those elusive memories of her childhood.

His mother, Lady Wardeaux, and Lady Emily Templemore were both in the hall waiting for them. Lady Wardeaux offered Henry her cheek so that he could place a kiss an inch away from it in the air. Lady Emily fluttered around Margery like a fulsome moth in a riot of draperies and clashing beads.

"My dear, I am your great-aunt Emily and so very happy to meet you. Let me look at you…such a happy day…my, what a striking resemblance you bear to your late grandmama…not your mama, she was tall. Do you recall anything about her?"

Margery smiled, pressed Lady Emily's hands and tried to answer her questions while she suffered herself to be hugged tightly.

Lady Wardeaux, elegant in coffee-colored silk and understated pearls, was considerably less effusive. She took Margery's hand and held it as though she was not sure whether it was clean or not.

"Welcome, my dear," she said. "We must not keep Lord Templemore waiting any longer. He has been fretting himself to flinders these three hours past, awaiting your arrival."

Henry saw Margery absorb his mother's tone and

the implication that this delay was entirely her fault. He saw her shoulders straighten and her chin come up. She was not going to be intimidated and Henry admired her very much for that.

"I am sorry to have kept my grandfather waiting, ma'am," Margery said politely. Her gaze swept over Henry and he felt her thoughts as clearly as though she had spoken aloud.

So this cold, empty creature is your mother. Now I understand your cold, empty heart.

"This way," he said, abruptly, gesturing to the west corridor. "I will take you to Lord Templemore."

The dome in the ceiling above them was dark as they walked beneath it. There was no scattering of colored light tonight. Nor did Henry pause to point out the Hoppner picture of Lady Marguerite Saint-Pierre as a child. There would be plenty of time for Margery to absorb the weight of history and find her place in this huge barn of a house.

He knocked on the library door. The earl's voice bade them enter.

Margery looked very small and unprotected as she stepped into the library. Henry allowed her to precede him then followed her in.

"Lady Marguerite, my lord," he said.

The earl was sitting before the fire, one of his spaniels at his feet, but as they came in he rose, holding himself upright more by force of will than physical strength, Henry thought. His gray gaze, sharp as a hawk, sought them out and fastened on Margery with a hunger and a desperation that was painful to see. Henry felt Margery pause, as though she was afraid. He wanted to reach out to her, to reassure her, but he kept his hands firmly at his sides.

"Come closer, my child." The earl's voice cracked with emotion. For the first time in his life Henry saw the old man's feelings completely naked, the hope and the fear and the longing.

Margery saw them, too. She hesitated a moment longer and then she did something that Henry would never have imagined, something that he, for all the years he had known Lord Templemore, would never have done. She ran to her grandfather and put her arms about him.

Henry heard the old man's breath catch in his throat and saw him go absolutely still. For a moment he wondered if the shock might actually have killed the earl, or if his godfather would chastize his granddaughter and tell her that no one at Templemore would dream of being so demonstrative, that it was not the done thing to show emotion and that she had a great deal to learn of the right way to behave.

The earl did no such thing. He put his arms about Margery and drew her close, slowly, with the rusty unfamiliarity of someone who had forgotten what it was to love. Margery was smiling and crying at the same time; she was speaking but Henry could not hear her words, and the earl's head was bent as he listened and held his granddaughter as though she was the most precious gift he had ever received.

Henry felt as though someone had punched him in the gut. In that moment, he saw the earl not as the dusty old autocrat who had ruled everyone's life like a minor despot but as a man with the same fears, hopes and failings as all other men and the same need for love.

He remembered the evening he had spent with Mar-

gery. He remembered her laughter and her generosity
of spirit, and how he had thought she could make the
world a warm, sweet place again. For her grandfather
she had done precisely that. He felt shaken, because
for a short moment, fiercer and more sharply than before, he wanted that same light in his life. There was
a dangerous ache in his throat. He waited for the cold
indifference to return and sweep away such thoughts.
Nothing happened. The ache remained. The longing
threatened to devour him whole.

He stepped back, closed the library door softly behind him, and left the earl and his granddaughter alone.

CHAPTER NINE

*The Seven of Swords: Malice. Be careful in whom
you place your trust*

MARGERY AWOKE IN A BEDROOM the size of Berkshire.
She had been so tired that she was convinced she would
sleep the clock around, but the habit of early waking was
ingrained in her and she could see that it was barely past
six. As soon as she was awake, her mind was already
busy with memories and impressions of the previous
day, of the journey and the house and her grandfather.
When she had first seen him she had been terrified,
for he had seemed so grand and so aloof. Then she had
seen beyond the superficial to the sick and lonely old
man, and in that moment she had loved him.

In some ways the earl reminded her of Henry. She
shifted restlessly under the weight of the bedcovers.
Henry, the real Henry Wardeaux and not the charming
man who had nearly seduced her, was driven by duty,
cold, ruthless and determined. There was a hard shell
to him that was impossible to penetrate. It was no surprise that he was so self-contained, she thought, if he
had grown up in this great empty house or somewhere
similar, with a mother who looked as though to smile
might crack her face, and with no love or laughter or

joy. She felt a pang of pity for the solemn child Henry must have been.

Then there was Lady Emily, her great-aunt, trailing scarves and reading the tarot cards. Over a late supper she had fixed Margery with her sorrowful gray eyes and had told her that she had drawn the Three of Wands in connection with her arrival. Margery had been unsure if this had been a good or a bad thing but thanked her aunt very carefully.

"It is a card of good luck and opportunity," Lady Emily said. "But one must beware of the reverse. It also signifies stubbornness."

"A defining Templemore characteristic," Henry had murmured, his eyes meeting Margery's across the tea-cups.

Margery was still a little hazy on the family rela-tionships but she already knew about the scandal in-volving Lady Emily. The previous Lord Templemore, her great-grandfather, had lived openly with his mis-tress after—or perhaps also before—his wife had died, finally marrying her and legitimizing their daughter. Lady Emily was considerably younger than her half brother, the earl, and seemed a timid creature, always on the edge of nervous speech.

Although Lady Emily was nominally her brother's hostess, it seemed that Lady Wardeaux took command when she was in the house. It was a most uncomfortable situation, and Margery was profoundly glad she had brought Chessie with her for some friendship and good advice. She had the feeling she was going to need it.

She slipped from the vast bed—it had almost en-gulfed her, and the mattress was so *soft*—and pulled back the heavy gold-velvet drapes at the window. It was going to be a beautiful spring day. The sun was already above the line of hills to the east and its light gleamed on the still waters of lake in front of her window. The Little Lake, Henry had called it. The Big Lake must be the size of an ocean.

There was an odd, piercing call below her window. Looking down, Margery could see a peacock strutting across the gravel, tail feathers spread in all their iridescent beauty toward a group of drab brown peahens. The peacock reminded her of Henry, as well. He was the elegant male and she the dull little female who, no matter how much she wished to deny it, was drawn to him by some sort of force of nature she would really rather ignore.

She turned her back on the window. In the morning light she could see all the elements of the room that she had missed the night before. It could have accommodated an entire army. The huge bed of dark wood, hung with heavy gold tapestry, dominated the space, complemented by two clothes chests and a writing table in the same gloomy dark style. There were acres of soft carpet beneath her bare feet.

No fewer than five windows looked out across the deer park, and four doors led out of the room. Turning the handles one by one, Margery found that the first led onto the landing, the second to a closet, the third to a dressing room and the fourth was locked. She stood in the middle of the room, revolving slowly, and decided that this simply would not do. She was a small woman and she required a small room.

In the dressing room she found her bag and unfolded her only spare gown. Lady Grant had assured her that a provincial dressmaker would come straight out to Templemore as soon as she was required, and that her services would do until Margery could return to Town to purchase a proper wardrobe.

The idea of summoning someone to come and clothe her had appalled Margery, but given that the alternative was to endure the sort of supercilious contempt that Lady Wardeaux had shown toward her gown the previous night, she could see that she had little choice.

Chessie had whispered to her that Henry's mother was aunt to the Duke of Farne, which was no doubt one of the reasons she was so high in the instep. The other reason, Margery thought, was probably just natural unpleasantness. She felt another wayward flicker of sympathy for Henry.

She dressed swiftly then slipped out of the room and down the staircase, running her hand absentmindedly down the shining mahogany surface, as she had been wont to do when she was a housemaid, to see if there was any dust.

There were so many faces looking down at her, so many portraits of her dead ancestors. They peered down from the walls, their eyes following her, staring down their aristocratic noses as though they could not quite believe that she, a maidservant, was the last of the Templemore line. She still could not quite believe it herself.

Her grandfather had told her the previous night that he rose late, and no doubt the household revolved around him. The only part of the house from which there was any sound of activity was beyond the green baize door at the end of the west corridor. On impulse Margery pushed open the door that led to the servants' hall and went down the steps.

It was a world that was immediately familiar. The

cook was lighting the range. A number of yawning housemaids were collecting their brushes and pans. A scullery maid, her sleeves rolled up to her elbows, was already scrubbing vegetables and one of the footmen was sitting with his feet up on the battered pine table flirting with a maid. When he saw Margery a look of utter horror came over his face and he swung his feet to the ground, leaping up, smoothing down his livery. Silence fell like a shroud. The clatter and bustle died. Everyone turned to look at Margery.

They all looked appalled.

It was in that moment that Margery realized she had dreamed of finding some friends here in the world below stairs, the world that she knew. But she had completely misjudged matters. The servants at Templemore were not pleased to welcome her as one of them. She was the earl's granddaughter, the heiress, and she was expected to behave as such. There would be no borrowing of the ovens to bake her confections or cleaning the chandeliers with the housemaid's feather duster.

She read the panic in their faces because they did not know what to do. This was up to her, she realized. It was her first test. She drew herself up and smiled. She hoped it looked gracious rather than terrified.

"I am very pleased to meet you all," she said. "Please don't let me interrupt."

She saw their faces break into smiles of relief. They bobbed curtsies, sketched bows and waited for her to leave. She was shaking as she went back up the stairs. She felt as though there was nowhere for her to go.

In the empty entrance hall the dome scattered light in colored shards over the tiled floor. Margery shuddered at the memory. She ran up the stairs and into her huge room, slamming the door. She ripped off her Sunday best—it was a maid's outfit and there was no place for it here—and ran into the dressing room. There was an ewer of cold water on the dressing table. Furiously she scrubbed at her body as though she was trying to wash away her very self.

Big fat tears fell on her bare skin, mingling with the cold of the water. She cried for herself and everything she had lost and for fear of the future.

Eventually she stopped crying because, really, it did no good and she had never been one for self-pity, and she went to the door to try to find something to dry herself. And realized she was locked in.

It was a perfect morning for a ride over the hills to drive out his demons. Henry gave Diabolo his head as they thundered down the chalk track toward Templemore. It was barely ten o'clock and already he had had an exceptionally trying morning. His mother, never an early riser, had made an entirely unexpected and unwelcome appearance at the breakfast table where he had been enjoying some peace and the *Oxford Morning Chronicle*.

"I don't like her," Lady Wardeaux said, without preamble.

"There was never any likelihood you would," Henry said, "since she is heir to Templemore. The earl likes her, and that is the salient point."

"I heard them laughing together last night," his mother complained. "If we are not careful we will find that his health will improve. He could live for years!"

"That would be no bad thing," Henry said.

"On the other hand," his mother continued, as though he had not spoken, "he could be so excited to find his granddaughter that he will have a heart attack and die. One simply cannot tell. Already he is speaking of going up to London in order to give Lady Marguerite a Season. A Season! Can you believe it? It would be a disaster!"

"She's hardly that unpresentable," Henry said.

His mother made an exasperated, flapping gesture. "That is not the point. She is sure to run off with some ne'er-do-well like her mother did. The Templemores are sadly unsteady." She tapped her fingers impatiently on the top of the table. "You must marry the girl at once, Henry, as soon as we can contrive it. We must not miss our chance."

Henry had slapped his paper down, drained his coffee cup and walked out without another word.

Marry Margery.

The words rang in his head now like temptation incarnate as his stallion crested the ridge and the whole of the Templemore estate was laid out before him. As ever, Henry felt a clutch of the heart to see it in all its neat perfection. He thought he would never grow tired of this view. He had wanted Templemore from the first moment he had seen it at the age of seven. The memory of these green fields was what had kept him sane through the horrors of war on the Peninsula.

If he married Margery he could keep Templemore. If he married Margery he could seduce her properly because his reaction to her had been very similar to his reaction to Templemore, give or take twenty years.

He had seen her and he had wanted her.

He set his teeth and set Diabolo to a gallop. Better to run off his energies out here on a ride than indulge in misplaced fantasies of ravishing the delectable Lady

Marguerite. Desire was a bad basis for marriage because in time it burned out, leaving nothing but ashes.

He looked at the view of Templemore. The view gazed back at him, golden and tempting and beautiful.

No.

He would not become a fortune hunter, not even to regain Templemore. He had too much pride to be his wife's pensioner, living off her money, forever in her shadow. He would leave for his estate at Wardeaux as soon as he could and put Margery, marriage and temptation behind him.

He took the track down to the River Cole at breakneck speed and splashed across the ford heading for the open fields beyond. By the time he turned back to the house and rode into the stable yard the morning sun was high.

Ned, the head groom, came hurrying to take his bridle.

"There's trouble, my lord," he said.

"Trouble?" Henry swung down from the saddle.

"Lady Marguerite," the groom said. "She's vanished. The house is at sixes and sevens, my lord. Your lady mother has been out here herself to see if Lady Marguerite might have taken a horse and run off."

"I assume she has not." Henry shot him a swift look.

"She's not taken a horse, my lord," the groom confirmed. "Though where milady is, I have no notion."

Cursing under his breath, Henry ran up the steps. He did not believe Margery had run away. She had too much courage. In the short time he had known her she had always chosen to stand and fight rather than to run. Nevertheless he hoped his faith in her was justified.

As soon as he entered the house he saw at once what

Ned meant. There was a feeling of suppressed panic in the air, a hum of anxiety just below the surface.

The dining room door opened and his mother hurried out closely followed by Lady Emily. "Henry—" Lady Wardeaux began.

"I've heard," Henry said briefly, forestalling her. "What happened?"

Lady Wardeaux shuddered. Lady Emily was dabbing at her eyes with the corner of a lacy handkerchief but there were no tears. On the contrary, Henry could see that her eyes were bright with pleasure and excitement.

"Lady Marguerite visited the servants' hall early this morning," Lady Wardeaux said. "The servants' hall, Henry!"

Henry merely raised his brows and waited.

"When her maid took her morning chocolate up there was no sign of her. We've searched everywhere."

"Everywhere!" Lady Emily confirmed eagerly. "I asked the cards," she added. "I drew the Eight of Cups reversed. The cards say she has run away."

"Did they say where?" Henry asked. "It might save us a lot of time if they could be more precise." He turned back to his mother. "Has anyone woken the earl?"

Lady Wardeaux looked scandalized. "Good gracious, of course not! Lady Alton did suggest it, but I would not dream of troubling him."

"It would be the first place that I would look," Henry said. "Lady Marguerite might be taking breakfast with him." He was glad that Francesca Alton at least seemed to have some common sense and kept a cool head. "I'll go myself."

"But what if she is not there?" Lady Wardeaux plucked

at his sleeve to detain him. "If you tell him she has run away he might die of the shock—"

Henry was saved the trouble of replying as Chessie Alton came hurrying down the stair. "I have found her! She is locked in her dressing room."

At his side Henry felt, rather than saw, Lady Emily make a slight move. "Locked in?" she quavered. "Why would she do such a thing? Doesn't she like us?"

"I think," Henry said impatiently, "Lady Alton means that someone else has locked Lady Marguerite in." He reached Chessie's side in a couple of strides. "Is the key not in the lock?"

"No." Chessie shook her head. "And I can hear Margery beating on the door although it sounds as though she is about half a mile away."

"The doors here are very thick," Henry said. "We shall need an ax if we have to break it down."

Lady Wardeaux gave a shocked gasp at the thought of violence being perpetrated against the fabric of Templemore.

"Don't worry, Mama," Henry said. "It will be a last resort." He took Chessie's arm and hurried her away up the stairs. Behind him he could hear Lady Emily's fluting tones rising to the rafters as she and his mother followed them up the stair.

"But I don't understand, Celia! The cards said quite clearly that she had run away. They never lie to me."

By this time they had also gained a retinue of interested servants. Henry half expected the earl himself to come out and join the crowd.

The door to Margery's bedroom stood open and one of the earl's spaniels was sitting patiently beside the dressing room door. The key was in the lock. "It was not there a moment ago," Chessie said, mystified. "Some-one is playing tricks."

Henry looked around. Lady Emily's face was blank. His mother looked pained and disapproving. The play-ing of anything, much less tricks, was not in her rep-ertoire. He wondered about the servants. It might be someone's idea of a practical joke but this seemed un-likely.

He turned the key in the lock and threw open the door. Margery was sitting curled up on the carpet. She was stark naked.

Behind him there was a concerted intake of breath and something approaching an outraged squawk from Lady Wardeaux. Henry tried to tear off his riding jacket to cover Margery but since he wore his jackets fitted to perfection this was easier said than done.

By the time he had struggled out of the jacket, Chessie, once again demonstrating admirable practi-cality, had rushed across to the bed and retrieved Mar-gery's robe. Henry flung it over her, then flung a curt dismissal to his aunt, his mother and the growing throng of servants. They departed with varying degrees of re-luctance.

"Margery." He drew her gently to her feet while at the same time trying not to dislodge the robe. It slipped and he only managed to retrieve it by pulling Margery hard against his body. For one long moment the warmth and softness of her was pressed against him, imprint-ing itself on both his mind and his body. Henry swal-lowed hard, wrapped her about more tightly with the robe and averted his eyes.

"What on earth are you doing?" he asked, hear-ing the strain in his voice. All he seemed able to see was Margery's exquisite nakedness, her dainty, perfect breasts, curvy buttocks and slender thighs. Even though she was now covered in both the robe and a shawl that Chessie had brought for her, he had to fight hard to try to expel those other images from his mind. He remembered the sensation of her breast against his palm that night in the park, the nipple hardening against his mouth, and almost groaned aloud.

"What does it look as though I'm doing?" Margery said wrathfully. "Someone locked me in. It is not amusing. And what are you staring at?" she added furiously as Henry found himself incapable of tearing his gaze away from the slender curve of her legs below the thin silk of the robe. "It is not chivalrous of you to stare."

Chivalrous? She expected him to behave with chivalry? Henry closed his eyes briefly while he fought another vicious battle with his imagination. When he opened them again Margery was still standing there, her hair streaming loose down her back, her bare feet peeping from beneath the robe and a stormy expression in her eyes that simply made Henry want to grab her and kiss her.

"Lord Wardeaux," Chessie interposed. "This is very improper. If you would withdraw I shall call Lady Marguerite's maid and help her to dress."

Henry jumped. "Oh. Of course." He risked another look at Margery and wished he had not. Her face was pink now with indignation and self-consciousness. Henry wondered how far down that blush extended. He remembered that there had been freckles dusted across her shoulders. He wondered where else she might have them. Perhaps they were scattered across her breasts or sprinkled along the soft skin of her inner thighs....

"Lord Wardeaux!" There was an irritated edge to Chessie's voice now. "Please leave us. Lady Marguerite needs to put some clothes on."

That did not help Henry at all. All he seemed able to think of was Margery with her clothes off rather than on. He heard the sensuous shift of the silk robe against her skin as she walked quickly across to the chest and started to pull out random undergarments. He caught sight of white lace and felt another thud of lust.

Damnation. In five brief minutes Margery had undone all the beneficial effects of his morning's ride. He felt the frustrated desire tighten like a vise in his belly.

He turned on his heel, went straight out into the yard and tipped a bucket of cold water over his head. The stable hands were looking at him with curiosity but he ignored them.

The ice-cold water did not help at all.

CHAPTER TEN

*The Empress: Abundance, material and
domestic comfort*

Reversed: Tyranny and overprotectiveness

"It is a pity that milady lacks height." The tall, thin,
frighteningly elegant French modiste whom Lady
Wardeaux had summoned that morning from Faringdon looked Margery over from head to toe and permitted a chilly smile to escape her lips. "She does however
have excellent taste and a delicate bone structure."

Margery had never applied the word *delicate* to any
part of herself. Nor did she appreciate being spoken
of in the third person as though she were either deaf
or absent. Not that either Madame or Lady Wardeaux
considered that to be important. At present she had as
much authority as a china doll, to be dressed and styled,
pinned and picked over, her opinion of no account and
her person held up to ruthless appraisal.

Margery found it even more galling because as a lady's maid she had developed excellent taste, whereas
Madame Estelle, she suspected, was no more a French
modiste than she was. In fact, Margery was almost certain that she had seen Madame in Wantage several years

back when she had been plain Esther Jones working in one of the haberdashers' shops.

They were in Margery's bedchamber and the entire room was crammed with clothes. They lay in piles on the bed and overflowed like a silken tide from the chest, the chairs and the window seat. Madame Estelle had brought with her a variety of ready-made gowns, which Lady Wardeaux had picked through like a costermonger at a fair, selecting a half dozen that were apparently intended to tide Margery over until the first of her originals were made.

Margery felt it was all appallingly extravagant but oh, she could not resist. It was a very special treat suddenly to be swamped in exquisite silk and lace after wearing nothing but coarse linens all her life.

Madame was busy with her tape measure.

"My lady has breasts too small and no décolletage," she mourned. "We shall need padding to fill out the bodice."

"Certainly not," Margery said. "I refuse to be padded out like a stuffed chicken. Stays will have to do."

Henry had had no complaints about her figure, she thought, when he had found her in the dressing room the previous morning. She had seen him looking at her, had felt for one disturbing moment the warmth of his hands branding her skin through the thin silk of her robe.

Her pulse fluttered and she felt heat unfurl within her. Indeed, she must be very wicked to be *glad* that Henry found her so attractive even if she knew that men were so often driven by lust and that it meant nothing at all. She remembered the seduction of Henry's kisses and the fierce ache they had aroused deep in her belly. She thought of his mouth tugging on her breast and felt

an echo of that delicious need pulse in a knot deep inside her. She closed her eyes.

"Milady is suffering the vapors?" Madame Estelle
had paused in her measuring to shoot Margery a sus-
picious look. "She is faint with the effort of trying on
so many gowns?"

"No, indeed," Margery said hastily, opening her eyes
and banishing the image of Henry making love to her.
"I am as strong as a carthorse."

Lady Wardeaux made a noise of disapproval. "My
dear Marguerite, a lady simply does not make such inelegant remarks."

Margery sighed. Lady Wardeaux had lost no time
in trying to improve her but it was going to be an up-
hill task.

"All is not lost with milady's figure, however," Madame Estelle said. "She has a tiny waist and a rounded
derriere. *Bien!*"

"I am shaped like a pear," Margery said, "albeit a
small one."

Lady Wardeaux shook her head "Nor is a lady of
quality ever shaped like a fruit," she said.

"I am." Chessie spoke up from where she was sort-
ing through scarves and gloves by the window. "I am
the shape of an apple."

"A lady of quality," Lady Wardeaux said, with emphasis, "resembles a pedigreed horse."

Madame Estelle was smiling sycophantically. "Just
so, madame. A lady must be a thoroughbred."

Since Lady Wardeaux herself bore a startling similarity to a bad-tempered racehorse, Margery was hard
put not to catch Chessie's eye and dissolve into giggles.

"I pray that you may do your best with such unpromising material, Madame," she said meekly to the modiste. "I know that I lack height, but I have been called a perfect miniature." Her grandfather had said so only the previous day.

Lady Wardeaux sniffed. "A very inferior form of art, the miniature," she said. Her cold dark gaze appraised Margery. "You take after your grandmama. She was very small. I am afraid she was the daughter of a banker."

"That explains everything then," Margery said. Evidently Lady Wardeaux thought that the earl had made a deplorable misalliance in marrying into trade, even though presumably his wife had brought wealth into the family. She wondered about her grandmother. The earl had talked about his daughter, Margery's mother, but had not mentioned his wife at all. Of course, there were so many things for them to talk about. They had barely started.

Tired of Madame Estelle's endless pinching and prodding, Margery excused herself and went across to the bed where the seamstress had laid out piles of different materials.

"This silk is beautiful," she said, gently touching a bolt of *eau de nil* shot through with silver thread. "I would like an evening gown in that color, please, and in the rose-pink."

Madame smiled. "Of course. As milady is not *une jeune fille* she may wear deeper colors than the debutantes."

"I do think that the cream would suit you, though, Margery," Chessie put in thoughtfully. She arranged a deliciously soft scarf about Margery's throat and stood back to admire the effect. "Oh, yes. Not white, that is so draining, but the cream is rich and very flattering to you."

Lady Wardeaux, stylish to a fault herself in a gown that reeked of the London salons, gave the tiniest nod of approval of Chessie's taste. "This will certainly do until Marguerite can travel to Town and buy some *proper* clothes."

Madame Estelle bristled at the slur on the quality of her work. Margery looked at Chessie. Chessie rolled her eyes.

"I doubt I shall be returning to London quite yet," Margery said quickly, to smooth matters over. "And Madame's collection is perfect for me. If I might also have two day dresses—"

"Two?" Lady Wardeaux looked scandalized. "My dear Marguerite, I have a list here. *Ten* day dresses, muslins and gauze, the cream muslin with metal thread embroidery, then six evening gowns, petticoats, colored and plain, three spencers, a green pelisse lined with blue, gloves, scarves, shawls, two riding habits, six bonnets…have I forgotten anything?"

"Slippers and half boots," Chessie said.

"For riding." Lady Wardeaux nodded. "Lady Marguerite will not be walking great distances. Energetic walking is not appropriate for a lady." She took hold of Margery's hands in both of hers, turning them over. "The gloves should not be too fine or Lady Marguerite's hands will spoil them. I am afraid she has the skin of a scullery maid." She dropped Margery's hands as though she were diseased. "I will send my maid along with some rosewater cream in the hope we may soften them."

"BETTER THE HANDS OF a scullery maid than the hide of an elephant," Margery said to Chessie over tea a couple of hours later, when the fitting was at last finished and Madame had departed with promises that the first of the day gowns would be delivered the following morning. She shook her head. "Of course I have the hands of a servant. That was my job!"

Chessie passed her a cup of tea and two chocolate pastries that Margery devoured one after the other. "Is it wrong of me to find Lady Wardeaux so difficult to like? She is so distant and disapproving! The more I get to know her the more puzzled I am that Henry was ever born."

"Why do you think Henry is an only child?" Chessie said expressively.

Margery snorted inelegantly into her teacup. "I suppose she saw it as her duty at least to produce an heir. Fortunate for both Lord and Lady Wardeaux that the firstborn was a boy and they did not need to keep trying."

"Such *froideur* would wither any man," Chessie said. "We should not laugh, though. I remember the late Lord Wardeaux. He was a frightful rake and his wife had a great deal to put up with. He humiliated her endlessly with his *affaires*." She sighed. "Many women do not seem to enjoy the marriage bed. I remember that Lady Patchet was delighted when her husband took a mistress. She said to me that they could split the burden of Lord Patchet's base demands between them. That was what she called them—base demands."

"How disheartening," Margery said. "I thought—" She stopped. Not even with Chessie would she discuss those forbidden moments she had spent in Henry's arms. She did not think that Chessie would be shocked, but it was too personal to share. Personal, intimate, *de-*

licious. She squirmed a little in the deep armchair. Either Lord Patchet had been doing it wrong, or Henry was very good or she was very wanton. Or perhaps all three were true.

She glanced out of the window and saw Henry striding toward the house from the direction of the lake. He had a fishing rod in one hand and his jacket slung over his shoulder. The breeze flattened his shirt against his broad chest and the sunlight was on his thick dark hair. Margery noticed with a jump of the heart that he looked different, relaxed and content. They were not emotions she associated with him. It must be Templemore that had wrought the change in him. She could tell he loved it here.

She wrenched her gaze away from Henry and tried to concentrate on what Chessie was saying.

"With Fitz, the marriage bed was the best thing about being wed," Chessie said. "But since our marriage was appalling in every other respect, that is not saying a great deal."

"Oh, dear," Margery said. "To think that there is nothing to look forward to if I choose to wed."

"Choose?" Chessie lifted an expressive eyebrow. "I suspect the earl already has a list of approved candidates for you, Margery. He will want the matter settled quickly." She looked up from stirring honey into her tea, a little frown between her brows. "You do understand that your marriage is almost as much of an issue as the royal succession? The continuation of the Earldom of Templemore is at stake."

"How medieval," Margery said. "I feel like a brood mare."

"Lady Wardeaux has quite settled on the fact that

you must marry Henry," Chessie said. "How do you like the idea?"

Margery jumped, splashing some of her tea onto the skirt of her new gown. "God forbid," she said. She scrubbed at the stain, head bent, a maneuver that allowed her to hide the pinkness of her cheeks. "Henry is too much like his mother," she said, by way of an excuse. "Too cold and stiff and formal for me."

"Do you think so?" Chessie looked thoughtful. "I think that underneath all that formality Henry positively seethes with passion. The fun would be in unlocking it."

Margery's entire body blushed. She was appalled to find that her fingers were shaking so much that her cup rattled in its saucer like artillery fire. She knew all about the passion beneath Henry's cool exterior.

The gold and bejeweled clock on the mantel struck twelve, making her jump, but at least allowing her to change the subject.

"I fear the clock is slow," Chessie said, looking up. "It keeps poor time."

"And it is so very ugly," Margery said. "Carved golden oxen for feet and jeweled butterflies on the dial! I would not give it house room."

"It must be worth at least twenty thousand pounds," Chessie said. "I believe it was made for King Louis XIV."

"What use is that if it cannot keep time properly?" Margery asked. "One of the things about taste I simply don't understand is how such an unsightly ornament can be considered so valuable." She jumped to her feet. "I must go. I promised to take luncheon with my grandfather today. Oh, I almost forgot." She gave Chessie a quick hug. "I purchased the cashmere shawl and a few other items for you. I hope you do not mind—I saw you admiring them."

Chessie turned quite pink with pleasure. "Oh, Margery! Thank you."

"I know we have not yet discussed your salary as my companion," Margery said, feeling very awkward. "And, indeed, Lady Wardeaux would think it inelegant for me even to mention something as vulgar as money—"

Chessie dismissed this with a wave of the hand. "I am not so refined as to refuse a wage," she said, laughing. "When one is penniless, one must also be practical."

"Then I shall ask Mr. Churchward to sort the matter out," Margery said, with great relief.

Lord Templemore was not in his parlor so Margery waited out in the hall between two enormous suits of armor that guarded the main entrance. The silence in the house was deep and oppressive. It was as though Templemore was asleep. Margery could see her reflection in the endless gilt mirrors that lined the walls, a neat little figure in Madame Estelle's hastily adapted creation of striped blue muslin. The room was enormous and she was so tiny. She felt utterly dwarfed by the scale of Templemore. It had been built for someone so much grander than she felt.

Over in the north corner of the hall she also saw the huge polished wooden stair stretching away up to the first floor, wide enough for three people to ascend abreast. The polished banisters gleamed enticingly. Margery felt a wayward spark of mischief. She picked up her skirts, ran up to the first landing, climbed up on to the top of the banister and slid all the way down. It was so much fun she did it again, going up to the second landing this time.

It was as she whizzed past the turn in the stairs that she realized she had miscalculated. She was going faster and faster, her skirts were flying up around her knees and the floor was approaching at nerve-racking speed.

She was just preparing herself for a very hard landing indeed when she saw Henry crossing the hall below. Immediately her racing heart performed another giddy somersault, quite different from the one induced by fear. Henry was still in his shirtsleeves, without his cravat, his pantaloons splashed, his boots muddy. He must have just come in from the estate rooms and be on his way to get changed. As she raced down the banister and shot off the end like a circus artist out of a cannon, she saw him break into a run.

His arms closed hard about her and he staggered backward. For one long moment she was held close against his chest and she could feel the warmth of him through the linen of his shirt. He brought with him the scent of fresh air and sunshine. It was in his tousled hair, and on his skin, and all of a sudden the hall at Templemore, for all its size, felt airless and stifling, and Margery did not seem to be able to breathe properly, as though a weight were pressing on her chest.

"It seems," Henry said in her ear, "that clothes do not make the lady after all." He placed her gently on her feet.

"It takes more than striped muslin to change me," Margery said.

"I can see that." His gaze traveled over her in slow appraisal. Then he smiled, a mocking smile that lit his dark brown eyes. "The stockings and the garters are very pretty, though. I had been wondering whether you had freckles on your thighs and now I know."

Margery, well aware that her petticoats, stockings and much more had been on display as she raced down the banister, turned scarlet. Her skin prickled all over with an odd sort of awareness. It was part embarrassment, part something far more potent. She smoothed down the offending skirts and tucked her feet away beneath the hem of her skirt. Henry's hands were still resting lightly on her shoulders.

"You need to slow down as you take the turn in the stair," he said. "Otherwise you have too much velocity."

"Velocity?" Margery said faintly.

"Too much speed," Henry said. "You go too quickly and do not have enough time to prepare to land. I know from painful experience. I broke my arm falling from the stair when I was nine years old."

Now he had surprised her. Margery had never envisaged that the solemn boy he must have been would ever have slid down the banisters.

"Did we know each other as children?" she asked abruptly. It had not occurred to her that they might, before now. The idea disturbed her because she could remember nothing of her early childhood at Templemore.

Henry nodded. "We met a few times."

"What was I like?" Margery asked on impulse.

"You were a baby," Henry said. "You had no personality at that stage."

"Even babies have personalities," Margery argued. "It is simply that you were not interested in me."

"I was a ten-year-old boy," Henry said dryly. "What do you expect?"

"Do you remember my mother?" Margery asked. "What was she like?"

She felt Henry stiffen beside her. It was only for a second, the very slightest of hesitations, and she felt it rather than saw it because, as always, his expression was quite impassive.

"Lady Rose was very beautiful," he said.

As an answer it was unsatisfactory, telling Margery only what she had already seen in the portraits and nothing of the woman she wanted to know. Something in Henry's face forbade her to question further, though, and she had the strangest feeling that he had held something back, not to hurt her but quite the reverse. She was already starting to suspect that she knew what it was. Her mother, she was certain, had not been a very nice person. She had been haughty and proud and spoiled. And no one wanted to tell her because they did not want to upset her.

Henry sketched a bow to her and set off up the staircase and Margery turned back toward Lord Templemore's private parlor. As she reached the door, she stopped and looked around. Henry was standing on the first landing, his hand resting on the banister and for one mad moment Margery thought he was going to emulate her and slide down to the bottom.

But that would be ridiculous. Henry had too much self-control, too much containment, ever to do so inappropriate a thing. Nevertheless she waited, almost holding her breath. She saw him shake his head slightly, and then he turned and disappeared from her view.

CHAPTER ELEVEN

The Devil: Lust

"How DELIGHTFUL THAT YOU are able to spare me the time to meet for tea, Marguerite," Lady Emily said, with her vague, sweet smile, beckoning Margery into her private sitting room and gesturing her to take the seat nearest the fire. The room was blisteringly hot. Sunlight falling through the mullioned panes fought with the heat from the grate. Margery could already feel the uncomfortable prickle of sweat on her forehead and she surreptitiously tried to push the old velvet wing chair a foot away from the fire. It refused to move.

Lady Emily seemed oblivious to the stuffy, airless atmosphere of the room. She wafted across to the little side table and poured tea into tiny china cups. A scent of jasmine arose. Lady Emily's bracelets clinked against the china and rattled against each other as she handed the cup to Margery.

"It's a pleasure to have some time with you, Aunt Emily," Margery said. She knew she sounded stiff and formal. There was something about Lady Emily that discomfited her and she could not explain why. She also felt guilty. It was all too easy to ignore Lady Emily, who fluttered around ineffectually in Lady Wardeaux's shadow, as insubstantial as her floating draperies. Margery had been at Templemore a week now and knew her aunt as little as when she had arrived.

"This is a charming room," Margery said, clutching desperately for a topic of conversation as Lady Emily settled opposite her and smiled benignly across the rim of her teacup. "You have a lovely view across the deer park."

"Oh, I am very lucky," Lady Emily said lightly. "Very, very lucky. I have lived at Templemore all my life, you know." She offered Margery a plate of little ginger biscuits. "Yes, indeed." Her eyes, gray as Lord Templemore's and Margery's own, were pale and inward-looking. "My mama came here as the housekeeper. Your great-grandfather took her as his mistress while his wife was still alive. He was in his seventies then, and my mama no more than five-and-twenty. It was quite a scandal!"

She laughed merrily, as though the sexual exploits of her parents were greatly entertaining. "Old Lady Templemore had been refusing papa her bed for years. She was very devout and would not sleep with him on saint's days, and of course every day of the year is dedicated to one saint or another."

"I see," Margery said, feeling vaguely uncomfortable at this insight into the intimate life of her ancestors.

"Oh, the Templemore men!" Lady Emily smiled indulgently. "Such rakes. Deplorable. Papa practically had a harem of mistresses. They called the women his game parlor. Casper, my brother, was the same. He married late and then he was unfaithful to your dear grandmama before the ink was dry on the wedding lines. Of course, he only married her for her money. Why do you think he never speaks of her?"

"Guilt, I imagine," Margery said dryly. She loved her grandfather but as she learned more about him she could not ignore his faults. She wondered how much the influence of a libidinous father had set him on the same track.

"Casper has always been a most generous brother to me," Lady Emily continued. "So much older, of course. Thirty years! I've always been the indulged little sister."

She started idly turning over the pile of tarot cards at her elbow. Margery's eyes were drawn to the vivid pictures and garish colors, the Hanged Man, smiling as he was strung upside down from a scaffold. The Devil horned and chained. Death the skeleton, riding a black horse, carrying his bloodred scythe.... Margery shuddered at the images of suppressed violence.

Lady Emily smiled. "Drink your tea, my dear," she said.

The tea tasted vile. Margery took one sip then quickly tipped the rest into a potted plant when Lady Emily was not looking.

"You must have been quite young when my mother was born, Aunt Emily," she said. "Were you not closer to her in age than you were to grandpapa?"

She saw Lady Emily's fingers check as she shuffled the pack of cards.

"I was twenty-three when dearest Rose was born," Lady Emily said after a moment. She smiled, wide and vague. "Such a beautiful child! She was almost like a sister to me. More tea, Marguerite?"

"Oh, no, thank you," Margery said hurriedly.

Lady Emily poured herself another cup. "Of course, dear Rose..." She paused and shook her head, while Margery wondered what on earth she was about to say.

"Such a tragedy," Lady Emily murmured. "So sad. First marrying that dreadful man and then…" She shuddered.

"You knew my father, then," Margery said. She thought she should probably leave well enough alone, since she had not met a single person with a good word to say about Comte Antoine de Saint-Pierre, but she could not help herself. The man was an enigma to her. She knew nothing of her father and it felt strange and lonely.

Lady Emily did not answer at once. She blinked, raising her hand to rub her eyes. One of the tarot cards fluttered down onto the rug.

"The sun," Lady Emily said vaguely. "It is very bright today." She looked up at Margery. "Your father? He was very handsome, my love. Poor dear Rose was so taken in by him. She was not the only one."

Margery remembered Henry referring to her father's roistering about Town, his drinking, his mistresses, his gambling. It was extremely lowering to think that she was descended from a haughty society beauty and a rakish spy. Between them, they appeared to have had few good qualities to endow her with.

"I don't suppose he was a very nice person," she said, a little wistfully.

"No," Lady Emily agreed with surprising firmness. "He was not. Vain, I fear. He and Rose were always competing for the mirror. And really quite cruel…" She was turning one of the tarot cards over and over between her fingers. "Best not to ask, my love," she said. Suddenly her eyes were very bright. "Best to let the past lie."

"I don't really remember it anyway," Margery said. "I think I was too young."

"Good," Lady Emily said, smiling. "That's very good." She frowned. "Are you happy at Templemore, Marguerite? I fear there are shades here, the ghosts of the past. They walk. It is not a happy house."

"It is certainly dark and gloomy," Margery agreed. "But I have not experienced any ghosts. I have no sensibility. No ghost would appear to me. I am far too practical." Suddenly she was desperate to be away from Lady Emily and her ceaseless turning of the tarot cards. The heat in the room was getting unbearable. Margery stood up and her head swam.

"Excuse me, Aunt Emily," she said. "I need some fresh air."

"Of course, Marguerite, my love," Lady Emily said vaguely. She waved a hand. Her bracelets clashed. "It was so charming of you to join me for tea." She raised her gaze to Margery's face. "I do hope that I have been able to tell you something of your parents."

"Yes, thank you," Margery said. Her hand slipped on the doorknob. Her palm was damp. She looked at Lady Emily sitting in a shaft of bright sunlight that pitilessly illuminated the faded gray of her hair and the tiredness of her face, and wondered why she was thanking her aunt for making her feel more miserable and lonely than she had been before.

"I HAVE BEEN GIVING some thought to the Templemore jewels," the earl announced at dinner that night. They were eating informally by Templemore standards, *en famille,* as Lady Wardeaux put it, which meant that the extra leaves on the long mahogany dinner table were not being used and they sat only four feet apart from one another, rather than six. It made conversation slightly

easier, although a chilly silence was apparently the normal environment around the Templemore dinner table.

Margery, who had been trying to disguise her disgust
with the turtle soup—there was no way that it could surreptitiously be fed to the dogs—saw everyone fall silent.
Lady Emily's pale gray eyes opened wide and her soup-
spoon was suspended on its way to her mouth. A quick
frown touched Lady Wardeaux's brow. Mr. Churchward
broke off in the middle of whatever he had been saying
to Chessie. Only Henry seemed unperturbed.

"Margery shall try them on after dinner," the earl
said. "Fine jewels are better admired by candlelight."
He smiled at Margery. "They glow."

"I doubt the Templemore jewels will glow in any
light," Henry said. "They have been in the vaults so
long they will surely need cleaning."

"Churchward may take them back to London with
him," Lord Templemore said, with a dismissive wave
of the hand. "Then they may be cleaned for Margery's
come-out and the Templemore diamonds reset."

"Come-out?" Margery said faintly. It had not once
occurred to her that she might have to return to London
and have one of those grand and thoroughly intimidat-
ing balls that were the fate of every young lady in society. She had thought that a local assembly would be
the extent of her social ordeal. "Surely I am too old,"
she said. "I have already been out, to all intents and
purposes, for twelve years."

She saw Henry smile. "Not as Lady Marguerite
Saint-Pierre," he said. "You must be introduced formally to ton society."

Margery's stomach lurched at the thought of being
the center of attention at a ton ball. There would be no-

where to hide and so many people watching her and talking about her. Henry's dark gaze was resting on her thoughtfully, and she was almost certain that he was remembering those foolish thoughts she had confided to him in London about how she preferred for no one to notice her.

Well, there was no chance of that in future. She might as well wear a large placard with her name on it. Suddenly sick with nerves she pushed away her soup plate and a footman swooped down to tidy it away.

"We will travel up in a month or so," the earl said, "before the end of the Season."

"I am so very glad that you feel well enough to make the trip to Town, Casper," Lady Emily trilled. "The cards told me we should be making a journey. I drew the Chariot in my reading today."

Silence fell again, since no one seemed able to find an adequate response to this. The plates were cleared and the roast beef served. Lord Templemore instructed his butler, Barnard, to fetch the jewels from the strong room and lay them out in the Red Saloon.

"The Templemore jewels are exquisite," Lady Wardeaux said to Margery. "You are most fortunate." Her tone implied that Margery scarcely deserved such good luck. "Of course, your grandfather is quite right to have the diamonds reset. You are far too small to carry them off."

"I am grateful," Margery said. "I am sure the mere weight of them would have squashed me flat."

"One requires stature to wear the Templemore diamonds," Lady Wardeaux said. "One needs Town bronze. They would have suited a beauty like Lady Antonia

Gristwood perfectly. Such a pity she will never wear them—"

"Mama!" Henry's voice cut like a whip and Lady Wardeaux fell silent.

Margery looked up.

"Who is Lady Antonia Gristwood?" she asked.

There was an odd silence around the table.

"Lady Antonia is the daughter of the Duke of Carlisle," Lady Emily said brightly. "She was going to marry Henry before she jilted him because he lost Templemore."

"The woman in the stripy gown," Margery murmured, remembering Joanna Grant's ball and the supercilious beauty who had so arrogantly demanded to be waited upon. The woman had been proud to a fault.

"Emily!" Now it was Lady Wardeaux's turn to snap a rebuke, but Margery could see a furtive spark of triumph in her eyes. She knew Lady Wardeaux had wanted her to hear about Lady Antonia, who would have carried off the Templemore diamonds with so much more style than she could ever hope to achieve. She felt upset, which was no doubt precisely what Lady Wardeaux had wanted. More disturbingly, she felt jealous of the woman Henry had apparently been going to marry. It had never occurred to her that he might have been betrothed. Nor that he might have lost his fiancée when he had lost his inheritance.

She looked at Henry. He was staring at his mother and he looked angry.

"I am very sorry," she said, addressing him directly. "Sorry that Lady Antonia jilted you, I mean."

Now everyone was looking at her as though she had committed some unspeakable act at the dining table.

She knew she was supposed to have ignored Lady Emily's comment and soldiered on chewing the tough roast beef, because that was what a lady would do. A lady would pretend to be selectively deaf.

Henry shrugged. "It was bound to happen," he said. "Carlisle would not have let his daughter throw herself away on a mere baron."

There was absolutely no emotion in his voice. Margery stared, wondering if he could truly be so unmoved.

"But did you love her?" she asked.

This time there was a distinct gasp of shock around the table, as though she had taken off her gown and danced naked amid the crockery. Lady Wardeaux had her eyes closed in horror. Lady Emily's mouth hung open. Even the footmen's wooden impassivity was threatened. The earl was smiling slightly as he fed some beef to one of the spaniels.

Henry's eyebrows shot up. "My dear Lady Marguerite," he drawled. "Marriage has nothing to do with love. It is a business agreement based on mutual benefit." His tone made Margery feel as naive as the little maidservant she had once been, reading penny romances in the attic. "I assure you my heart is not broken and neither is Lady Antonia's, assuming she has a heart, which I beg leave to doubt."

"Well, then," Margery said, "it is a great pity the wedding did not come off because it sounds as though you would have been ideally suited."

She sawed furiously at her beef. Of all the cold, indifferent, stiff-necked, stuffed-shirted pomposity. She would never understand the aristocracy and she did not want to be one of them.

The beef was removed and pudding served. Gradually the room resumed what passed for a normal air. The ladies withdrew for tea; the gentlemen were left to their port. Lady Wardeaux delicately ignored Margery's social gaffe and chatted about the warm spring-like weather until Barnard came to tell them that the jewels had been laid out for them to try on in the Red Saloon.

"I know I did a bad thing," Margery whispered to Chessie, catching her arm as they made their way past the library. "But I cannot quite work out whether it was worse to mention love, or to do so in front of the servants."

Chessie gave a snort of laughter. "It is Lady Wardeaux who showed bad manners," she whispered back.

"I bumped into Lady Antonia at Lady Grant's most recent ball," Margery said. "She was vile."

Chessie pulled an expressive face. "She has vileness perfected to an art form," she agreed. "Not even Henry deserved that."

The Red Saloon glittered, the light from the chandeliers throwing back the sparkle and gleam of a dozen different items of jewelry Barnard had laid out in their velvet cases. Edith, Margery's maid, had set out a table with a mirror and a stand of candles.

Lady Wardeaux fell on the jewels rather like a magpie, picking them up, holding them to the light, exclaiming over them. Margery, catching Chessie's eye, tried not to laugh, but there was no denying that they were a stunning collection. She simply could not accept that one day they would all be hers, especially not the earl's coronet with its ermine trim and eight silver balls.

"Am I going to have to wear that barbaric thing?" she whispered to Chessie in abject horror.

"Only for state occasions such as the coronation of monarchs," Chessie said comfortingly and Margery almost fainted at the thought of it.

"Let us hope the King has many more years in him, then," she said.

"I think that might be a vain hope." It was Henry's voice. Margery looked up to see that he and Lord Templemore had joined them. Her grandfather was settling himself in one of the wide armchairs near the fire, a brandy glass at his elbow and the inevitable spaniel at his feet.

"Henry will help you try on the jewels," Lord Templemore said.

A little shiver ran through Margery at the thought of Henry placing the stones about her neck. She felt self-conscious enough without him near her. Already the skin of her neck and shoulders, uncovered by the modestly low bodice of her evening gown, felt strangely sensitized as though it was only awaiting his touch.

"How singular," she said. "I did not imagine you as a lady's maid, Lord Wardeaux."

A spark of wicked amusement leapt into Henry's eyes. "My experience is quite extensive," he murmured.

"That I do not doubt," Margery snapped. "You shall not be extending it further at my expense, however."

Henry smiled. "I assure you, you will not find it an unpleasant experience. Shall we?" He gestured to the chair that Edith had placed in front of the mirror. Gritting her teeth, Margery sat as he took up a position behind her left shoulder. A tapestry panel embroidered with dragons in red and green stood to one side, partially screening the table from the room.

"Try this." Chessie was offering a pretty little silver

tiara that sparkled with tiny rubies. Henry placed it gently on Margery's head, his fingers entangling for one brief moment in her hair, loosening the pins. Margery's scalp tingled. Little shivers skipped through her and her toes curled in her satin slippers. She felt hot and flustered. A strand of her fine honey-dark hair slid down her neck like a caress to feather over one bare shoulder, satin soft against her skin. She felt Henry's fingers move again and another curl slid surreptitiously from its carefully arranged pins to tease her nape.

Margery shifted on the chair, feeling a dangerous excitement squeeze all the air from her lungs. She knew that Henry was doing this on purpose and she was determined to resist this seduction of her senses but it was not easy. The combination of Henry's touch and the caress of the jewels was a potent one.

The room seemed too bright, hot and airless. Already she felt a little light-headed and she was achingly aware of Henry standing directly behind her, his body close to hers. She knew she was susceptible to him but she had had no idea that she would also find the trappings of luxury so seductive, that she would be bewitched by the sensual shift of silk against her skin and the heavy glitter of the priceless jewels. With each step she seemed to move further away from the life she had known and into a new world of lavish excess. And she liked it. She could feel it tempting her, drawing her in. She shivered voluptuously, closing her eyes.

"Here is the matching ruby necklace." Chessie had evidently seen nothing strange in her for she was smiling, holding out a delicate silver-and-ruby filigree necklace that Henry fastened about Margery's throat. She felt the cool silver against her skin then she felt Henry's hand slide down from her nape, down the exposed line of her spine, slow and sure, in a deliberate stroke that had her quivering.

Chessie was saying something about the ruby necklace being too insipid but Margery could not concentrate on the words, could concentrate on nothing but the sly downward glide of Henry's fingertips against her bare back. They reached the first button and paused, again very deliberately.

Margery caught her breath on a gasp. Surely he was not going to undress her here and now, slide the buttons from their moorings and leave her exposed in her petticoats and drawers in front of everyone. But of course not. He was teasing her. His fingers moved on to brush against the top edge of her gown, over the tender line of her shoulder blade, and in a devastating flash of understanding Margery realized exactly what he was doing. He was seducing her in full view of the assembled company, reducing her to a state of desperate longing that she was finding it increasingly difficult to hide. And he had only just started. A heavy pulse started to beat in her blood, primitive and insistent.

Her gaze flew up to meet Henry's in the mirror. His was dark and impassive, completely unreadable. He unhooked the silver necklace and passed it back to Chessie, who exchanged it for a river of emeralds that flashed green fire. Chessie took the rubies away and Henry hung the emeralds gently about Margery's throat in their place. Once again she felt his fingers, warm and strong, brush the nape of her neck as he fastened the clasp. Once again his eyes rose to meet hers in the glass, then his gaze dropped very purposefully to where the huge center stone of the necklace was cradled between her breasts.

Margery could feel the cold, hard emerald against her warm skin. A shiver racked her and she felt the heat rise in her like a furnace. Soon she would be burning up.

"You look quite delicious," Henry murmured.

Margery grabbed the matching eardrops, her fingers shaking a little as she tried to fasten them. She wondered that nobody could see the state she was in, ruffled, disturbed and thoroughly aroused. But no one was watching them. Her grandfather appeared to have fallen asleep before the fire with the spaniels at his feet, Lady Wardeaux and Lady Emily were still trying on a variety of coronets and bracelets, chattering together farther down the room, and Chessie, too, had been distracted by a splendid sapphire necklace that matched her eyes.

Besides, the table was a little turned at an angle from the room and the mirror was wide and Henry's body shielded her from sight. The dragon screen hid them from the side and suddenly it was as though they were alone. It felt strange but utterly compelling that in a room full of people she was only aware of Henry, of the dark, heavy heat now in his eyes and the sensual brush of his hands on her.

"Let me help you with those," Henry said, seeing her struggles with the eardrops. His voice was quite indifferent but his fingers brushed lightly up her throat to her earlobe, tugging it gently down so that it accepted the weight of the huge, heavy emerald stone. The clip snapped shut on Margery's skin with a sharp bite that was half pleasure, half pain.

Margery caught her breath on a tiny moan as a bolt of pure carnal desire shot through her to center between her thighs. Her nipples hardened instantly to tight peaks beneath the pink silk of her evening gown. She jerked on the chair. She could not help herself. Her gaze, shocked, sought Henry's in the glass, but his head was bent as he took the other stone in the palm of his hand. He waited and Margery could feel anticipation tighten like a knot in her belly.

"You will have to be very quiet." Henry's voice was a dark whisper.

His hand came up. Margery felt a long ripple of arousal shimmer through her and the throb of sharp lust in the pit of her stomach. Henry's fingers tugged her earlobe down. Margery's body jolted again in response and then the clasp snapped shut and the delicious, painful sting of it pulsated through her. This time the carnal pleasure was sharper and deeper. The ache in her belly was a torment, demanding satisfaction. Her skin felt hot and damp, the dark green emerald flashing between her breasts as she took a shaken breath.

The emeralds swung, huge and heavy in her ears, each tiny movement setting up an echo of sensual delight through her entire body. It was exquisite. It tortured her. She was both appalled and fascinated, wanting to run from the room but held in her seat by the fact that she was not sure her legs would be able to carry her as far as the door.

Henry's hands came to rest on her shoulders. His gaze was on her reflection, on the rise and fall of her breasts and the outline of her nipples so shamelessly hard beneath the thin silk. About her neck and between her breasts the opulent emeralds gleamed against her skin. Margery had never felt more aware of her body, of its heat and tightness, and of the sleek, taut pleasure bound up so fast inside her that it positively screamed for release.

Henry bent down so that his lips brushed her ear and his breath stirred the stray curls at her nape. Margery almost moaned aloud, remembering at the last moment to stifle the sound.

"Some people find jewels extremely arousing," Henry murmured, "and it seems you are more responsive to them than most." His lips touched the curve of her neck and he bit down, very gently, against her bare skin. Margery squirmed, her nipples unbearably tight and hard, stimulated by the silken slide of her gown and the soft chemise beneath.

"Who would have thought that such decadence would so excite you?" Henry's tongue salved the sting of the bite and this time a tiny moan did escape Margery's lips.

"Here are the Templemore diamonds!" Lady Wardeaux's voice sounded too loud, too triumphant, shattering the moment. Margery jumped. Henry's expression changed, the sensual darkness in his eyes replaced by blank impassivity.

Inside Margery was shaking. Suddenly the lights were too bright and the chatter too loud. She felt stripped bare, exposed. She could not understand how she could have behaved in so abandoned a fashion in a room full of people. She had been lost to all propriety, swept away by the sensual caress of the emeralds against her skin and the disturbing heat in Henry's eyes.

She looked at him. He had strategically retreated behind the table, and innocent as she was, she knew exactly why. Male arousal was impossible to hide, particularly in such well-fitting evening trousers. It served him right. She felt glad that he was suffering, too.

She stood up. Her legs felt a little shaky and she steadied herself by grabbing the edge of the table.

"If you will excuse me...." Her voice sounded very odd. Suddenly everyone was looking at her, which was exactly the opposite of what she wanted.

"I'm very tired," she said, hoping she looked exhausted rather than aroused.

Chessie hurried over to help her remove the emerald necklace. Margery pulled off the ear bobs and dropped them in the velvet case. The walk to the door seemed very long and once out in the hall, in the safety of the shadows, she stopped to draw a steadying breath. Her body still felt restless and on edge, quickened with desire. She slumped to sit on the bottom step of the grand stairs. In front of her on the wall was a huge portrait of her mother. Margery did not particularly like it because Lady Rose looked faintly supercilious, as she did in a great many of her portraits, so much so that Margery was beginning to suspect that she would not have liked her mother very much at all.

She sighed and leaned her head against the newel post. If ever there was a warning to her to be careful in her affections, then Lady Rose embodied it. Her mother had loved unwisely and Margery had no intention of following in her footsteps.

CHAPTER TWELVE

Temperance Reversed: Quarrels

HENRY SAT IN THE GOLD SALON and watched Margery hold court. It was the only way to describe it; every man of marriageable age in the neighborhood—and some who fancied themselves to be marriageable and frankly were not—was sitting in a rapt circle about her chair. It had not taken long for the richest heiress in England to attract the suitors.

On Margery's left was young Hugo Wentworth, the son of a merchant from Bristol who had bought himself a knighthood and a local manor. Hugo was barely out of Eton. On Margery's right was Dr. Fox, the local physician. The squire Sir Reggie Radnor had also come to pay his respects.

Radnor was not generally interested in anything that he could not shoot or hunt, but his terrifying mama had positively whipped him into the salon. Henry had heard that the Radnor pockets were to let and a rich marriage would set Reggie up to maim and kill many more feathered and furry creatures in the neighborhood.

Holding the floor at present was the aged Lord Blunt, who had buried three wives already and was boasting loudly to Margery that he still had all his own teeth, a fact that she was pretending to find fascinating. Out in the cold on the window seat was another youth, barely out of the nursery, whose mama had tricked him out in his highest shirt points for the occasion. None of them were remotely credible as suitors for the Templemore heiress and Henry was not at all sure why the sight of them panting after Margery put him in such a bad humor.

It was a fortnight since he had practically seduced Margery in the Red Saloon in front of everyone, a fortnight in which he had scrupulously kept out of her way as much for his own sanity as for her good. The swift and devastating descent into desire that night had taken him by surprise as much as it had her.

He had spent most of his time in London at the Board of Ordnance, only returning because the earl had said that he had an urgent business proposition he wished to discuss with him.

Henry needed his godfather's investment in the Wardeaux estate, but he would have preferred not to return to Templemore to discuss the matter. As it was, his nights in London had been largely sleepless, and when he had dreamed it had often been of Margery. They were hot, explicit dreams that had left him hard and aching for her, and on one occasion spent, only to realize as he woke that her presence in his bed had been an illusion.

And now he had come back and it was clear that Margery was avoiding him. For some reason, that simply made the awareness between them more scalding-hot and uncomfortable.

He caught Chessie Alton's eyes upon him. She smiled sympathetically. Henry shifted slightly. He did not want Chessie or indeed anyone else sympathizing with him.

He doubted that she would, in fact, be sympathetic if she could read his thoughts. He was sitting here, sipping tea from a china cup and pressing the rector to a ginger biscuit, but all the time he was hearing Margery's gasp of pleasure as the heavy weight of the ear bobs pulled on her flesh, and imagining stripping the clothes from her to leave her naked but for the Templemore emeralds.

He shifted again. The room felt hot. Margery was wearing a pretty gown of jonquil-yellow with a scalloped neck that only hinted at the curves beneath. The very demureness of it was strangely enticing. Henry rubbed the back of his neck, wondering yet again if Margery's forbidden state was working some inverse attraction upon him. His body felt on the edge of arousal.

He stared at the yellow ribbon threaded through Margery's gleaming golden-brown hair and wanted to grab it and pull it, pull the matching ribbons on the dress as well until she was unlaced and unwrapped, warm and willing under his hands. How galling it was to be so undone by such an innocent and how much more self-control he would need to find each day he remained at Templemore.

"Of course the Radnors were lords of the manor here when the Templemores were still herding sheep," Henry heard the Dowager Lady Radnor say *sotto voce* to Mrs. Wentworth. "But one must be civil to rich upstarts."

Reggie Radnor was being more than civil to Margery, Henry thought. He had managed to possess himself of one of her hands and was running his tongue over her knuckles in what he no doubt thought was a rakishly seductive move. Henry felt revolted. Margery, smiling grimly, wiped the back of her hand against her skirts.

"Dearest Lady Marguerite," Reggie said. "I am so

delighted to make your acquaintance. *Enchanté!* Which means—"

"Please do not explain your compliments, Sir Reggie," Margery said. "It quite spoils their impact."

"Alas, dear Marguerite is looking a little peaky today," Lady Wardeaux whispered in Henry's ear.

"Her money is still looking frightfully attractive, however," Henry said, as Lord Blunt maneuvered his chair even closer to Margery.

He was not jealous. He was not possessive. Such emotions were irrational.

"Fetching little filly, ain't you!" Blunt said, staring down the front of Margery's gown. "I used to go wenching with your papa."

"How charming, Lord Blunt," Margery said. "I have often wanted to learn more about him, but now I am not so sure."

The door opened. Henry stiffened. Barnard was ushering in three gentlemen who were of a very different complexion from the rustic gentry of the shire. One was a dandy in an embroidered silk waistcoat and high shirt points, the second was a sporting gentleman and the third was a Byronic-looking youth wearing black and a rather intense expression. They brought with them an indefinable air of fashionable society. Henry saw the other gentlemen in the room shift and bristle at the invasion of the ton.

"The Marquis of Bryson, Lord Stephen Kestrel, Lord Fane," Barnard announced, with the air of a man who at last had something important to say. Henry stood up.

"Bryson." He offered his hand to the elegant peer who was making his way into the room. "London lost its charm for you?"

"Visiting m'sister," The Marquis said with a bland smile. "How do you do, Wardeaux?"

"I thought Lady Belton lived in Devon," Henry said.

"This is on my way," Bryson said vaguely. He nodded to Henry and moved across to the sofa where with utter ruthlessness he displaced Sir Reggie from Margery's side, took her hand and held it between both of his in a manner that made Henry want to punch him.

"I hear there is to be an assembly in Faringdon tomorrow night, Lady Marguerite," Lord Fane put in eagerly. "I do hope you will be gracing it with your presence."

Suddenly the room seemed to have woken from its rather sleepy pleasantries and was full of chatter and masculine laughter. Lord Stephen Kestrel, gracefully acceding to Bryson's claim on Margery, had taken a chair beside Chessie, perhaps thinking he might get to the heiress through her companion. Or perhaps Margery was not his objective at all. Henry noted that Chessie blushed and smiled at Lord Stephen, and Lord Stephen in turn seemed extremely pleased to see her. Kestrel was a good man, Henry thought. He was glad he was not dangling after Margery because, unlike Bryson, there was nothing about him to object to at all.

Lord Fane was hanging on the back of Margery's chair and hanging on her every word. Rather cunningly he was claiming to be a distant cousin to her and therefore to have a prior claim on her attention.

"I knew this would happen!" Lady Wardeaux hissed in Henry's ear. "The gentlemen of the ton simply could not wait for Marguerite to return to London so they have come courting here. She will be wed in a trice! Henry, do something!"

"I am not sure what you expect me to do," Henry said, "other than carry Lady Marguerite off."

"Would you?" his mother asked hopefully.

The idea held a certain degree of appeal, Henry thought. But he could not act on it. Marriage to Margery, aside from branding him the biggest fortune hunter in the ton, would be a helter-skelter mix of lust and argument until the lust died and the argument turned rancid. He shuddered at the thought of all that chaos.

He realized that Margery was looking at him. This was in itself unusual, since she had made a point of keeping out of his way ever since his return. Now, though, there was quite definitely a plea in the silver depths of her eyes. Henry found it oddly difficult to resist that appeal. He strode languidly over to her sofa, edged Lord Fane out of the way and rested his hands on the back directly behind her. If his fellow peers chose to interpret that as a sign that he exercised a prior claim, he was not averse to that in order to chase them away.

"Gentlemen," he said. "Pleasant as it has been to see you all, I fear that Lady Marguerite is about to expire beneath the weight of your attentions. So if you would not mind…"

"Thank you," Margery whispered to him and when she smiled Henry felt a ridiculous pleasure.

His words created a certain amount of resentment. "So, Wardeaux thinks to steal a march," he heard Fane say to Bryson as Barnard ushered the overzealous suitors from the room. "Good luck to him—I suppose she is quite a fetching little piece if one can ignore the smell of the servants' hall, but she is not good enough for me."

Henry found himself possessed of such a white-hot fury that his hands itched to take Fane by the cravat and strangle the life out of him. He balled his fists at his sides, and instead derived a certain pleasure from sticking his foot out as Fane passed him, sending the peer sprawling in the entrance hall in front of everyone.

"In your proper place, Fane," Henry said pleasantly. "Beneath Lady Marguerite's feet." He strolled back into the saloon feeling absurdly pleased with himself.

"The local gentry are small fry," Lady Wardeaux was saying to Margery, "but one must keep in with them. As for the others—" Her face creased with displeasure. "It is most unfortunate that they did not see fit to wait until you went to London, Marguerite."

"The local innkeepers must be delighted," Henry said. It would be like this from here on in, he thought. There would be an endless troop of hopeful peers through the house until Margery made her choice. He wondered if she realized just how besieged she would be. Drawing a deep breath, he tried to drive out all the inappropriately possessive feelings the thought engendered.

Margery had started to collect the plates and teacups, stacking them neatly on the table.

"Marguerite, my dear—" An expression of abject horror crossed Lady Wardeaux's features. "Pray do not remove the cups. That is the footman's task."

She went out to chivvy the servants and Margery sat back with a sigh, picking up a copy of *La Belle Assemblée* and flicking through it. A silence descended on the drawing room but it was a silence sharp with awareness. Margery broke it after a moment.

"I quite had it in mind to wed Sir Reggie," she said lightly, "until the Marquis of Bryson arrived." Her silver-gray gaze was guileless. "He is *extremely* handsome."

Henry looked at her. It was impossible to tell whether she was sincere or not. He supposed that two weeks might completely change her beliefs about marriage, but it would be surprising, since one of Margery's abiding characteristics was stubbornness. On the other hand, this elegant creature before him, so fresh and pretty in her bright yellow muslin, had a certain brittle air of sophistication about her that the Margery Mallon he had known a month before had definitely lacked.

The bright candor that had so warmed him had vanished. Henry felt a lurch in his stomach to think that a mere four weeks might have changed Margery so fundamentally. Yet it was not impossible. She was the richest heiress in the ton now, and might have developed attitudes to match. Not every young woman coming into such an inheritance would remain unspoiled.

"Bryson keeps a stable of mistresses the way that most men keep a stable of horses," he said.

"I thought that was *de rigueur* in the ton," Margery said, her eyes mocking him over the top of the magazine. "I understand that you had an opera singer in keeping. Just the one, so I believe. Perhaps you do not have Lord Bryson's stamina?"

Minx. Henry, who had resolved not to be drawn into a dispute with Margery any more than he was going to make love to her, was tempted to break his vow on the spot.

"I thought you believed that love was a prerequisite for marriage," he said. "Did you then fall in love with Lord Bryson at first sight?"

Margery raised a shoulder in a dismissive shrug.

"Perhaps I was a little naive about that. I do not believe that love matches sit well with the ton. If I am to make a marriage of convenience, then is not any man as good as another?"

She sounded sincere. She looked sincere. Henry felt anger and disillusion stir in him that she had so easily, so carelessly, dismissed the principles that had been important to her and was now as vapid and shallow as any spoiled debutante. He took the magazine from her hand and tossed it down onto the sofa. Margery's eyes widened with surprise and annoyance.

"If you are to make a marriage of convenience," Henry said, "it would be better to settle for Lord Blunt. At least he might die soon."

"I do not see that it matters much," Margery said dismissively. "Whoever I choose will have no real respect for me. He will deplore my upbringing while spending my money. You heard Lord Fane's comment."

"All the more reason to find a worthy man." Henry felt that ungovernable fury again for Fane's boorishness, and with it a fierce protectiveness for her. He wanted to defend her against the slights and the snobbery of the ton. At the same time, he wanted to shake her for even considering abandoning her principles and selling herself into an advantageous marriage.

"That is unexpected advice coming from you," Margery said. She had sprung to her feet and was confronting him. "You intend to make a passionless match with some equally cold-blooded aristocrat. Why criticize me for doing the best I can?"

"That was different," Henry said, keeping a tight hold on his temper and his self-control. "That was what

I wanted. I do not want to marry for love, but you are denying what you want."

Margery's slender shoulders lifted in another shrug. "A love match was what I used to want before I understood how the world worked. The best thing I can do now is to marry a man whose estate and title match my own. In that way, we will both understand the bargain we have made." She smiled. "Perhaps I could even catch myself a duke."

"Perhaps you could," Henry said, through his teeth. She looked so fresh and pretty in her springlike dress, and she sounded so spoiled, corrupted by all she had gained. He felt a violent wave of anger.

"Since you outrank me, and I am not suitable to put myself forward as a husband, pray remember to call on me as your lover when you have produced the heir and the spare," he said. "No doubt you are aware that that is the way fashionable society operates. If you are to adopt some of its customs, why not all of them?"

He found he had already taken a step toward her. He took another. She did not retreat because it was not in her nature. She stood her ground and looked at him, looked down her nose at him, in fact, with all the disdain of the Templemores. Henry had never found disdain arousing before; in Margery he found it provocative in the extreme. He wanted to toss her onto the sofa so recently occupied by his mother and the Dowager Lady Radnor and make wild love to her.

"How odious you can be," Margery said. "I wish you had not come back."

"I doubt you would think me odious if you were in my bed," Henry said. "You may be above me, but you might find it stimulating to have me under you."

Margery's mouth rounded into a small outraged O. "If I wished to take a lover," she said, rallying, "I am sure I could do a great deal better than you."

That was fighting talk, and Henry could see that Margery knew full well it was dangerous. There was trepidation as well as defiance in her eyes now.

That was the trouble with the Templemores; they had always been reckless in the extreme. He had simply not expected to see that recklessness in Margery. Nor had he expected to find it so stimulating. Not that his behavior was any better. He was already halfway down the road to ruin—Margery's ruin—and riding hell for leather. He knew it. He could feel his self-control slipping. There was a devil in him, the same one that had possessed his father, the one he had fought so hard for so long to deny with his devotion to duty and his rejection of all that was rakish and unprincipled.

The devil won. He put out a negligent hand and caught Margery's elbow, drawing her toward him. The sleeve of her gown felt smooth beneath his fingers and her arm was warm, soft and rounded beneath the light muslin. He heard her intake of breath, a tiny catch in the throat. Her eyes were still wide and defiant but beneath the surface lurked all manner of fascinating emotions. She knew she was pushing the edge of his control but that in itself was enough to excite her. He could see it in the smoky silver of her eyes, and that knowledge brought him back to the edge of arousal, tempting him almost beyond endurance.

"You think that you could find a better lover than me," he said very softly. "And you are basing that assumption on...what, precisely? Given that you were a virgin a month ago, I imagine your means of comparison would be decidedly limited."

Margery gasped. "A gentleman would not mention such a thing."

"I beg your pardon," Henry said. "I was simply stating a fact. If you have managed to extend your amorous education in the past few weeks, as well as becoming heiress to the richest earldom in the country, then do enlighten me. After all, I have not been here to follow your progress."

"What I have been doing in the past few weeks is not your business," Margery said. She looked at him with cold, hard dislike. "I wish you had not come back," she repeated.

She tweaked her sleeve from his grip and whisked past him and out of the room. The door closed softly behind her.

Henry swore under his breath. He walked slowly across to the window. The last of the visitors were departing, the carriage wheels spattering the gravel. Bryson handled his team well. He was a very accomplished whip. And he would make Margery very unhappy as a husband.

Henry swore again. Margery was right; it was none of his business. The fact that he wanted her future to be his business meant that he was deep in trouble, deeper than when he had gone away two weeks before. He had come back fully intending to speak with Lord Templemore and be gone. He had not planned to be drawn into Margery's life at all.

That was the trouble with good intentions, Henry thought. The road to hell was paved with them.

CHAPTER THIRTEEN

The Ace of Cups: The start of love

THAT AFTERNOON MARGERY was sitting by the fountain watching the goldfish flirting their lazy fins beneath the lily leaves. She had brought a book with her, a Gothic romance by Clara Reeve called *The Old English Baron*. She had found it in her grandfather's extensive library, a room that had overawed her when she had first seen it, with its floor-to-ceiling bookshelves and well-thumbed collection.

Lord Templemore had been delighted to find her browsing. Her mother, he said, had read nothing other than the fashionable magazines. Margery hardly felt qualified to call herself bookish but she did enjoy having the leisure to read. As a maid, she had only been able to snatch moments between her duties and so often fell asleep at night over her books.

One of the peacocks strutted up to her across the gravel. It gave a loud cry and spread its tail feathers in shimmering display, turning back and forth so that she might admire it. Margery smiled. She was starting to get quite fond of the bad-tempered birds. Perhaps the poor thing wanted to mate and felt frustrated. She sympathized.

She wished Henry had not come back. Except that

she had missed him quite desperately every single day of his absence. She had felt bereft and lonely, angry with herself for the weakness but powerless to prevent it.

She had been so pleased to see him and so *angry* to see him. Her heart had felt as though it might burst and she had been quite breathless. She did not quite understand her own emotions but she understood all too well why she had tried to provoke him this morning in an attempt to appear as though she did not care. It had been a spectacularly bad idea that had left her feeling more miserable than ever.

Lust and passion. That was all Henry could offer her. She wanted it, but she could not have it with honor and never with love.

She sighed. Being Lady Marguerite Saint-Pierre was decidedly more a bed of thorns than roses at the moment. On the outside, the expensive gowns made her a lady, but she was still grappling with her new role. She was learning about the estate and the way that Templemore was run. She was also learning the social graces. It felt as though she had spent an inordinate amount of time with Lady Wardeaux and Lady Emily learning how to arrange flowers and how to supervise dinner menus.

Lady Wardeaux had also tutored her in the superficial discourse required on social occasions. She could chat comfortably to the neighbors about the weather or the state of the roads. She could offer the vicar tea and discuss feminine accomplishments with his wife. She could even, at a pinch, act as hostess for her grandfather if he chose to hold a formal dinner.

In other ways, however, she was sadly lacking. She possessed few feminine accomplishments such as painting watercolors or playing the piano. She could sew, of course, since it had been one of the skills she needed as a lady's maid, but she had had only the most basic of educations and knew no languages and precious little about history or geography. Lady Wardeaux, in a rare moment of encouragement, had pointed out to her that no one liked a bluestocking, but Margery still felt inadequate.

She was not sure what she was supposed to do all day either. According to Lady Wardeaux she was already doing it, but being Lady Marguerite was not really a job. It did not require her to get up at five in the morning to clean grates or to carry hot water.

She had hoped that her brothers might come to visit her so that she could recapture something of her old self and her old life, but Jed had not replied to her letter. Billy had congratulated her on her good fortune and asked for a loan, but had made no mention of visiting her. That only left Jem, who was apparently out of London on some typically vague business that was bound to be illegal, immoral or both. Margery felt a little hurt to be so abandoned. She had thought she was close to her brothers and she needed them.

This morning she had stood before the enormous portrait of her mother in the Blue Saloon and tried to draw something, anything, from the pretty painted face that looked down at her with such unconscious arrogance. Lady Rose, Margery now realized, had been the sort of spoiled little rich girl whom she had deplored when she was a maidservant, the type of woman who had taken her material comforts for granted and who had ignored those she thought of as beneath her. As for Margery's father, there were no pictures of him in the house, not even a miniature, because he had been a thoroughly bad lot and an utter cad. No one mentioned his name. He had even been crossed out of the family bible where the names of the Templemores were recorded back through several centuries.

"Excuse me, milady." William, one of Templemore's many footmen, was approaching her over the gravel. The peacocks scattered, squawking and shedding their tail feathers. William bowed to her. "Lord Templemore requests that you join him in his study, ma'am."

"Thank you." Margery got to her feet and dusted down her skirts. "How is your mama, William?" she asked as the footman followed her deferentially indoors. "I heard that she has not been well."

"She is much recovered now, thank you, ma'am," William said, holding the garden door open for her. "She asked me to thank you for the fruit you sent."

Margery nodded. "It was a pleasure. The hothouses produce far more than we can use here, so it is nice to share."

"Lady Templemore used to do the same," William said. "His lordship's late wife. You are the spitting image of her, ma'am." He blushed as though he had spoken out of turn. "Begging your pardon, ma'am, but she was a lovely lady, your grandmama, so I heard."

No one ever said that about her mother, Margery thought.

She blinked as she went into the darkness of the West Passage with its stone-flagged hall and hideous gold furniture. Chessie had told her that, like the ugly gilt clock in the Red Saloon, the tables and spindly chairs were from the palace of King Louis XIV of France and were worth a fortune. Personally she considered them a crime against good taste and impractical into the bargain. No one could sit on a chair like that. It would collapse.

She knocked on the door of her grandfather's parlor. He bade her enter.

Henry was with him. There was a pile of drawings and diagrams on the big cherrywood table in the center of the room, but these had been temporarily abandoned and the two men were playing chess at the smaller table in the window. Margery stopped abruptly just inside the door. She had not imagined that Henry's relationship with his godfather would involve something so frivolous as a game. They had always seemed so formal with each other. Now the earl was smiling as he put Henry's queen in check and Margery felt a pang of something close to jealousy. Then she felt ashamed. Lord Templemore was her grandfather and he loved her. She should not grudge Henry a relationship with him, too.

The sunlight played over Henry's glossy black hair, and when he looked up Margery was conscious of a strange tumbling feeling in her stomach.

"Checkmate," Lord Templemore said with considerable satisfaction.

"I concede the game." Henry stood and bowed to Margery. "Lady Marguerite? Would you care to take my place?"

"I don't play games of skill and cunning," Margery said. "I am far too honest."

Henry laughed. "You don't play games," he said. "Is that so?"

Already it was there, that undercurrent of awareness that always flared between them. Margery tried to ignore it. She went over to the window seat and curled up on the cushion, welcoming the warmth of the May sunshine on her back. There were far too many places in the depths of Templemore that the light and warmth did not penetrate. It did not feel like a home.

"Stay, Henry," Lord Templemore said, as Henry pushed back his chair and started to walk toward the door. "I wish to speak with you both."

"Sir," Henry said. He shot Margery a look she could not read but that sent more prickles of response down her spine. He resumed his seat, his dark gaze steady and watchful.

"I have been thinking," the earl said, "that it would be useful for Margery to see more of the estate. She has been here a month now and is finding her feet. I would like you to show her around."

Margery's stomach lurched. She had taken it for granted that Henry would be returning to London or Wardeaux once his business at Templemore was finished. The last thing she required was her grandfather issuing him with orders to stay.

She looked up, saw tht Henry was smiling quizzically at her and realized that every last one of her thoughts had shown on her face. She knew in that moment that Henry had planned to refuse Lord Templemore's request but now, given her reaction, he would agree to the earl's request. Margery frowned fiercely at him. He met the look with a bland smile.

He opened his mouth. Margery forestalled him.

"I would not dream of inconveniencing Lord Wardeaux any further, Grandpapa," she said lightly. "I am persuaded that he has plenty of other matters demanding his attention and we shall manage very well without him." She looked at Henry. "Do you not have a home to go to, Lord Wardeaux?"

"I have my estate at Wardeaux, as you are well aware, Lady Marguerite," Henry said. "However nothing would give me greater delight than to show you around the Templemore estate. You will find my help invaluable, I am sure." His smile deepened. "Templemore it is no plaything for a girl."

Oh. It was a very deliberate challenge and Margery felt it like a jab in the ribs. She was helpless to resist. There was something about Henry that was so provocative. He got under her skin every single time.

"I am well aware of that, Lord Wardeaux," she said coldly. "That is why I asked Mr. Churchward to spend so much time taking me through all the details of the estate so that I would be as well versed in its operation as any *man* might be."

"You will need to ride about the estate to see how it works in practice," Henry said. "You do ride?" he added with an expressive lift of the brows. It was clear he thought she could not.

Margery smiled triumphantly. "My adoptive father was a blacksmith, Lord Wardeaux," she said. "I have been around horses since I could walk. I may not ride in the fashion prescribed for ladies, but we are in the country now, not in Hyde Park."

"Splendid," Henry said. "We shall ride out tomorrow and I may admire your seat."

"If we must," Margery said, through gritted teeth.

"What about dancing?" The earl was watching them, a little smile playing about his mouth. "Dancing is a social grace you will require in London."

Margery's eyes met Henry's. She was remembering the dance they had shared on the darkened terrace, before she had known who he was. Desolation swept through her. It felt as though that had been another world.

"I dance very poorly," she said.

"Henry will teach you," the earl said, waving a hand in his lordly manner.

"I would prefer to learn from a proper dancing master," Margery said. She was starting to feel like a kettle coming slowly to the boil. She could feel the anger bubbling inside at the way in which the earl and his godson were ordering her life in so superior and patronizing a fashion. "For all I know, Lord Wardeaux might be an appallingly bad dancer."

"I promise you I dance very well, Lady Marguerite," Henry said, smiling at her in a way that told her he had not forgotten one stolen moment of their forbidden waltz. "All the Duke of Lord Wellington's officers do. I would not dream of stepping on your feet."

"God forbid," Margery said. "And I would not dream of putting you to so much trouble, Lord Wardeaux."

"No trouble at all," Henry said smoothly.

Their gazes locked. "I fear you underestimate me," Margery said sweetly. "I shall be a very great deal of trouble. You have no idea how much trouble I can be."

Henry's smile was for her alone and promised all manner of sinful retribution. "I shall do my best to deal with you," he said.

"Was that what you wished to discuss, Grandpapa?" Margery asked. "My proficiency at riding and dancing, or lack of it? I do not wish to keep Lord Wardeaux any longer than necessary."

"No," Lord Templemore said, his lips twitching.

"There was another matter that I have been discussing with Mr. Churchward."

"I do hope," Margery said, looking directly at Henry, "that you have not asked Mr. Churchward to draw up a marriage settlement, Grandpapa."

"God forbid," Henry said. He turned to the earl. "I have no designs on Templemore and even fewer on your granddaughter, sir."

Margery glared at him. "Tell me, Lord Wardeaux, do you practice being so rude or is it a natural accomplishment?"

"You are both ahead of me," the earl said, a twinkle in his eye. "Do you wish to wed? If only you had mentioned it, I would have asked Churchward to arrange matters before he set off for London—"

"You are teasing me, Grandpapa," Margery said. "Lord Wardeaux and I would not suit."

"A pity," the earl said. He reached for the sheaf of papers resting on the rosewood table at his elbow and perched a pair of half-moon glasses on the end of his nose.

"Now, Margery, my dear child," he said. "I have asked Mr. Churchward to devise this new arrangement so that in the event of my death—"

"You're not going to die, Grandpapa," Margery interrupted. She felt cold all of a sudden. She knew that the earl had been very ill; the doctors had been frank with her that his heart was weak and his health poor, but she had persuaded herself that her arrival had so lifted his spirits that he would recover. In all of her new life the only warmth and affection she felt was from her grandfather. She simply could not countenance losing him so soon and rattling around in the big, dark rooms of Templemore all alone. She would be utterly lost.

She grabbed his hand. "Don't," she said, her voice cracking. The tears stung her throat. "I can't bear it."

Henry was watching her, his dark gaze steady and impassive. Suddenly she did not want him to see her feelings; he would judge it a weakness to show such emotion. For Henry, everything came back to duty, not love. She turned her face away, trying to hide from him.

Her grandfather squeezed her hand gently. "I hope to be with you a good while yet, Margery, but one must make plans," he said. "Now, the terms of your inheritance of Templemore are that your fortune remains in trust until you are thirty years of age or until you wed."

"How typical," Margery said, so incensed that she forgot to be upset. "I suppose that is because I am a female? I cannot be expected to manage the estate before I attain a vast age or before my husband takes it all in marriage!"

"It was indeed thoughtless of your great-great-grandfather to set up such a stipulation," Henry murmured, leaning back in his chair and crossing his elegantly booted legs at the ankle. "But I believe he had no sons and three very unruly daughters." His dark gaze mocked her. "Perhaps that is where you have inherited your character from, Lady Marguerite."

"One does not have to look far to see where yours derives from!" Margery snapped back.

"I have appointed Henry as your trustee alongside Mr. Churchward," the earl continued, unperturbed. "He will take on the role of guardian—"

"Guardian!" All the pent-up frustration within Margery exploded. "I don't need a guardian," she said. "I may not be thirty years old but I am not a child!" Her gaze picked Henry out and accused him. "You knew about this!"

"I did not," Henry said. He was frowning now. He drove his hands into the pockets of his coat, spoiling the beautiful line. His eyes lifted to hers. "I can think of nothing I would like less than to be your guardian, Lady Marguerite."

"Of course you can," Margery said sweetly, the anger and resentment fizzing inside her. "You would abhor to be my husband!"

They stared at one another while the air between them hummed and crackled with antagonism.

"I was about to say guardian of the estate," the earl said calmly. He looked at Margery over the top of his glasses. "In the event of my death, Henry and Mr. Churchward will advise you on the running of Templemore, Margery. It is Churchward who will act as your treasurer."

Margery jumped to her feet. "I suppose I have no say in this at all," she said. "I'm no more than a pawn. I had more freedom when I was a lady's maid."

With one swing of her hand she sent the chessmen tumbling from the table. They rolled across the floor to clatter against the skirting board. Tears stung her eyes and swelled her throat. She was furious with her grandfather. She already loved him so dearly that she could not bear to lose him. Yet it was intolerable to be treated like this, as though she was of no account.

First there was Lady Wardeaux, dressing her like a doll, telling her how to behave, and now her grandfather and Henry and Mr. Churchward, drawing up settlements and trusteeships and parceling out her life as though she had no mind of her own.

The angry beat of her blood was in her ears. Her head sang with the effort of repressing her fury. She stalked from the room and along the West Passage, the soft tap of her slippers on the tiled floor of the hall echoing to the dome in the roof and back. She had no notion where she was going, only that she had to get out of this stifling old mausoleum before she ran quite mad.

"Lady Marguerite!"

She heard Henry's voice behind her and the echo of his boots on the floor. She did not turn. The last thing she wanted was to listen to Henry preaching her duty to her. It was no wonder that her mama had run away if she had had to bear so much interference in her life. Suddenly the idea of running off with a notorious scoundrel seemed positively appealing.

She picked up speed. So did Henry. She could hear him getting closer, his long strides eating up the distance between them. He seized her arm from behind and whirled her around. Margery caught her breath. His face was set and hard and he held her wrist tightly as though he thought she was about to run away.

"Your grandfather is doing this because he loves you," Henry said. "He wants to protect you."

"He is going about it quite the wrong way," Margery said.

"He always does." Henry dropped her arm. "That does not mean that he does not care for you."

Margery rubbed her wrist where he had held her. She noticed with detached interest that she was shaking.

"I can allow that Grandpapa may have honorable motives," she said. "But what about you, Lord Wardeaux?

Would you be my trustee so that you can regain control over Templemore? Is that what prompted you to agree to his plans?"

She saw Henry go very still. "I accepted Lord Templemore's charge out of duty, Lady Marguerite," he said very quietly. "Don't ever insult me like that again. If you do I promise I shall not be a gentleman about it."

Margery's anger was acting on her like wine. She felt dizzy, out of control, drunk with frustration and fury. All the feelings she had repressed in her grandfather's presence came bubbling up and there was no stopping them.

"I do not see that my suspicions are so misplaced," she said. "I know that you must resent my coming here and taking Templemore from you!"

"That," Henry said, "is not true. I never resented you."

"You must have done," Margery said. "It would be unnatural not to. Why do you never speak of how you feel?"

Henry made a sharp movement and she flinched. "Because it makes no difference how I feel," he said. His voice was still level, betraying nothing. "Templemore is yours now. Nothing changes that. How I feel does not matter. My role is to fulfill your grandfather's commission and protect his heir. You."

"It seems to me that asking you to be my guardian would be like setting a fox to protect the chickens!" Margery burst out.

She knew she had gone too far as soon as the words were out. She wished she could take them back now, because she did not mean them for one moment. But it was too late. The atmosphere in the hall had changed. It had cooled, hardened. They were on the edge of something dangerous and one small step would push them over. She felt frightened. She wanted to run.

"What do you mean by that?" Henry asked very softly.

"Nothing!" Margery said. She could feel her heart beating a suffocating pulse in her throat.

"You implied that you are not safe with me, that I might be a danger to you because I want Templemore back," Henry said.

Margery could not look away from the compelling darkness in his eyes.

"I'm sorry—" she started to say, but he shook his head.

He put a hand about her waist and pulled her hard against his body. His frame was taut with fury and his eyes blazed. "That is not the danger that you are in from me," he said.

All the emotion that had burned between them since he had walked into her life blazed into vivid being. Margery could feel the elemental anger in him, all the more frightening because it was held under such absolute control. For one long, heart-stopping moment he looked down into her eyes. Then he started to lower his head.

"Don't you dare—" Margery began. Her heart was beating so violently against her bodice that she could feel the batter if it through her entire body.

"I do," Henry said. "I do dare."

He covered her mouth with his. The touch of his lips instantly obliterated everything except sensation. There was the stunning shock and pleasure of gaining what she knew she wanted, the sense of rightness, the consuming need that made a mockery of her defiance.

She could feel the hunger in him and something that felt almost like desperation. It was a match for hers.

There was a raw edge of anger in him, too, and it elated her. Henry seldom showed emotion and she felt a wicked pleasure in driving him to this. She gasped and opened her lips to his, and felt the fury in the kiss transmute almost immediately into sweetness.

She drove one hand into his hair so that she could pull him closer and for long moments she lost herself in him, careless that they might be seen. She was far, far beyond anything she understood or could control. She was swept by a desire that became more familiar and more demanding each time Henry touched her. She only knew that she wanted him and that the need was so acute it hurt.

Then he let her go so abruptly she almost fell.

"Don't ever doubt me again," he said abruptly and this time he was the one who turned and walked away.

MARGERY STOOD BY HER bedroom window watching the moon chase patterns across the lawns. Her window was open, letting in the cool night air. Somewhere away in the woods a deer barked in sharp alarm. The wind was rising, tossing the shadows of the lime trees across the grass and ruffling the surface of the lake.

With a sigh, Margery let the curtain fall and curled up on the cushioned window seat. Her toes were cold and she tucked them under the hem of her nightgown. The huge bedroom was lit by a roaring fire and looked cozy and welcoming, but still she shivered.

The house was quiet. Margery remembered the chatter and camaraderie of the servants' hall, the yawning as they all made their way to bed, the ache in her bones.

Sometimes she had been weary to her soul but she had
felt more alive, more a part of something than she did
here. At Templemore she was lonely and more than a
little lost. The size of Templemore still daunted her.

She fell asleep dozing over *The Old English Baron*
and her dreams were filled with ruined castles and
ghosts. She woke to the sound of the dog barking and
a hammering at the door, and for a moment the noise,
the heat and the tangle of her bedclothes formed a nightmarish prison from which she could not escape. Then
she came awake with a violent start.

Her bed curtains were on fire, the flames leaping toward the ceiling, the whole of the wooden four-poster
creaking and groaning like a foundering ship. The spaniel was already by the door, barking urgently.

With a scream Margery leapt from the bed, ran to
the dressing room and grabbed the ewer of water on the
stand there. She hurled it over the bed and in the same
moment the door of her room burst open and Henry
erupted through it, Chessie and several of the servants
hot on his heels.

He grabbed Margery and pulled her clear of the
smoldering ruin of the bed while Chessie, with enormous presence of mind, beat out the remaining flames
with Margery's dressing robe. Henry pulled her close
to him, swearing, a thing that she had imagined he
would never do, and there was raw fury and something
else, something far more disturbing, in his voice and
in his touch.

"Of all the *stupid,* irresponsible and downright dangerous things!" Henry's arms were about her and Margery could feel him shaking with rage. His eyes were
black with it.

"I don't think you should be so rude," Margery said. "After all I put it out myself."

"After starting it yourself!" Henry's gaze went to the candle, tumbled on the floor, and from there to the book, lying half-open on the table by the bed, its pages charred and blackened now. "God Almighty, you could have burned the house down and yourself with it!"

Margery was starting to shake now, too. The acrid smoke from the burnt draperies filled her throat. Her eyes smarted with smoke and tears. And still Henry held her with arms as tight as steel bands. She could feel the fury elemental in him but somehow she knew instinctively that it was anger born of fear for her. Her hands were pressed against the silk of his dressing robe and she could feel the heat of him through the thin material and feel, too, his heart racing against her palm.

For one brief moment his cheek rested against hers and she breathed in the scent of his skin and felt the tumult of emotion in him. Then he loosed her and she stepped back, very aware of her hair tumbled about her shoulders and the thinness of her cotton nightgown. She felt an acute sense of loss without his warmth and his touch.

Lady Wardeaux was hurrying forward with a blanket, more to cover her up respectably than give her comfort, Margery thought. Edith had gone to heat some milk for her and everyone else was talking at once. Lady Emily, white and frightened, was twisting her fingers anxiously in her shawl.

"How could this happen?" she was asking of no one in particular. For once, the tarot cards did not appear to have furnished her with an answer.

"It was fortunate that Lord Wardeaux smelled the smoke," Chessie said.

"I was on my way to the library for a book." Henry's gaze touched Margery's briefly. "I could not sleep."

"The door was locked again," Chessie said, and Margery caught the sharp glance Henry threw at her with its unmistakable order to keep quiet. She shivered and immediately Chessie was by her side.

"Come along," she said. "There is another bed in my chamber. You can have that, for tonight at least."

Chessie's room was another huge space lit by a pitifully inadequate fire and with dramatic wall hangings depicting a medieval scene. Margery shivered harder, whether from cold or shock, she was not sure.

"You've got one, as well," she said, pointing to another of the spaniels that was snoring on Chessie's bed cover, oblivious to the drama.

"I always keep a dog with me in country houses," Chessie said. "It's far too cold otherwise." She shepherded Margery into the enormous four-poster and Margery burrowed under the comforting weight of the bedclothes.

"Was the door really locked?" she asked as she drank her hot milk.

Chessie looked troubled. "Yes, it was," she said. "Lord Wardeaux kicked it in."

Margery frowned, remembering the hammering. "I had not locked it myself."

Chessie stilled. "Are you quite sure?"

"Certain," Margery said. "Perhaps it was simply jammed shut. I did leave the candle burning," she added, feeling dreadfully guilty. "I fell asleep over my book so I suppose it was my fault."

She did not sleep well and was wan and heavy-eyed when she went down to breakfast. Lady Wardeaux exclaimed that she was out of bed at all.

"I am not ill," Margery said, "and I agreed to ride out with Lord Wardeaux this morning."

"Riding!" Lady Wardeaux said. "You would do better to take the carriage."

The thought of parading about the countryside in the Templemore coach seemed ridiculously pompous to Margery. Besides, she needed to ride. She wanted to gallop across the hills and run off some of her frustrations.

Before she was allowed out, however, she had to choose a new bedchamber from the twenty-two on offer. Her own was largely undamaged but for the ruin of the bed curtains, but the unpleasant smell of stale smoke hung about it, reminding Margery of how close she had come to disaster.

"You must never read in bed again," Lady Wardeaux scolded. "In fact, it would be better if you never read at all. No good can come of a book."

Eventually Margery was installed in the north tower room, a circular chamber with walls covered in yet more family portraits and a spiral stair leading down to the ground floor.

"I wanted something smaller," she wailed, feeling like a marble rattling around in a huge box.

"I've explained that there is nothing smaller," Lady Wardeaux said, with barely concealed exasperation. "We do not have small rooms at Templemore, and this is the traditional room of the heir."

It had not occurred to Margery that this would previously have been Henry's room until she found a copy of *Tristram Shandy* with his initials on the bookplate.

She held it in her hand and looked at the strong black slashes of his name. She really had taken everything from Henry, his place at Templemore, his future itself. In return he had saved her from a burning bedchamber. She felt humbled and deeply ashamed that she had previously questioned his integrity. She remembered the clasp of his arms about her, strong and sure. She was coming to rely more and more on Henry's strength and it frightened her. But she was powerless to resist.

CHAPTER FOURTEEN

The Two of Swords: Balance, a duel between two equally matched opponents

IT WAS WITH A LIGHTER SPIRIT that Margery ran downstairs after luncheon and out into the bright sunshine of the May afternoon.

"Lord Wardeaux requested the most docile mare for you, milady," Ned said, when Margery arrived in the stable block. There was a twinkle in his eye as he gestured toward a piebald nag with graying whiskers who looked as though all he wanted to do was stay in the warmth of the stable pulling the hay through his rack.

"I could outrun Lord Wardeaux any day," Margery said. She looked out of the door to where a groom was leading out Diabolo. The sun gleamed black fire along the stallion's coat. He was bursting out of his skin with energy.

"I'll have a horse like that, please," Margery said.

Ned laughed. "There's no horse like Diabolo, but I'll do my best for you, milady. Your lady mother did not ride," he added. "It's good to see you here in the stables."

His gruff approval warmed Margery. "Wait until you see whether I can ride first," she said with a smile.

While Ned went off to saddle a horse for her, Mar-

gery watched Diabolo. It seemed curious to her that
Henry would choose a horse so wild and with a name
to match. He must be an incomparable rider. The Henry
who was bound by duty and obligation would surely
choose a steadier mount, but perhaps the Henry she had
known in London, the rake with charm to burn, would
be perfectly matched with this magnificent stallion.

She turned to find Henry at her shoulder. The sight
of him in his perfectly cut riding garb stole her breath,
and when he took her hand unexpectedly in his gloved
one she thought her breathing might stop altogether.

His dark eyes appraised her. "You are well today,
Lady Marguerite?"

"I am very well, thank you," Margery said, suddenly
feeling extremely shy and aware that the grooms were
watching with avid curiosity. "I wanted to thank you
for…for rescuing me last night." She waited for Henry
to tell her off again for being so careless, but he just
looked at her and the expression in his eyes made her
feel dizzy. When he smiled, the effect on Margery increased accordingly.

"It was my pleasure," he said. He gave a brief nod
and released her hand, leaving her feeling light-headed
and oddly confused.

"I see Ned is saddling Star for you," he added. "She's
something of a handful. Do you think you can deal
with her?"

"I'll leave you standing," Margery promised reck-
lessly. She saw Henry's eyes light with challenge.

"I'll take your wager," he said.

Ned gave Margery a leg up into the saddle. It was a
long time since she had ridden and suddenly she felt a
little apprehensive, but it was too late. Star was fresh

and bursting to go, and they clattered out through the gates and onto the drive before Henry was barely in the saddle. After that it was all a haze of color and the wind on Margery's face and the beat of the sun.

She clung for dear life and tried to remember all she had learned about riding to bring at least some semblance of control to the headlong flight. Star galloped across the formal lawns and jumped the ha-ha and was away through the deer park while Lady Wardeaux's face was still a blur of shocked disapproval at the drawing room window.

Behind her, Margery could hear the thunder of Diabolo's hooves spattering gravel and then turf as Henry followed her across the park and up onto the downs. Margery was fairly certain that he would be furious with her for behaving like a hoyden, so she spun out the ride for as long as possible. Eventually Star began to tire a little, so she drew rein on the hill above Templemore village, flushed and exhilarated with the primitive beat of the chase still in her blood.

"That was wonderful!" she said, turning a smile on Henry.

"You really can ride," Henry said. She was astonished to see he was laughing. He brought Diabolo alongside Star. "Like a circus performer."

"I know I'm not elegant," Margery said. "But I am good."

"You're out of control," Henry said. "Wild." Something fierce and hot burned in his eyes to rival the sun. His gaze trapped hers and she felt her stomach drop.

"Don't pretend you don't like it," she said.

"Oh, I do," Henry said. His voice was rough now. "I like it far too much."

The horses shifted, bridles jingling, and the moment was broken. The light died from Henry's eyes. He turned Diabolo toward Templemore village.

"Come on," he said, over his shoulder. "There's work to be done."

After only a few hours, it felt to Margery as though he had presented her to a bewildering array of tenants and villagers. Her head was spinning. She tried to remember all their names but so many people were introduced to her, one after another, that it was impossible. Babies were thrust into her arms, little alien creatures that she did not even know how to hold. She felt awkward and clumsy, and the babies invariably cried and needed to be handed back to their mothers.

The older folk went misty-eyed when they saw her and told her she was the image of her grandmama. They related long, complicated stories of their families and Margery nodded, and tried to ask the right questions and smiled until her head ached. Through it all she was aware of Henry watching her, prompting her if she forgot a name or a connection.

And she saw the villagers look at him, and look at her, and she felt the wariness in their manner. She knew it was through loyalty to Henry that they were not prepared to take her unconditionally to their hearts.

The next day they rode out again, and then the next, this time to Temple Parva and Temple Hollow. With the villagers and the tenants, Margery was beginning to see a completely different side to Henry, a man who was concerned, thoughtful and deeply involved in the life of the estate. She knew he had built up such knowledge and involvement over many years but she envied him fiercely the history he shared with this place, its land and its people.

On one occasion she saw him strip off his jacket to help one of the tenant farmers wrestle an unruly sheep into the stockyard. On another she saw him squat down to talk to the children of the local blacksmith who wanted to show him their puppies. He had a word for everyone who needed him and as she watched him she felt both humbled and inadequate. She had thought that her natural friendliness would carry her through all the ordeals that being heir to Templemore might throw at her. Now, she was not so sure. She felt frighteningly lost under such a weight of responsibility.

"I don't know what to say to them," she burst out suddenly, on the way home that day. "I don't know what to *do!*"

They were riding along a narrow path through thick woodland, ancient forest with huge spreading oak trees and beech in fresh green leaf. Fat rain clouds were building overhead. The sun had disappeared and there was an odd quiet in the air, the prelude to a rainstorm that had been threatening all day.

"Just be yourself," Henry said. He glanced sideways at her. "All they want is someone to listen to their concerns, someone who cares about their welfare."

"You are very good at that," Margery said. She reined Star in and sat looking at him. "I wish…" She stopped. There had been a wistful tone in her voice and Henry had heard it. He cast her a searching glance.

"I wish you did not have to give it all up," Margery said, in a rush. Then she blushed scarlet. "I'm not proposing to you," she said, even more hurriedly. "I only meant…" She risked a glance at Henry through her lashes and saw with relief that he was laughing.

"I know what you meant, and thank you for your generosity." His voice changed, gentled. "You have so much warmth and kindness in you," he said. "That is all you need." He reached out and touched her cheek. "In time they will take you completely to their hearts and I think that you will be very good for Templemore. You light it up."

"Almost literally, the other night," Margery said. She was very aware of the soft brush of the leather of his glove against her cheek. Her skin tingled from his touch. She could hear the whisper of the wind in the leaves and feel it stirring her hair. The trees pressed close, secret and dark, and the air felt alive with awareness. She held her breath and felt as though she was waiting, waiting for Henry's kiss because she wanted it, because her entire body ached for him.

Another breath of wind brushed her cheek, followed by a loud thud. As the air sang with reverberations, she stared uncomprehending at an arrow that had pieced the trunk of an oak just two feet from her head. It was still quivering.

Henry's reactions were quicker than hers. "Ride!" he shouted. They thundered down the path, the earth flying from the horses' hooves, Henry forcing her mare ahead of his bigger stallion so that he could protect her back. At any moment Margery expected to feel the next arrow between her shoulder blades. She crouched low over Star's neck, clinging for dear life.

Perhaps it was because she was too preoccupied to watch where she was going, but a low branch caught her a glancing blow on the arm and she teetered in the saddle then lost her balance completely and tumbled from Star's back. She heard Henry swear before he followed her down to the ground, rolling her over and down into a ditch in a swirl of petticoats and tangled limbs. She was blinded; her hat came off and her hair fell from its pins. She felt the sting of nettles above her half boot. The ditch had several inches of water in it and at that moment it started to rain, huge drops pattering down from the heavy gray clouds.

Margery pushed the matted hair away from her face and tried to sit up, but Henry's weight held her down. She glared up into his face, so close to hers.

"What the—" she began.

He put a hand over her mouth. "Quiet!" he whispered.

She did not like being told what to do, especially by him. She wriggled. Immediately Henry allowed his full weight to rest on her so that she could not move. Margery gave a muffled squeak against the leather of his glove and he shook his head slightly. He was tensed, his head tilted, listening.

The rain was falling harder now, pattering on the leaves above them. Margery strained her ears, but she could hear no sound of footsteps or horses. It was dark under the trees now. Henry's face was in shadow, a bare few inches from hers. He took his hand from her mouth and this time she made no sound but lay as still as a hunted mouse, all senses alert to danger.

How long they lay there she had no notion. Her skirts were soaked now and the spiky grass prickled her back through her riding habit. One of Henry's legs was pressed between hers, their bodies intimately close at hip and thigh. She could feel the beat of his heart mingle with her own. The rain had drenched his dark hair and it lay plastered against his head, droplets of water running down his cheek and the strong column of his throat. Margery watched the progress of one drop and felt an urge to trace its course with her tongue. Awareness flared between her thighs and she would have squirmed had she been able to move.

Their eyes met. His were darker than the forest shadows, his gaze intent and concentrated as it moved over her face. Margery felt the heat swamp her. Hastily she shifted her gaze to Henry's lips. They were firm, chiseled and damp. This was even worse than staring into his eyes. It put all sorts of shocking ideas into her head. She felt as though she had a fever now, soaking wet and chilled and yet shivering for quite a different reason. Henry dipped his head a little toward her. In a second he would kiss her.

Or perhaps he would not. From the spark now in his eyes she divined that Henry was enjoying this soaring tension between them. She could feel his erection pressing against her thigh through all the wet and cumbersome layers of material between them. Shockingly, the sensation made her want to shift her hips to cradle him against her, to part her thighs wider still.

Margery gave a little gasp, a drop of rainwater ran to the corner of her mouth and Henry licked it up, the bright light in his eyes even more intense now. With great deliberation he started to lap up the beads of water that lay on her skin, flicking his tongue over the curve of her ear and the hollow of her throat.

He bit gently on her earlobe and Margery wriggled helplessly. Goose bumps covered her body. Her nipples chafed against the soaking-wet linen of her chemise.

She felt hot and light-headed, her ears filled with the sound of the rain, every inch of her skin sensitive and raw to Henry's touch, begging for it, her body aching.

When he folded back the lapels of her shirt and exposed the wet skin of her collarbone, licking and sucking at it, Margery arched upward to meet him. His teeth bit down on her nipple through the damp cloth of her riding habit, not too gentle, not too hard. He tugged on her breast and fire streaked through her, pleasure flowering all the more with the slight sting of pain. Her nipples rose tightly and he pulled on them again and again, pressing the wet linen against her with his tongue, his hands at her waist holding her arched upward to meet his mouth. The rough caress was exquisite yet utterly frustrating. Margery wanted to rip off the heavy weight of her clothes and his, as well.

And still Henry did not kiss her. His lips hovered over hers and she saw them curve into a smile. There was a fierce heat low in her belly that demanded satisfaction and she was so angry with Henry for denying it to her. She frowned, reaching to pull his head down to hers. He drew back. Now she was so furious with him for refusing to kiss her that she wanted to bite him instead, to punish him for withholding pleasure from her.

Suddenly he pounced on her, kissing her so deeply and so possessively that she forgot her anger in the wave of urgency that swamped her. She felt as though she was falling into darkness, felt as though her whole body was rising and opening to him. In that moment she was his completely without pretense or calculation and it felt so undeniably right that she trembled with it.

Two deer crashed through the undergrowth beside them and out onto the path, and Henry let go of her so abruptly that she gasped. Pleasure fled and she became aware of the rain that was still falling and the chill of her body. She started to shake with a mixture of cold and shock.

She heard Henry swear softly. He drew her to her feet. His expression was dark and closed and, as ever, Margery had no idea what he was thinking. He looked her over and she was acutely conscious of the way her sopping-wet riding habit clung to every curve. Henry pressed his lips together in a thin line. He looked angry.

She started to brush the old leaves from her riding habit, her fingers shaking a little. Henry was gently removing the twigs from her hair and she was devastatingly aware of the stir of his fingers through the tangled strands. He passed her hat to her while she self-consciously smoothed down her crumpled skirts. She felt stiff and soaked and bewildered.

"I don't understand!" she burst out. Her eyes searched his face. "What happened?"

"Lust," Henry said. "The natural consequence of proximity and—" his gaze traveled over her thoughtfully and she blushed all over "—your delightfully disheveled state."

Margery felt a flare of annoyance that she had even bothered to ask. "How very *primitive* you are, Lord Wardeaux," she said.

"I'm no different from most men," Henry said. A smile touched the corner of his mouth. "I only tell the truth. Why dress it up as something it is not, Lady Marguerite?"

"You mean something like love?" Margery said tartly. "God forbid. Sometimes I don't even *like* you very much."

"You don't need to like me to kiss me," Henry said.

"Clearly," Margery snapped. Misery fluttered inside her. It felt like a betrayal to dismiss her response to Henry so casually. What had happened between them had felt too intimate and special to be nothing more than base nature. She could have sworn that there had been true emotion. Yet it had meant nothing to Henry so it could only be her inexperience that made her give the kiss more significance than it possessed.

She stole a glance at him but he had turned away to climb back up onto the track. He was scanning the shadowy depths beneath the trees.

"Come along," he said abruptly. "We should not linger here. I imagine the horses will have run for home but it is not far."

"Who was shooting at us?" Margery was shocked that she had almost forgotten the panic and fear of their flight in the heat of what had happened afterward.

"Poachers, I expect," Henry said. She saw a muscle flicker in his cheek. "We have had trouble with them in the last few months—although normally they do not attack anyone."

Fifty yards farther along, the woods fell back and Margery was astonished to see that they were at the edge of the Templemore deer park. She had not imagined the house to be so close.

"I need to take some of the men and find this poacher of ours," Henry said. He was already turning away.

Unexpected fear clutched at Margery's heart. She grabbed his sleeve between her fingers, the words tumbling out before she could stop them.

"Don't go back," she said. "It might be dangerous."

Henry stopped. Very slowly he turned to look at

her. There was an arrested look in his eyes as he stared down into her face, a look that suddenly stripped away all pretense. Margery felt her stomach drop as though she had missed a step in the dark. She felt confused and vulnerable, and she did not want Henry to read that in her eyes. Her feelings were too naked.

She would have allowed her hand to fall but it was too late. He covered it with his own. His fingers were warm and strong over hers.

"I shall be quite safe," he said softly and Margery's heart gave an errant thump.

She wanted to resume the pretense and claim that she was not worried for him but the light words would not come. Instead, she simply looked at him and could not look away. "Be careful," she whispered. "Please."

Something moved and shifted in his eyes. "Margery," he said, and there was a tone in his voice that she had not heard before. Her heart fluttered.

Henry leaned forward very slowly and gave her a brief, hard kiss. Her lips clung to his, parted. The caress, so short and yet so potent, set up a trembling deep inside her. Henry's fingers slid from hers reluctantly as he stepped back. There was a baffled look in his eyes now as he looked down at her.

"I should go—" He made a vague gesture in the general direction of the stables. He sounded slightly confused, as though someone had hit him over the head with a heavy object.

Margery cleared her throat. "Oh, yes. Yes, of course."

She watched him walk away. After a few paces he turned to look back at her. He stood staring at her for a very long moment.

Margery picked up her mud-spattered skirts and

headed for the door. The ache in her ankle had dulled
now. The footman, wooden-faced, bowed her inside.
The long gilt mirrors bounced her reflection back at
her, wet, muddy, hair bedraggled, cheeks radiantly pink,
eyes like stars. She paused. She looked happy. Which
was odd, given that she had just had such a distress-
ing experience. In fact, not only did she look happy,
she looked…

Her heart gave another errant thump. She remembered the slide of Henry's fingers in hers and the sweetness of his kiss.

Oh, no.

She could not be.

She could *not* be in love with Henry Wardeaux.

But there was no arguing with it.

Because she was.

WHAT THE HELL HAD happened there?

As Henry directed the grooms and estate workers to
fan out through the woods in the hunt for any poachers, a large part of his mind was still preoccupied with
the moment he had kissed Margery on the steps of the
house. The kiss in the woods had been easier to understand; tension, proximity and the wet riding habit
clinging to Margery's every curve had overcome his
self-control, which these days hung by an increasingly
slender thread. That, in itself, was troubling enough.
But the second kiss had been even more disturbing.
When Margery had begged him to take care he had been
thrown completely off balance. He had felt as though
the world tipped on its axis and had not quite steadied again.

He felt the shift and slide of some emotion deep inside. It was disconcerting. His disliked it intensely because it was incomprehensible and irrational. Yet he could not deny it. Nor could he banish it. It followed on from the equally disturbing experience of the previous week and the violent clutch of fear he had felt when he had realized that Margery was trapped in her burning bedchamber. No power on earth could have prevented him from breaking that door down to get to her. He had wanted to shake her then for being so careless and endangering herself. He had wanted to hold her close and never let her go again.

He gave his head an impatient shake. These were disturbing thoughts. When Margery had spoken so candidly of her fears about her inheritance and when she had been so generous in recognizing how important Templemore was to him, he had felt again that warmth and sweetness he was afraid she had lost. His hunger for her had returned fourfold, and not just his desire for her, but a hunger to possess her utterly and draw on that sweetness for his strength.

One of the search party crashed through the brambles ahead of him, beating the undergrowth back for any sign of poachers or their prey, and Henry turned his attention to the search. He realized that he had been riding along the path so deep in thought that a dozen poachers could have marched past him carrying a brace of pheasants each and he would not have noticed because he had been too busy thinking about Margery. It was hard not to believe that something more than bad luck was at work here. Margery was becoming remarkably accident-prone and he remembered Garrick's words to him in London.

I don't believe in random coincidence....

In this situation, neither did Henry. There had been the fire and now this. It seemed that someone at Templemore did not wish Margery to inherit.

"There's no sign, sir." Ned had come up to him and put his hand on Diabolo's bridle to catch Henry's attention. Henry was not surprised. He was starting to think that their mystery assailant had been no thief. In the past, he had caught enough men roaming the woods in search of game and not one of them had been armed with an old-fashioned bow and arrow.

"Thank you, Ned," he said. "Take a half dozen men and search the Upper Wood."

The groom nodded and stood back, and Henry eased Diabolo to a trot until he reached the point in the path where he estimated the first arrow had struck. He stopped, looked around. Twenty feet away was a broad oak and halfway up the trunk the wood was split. A few splinters dusted the ground beneath.

Henry's skin prickled. So someone had come back and removed the arrow after he and Margery had galloped away. There could be only one reason for that: there was a danger it might be recognized. He closed his eyes and tried to remember everything he could about the attack. The problem was that instinct had taken over and all he had wanted to do was protect Margery. Keeping her safe had been the most important thing on his mind.

He ran his gloved fingers over the wound in the bark, feeling the sharp edges of the cut even through the leather. The arrow had gone in deep. If it had hit Margery she would have been badly injured, even killed. And that was the thing that puzzled him the most. Both he and Margery had been sitting ducks. A good marksman would not have missed his target.

He urged Diabolo out from under the trees and continued to trace their path along the track, knowing even as he did so that the second arrow would also have vanished. Someone had gone to a lot of trouble to cover his—or her—tracks.

A cold hard weight settled in his gut as he considered the danger to Margery. Whatever happened, he had to keep her safe. It was his responsibility to do so, an obligation he owed to Margery, to her grandfather, to Templemore.

The use of such words reassured him. The curious emotion he had felt earlier when Margery had caught his hand and begged him to take care was tempered now by a sense of duty. Yet even so, he could not quite shake the feeling that he was in danger and it was not the sort that was delivered at the point of a poacher's arrow.

CHAPTER FIFTEEN

The Knight of Wands: A robust young man, an energetic warrior, a generous friend or lover. He has a hasty personality

JEM MALLON RODE THE STAGE to Faringdon and then walked the seven miles out to Templemore, turning in at the gates and standing for a moment to take in the sheer scale of the estate. Before him was an extremely pretty drive. It was shaded by lime trees on this humid spring day, but he could have done with it being a bit shorter. By the time he was close to the house he had taken off his jacket, loosened his neck cloth and was aware that his linen shirt—especially laundered for the important occasion of greeting his sister, the heiress— was sticking to his broad back.

As he approached the little stone bridge over the stream, he saw a lady standing on the parapet looking down into the water below. She was dressed in a pink muslin gown with a matching pink parasol. Her hair was a rich chestnut color threaded with pink ribbon. She was tall and slender, and as she turned to look at him he saw she had the biggest blue eyes that he had ever seen.

Jem felt a little odd, light-headed, as though he was parched for a drink. Perhaps it was the heat of the day or perhaps it was those blue eyes that were now appraising him from his scuffed boots to his tousled hair. Never in his life had Jem Mallon felt at a disadvantage with a woman but this was, without a doubt, the most beautiful woman in the entire world. He should know. He had met plenty of beautiful women, but none could hold a candle to this one.

"Good afternoon," she said, as he reached her side. Her voice was cool and perfectly modulated, like a refreshing shower of water on a hot afternoon. "You must be Mr. Jem Mallon. Margery said you would be coming." She smiled, straightened up and extended a hand. "How do you do? I am Francesca Alton. I am Margery's companion."

Companion?

Jem had thought that only old women had companions, desiccated old spinsters who sat around playing at whist. He took Francesca Alton's hand, small and cool in its lace glove. He felt an overwhelming urge to kiss the back of it. He had never done such a thing in his life. He bowed, a little awkwardly. Francesca Alton smiled at him again and he felt as though the sun had doubled in strength.

"I am afraid that Margery is out at the moment visiting about the estate," she said. She withdrew her hand gently from his. Jem had not even been aware that he was hanging on to it. "If you would care to come up to the house to take tea while you wait for her to return…"

"That would be delightful," Jem said, recovering his powers of speech. "Thank you."

He had never taken tea in his life but he was quite willing to start now. In fact he was prepared to drink anything that Francesca suggested as long as she kept him company while he did it.

Francesca was waiting and after a moment Jem realized that he was expected to offer his arm, dusty and travel-stained as his sleeve was. He did so, and she laid her hand delicately on it and they walked slowly up to the house. Jem was very aware of the sway of Francesca's hips and the way that the pink muslin of her skirts brushed against his thigh as they walked. He was also aware that this was a proper lady, a very proper lady, and so to harbor any improper desires toward her was utterly pointless. She was far above him.

"Is your husband also staying at Templemore?" he asked.

For a second she looked startled. "I am a widow," she said. "Lord Alton died last year."

So she was *that* Lady Alton. That changed everything. Jem felt a doubling of interest. He had heard about Francesca Alton and her shocking marriage to the late marquis. No doubt the whole of London knew about it. She was without a doubt a very racy widow, indeed, just the type he liked.

He put his hand over hers where it rested on his arm and gave her fingers a little squeeze.

"I do hope that you have been able to find sufficient comfort in your widowhood."

Lady Alton gave him a look so cold that his ambitions and a great deal else froze in that moment despite the heat of the day.

"How very thoughtful of you to be so concerned for my comfort," she said, in arctic tones. "I assure you that there is absolutely nothing you can contribute to it."

Ouch.

Jem winced. He acknowledged that he had grossly miscalculated. Lady Alton was not a fast widow to be tumbled in the bushes on the basis of five minutes acquaintance. Perhaps all the stories about her were not true. One could not believe anything the papers wrote nowadays.

They walked on in silence until Lady Alton unbent sufficiently to comment on the weather and to point out to him various items of interest about the estate: the dovecote, the walled garden and the fountain. Jem found it all fairly boring except as an indication of just how rich Margery must be now, which interested him very much indeed.

They reached the gravel sweep where a number of peacocks stared balefully at him, as though they knew he was no gentleman and should not be permitted to set foot on Templemore turf. A footman bowed him inside the house. The sudden shade after the dazzling sunlight was blinding for a moment. Jem found himself standing in an enormous hallway dominated by a picture of Margery as a small child. It was the same image that his brother Billy had found on a miniature painting in their mother's effects after she had died, a miniature that had set Billy on his unfortunate quest to reunite Margery with her inheritance. If only he had left well enough alone....

"Mr. Mallon will take tea in the drawing room, Barnard." Lady Alton was addressing the butler. "Pray tell Lady Wardeaux that he has arrived." She gave Jem a cool smile. "Good day, Mr. Mallon. I will see you later."

"Oh," Jem said, realizing that his chances of recovering lost ground over a cup of tea were lost. "But—"

But she was gone. Jem realized that he would have to work a great deal harder in order to fix the interest of the lovely Lady Alton, but he was not a man who accepted defeat lightly. The situation still held intriguing possibilities.

"This way, sir." The butler ushered him into the drawing room and Jem paused to admire the high ceilings with their exquisite plasterwork, the thick carpet beneath his feet and the soft glow of the sun on the rosewood furniture. The room reeked of money, but in the most discreet and tasteful way imaginable. It was a great pity, Jem thought, that he was going to have to put a stop to all of this. But not before he had taken advantage of it first.

"MOLL!"

Margery had been in the hall for no more than twenty seconds when the door of the drawing room opened and Jem hurried out and enveloped her in a bear hug. She hugged him back fiercely, then surprised them both by bursting into tears.

"What's this?" Jem, looking comically bewildered, held her at arm's length. "Aren't you pleased to see me?"

"Don't be daft." Margery felt a huge swell of gladness in her heart. Jem looked so familiar, so reassuring, at a time when her heart and life felt in total turmoil. She grabbed him again, drawing comfort from his sold strength. "What took you so long?" she scolded. "I wrote to you weeks ago."

"Sorry," Jem said. "I had business to attend to." His bright blue gaze traveled over her, taking in her soaking clothes and general air of dishevelment. "What on earth has happened to you?" he added, releasing her and looking down at the smears of mud that were now adorning his beautifully cut jacket. "You look as though you have been pulled through a hedge, and you've spoiled my new jacket."

"I fell off my horse," Margery said. She had already decided to say nothing about the poachers for fear that word would get to her grandfather and upset him. Now she was doubly glad to hold her tongue. The last thing she wanted was Jem rushing off to confront Henry about what had happened and demanding to know why he had not taken better care of her. There would be quite enough antagonism between the two of them without that, especially when Jem realized that Henry was the man she had been with that night in London.

"If you will buy expensive clothes," she said lightly, "what do you expect?"

"I got it on tick," Jem said with satisfaction. "Now my sister's going to be a countess I've got great expectations."

Margery laughed. She could see Lady Wardeaux hovering behind them, her expression creased with disgust at Jem's vulgarity. She wondered whether Lady Wardeaux would attempt to refine her brother in the way that she had tried to improve Margery herself, or whether she would simply consider that a task too challenging even for her talents.

She grabbed Jem's sleeve.

"Walk with me to my room," she said. "We've got so much to catch up on."

Jem offered her his arm and they walked through the hall toward the grand stair. "That old trout is determined to send me away," he said as the drawing room door closed behind Lady Wardeaux. "While we were taking tea she asked me whether I wouldn't feel more at home staying at the Templemore Arms in the village."

"Well, I am sure you would," Margery said. She gave a little giggle. "If you stay for dinner she will probably make you take it in the servants' hall."

"I'd have more fun down there," Jem said. "I had no notion that being a nob was so deadly dull. What do you do all day, Moll?"

"Lots of things," Margery said tartly. "Being Lady Marguerite is my job now. I ride out and meet the villagers and listen to their concerns and learn all there is to know about the estate. I receive visitors, I plan menus, I arrange flowers and I change my gown five times a day. There isn't much time for anything else."

Jem yawned ostentatiously. "Well, don't overdo the excitement, Moll."

"You can always go back to Town if you find it so tedious here," Margery said.

"Oh, I'm in no hurry to leave," Jem said quickly. "I fancy a taste of the high life."

Following his gaze, Margery saw that Chessie was approaching from the hothouses, a basket of early roses over her arm. She looked beautiful, a vision in pink with the cream haze of the flowers only serving to accentuate her prettiness. To Margery's amusement Jem stopped dead in his tracks.

"I'm definitely in no hurry to go," he repeated.

"You have already met Lady Alton then?" Margery said. "I might have guessed."

Jem glanced down at her but she had the impression he was not really seeing her. "Do you mind if I leave you here?" he asked. "Lady Alton might require my help with the flowers."

"I doubt that," Margery said "Especially as flower arranging has never been one of your talents."

"She's lovely." Jem was still staring as Chessie came toward them down the West Passage. "Like a flower herself."

"Poetry is not your forte either," Margery said. "For goodness' sake, Jem, you sound ridiculous."

"I can't help it," Jem said. "I think I fell in love with her at first sight."

"Love, is it?" Margery said sharply. "I thought it was something rather less profound. It usually is with you."

"You can be so harsh, Moll," Jem said, grinning.

The front door opened and Henry came in. Fortunately Jem was still distracted watching Chessie so Margery seized her moment.

"Jem, about Henry—" Margery began.

"Who?" Jem said vaguely.

"Lord Wardeaux," Margery said sharply, still failing to reclaim his attention. "You met him in London. At the Hoop and Grapes."

For a moment Jem looked completely bemused, then his expression cleared. "Oh, the nob. Yes. What about him?"

"He's here," Margery said. "He's Lord Templemore's godson. That was his mother you took tea with this afternoon."

Jem's expression changed. "No wonder he behaves as though he has a poker up his—"

"Yes, thank you," Margery said quickly. "Could you try to be civil to him? We have guests tonight and my grandfather would not care for it if you took a swing at Henry during dinner."

"Might liven things up around here," Jem said, looking unfavorably at the suit of armor and the marble busts of long-dead Roman emperors that guarded the top of the stair. He caught Margery's agonized expression and sighed. "Oh, all right," he said. "I'll do it for you, Moll."

"Thank you," Margery said, feeling a rush of relief. She left Jem at her chamber door and went in to change. It was raining in earnest now, a shroud of mist hanging over the deer park, the water gurgling down the old lead pipes and pouring from the gargoyles on the roof. The peacocks, soaking and bad-tempered, were huddled in a corner beneath Margery's window.

Margery stripped off her filthy riding habit and rang the bell for Edith to bring her some hot water to bathe. She wanted to look her best this evening. Her beautiful golden gauze gown would make her look every inch an heiress and give her confidence. She lay in the steaming, scented water, enjoying the heat of it and the soft rub of the soap on her skin. It felt rich and decadent and her body felt awake and alive, still humming with awareness from Henry's kiss.

Dinner was an even more uncomfortable experience than she had expected. Lord Templemore presided, the first time he had hosted a dinner for a number of years. The neighborhood turned out in style. There was a distinct current of antagonism in the air between Jem and Henry, but as Lady Wardeaux had seated Jem at the far end of the table and Henry at the top, they had no conversation. Lady Emily also seemed to have taken exception to Jem, casting him dark glances.

"The cards foretell bad things, Celia," Margery heard her mutter to Lady Wardeaux. "Are we to be visited by every one of dear Marguerite's disreputable relatives?"

Lady Wardeaux spent much of dinner telling Lady Radnor her plans for their trip to London for the remains of the Season. As Margery had not been consulted she could feel little prickles of annoyance jabbing her at regular intervals.

Jem was exerting himself to be pleasant to Mrs. Bunn, the vicar's elderly mother, who was placed on his right, and Miss Fox, the doctor's dowdy sister, who was on his left. In between he watched Chessie, who ignored him with polite indifference. It amused Margery. Such lack of interest from a beautiful woman was a very new experience for Jem.

She felt only slightly less self-conscious herself. Discovering her feelings for Henry had had a disastrous effect on her composure, making her as gauche as a schoolgirl in his presence.

The ladies withdrew while the gentlemen took their port. The talk was of the humid weather and an outbreak of typhus in the village. Miss Fox commented that a traveling fair was encamped on the green, so no doubt the village would be a hotbed of crime and was it not a disgrace? She seemed overly excited at the prospect of so many potential thieves and pickpockets in the neighborhood. Margery thought she would probably swoon if she realized she had been sitting next to one at dinner.

"We should make up a party and go," Margery said. "I love the fair."

As with so many of her comments, this one was met with utter consternation.

"Oh, Lady Marguerite!" Miss Fox twittered. "We could not possibly! It would be most scandalous and quite, quite wrong!"

"It would be very inappropriate," Lady Wardeaux confirmed with a grim smile as though appealing to all the local ladies to sympathize with quite how much she had to put up with in trying to educate her charge in the manner befitting a lady.

Later, when the guests had departed and the family had collected their candles and made their way up to bed, Margery stood by the window in the tower room and looked out into the spring darkness, across Templemore's manicured lawns to where the lanterns of the fair swung in the distance. She was so tempted to go. Except that she knew that if she disappeared to the fair her grandfather would worry.

She felt intolerably hemmed in tonight, both held captive in a gilded cage and hostage to her feelings for Henry. They made her feel restless and pent up. She glanced toward the door in the corner tower. It seemed to beckon to her. Suddenly, she made her decision. Tonight she would escape, if only for a little while. Tonight she was going to be Margery Mallon again.

CHAPTER SIXTEEN

The Lovers: Strong emotions, a choice of the heart, the power of attraction

TWO HOURS LATER, MARGERY was as happy as she had ever been at Templemore, a capacious white apron over the top of her golden evening gown, her hair bundled up under the cook's spare cap, up to her elbows in flour and sugar with a batch of marzipan cakes cooling on the table and some ginger biscuits cooking in the range. The air was thick with the scent of spices and steam. All the servants were crowded around the long pine table sampling the almond drops and the Naples biscuits. Mrs. Bow, the cook, had been completely won over by Margery's sponge roll, declaring it the best she had ever tasted. The hall boy had taken a parcel of cakes out to the stables for the grooms and the coachman to try, and even Barnard the butler had biscuit crumbs trailing a guilty path down his livery.

After the initial half hour he had cracked open the second-best bottle of sherry, supposedly for cooking purposes only, but it was not long before one of the footmen had surreptitiously passed the bottle around. From the sherry they had somehow progressed to port and from there to champagne and so the confidences had started to flow along with the wine.

Daisy, the second housemaid, had told Margery all about her younger sister who did not want to go into service but wanted instead to be an actress, and how their mother thought that was more likely to be the start of a career as a lightskirt than anything else.

William the footman told Margery about his father's farm over near Faringdon and how it was losing money hand over fist because his father converted the barley into beer and then promptly drank the lot. Even Mrs. Bow had confided her worries about her sister who was sick with the typhus and had four children to care for.

Margery listened and chatted, and drank from the bottle, and felt that at last she was accepted below stairs, not as someone with a background in common with the servants, but entirely for herself. It was lovely.

Then, suddenly, the door of the kitchen swung open and Henry stood there, wet hair plastered to his head, water droplets scattered over the shoulders of his coat, looking formidably furious.

Silence descended on the kitchen like a shroud falling. Those servants who had been sitting at the table scrambled to their feet and executed hasty bows and curtsies. Barnard tried to brush the stray crumbs from his livery.

"My lord," he spluttered.

Margery hastily pushed the empty champagne bottles out of sight behind the dresser.

Henry strode into the room. "I am sure," he said, glancing around at the guilty faces, "that you must all have work to attend to." His voice cut like a whip.

"We'd finished—" Daisy the housemaid began, only to be hushed by Mrs. Bow.

"Then you can go," Henry said curtly.

No one argued. One by one they melted away.

"You did not need to spoil their fun," Margery said reproachfully. She felt miserable, all the pleasure she had taken in the baking and the camaraderie of the evening leaking away like gas from a balloon.

Henry's gaze focused on her hard and fast, and she felt her stomach drop with nervousness at the anger she saw there. "What the devil do you think you are doing?" he demanded.

"I am baking cakes," Margery said, "as you can see." She gestured to the scatter of pastries, marzipan and ginger across the table. "I like it," she added defiantly. She was scared by the anger she saw in Henry's face but she felt mutinous, as well. Henry was so good at spoiling her fun. "It makes me happy," she said.

"You were distracting the servants from their work," Henry said. His gaze picked out the bottles lurking behind the dresser. "And I see you are drunk, as well."

"No, I am not!" Margery said, stung.

Henry simply looked at her. He came up to her and took her by the shoulders. Margery's stomach swooped down to her toes with a mixture of fear and anticipation. Henry bent his head and, without any preamble at all, he kissed her. Shock skittered through Margery's veins at the rough possession. She gasped in outrage as he slid his tongue into her mouth, tasting her. It was deliberate and insolent and she felt it all the way through her body. A heat that was different from that radiating out from the ovens lit her from within.

"You taste of champagne," Henry said. There was something dark and heavy in his eyes now. His gaze lingered on her lips.

"We were only having a little glass," Margery said.

She wiped her damp palms down her apron, willing her hands to stop shaking. "The servants had finished for the night," she said. "You heard Daisy—"

"Who?" Henry said.

"The housemaid," Margery said. "She is sister to one of the grooms. You know their father. He is grandpapa's chief gamekeeper—"

Henry made a brief gesture, cutting her off. "I am not concerned with that," he said shortly. "I am concerned with you disappearing and letting no one know where you were."

"I don't see why it matters," Margery said.

Anger flared again in Henry's eyes. She could feel it in him, banked down, under control, but burning fiercely for all that. His fists were clenched at his side as though he wanted to catch her to him and shake her. She could feel his fury and his frustration but she could not understand it.

"It matters because it is dangerous," he said. "Do you know where I have been?" He flung out a hand. "I have been out looking for you because I thought that you had run away to the fair! Anything might have happened to you—" For a second there was raw anguish in his voice, then he took a steadying breath and moderated his tone. "It was foolish of you not to tell anyone what you were doing."

"I am sorry," Margery said. She felt shaken and confused by his anger but she sensed something deeper, something that tormented him.

"Sorry is not good enough!" Henry said. His voice shook with repressed feeling. "Someone is running around taking pot shots at you with a bow and arrow and yet you vanish for several hours without explanation. You have become so spoiled that you do not have any sense, nor do you stop to consider other people's feelings!"

The blatant unfairness of this made Margery's temper snap. "That," she said furiously, "is completely unjust."

She walked over to the sink and washed the flour off her arms. She did it very deliberately, keeping her back turned to him. Inside she was fizzing with indignation at Henry's criticism. All he ever seemed to do was tell her off and drag her back to face her unremitting duty. He drained the joy and the color out of everything.

"I did not even leave the house." She swung back to face him. She could feel her cheeks burning with heat and fury. Her whole body was shaking. "The reason you did not realize that I was here was because you are so stiff-necked and proper that you would never visit the kitchens yourself!" She threw down the cloth she had been using to dry her arms and stalked straight up to him. "You claim to care for the people of Templemore, but I think you are a fraud, Henry. You don't even know the servants by name! I think all you care for is to be seen to fulfill your obligations. The people themselves do not matter to you at all. They are just another means by which you can demonstrate that you do your cold duty!"

There was a frozen silence. Henry's eyes had gone as icy as a winter night, his expression terrifyingly aloof.

"Is that all you have to say?" His tone was extremely polite.

"No," Margery said. She felt like a runaway carriage careening down a hill; now she had started, she could not stop until the inevitable crash at the end. "You show your mother not a single jot of affection," she said. "You call your godfather 'sir.' You care for no one. You have not a drop of love in you and you never have—"

She stopped. For one brief second she had seen in Henry's eyes a pain so searing, so vivid, that it stole her breath.

"You have no idea," he said, very quietly. "No idea at all."

He turned and walked away. The sound of his footsteps echoed on the stone flags of the floor. Margery heard the soft swish of the green baize door closing. Then there was nothing but silence.

She stood irresolute for a moment. Already, the anger draining from her, she felt completely wretched. Stung by Henry's criticism, weary of always being forced to put duty before pleasure, she had lashed out at him in frustration and hurt, and in doing so had hurt Henry in turn. She had been unfair to him. The one thing she could not question was his devotion to Templemore and its people. She had seen his kindness to them and seen, too, the respect in which they held him.

She grabbed the candlestick and hurried from the kitchen, her quick steps pattering on the stone stairs up to the green baize door. If she left this now and went to bed she knew what would happen in the morning. Henry would be his usual courteous but distant self. He would behave as though nothing had happened. They would continue in this state of remoteness and yet another brick—an entire row of bricks—would have been erected in the wall between them.

She did not want that.

She realized it with a little jump of the heart. She did not want Henry to treat her like a stranger. She could not bear such coldness between them. She wanted more than that.

The house was very still. A light showed beneath her grandfather's door and from within Lady Wardeaux's chamber came the sound of voices. No servants were about. At times like this, Templemore echoed with emptiness.

Henry's chamber was at the end of a long, dark passage shrouded in tapestries and wreathed in shadow. Margery paused outside his bedroom, listening for voices, but there was no sound from behind the heavy panels of the oak door, no sound other than a faint crash and Henry giving voice to a muffled curse. Margery stood listening some more. She pressed her ear to the door. And then she turned the handle.

The room was almost as large as hers, with a stone window embrasure smothered in heavy curtains and a roaring fire even on this mild May evening, but where her room was brightened by flowers and colored hangings, Henry's was as sparse and masculine as he was himself. The wide, unruffled expanse of the bed stood before her. There was no sign of Henry.

Margery's racing heart steadied slightly. She heard another crash from the dressing room. Shadows moved. She crept forward to the doorway.

Henry was throwing random items in the direction of a portmanteau that stood by the dresser: boots, a shaving brush and stand, a shirt. There was repressed violence in every movement he made. Fear curled in Margery's stomach. Her nerve deserted her. This had been a mistake. She turned to creep out of the room as quietly as she had come but she was in such a hurry that she tripped over a chair.

Henry pounced on her as quickly as a hawk. His hand bit into her arm and he spun her around so that she was facing him.

"What the hell are you doing here?"

The expression in his eyes was harder than she had ever seen.

"You're leaving," Margery said. The desolation ripped through her, taking her by surprise. "Why?" she said. "Why are you going?"

A veil of darkness had fallen across his eyes. "It is for the best. I should never have come back."

"No," Margery said. "Please." She stopped and took a deep breath. If she was not careful she would make this worse not better.

"I came to apologize," she said. Her voice wobbled. She wanted to sound strong but she was not sure she was going to achieve it. "I was wrong. I'm sorry. I know you care deeply about Templemore—"

Henry turned away. "I don't want to talk about it. You had better go."

"No," Margery said. Her stubbornness was returning. "I am not going. You always turn people away, Henry. Well, I'm not going. I came to say I am sorry."

The silence was absolute. Margery was trembling but she was not sure why. She could see tension tight as a drum in every line of Henry's body. His jaw was tense.

"Very well," Henry said after a moment. His tone was indifferent. "Thank you, Lady Marguerite. I accept your apology."

Margery felt dismay crash through her. So that was that. She had not reached him. His tone and the formal use of her name told her so. His formidable defenses were back in place. She had not even made the slightest impression on them.

She went up to him and put her hands against his chest. He went very still. She could feel his heart thudding beneath her palm.

"Don't push me away," she said.

She thought that he was going to dismiss her again, but something flickered in his eyes. The tension between them simmered, feral and hot.

"You had better leave," Henry said again, but this time there was a warning in his voice. His tone was rough. He took Margery's wrists, forcing her hands back down to her sides. His gaze was on her face, intent, focused. "Go," he said quietly.

Margery did not move.

Henry took the final step that brought their bodies into contact and then he kissed her. It felt different, as though he was perilously close to the edge of control, desperate for her, with a complicated hunger that he could neither understand nor control. Margery felt it, too. She had known only that she could not withdraw, that she could not walk away and leave him because under that self-containment and control she sensed the absolute solitariness and loneliness in his soul.

"Margery," he said. He sounded dazed now. She knew he was searching for the words to make her go, but she knew equally intensely that she would never leave him now. This was her decision to take and for the first time she felt as though she was close to him, within touching distance of his heart, able finally to break down all the barriers he had erected against her and against the world. The love swept through her so violently that it made her shake.

She put one hand on the nape of his neck and brought his head down to hers, biting his lower lip, tentatively sliding her tongue into his mouth. She heard him give a shaken laugh against her mouth and then, suddenly, there was no more laughter, only heat and fierceness and longing that sent them spinning into another dimension entirely. It lit a wicked excitement within Margery to be able to do this to a man whose life was ruled by such powerful restraint. She alone could strike this response in him. She alone could meet his need.

Henry grabbed the cap from her curls and threw it aside. He ran his hands into her hair, holding her head still, her mouth tilted up to his, and his kiss was as greedy and demanding as a starving man. His tongue plundered her mouth. The kiss that Margery had offered up so hesitantly he took and turned into something ferocious in its need. She knew that his self-control was gone now and she was filled with wanton delight. There was no virginal hesitation in her, only a dazzling sense of urgency and sweet, seductive desire.

"You taste of sugar and cinnamon." Henry licked the corner of her mouth and Margery's knees weakened as she grabbed his forearms for support.

Henry tugged on the ribbons of her apron and threw it aside. He spun her around, his hands on her waist. His mouth was in the curve of her neck now, hot against her skin like a brand. She felt his fingers on the buttons of her golden evening gown. The dress ripped as his impatience got the better of him. Margery felt a rush of dismay.

"It's my favorite—"

He laughed. His lips moved against the tender line

of her throat. "My apologies. Buy another. You're the richest heiress in the country."

The jibe stung, and in response Margery grabbed him and kissed him angrily, feverishly. It was always like this between them, the current of desire laced with antagonism. But this time he was the master. He drew back and turned her around again. A tug of his hands, two, and she was stripped of the golden gown. Her heart missed a beat at the ruthlessness of it. She felt hot. There was a tingling between her thighs. He was still behind her. His hands cupped her breasts now. Dizzy pleasure flowered through her, dispelling all other thought.

He bit down softly on her neck, and her nipples hardened against his fingers as the exquisite shivers racked her. He was playing her body so sweetly now. It rose to the demand of his hands, his lips and his tongue as over and over he stroked and caressed; the underside of her breasts, the curve of her stomach, the flare of her hips. She was adrift, lost in pleasure, and when he laid her down on the bed she was glad of the support it gave her.

Henry kissed her again and it seemed as though her whole body was rising to his touch, begging for release, consumed. He raised himself. His mouth was at her breast and she arched, turning her head restlessly against the covers, seeking surcease. The assault on her senses was relentless. She felt his hands on her thighs, gently drawing them wider apart. There was a pillow beneath her hips now, raising her up. Her mind acknowledged the intimacy of her position, recognizing that he had exposed her completely to his gaze and to his touch. It was wildly exciting. She could not believe what was happening to her and yet there was no space left in her mind for shame or apprehension. She wanted nothing more than him.

Her thoughts fractured as she felt Henry part her, then touch the core of her. His lips grazed her softly. His tongue entered her in a hard thrust. Margery cried out in shock and climaxed at once, shaking, helpless, scorched by irresistible desire. Her body clenched violently, spinning her into a vortex of vivid pleasure.

She was gasping and still trembling with shock and reaction as Henry gathered her into his arms. He had shed his clothes now and the heat and hardness of him against her had her body tightening with demand. She reached out to him blindly, wanting to give as much as she had taken, and heard him laugh, a low, strained sound.

"Presently, sweetheart."

He laid her back on the bed and kissed her, and she tasted herself on his tongue and almost fainted at the intimacy of it. Their kisses were deep, feverishly greedy. Margery could feel the pleasure she had taken twist and tighten into a renewed need. The rekindling of such desire startled her. Her body felt so unfamiliar, sleek and sensual, possessed of such a driving hunger. She could feel the hunger in Henry, too. It was present in each stroke, each touch and each kiss.

His lips caressed the curve of her shoulder and dropped to her breast. At the same time, she felt his fingers within her, penetrating her, feeling her warmth and her wetness. She parted her thighs wide, shameless now in her need for him. His lips touched her exposed belly and then he slid his hands under her hips and lifted her up. She felt delirious with pleasure, her legs falling farther apart as he slid inside her.

There was pain, a short, sharp stab of it that cut through the pleasure and made her gasp. She felt Henry hesitate and withdraw a little, and she thought he might stop and suddenly she was desperate to prevent it. She scored her fingers down his back and heard him groan. He thrust into her again and the pain flowered and she felt sore and tight, too small to take him. Then, as she faltered on the edge of discomfort and misery, her body seemed to give and to stretch and the pain started to fade.

Henry lay quite still inside her and she adjusted to the sensation of being so completely filled. It was strange, but it awed her, as well. And just as she was starting to wonder what should happen next, Henry's lips were at her breast again and the hot, wicked sensations started to flow back.

He sucked at her nipple, tugged, licked in tiny circles that made her quiver, and all the time he lay hot and hard, buried inside her until Margery's body stretched and shimmered and tautened again. She felt the muscles of her stomach jump and jerk, and at last Henry moved within her in response. This time it was sleek and smooth with an undercurrent of friction that had her gasping in startled pleasure.

She ran her hands into Henry's hair and pulled his mouth to hers again, opening for him. She found herself clutching greedily at each stroke of his body, chasing that elusive bliss she had felt before. She wanted more from him, deeper and harder. She was learning all the time and she was greedy for more. She had more to give, more to take. She dug her fingers into his buttocks to pull him closer inside her.

"Don't be gentle," she whispered. "I want it. Please."

She felt his self-control shatter.

He shifted, lifting her up so that her hips were almost entirely clear of the bed. She was so small that he could hold her up easily and she realized faintly that she was lying across the bed, her head falling back over the edge, her hair tumbling down to brush the floor. Her mind spun. She was entirely in Henry's hands now, her position helpless and open to him as he knelt between her thighs and plundered her body with his at each stroke.

The softness of the bedclothes rubbed against her shoulders. Her breasts jolted with each sure thrust. Her back arched. She was ravished, taken and achingly aware that she had pushed him to this extreme of possession. She had driven from his mind all thoughts of gentleness and control. She had demanded this invasion that took her body and soul.

It was astonishing, brazenly exciting; she could not comprehend how she felt, could do nothing but surrender to sensation. As Henry came to climax in hard, shuddering thrusts she felt her body grasp his tightly and she split apart into an orgasm so fierce that she cried out over and over again.

She felt Henry withdraw from her and gently lift her so that she was lying with her head on the pillow. She lay quite still as her breathing steadied. Light danced against her closed eyelids. Her mind still spun in hazy circles as her body absorbed the last sleek, sensual ripples of pleasure.

She felt stunned and exhilarated. She waited to feel shock or shame for her unvirginal eagerness, but those emotions never came. There was nothing but happiness, like a shower of light, and a deep sense of peace and rightness. She loved Henry. She had wanted to break through his cold facade and reach him, and now she had done so in the most fundamental and shattering way possible.

Everything would be different now.

She heard him move across to the washstand and splash water into a dish. Then he was beside her again, and she could feel him gently cleaning the stickiness from her thighs.

It was such an unexpected and tender thing for him to do that her throat closed with emotion. He put aside the cloth and covered her with the bedclothes. Margery rolled over onto her side, reaching for him. She wanted warmth and intimacy, wanted to cuddle him. But then he moved away from her, fumbling for his clothes. His back was to her as he slid on his breeches. The candle-light played in slabs of golden light across the muscles of his shoulders and back and gave his tousled black hair a sheen of blue. Margery felt a pang of tenderness so potent it shook her to the core. She sat up, the sheet slipping to her waist.

"Henry—"

He turned and the words died on her lips as she saw his face.

He looked as cold and remote as he had always done. More so, for there was a terrifying distance in his eyes that chilled her to her bones. She had thought that she had touched him. She had thought that everything would be different because she loved him and she had shown him her love without pretense or evasion. She had opened herself up to him wholly, hiding nothing in the honesty of their lovemaking. Her mistake had been to think that Henry felt the same in return.

He had not. She could see it in his eyes. He did not love her.

Oh, he had wanted her. She knew that. He had wanted her with an urgency that had overridden caution, care and gentleness. He had needed her. She knew that, too. She had felt it and she had fed that desperate hunger in him and had thought it would bind them closer. She had been shamelessly wanton, but her real mistake was that she had been hopelessly naive in confusing her love with Henry's physical pleasure and thinking they were the same thing.

Horror clogged Margery's throat. She felt the sting of tears at the back of her eyes. The tenderness inside her withered and fell apart, leaving nothing but emptiness. She was not sure how long she stared at him but then she grabbed her clothes, holding them protectively in front of her as she slid from the bed and backed away from him. She saw the expression in Henry's eyes change as he realized that she was going to run away. He moved fast but this time she was quicker. As far as she was concerned all the servants in the entire house could have been lined up outside Henry's bedroom door and she would have streaked past them all, so urgent was her need to escape.

"Margery, wait!" Henry's tone was sharp but she ignored him. She whisked around the door, flinging her clothes on helter-skelter as she ran. She thought she heard Henry behind her and panic caught at her chest; she almost stumbled but she was not going to stop.

All she knew was that she could not talk to Henry now. She felt unprotected, with her emotions hideously exposed. Her physical nakedness was nothing in comparison. She had no defenses and she needed time to compose herself and find some way of hiding her vulnerability from Henry.

She ran to her chamber, slammed the door and turned the key in the lock. She waited, her breath loud in her own ears, straining for the sound of footsteps and the knock at the door. Nothing happened. Henry did not come. And although she had not wanted him to do so, disappointment struck Margery so sharply that she caught her breath on a sob.

The room was warm and bright, lit by a stand of candles and the comforting glow of the fire. Margery stripped off her clothes again, her hands shaking so much this time that she could barely remove them, haphazard as they were. There was a huge wave of grief building within her. She could feel the misery and the shame grow and grow inside until it was too big for her body and it threatened to consume her.

She had begun to think that she was not like her mama, that flighty, foolish, spoiled girl, but now she knew that in one matter they were both the same. They both loved men who did not love them back. In her mother's case, it had destroyed her. Margery would never allow the same.

She scrambled into her nightgown and burrowed beneath the bedcovers, seeking the anonymity of the dark. She felt suddenly exhausted as though all the energy and life had drained from her in the space of a moment. Her body ached in unfamiliar places. It felt a little sore but not in an uncomfortable way.

In fact, she felt knowing and pleasantly used. Her body, so much less complicated than her emotions, wanted Henry again. Until she had met him she had never suspected that her neat, practical mind could cloak such outrageously passionate desires. And just at the moment she hated that it did, that her body could betray her.

CHAPTER SEVENTEEN

The Three of Swords: Heartache

HENRY STOOD BY THE WINDOW, staring out into the inky blackness of the night. The rain had gone and a slice of the view was now lit by a full moon riding high in the starry sky.

He tried to think. He found it a great deal more difficult than he had expected.

He did not recognize any of the emotions inside him, for he had shared far more than he had intended. He had shared himself, so much so that he was left feeling acutely vulnerable, shocked by his lack of restraint.

Margery…

He had followed her to her room and heard the key turn in the lock. He knew she was safe. But it was a little late for locking doors. She should have been safe with him. He should have protected her. Instead he had seduced her, thoroughly, ruthlessly, as though in the act of possession he could bind her to him forever. Why he had wanted that he did not know. It ran contrary to everything he believed in. All he knew was that from the moment he had thought Margery gone, he had been possessed with a fear that eclipsed everything else. When he had found her safe and well he had been as angry as he had been relieved, and that fierce mix of emotions had burned out all other feeling.

Emotion. He did not like it and he was not going to succumb to it or even analyze its causes. Instead, he would focus on facts and on actions.

Fact one. He had made love to Margery. He had wanted her from the first moment he had seen her in Mrs. Tong's brothel and his determination to resist her had simply not been strong enough. Instead, his self-control had snapped and his desire had led inexorably to this moment when he had taken what he wanted.

He could not understand this driving hunger for her. It was as inexplicable to him as it was compelling. He had tried damned hard to resist that need, but tonight he had failed. He had failed in his self-control and he had failed to act as a gentleman. He could continue to reproach himself for his actions, but it was done now. The important thing was to take responsibility and put matters right.

He reached for his shirt, pulling it absentmindedly over his head. Facts. He forced himself to concentrate, shutting down the emotion again.

Fact two. Making love to Margery had been rapturous, the most exquisitely pleasurable experience of his life. Margery had responded to him in ways he could not have imagined in his wildest fantasies. She had been as generous and open in giving herself as she was in all other aspects of her life.

Henry shifted uncomfortably, aware that the need he had for Margery still felt disturbingly powerful. In fact, it felt even more intense than it had before they had made love, as though the mere taste of what he wanted had reinforced his need. This was not a lust that had burned itself out in the taking. Instead, it had come back, more forceful, more dangerous.

Once again he felt the need to hold and possess. It was mystifying to him.

The third fact was that someone would know that Margery had been in his chamber that night. She had run from him stark naked, and even if there had been no obvious witnesses—and for all he knew, the corridors might have been packed with servants and family members—someone would have seen her because in a house like Templemore it was impossible to keep secrets. There would be rumors. Margery's reputation would be compromised and it was entirely his fault.

He threw himself down on the bed, then stood up again almost immediately as Margery's scent invaded his senses with its sweetness and warmth. He went back to the half-open window where the cool night air soothed his mind.

Fact four. Margery might have conceived his child tonight. It was unlikely but not impossible. He rested his hands on the cold stone of the window embrasure. There was only one way forward and he had known it from the start. He would marry Margery. There would be those who called him a fortune hunter but that was of no importance anymore. The only thing that mattered was that he put this situation right and bring order out of this chaos. Marriage was the only way.

The decision calmed him. It was the honorable course to take. It also felt like the right thing to do, right because it was meant to be. Such a notion was fanciful but he could not shift it, so instead he tried to ignore it. He told himself that if he married Margery he could make love to her again and slake this disturbing hunger he had for her. His body was already hardening again at the thought of having her in his bed. He wanted to feel her beneath him, to claim her and possess her. If he married her, she would be his before the whole world and his to claim in the hot darkness of the night, as well.

He walked over to the bowl of water on the chest and splashed water on his face again, trying to wash away the dark and complicated emotions he could still feel inside. He could not quite understand what disturbed him, for the issue was very simple. He had made a mistake; now, he was going to put it right. He had a duty to wed Margery. Duty, responsibility... The words had always comforted him in the past, devoid as they were of emotion and pain. But now they seemed to have lost their power.

It was as though he no longer quite believed in them.

MARGERY HAD NEVER previously thought of breakfast as an interminable meal, but on this particular morning it seemed to go on for several centuries. She had no appetite. The bread tasted of sawdust, the footmen seemed to be moving in excruciating slow motion and she could not concentrate on the conversation, even though it was of the most mundane type, centering on the weather.

She had wanted to cry off from breakfast that morning and hide like a coward in her room. She had not slept a wink and her feelings felt so bruised and battered that she was afraid it might show on her face.

Yet when she had finally forced herself from her bed and dressed in a bright blue muslin gown, she had glanced in the mirror and seen that she looked exactly the same as she did the day before. She was bemused

at how she could feel so different inside, as though all
her awareness and perceptions had changed, and yet to
all intents and purposes, look no different.

Sex was a curious business. It had turned her heart
and her mind inside out, it had taught her things about
her body that she could never have believed. And it had
left no outward sign that her life was changed.

She looked up from pushing a piece of bread roll
about her plate and saw that Henry's eyes were fixed
on her. She felt a wayward quiver of awareness mixed
with a flutter of fierce apprehension in her stomach. She
knew Henry was only waiting for the right moment to
get her alone and confront her, and she knew exactly
what he was going to say.

He was going to propose marriage to her and she
was going to refuse him.

The meal was over at last. Lady Wardeaux was chattering about taking the carriage and visiting Mrs. Bunn
and Miss Fox in the village. Her words washed over
Margery in a confused litany that made little sense.
Lady Emily was laying out the tarot cards in the midst
of the breakfast crumbs. She looked at the cards then
up at Margery's face with a strange, myopic expression.
Margery blushed. It was ridiculous to believe that the
cards knew what she had done and yet she felt guilty.
Hot, guilty and embarrassed in case anyone had seen
her running half-naked from Henry's chamber the night
before, and what a disaster it would be if they had. She
did not want to think about that.

"Lady Marguerite." Henry was waiting for her by
the door. There was no avoiding him. "May we speak?"

"Certainly, Lord Wardeaux," Margery said. Her
voice sounded a little squeaky. She feigned a bright

smile but suspected that it had not come out quite right when she saw Chessie looking at her with a mixture of puzzlement and concern.

"Shall we use the library?" she asked. "I am sure we may be undisturbed there."

Now Lady Wardeaux was looking both intrigued and speculative. She opened her mouth to comment but Henry seized Margery's arm and hustled her from the room, his imperative touch making it clear that he could not care less if they met in the library or the cowshed as long as they were undisturbed.

He opened the door for her and ushered her inside, closed the door and stood leaning back against it. He looked so stern and unyielding that Margery's heart did a wayward skip. She was not sure that she could go through with this if Henry was going to be so terrifyingly autocratic. It quite unnerved her. She folded her hands in front of her and tried to look assured rather than defensive.

He crossed the room and took her hands in his, demolishing all her good intentions in one fell swoop. Her heart did a positive somersault.

"You are well?" he asked.

"Of course not," Margery said. "Was it likely that I would be well this morning?"

Henry looked taken aback. Margery wondered whether the women he habitually slept with assured him the following morning that they felt absolutely marvelous. Probably they did, since they would all be sophisticated widows or elegant courtesans who would have been well able to cope with a night of unbridled passion uncomplicated by any emotion other than lust.

"Please do not misunderstand me," she added, anxious to be scrupulously truthful. "It was not that I did not enjoy——" She stopped. Henry raised a brow. He was still holding her hands and she imagined he could feel her pulse racing against his fingers. "I mean," she said desperately, "that it in some ways it was quite delightful——"

"Indeed?" Henry murmured.

"But not the type of activity that I should probably have been indulging in," Margery finished in a rush.

"Probably not," Henry agreed. A smile that was positively wicked curled his lips. "But I am relieved that you found it…ah…*delightful* was the word I think you used. That might predispose you to wish to do it again."

"Which is nothing to the purpose," Margery said hastily. She was starting to feel very hot. Matters were not working out at all as she had planned them. For a start she had not anticipated that simply seeing Henry alone and talking about what had happened between them would make her feel so stirred up, as though she wanted to grab him by his pristine neck cloth and kiss the life out of him. The fact that he looked so severe, so buttoned up, seemed only to make it worse because she knew now just what depths of passion and decidedly improper behavior lurked beneath that so-proper exterior. She closed her eyes and took a deep breath.

Concentrate.

"I wanted to ask you…" Henry said.

Oh, dear, here it comes.

Margery opened her eyes. Henry paused, looking at her. For a moment she thought he looked nervous. She had never seen him look nervous once in the whole of their acquaintance. It made her feel ridiculously tender toward him and that, of course, was dangerous because she loved him and she had to remember that he most certainly did not love her.

"I would like to ask for your hand in marriage, Lady Marguerite," Henry said, very formally. "Will you do me the honor of becoming my wife?"

It was impossible not to feel affected by that. It was tempting, so very tempting. If he had loved her, Margery would not have hesitated for a second. But he did not. Suddenly she remembered the coolness in his eyes the previous night and the complete absence of emotion. She almost shivered. She could see herself, a vision in her wedding gown, floating up the aisle on her grandfather's arm and Henry turning to watch her with the same detached indifference. It chilled her to the soul.

It was also enough to strengthen her resolve, because she had so much love to give but she would wither and die if she received nothing in return. Not even the hottest lust could compensate for the lack of love. She might have little worldly experience, but that she knew.

"Thank you, Lord Wardeaux," Margery said. "I am honored by your proposal but I fear I must decline."

She saw the stupefaction in Henry's eyes and realized that he had not for a moment imagined that she might refuse him. Under other circumstances it might have been amusing to see his confidence take such a knock. Now, though, she simply felt miserable. She saw him master his surprise, saw the way that he controlled his immediate reaction, which had been to demand rather than request an explanation. When he spoke his tone was still easy and smooth but she could feel the tension beneath it.

"Might I enquire as to why?"

"I have no plans to wed."

Henry raised his brows in patent disbelief. "Only last week you were speaking of marrying Reggie Radnor."

"That was different."

"I should hope so. You have not slept with him."

Margery blushed. "That is none of your affair."

Henry stepped close to her. "On the contrary," he said. "It is entirely my affair. Do you think that I do not know you were a virgin?" Then, as she took a breath, he leaned closer. His cheek brushed hers, his fingers touched the nape of her neck, and the warmth of his touch and the scent of his skin assailed her simultaneously. She felt dizzy with longing.

"Please do not tell me," he said, very softly, "that I was not the first."

Her face flaming, Margery backed away. "Whether you were the first or the tenth is not the material point, Lord Wardeaux. I do not wish to wed you."

There was a silence. It felt uncomfortable. Margery gritted her teeth and waited it out. It was foreign to her nature to keep quiet but somehow she managed it. She wanted love. She needed love. She could not compromise on something so huge and important. Even so, it hurt to refuse him. It hurt more than she had ever imagined.

"A gently bred young woman," Henry said, an edge to his voice now, "does not give herself to a man as you did with me last night and then refuse to marry him, unless she has very good reason. So I ask again—" His tone hardened further still. "Why are you refusing me?"

Margery clutched at the straw offered. "I am not a gently bred woman," she said quickly. "I do not behave as a lady would. I do not see marriage as a necessity."

This was getting more and more difficult. She could

see that he did not believe her and he had every reason not to do so. In London she had told him point blank that she was a virgin and would never accept carte blanche. He knew she was not wanton; she had had every opportunity to make a different life for herself through selling her body and had never chosen to do so.

His eyes searched her face and it felt like a physical touch.

"That's nonsense and you know it," Henry said. "You are in every way a lady. Don't demean yourself so."

Tears prickled Margery's eyes. He sounded so angry, as though he would confront anyone who dared to suggest she was anything less than a gentlewoman.

He was waiting for her to say something else, to explain. She could feel his frustration and his bafflement. She could not bear it. She turned away, and to her inexpressible relief Henry moved away, too, but only as far as the rug before the hearth where he paced as though he would wear a path in it.

"You have thought of the scandal, I assume," he said, after a moment. "It is inevitable that someone would have seen you leave my rooms last night. Your reputation is ruined."

Margery felt a flicker of fear deep down. She had thought of that in the long hours of the night. Templemore's endless dark corridors could contain any number of gossiping servants. She knew exactly what it was like to live and work in a house like this. There were no secrets.

"That's impossible," she said, denying facts she knew to be true since she would rather not accept them. "There was no one about. No one saw me."

Henry shook his head, a faint smile on his lips. "You,

of all people, should know that servants see everything. Someone will know. The scandal of it would kill your grandfather for sure."

"That's blackmail!" Margery said.

Henry shrugged. "Call it what you will. It is fact."

Margery stared at him. "I won't do it," she said stubbornly. "I will not marry you." She could see his reasoning all too plainly and it lit her with despair. He saw their situation—he saw *her*—as his responsibility. He had to protect her, do his duty, because he had made such a profound mistake in taking her virginity. He was a man of honor and that very fact made her heart turn over with misery because she admired him for his principles. They made her regret all the more fiercely that he could not love her, because to have the love of a man like that would be wonderful.

Henry came back to her side in one swift stride. He pulled her around to look at him. She sensed the puzzlement in him and the frustration.

"I do not understand why you are refusing me."

The pain twisted in Margery. She was refusing him because she loved him and because without his love the match was so unequal that she could not bear it. She remembered Chessie saying once that she had tried to change Fitz after marriage and tried to make him love her, to no avail. She remembered her mother, another Templemore woman, who had loved unwisely and lost everything. Her stomach dropped with desolation.

"Last night," Henry said. "You wanted me then. You responded to me then." His lips brushed her cheek, touched the corner of her mouth. It was instantly disarming. She could feel her body weakening and melting into warmth. She felt a fierce longing for his touch, his kiss, and jerked herself away. She could not bear for Henry to seduce her into agreement. She was all too likely to surrender, and embarrassingly quickly.

"Lust," she said. She forced the word out between dry lips. "You said it yourself before, my lord. We have a certain attraction to one another. Last night—" She swallowed hard. "It was most enjoyable, but scarcely sufficient to base a life upon. So…" She forced another shrug, making certain that she was sounding as hard and uncaring as she could. "It is best not to compound our mistake with the greater one of marriage."

She withdrew her hands from his and turned away from him. The distance yawned between then and with every word she pushed him farther away.

"I understand that you have business at Wardeaux," she said. "We have kept you from it for far too long. And as my grandfather plans our return to London in a few days, I think we shall not see much of each other."

For a moment she thought Henry was going to refuse to accept his dismissal. Her body was clenched tight with the tension as she waited. The ticking of the ugly clock on the mantel filled her ears as she waited for him to go, waited for him to leave her.

He paused with his hand on the doorknob. Margery held her breath. She wanted to hear him to say that he loved her but she knew he would not. He would not say it because it was not true.

"Send for me if you need me," Henry said. "I will always come to you." And although they had not been the words Margery had wanted to hear, she felt the tears close her throat. The door shut behind him. He had gone. She did not know why she wanted to cry. She had done the right thing. She knew it. But it did not seem to help.

HENRY RODE SO HARD it took only a couple of hours to reach Wardeaux. His luggage, his valet, everything else he had left in the dust to follow when they could. He wanted to be alone. He would have been filthy company anyway. He was angry and frustrated. It had never once occurred to him that Margery would refuse his suit and he was not prepared to accept her decision.

By now, the sun was up and the air was warm. The old Elizabethan manor of Wardeaux Court looked timeless and peaceful and very much like home, nestled in the curve of the river, its mullioned windows reflecting the light. Henry left Diabolo in his stall with a bag of oats and a trough of water, and walked down to the river where it ran narrow and deep through the water meadows, and all the time he was thinking of Margery.

He remembered the time they had spent together in London—which seemed as though it had happened years before, rather than months—and the bright, honest, fearless qualities he had seen in Margery then. It had been her warmth and generosity of spirit that had drawn him to her in the first place, helpless to resist the need he had for her, wanting her sweetness to illuminate his own life.

Becoming Lady Marguerite had changed her, not merely superficially with the clothes, the jewels, the dancing and the patina of polite conversation. She had become more wary of people, more guarded. Henry felt a pang of shame that he had played his part in that, in trying to make Margery into someone different. The truth was that she had always been more than good enough for any role, be it lady's maid or countess. Her grandfather had been wise enough to recognize that. He had not.

Yet beneath the silks and laces, Margery was still the same person. Last night he had tasted again that warmth and generosity in her. She had given herself to him wholly and without reservation. She had reached out to him. She had held nothing back and he had taken because he had such a hunger for her.

He knew, although she had not said so, that she must love him. Despite her claim that she had been motivated by no more than lust, he knew differently. She argued that she was no lady and so was not governed by the moral precepts of society, but Henry knew in his heart that Margery would never give herself to a man she did not love. It was not in her nature. She was too generous to hold anything back, so when she had given her body she had also given him her love.

She loved him but she would not marry him.

He rested a hand on the top bar of the fence and looked out across the river. The sunlight on the water dazzled him. The house slumbered in its hollow. Wardeaux was beautiful. He did not need Templemore.

But he did need Margery. There was a longing in him that only she could satisfy. It was not love, that brittle, foolish emotion that he had felt for Isobel so long ago, and he was grateful for that. Love was not something he recognized or wanted in his life. He had surrendered everything when he had been young and in love, he had lost his good sense and his self-respect, his name and his honor. Isobel had taken them all and tarnished them beyond recognition, and he would never allow anyone to do that again.

His feelings for Margery were different. They were not something he had ever felt before. They were compounded of a raging desire that could not be sated and a need to protect and care for her, to claim her and hold her safe. He did not like the way it made him feel. It made him vulnerable and he detested that but he had to accept it. He needed Margery by his side.

Margery wanted love. It was the one thing that he could not give her. He paused for a moment, wondering if it was selfish in him to insist on marrying her when there might be another man prepared to give her his love. He decided that it was selfish. And that it made no difference.

He had to persuade Margery to change her mind about marriage. The action he had been too scrupulous to take that morning had become a necessity. He would have to seduce her into accepting him.

CHAPTER EIGHTEEN

The High Priestess: A secret is revealed

LONDON FELT DIFFERENT.

It was not simply that it was June now, and all the trees bore fresh green leaves and some were ridiculously pretty in their pink and white blossoms. Margery was accustomed to seeing London in all seasons, wreathed in the fog of winter or when the dusty heat of August had taken the shine off summer.

It was not even that she was now one of the richest heiresses in the ton, and so of course everything looked different, from the pile of invitation cards that threatened the mantelpiece with collapse to the displays of flowers that the cart delivered fresh each morning, from the smart open phaeton in which she went driving in the park to the rainbow array of gowns folded in her wardrobe.

No, the difference, of course, was Henry. He was gone from her life and it seemed bleak and lacking color without him.

Margery tried to pretend. She went to dress fittings in Bond Street where the modistes tried to give her clothes rather than sell them to her because she was the sensation of the Season. She wore the Templemore diamonds in their new setting, and all the other jewels that had graced the necks of her mother and her grandmother before her.

She had the best box at the opera and the theater and anywhere else she chose to go. She rode on Rotten Row with Chessie and Jem and she drove with her grandfather to the exhibition at the Royal Academy of Art and to lectures and concerts.

The Prince Regent entertained her at Carlton House and declared her to be utterly charming. People begged for invitations to the balls she attended and crowds thronged the streets to catch a glimpse of her, and all of it was worth less than nothing because Henry was not there.

She had met a number of people who had known her mother and some who even remembered her as a child. It was odd and disconcerting to hear them speak of her, because she still had recovered no more memories of her childhood and wondered if she ever would. There had been no more strange accidents since she had come to London. She had told Jem about the fire and the shooting in the woods and he had said that, from what he had heard, Lord Templemore had probably sired a host of bastards who were jealous of her because they were not inheriting the family estate, and that she should not regard it because he was sticking close enough to protect her from anyone. He was indeed attentive to her, and he was also relishing the influence his position gave him in the ton. The ladies swooned over him.

Margery's come-out ball had been arranged to take place at the end of June, a fortnight after her arrival in Town. It would be one of the last balls, the culmination of a glittering round of social events and activities. The cream of the ton had been invited and there were reports that those who had not received one of the gold-embossed cards had wept tears of rage and frustration. Some had begged, stolen or bought tickets. It promised to be the crush of the Season.

"You look lovely," Chessie whispered to Margery as they paused at the top of Templemore House's grand stair. She tweaked a wayward curl back into Margery's diamond tiara and beamed at her. "Truly, Margery, you are the most beautiful debutante."

"And the oldest one London has ever seen," Margery said wryly. She looked at her reflection in the long pier glass and a stranger stared back at her. The girl in the mirror was tiny but elegant, a perfect miniature, as her grandfather had once said.

She was wearing a gown of cream silk with silver gauze embroidered with tiny diamond stars. They caught the light and shone like glittering raindrops. There were diamonds in her tiara and around her neck. Her feet were clad in cream evening slippers with diamond heels. Her hair was a fine golden-brown and shone like a swatch of rich silk. Her gray eyes were sparkling, her complexion was pink and cream as a china doll's. She looked happy. She looked *rich*. Even Lady Wardeaux was smiling with approval.

Margery almost stretched out her hand to touch the mirror, to check that she really was the girl standing there under the gleaming candlelight of a hundred chandeliers. It seemed impossible, but it was true.

In a change from normal etiquette, her grandfather had decreed that the guests should arrive first and then he would escort Margery down the stairs and present her to them. It seemed like the most pretentious nonsense to Margery and as she listened to the roar of the crowd in the huge hall and reception rooms below she almost turned tail and ran.

Suddenly she longed for Henry with a sharpness that caught her breath and left a hollow beneath her heart. She wanted to lean on his strength and feel safe and protected. She wanted him by her side. The force of the impulse shocked her. She missed him dreadfully.

Her grandfather came to join her, handsome in a claret-colored velvet evening jacket that was, so Lady Wardeaux muttered, at least fifty years out of date. They started to descend the broad and sweeping stair together with Lady Wardeaux, Chessie and Lady Emily following them down. A sea of faces swam before Margery's eyes. Everyone was gazing upward, staring at her. Over the past fortnight she had attended balls every night of the week, and met everyone from royal dukes to politicians to poets to men who had made their fortunes in trade. This was her greatest ordeal, for they were all waiting for her now, all watching her. There was a tight band about her chest. The tiara pinched her temples. The candlelight swam before her eyes. She was terrified.

A wave of applause started to ripple through the assembled guests, swelling and rolling toward Margery like the tide. Her grandfather was smiling; he looked so proud. And suddenly Margery did not care if it was all pretense, if people were only smiling and clapping because she was rich and eligible and her grandfather was one of the most influential peers in England. He was happy and that was all that mattered to her now.

She stood on tiptoe to kiss his cheek and the applause doubled as the guests roared their approval. They reached the bottom of the stairs and were immediately engulfed. The press of people was overwhelming, all wanting to congratulate her and to shake her grandfather's hand. Margery smiled until her face ached, smiled and chatted and felt an increasing sense of unreality. The noise was deafening. There were so many faces.

Gradually she came to realize that while everyone smiled and complimented her, many of those smiles did not reach the eyes. People watched her for the slightest slip that might betray her upbringing. She knew that behind her back they laughed at her. She had seen some of the caricatures of herself in the papers, dressed as a maidservant cleaning the Templemore diamonds with a feather duster.

There had been other cartoons making fun of her childhood and her career in service. Her grandfather had told her not to regard them, to treat them with aristocratic disdain, but that did not come easily to Margery.

It was with some relief that she saw the Duke and Duchess of Farne, Lord and Lady Rothbury and Lord and Lady Grant approaching her.

"Thank goodness!" she said, as Joanna Grant came over and gave her a hug, followed by her sisters, all chattering and smiling, glorious in their cascade of silks and jewels.

"This is all so splendid, Margery, my love," Joanna said, grabbing Margery's hands and spinning her around. "You are the success of the Season!"

"I feel such a fraud," Margery confessed. "These grand occasions terrify me."

"Well, you carry it off perfectly," Tess Rothbury said, eyeing the silver-and-cream gown with the greatest approval. "And you look simply stunning. There isn't a bachelor in the room who doesn't want to elope with you on the spot."

"I think they would rather bundle my money into the carriage to Gretna than me," Margery said, laughing.

"The word is that you are very choosy," Joanna said. "Can it be true that you have had nineteen proposals of marriage?"

"Twenty," Margery said, shame-faced. "Viscount Port proposed this morning."

"They say you will marry either Plumley or Cumnor," Tess said. "They are taking bets on it at Whites. Of course, Lord Plumley is rich as Croesus, but they say that he snores fit to wake the dead. Happily I would not know, but the neighbors do complain."

"The Duke of Cumnor is the most eligible peer in Town," Joanna put in. "But he is still tied to his mama's apron strings." She gave a little shrug. "Not a promising sign."

"It is a sad fact that almost no gentleman meets my sisters' stringent criteria," Merryn Farne murmured. "Apart from their own husbands, of course. It seems that between us we have already snapped up all the most desirable gentlemen in the ton."

"There is Lord Stephen Kestrel," Joanna said. "But I do believe he has a *tendre* for Chessie Alton."

"I hope so," Margery said. "Chessie deserves to be very happy."

"Well," Tess said, "then it seems you are destined to remain a spinster, Margery. Oh, but wait!" Her eyes lit up. "We forgot the most eligible choice. Lord Wardeaux, of course. By door of the refreshment room, talking to Garrick."

Lord Wardeaux.

Margery turned hot. Then she turned icy cold. She looked up. Tess had not been mistaken. Henry was leaning against a pillar, looking breathtakingly splendid in his black-and-white evening dress. He was indeed talking to the Duke of Farne but he was looking directly across the room at her and his gaze never wavered from her face.

Margery was not at all sure how a mere look could make her feel so dizzy, as though she had forgotten to breathe. But it did. And as Henry started to cross the floor toward her she felt even dizzier and more breathless still.

She heard Tess give a little sigh. "Is he not *sinfully* handsome? So dark and intense!"

"He must be," Joanna said dryly. "Normally you never notice any man apart from your husband."

"I had quite a *tendre* for Lord Wardeaux myself when I was younger," Merryn admitted. "Naturally it was his engineering projects that I admired the most."

"Of course you did," Tess said. "His engineering projects were frightfully attractive."

Henry was bowing to them.

"How are you, Henry?" Merryn said, reaching up to kiss his cheek. She caught Tess's eye. "What?" she protested. "He is Garrick's cousin. It is perfectly acceptable for me to kiss him!"

Henry was still looking directly at Margery. He took her hand and pressed his lips to the back of it. Margery worked extremely hard to repress the quiver of sensation that flickered along her nerve endings. One touch was all it had taken to reawaken her longing for him.

"Madam," Henry said. She suspected he could read all too well the effect he had on her. There was a glint of wicked amusement in his dark eyes.

"Ladies, we are *de trop*," Joanna Grant said, smiling mischievously as she shepherded her sisters away.

"Dance with me," Henry said to Margery. He was already guiding her toward the floor.

"I am to open the dancing with the Duke of Cley," Margery said, looking around. The Duke was nowhere to be seen and Henry seemed disinclined to accept a refusal anyway.

"Cley should have been more attentive," Henry said, "if he did not wish to lose his chance." Other couples were following them onto the floor, taking their place in the set.

"I like your gown," Henry said. His fingers touched her sleeve lightly and brushed her bare arm below the band of embroidered satin. "Cream rather than white." His eyes met hers. "Almost virginal, but not quite."

Margery blushed hotly. She glared at him. "You have been here two minutes and already you are behaving very badly, my lord."

Henry's fingers, warm and strong, interlocked with hers. His hand was sure on her waist as he spun her down the set of the first country-dance. Margery repressed a little shiver of longing. This was the Henry Wardeaux she remembered from their first meeting, the charming rake who could have taken anything from her, her heart, her soul, her love. One touch of his hand, one look, was all it had taken to undo all her efforts to forget him. She did not want to feel so vulnerable. It hurt too much.

"I do not recall inviting you tonight," she said, reaching for hauteur to defend herself against the emotional onslaught.

"You did not," Henry said. "Your grandfather did. He still outranks you, I think."

"I do not know why he would do such a thing," Margery said.

"He thought you were missing me," Henry said. He raised his brows. "Were you?"

The music separated them for a moment.

"Well?" Henry said, as they came back together again. "You did not answer me."

"No," Margery said. "I did not. I did not miss you at all."

Henry laughed. His fingers tightened on hers. She almost lost the beat of the music because she was assailed by so sharp a longing that it felt like pain.

"You always did lie badly," he said softly.

Margery did not answer. She could not. She was aware only of the touch of his hand in hers and the way in which her willful heart sang to be near him again, ready to betray her in an instant.

"When did you return to London?" She was aware that the other dancers in the set were watching them and that polite conversation, as Lady Wardeaux had been at pains to teach her, was a requirement of any couple in the dance.

"I have been here almost a fortnight," Henry said.

Margery almost missed her step. Her heart was sore to realize that Henry had been in London almost as long as she had.

"You did not come to see us—" she began, then broke off as she realized just how much of her feelings she had betrayed.

"You have had so many admirers vying for your attention," Henry said, "I am surprised you noticed."

The music had stopped. Around them the crowd ebbed and flowed. Henry took her elbow and steered her gently off the dance floor toward the open doors leading onto the terrace. Couples were strolling along its width, taking the summer air, so fresh and cool after the overheated press of the ballroom. Beyond the walls of the garden stretched the expanse of Hyde Park, falling into twilight, the shadows gathering beneath the trees. The sky overhead was a deep, dark blue, studded with stars to rival Margery's diamonds.

Henry took a glass of champagne from a passing footman and handed it to her. Margery took a gulp, feeling the bubbles burst on her tongue and fizz up her nose. She almost choked and wondered if she would ever master the art of being the elegant society lady.

"So, have you chosen between the dozens of suitors begging for your hand?" Henry asked. "Fairness might prompt you to put them out of their misery."

"No," Margery said. "I haven't made my choice."

"Do you intend to?" Henry asked. He had turned slightly away from her, resting one hand on the stone parapet. "I remember you saying that you saw no necessity for marriage. But perhaps—" he tilted his head "—that was just with me?"

Margery hesitated. The simple truth was that Henry had gotten into her blood so that she compared every man she met to him and found every last one of them lacking.

"It is not that," she said. "I have yet to discover a man—"

"Whose lovemaking you would find delightful?"

Margery gasped aloud. "My lord!"

The smile in Henry's dark eyes deepened, making her feel positively scorching.

"I want more from marriage than that," she said stubbornly. "I was going to say a man who loves me."

Instantly she saw the expression in Henry's eyes flatten and go dark, and she felt desolation possess her soul. Secretly she had thought—hoped—that he had come to find her tonight because his feelings for her had changed. But they had not. She could see they had not and his next words confirmed it.

"If you cannot find love in marriage," he said, "why not settle for desire instead?"

Margery heart was bumping against her cream satin bodice. "Because I am not in the habit of settling for second best," she said.

"There was nothing in the least second best about what we shared that night," Henry murmured. He took the champagne glass from her hand and placed it gently on the parapet. Margery's senses were so aware that she heard the tiny scrape of glass on stone. She heard her own unsteady breath. She felt the caress of the cool evening air on her skin and shivered at the contrast of Henry's touch, his hand warm on her bare arm above her glove. The intense darkness in his eyes was so forceful that she felt trapped, captured and quite unable to look away.

The terrace was momentarily empty. Henry leaned forward and touched his lips to hers in the sweetest of kisses. His fingers brushed her cheek very gently. Margery's lips parted and clung to his. She felt helpless, swept with sensation so powerful that she trembled. It was all over in an instant. Henry released her and she stared at his face, so clear-cut in the rising moonlight.

She cleared her throat. "This really is not fair, my lord."

She saw him smile. "How so?"

"You know how," Margery said. "You take advantage of my feelings for you."

"Let's talk about it," Henry said. He drew her along the terrace away from the ballroom. The sound of the music and the crowd died away behind them, falling to a murmur, then to quiet. Henry pushed open the door of the room at the end and it opened with a tiny click. He waited for her to precede him inside.

Margery hesitated again. She suspected that talking was not high on Henry's list of current priorities. She was scarcely that naive. Nor was she coy. She knew the risk she was taking.

She cast one glance at his face, half nervous, half anticipatory, but his expression gave nothing away. As she stepped into the room he closed and locked the door behind them, pulling the heavy gold velvet curtains closed against the night. The room was warm and intimate, lit by candles and thick with long shadows.

Henry turned to face her. "I would like to renew the offer I made you at Templemore," he said formally. "I would like you to marry me."

"Why?" Margery said bluntly.

She saw his eyes widen. It was always a pleasure to disconcert Henry.

"You're not a fortune hunter," she said. "I know you are not. You don't want the money. So why would you marry me?"

"I want you," Henry said. He was frowning now. "I need you."

There was tension latent in all the lines of his body.

If it had not been so ridiculous, Margery would have thought he did not truly know his own feelings. But this was Henry, cold, dutiful Henry, who had no difficulty in separating passionate lust and true love, because while he was masterful at creating the first he never wanted to feel the second.

And need…well, need and longing and the other pretty words were all very nice but they were not love. This was a declaration of sorts, but it was still not enough for her. Perhaps she was wrong to ask for the whole world when Henry was offering her more than he had ever offered before. But still, she would not settle for less than everything.

"No, thank you," Margery said.

"You are always direct," Henry said.

"I don't want to waste your time," Margery said politely.

Henry's gaze appraised her, making her feel quite faint. "I doubt that you could do that," he said with a slight smile. He took a step toward her. It was a very purposeful step. Margery took a step away. She backed up against the enormous mirrored display case containing the china that had been a wedding present to her grandparents from King George II. Her palms pressed against the cold glass.

"You can't seduce me here," she said.

"I beg your pardon," Henry said, still immaculately polite. "But I can."

Margery's stomach dropped in shock, her lips parted on a gasp, but before she could speak he had covered her mouth with his own. He kissed her with deliberation, purpose and a fierce control that was intensely exciting. It told her that he was determined to gain what he wanted and he would brook no refusal. The kiss, relentless in its demand, sent spikes of awareness instantly coursing through her. Margery's insides turned to liquid fire. She felt shame all the way down to her perfidious soul that she was so susceptible to him and then, less than a split second later, she felt a burst of wicked anticipation replace all other sensation.

The kiss deepened, then deepened again. Margery felt as though she was falling into it, powerless to stop. She had been denying her feelings for weeks, starved of Henry's touch, and now she was lost as love and desire fused into one. She was captivated by the passion that flared between them, so sweet and hot. It called to all that was wild in her, brazenly reminding her of how it had been between them at Templemore.

When Henry raised his head, they were both panting and Margery felt hot and alight with the desire that shimmered around them. Henry's hands slid down her arms to clasp her lightly by the wrists. She thought he would kiss her again then but he did not. His gaze searched her face and it felt like a caress, as though he was committing every feature to memory.

"I made a mistake at Templemore," he said softly. "I let you go. I won't do that again."

Margery's heartbeat increased its pace even further. "You don't love me," she said stubbornly. "You want me but you do not love me and I will not marry a man who does not love me."

Henry leaned in; his breath feathered softly across her cheek. "I could persuade you to change your mind."

She was afraid he could, that in the heat of the moment she would forget everything but her love for him.

Her knees trembled. "I am not open to persuasion," she said. "You cannot seduce me into agreement."

"Let's test your willpower then." He captured her lips with his again and slid his tongue into her mouth. The dance began again, fevered and deliciously sweet. There was an edge of something fierce and blistering to the kiss now and it spun out until Margery's head was whirling and her body felt heavy and languorous and there was such an ache between her thighs. She wanted him. The love she had for him felt huge and overwhelming, painful in its intensity, dazzling her. She fought for control, fought for even some grain of sense.

"Someone will notice we are gone," she whispered. "They will know."

She felt Henry's fingers on the thick cream ribbons that fastened her bodice at the front and matched the intricate embroidery on the sleeves and hem. He was loosening the ties. Her body quaked at the knowledge of what would happen next.

"There are two hundred and fifty people here tonight," he said. "No one will notice you are gone. They will all assume you are talking to someone else, hidden in the crowd."

Henry slid his hand into her chemise and drew down the fine silk. It slipped from Margery's breasts and he pulled her bodice wide, leaving her naked to the waist in nothing but the Templemore diamonds. He spun her around so that she had her back to him, facing her reflection in the mirrored display case. His hands were hot on her bare waist.

The room was warm but Margery shivered violently. The candlelight caught the diamonds and shimmered in a glittering cascade of light, reflecting her image back

from the mirrors; her eyes wide and bright, her lips
stung red from Henry's kisses, her cheeks flushed pink,
the scatter of freckles across her bare shoulders, the diamonds heavy against her hot skin, her nipples small
and tight, her breasts rising and falling rapidly as she
tried to steady her breathing. The beautiful cream-and-
silver gown was about her waist, the ribbons trailing.
It looked so innocent in its pale allure and she looked
so abandoned, half-naked in it.

She heard Henry's breath hiss in between his teeth.
"I remember how arousing you find precious jewels,"
he said.

One of his hands held her still, facing the mirror,
with him braced behind her. His other hand closed
warm and hard over her breast. Margery felt her legs
tremble.

"Don't cry out," Henry whispered. "And don't close
your eyes." His lips were against the skin of her neck.
He squeezed her breast gently, taking the nipple between his finger and thumb, teasing and tugging until
she ached with carnal pleasure. The diamonds flickered
with each unsteady breath she took.

She tilted her head back shamelessly to give Henry
greater access to the tender skin of her throat and arched
her breasts to his hands as they plucked and tormented.
Desire rolled over and through her in a great shuddering tide. She closed her eyes in wanton delight and
Henry's teeth nipped her neck in a silent order to open
them again. She watched, her gaze slumberous as he
caressed her, one hand still at her breast the other sliding low now over the plane of her bare stomach.

"I won't give in," she said. Her voice was a broken whisper. She could scarcely believe that he walked

straight back into her life and that she was here with him, like this. "I won't agree," she said. "I won't marry you."

Henry gave her the tiniest of nudges forward and she almost fell, bracing herself at the last minute with her palms against the flat top of the glass case. She felt him move behind her.

"My gown—" She forced the words out against the beating of her heart. "Everyone will see the creases."

In response he tossed her skirts and petticoats up about her waist so that they frothed over the surface of the cabinet. His fingers were at the gap in her drawers. Margery gasped in shock. She had not really thought he would dare to make love to her here, now. It was too shocking to comprehend and yet so blissfully, so terrifyingly what she wanted.

"How?" She could barely get the word out. Her insides tumbled. Her whole body washed with heat. She was shaking. Only the brightly lit glass under her palms held her steady.

"I'll show you." He spoke softly in her ear. "Trust me. And…" There was wicked amusement in his voice. His fingers brushed the inside of her thighs, inside the drawers. "Don't break the china. That would be very difficult to explain."

He had found the core of her, moist and damp, and his fingers slid over it and then inside her. Margery shook all the harder, flattening her palms against the glass, stifling her moans as he explored her slowly, deliberately, seeking out the most sensitive places, stroking, drawing out her pleasure until she was drowning in the most tortuous rapture imaginable.

"I will have you," he whispered and she knew he

meant in marriage as well as here and now. She sensed
the absolute will in him, the determination and beneath
that the hunger and the need. It was almost enough to
convince her. But it was not love. She struggled to hold
on to that thought, fighting wave upon wave of pure
carnal delight that lapped at her and threatened to steal
her very will.

"I will not marry you." Her voice was a mere thread.
His fingers paused in their caresses. She gasped.

"Then do you wish me to stop now?" He still
sounded amused.

"No!" She could not stop herself begging. "Please,"
she said. "I want—" She bit off the words. She hung
on the very edge of pleasure, cursing him. She felt her
body twitch; so did Henry, and he gave her one small
stroke. It was not enough. It was not nearly enough. Her
hips jerked. Henry laughed and brought one hand up to
her breast, squeezing so that the unendurable pleasure
racked her again.

"You want to be my mistress but not my wife?" His
words were a dark, heavy whisper.

"Yes! No!" Margery writhed against his hands. "I
will not marry a man who does not love me."

"And I will not stop making love to you until you
agree to marry me."

It was a measure of Margery's desperation that she
felt nothing but relief in that moment. She felt him move
behind her, felt the hard length of him sink into her
slowly, filling her completely and sending her senses
tumbling into an abyss of pleasure. She gasped, shocked
at the intensity of the sensation, as he pulled back, withdrew from her and slid in deep again.

There was urgency in him but he did not hurry as

he allowed her body to adjust to the penetration of his. His hand was at her waist, holding her steady. Over and over he took her and Margery's emotions as well as her senses were captured and burned in a tight spiral of desire, higher and higher with each thrust. It was wild, it was completely abandoned, and yet it was the ultimate in her most tender desires.

"Open your eyes."

Again she obeyed him and the sight robbed what little was left of her will. She was braced against the cabinet, hands flat on the glass, her skirts spread like a bell about her waist, naked above but for the flash of the diamonds about her neck. They moved with every stroke of Henry's body into hers. Her breasts rocked gently with each slide of him inside her. The light played over her skin in gold and shadow. She looked utterly ravished, deliciously debauched and wanton. The sight made her cry out with disbelief and wicked delight.

She watched in the mirror as Henry pressed down gently on the small of her back, his hand warm and sure. She obeyed the pressure, parting her thighs wider, then she cried out again, overwhelmed, as he penetrated even deeper, even harder. She strained forward as she took all of him in. It was blissful beyond her dreams. She was desperate to come, her body aching for surcease, but he would not hurry. She begged him, abandoning all pride and modesty. He laughed. She cursed him roundly in language most inappropriate to the heiress to Templemore.

Gradually, with tantalizing slowness, he drove her toward the zenith. Whenever she thought she would surely tumble over the edge he would draw back, once again denying her the ultimate release.

"You will take me," he whispered, his lips against the damp skin of her neck. He stroked her core once, twice, a final time. She squirmed.

"Make your surrender," he said. "You know you are mine."

She did know. She knew it deep in her heart, in her soul. But he was not hers. Not wholly. He always held something back.

"I will not," she said. "I'll never agree." The words fractured as she felt him thrust inside her one last time, as ecstasy became dream, as he took her completely and she shattered into a climax as bright and sharp as the diamonds. Her knees buckled. She felt him catch her and hold her up while the pleasure rocked through her, and her body shimmered and heated, and finally softened into abject capitulation. He had made her his again, as thoroughly as he had promised. She trembled all over.

It was then that she realized that he was still as hard and hot as before. He had not achieved his release. He had, in fact, deliberately denied himself. She saw his face; she realized it was not over. She gave a little whimper of protest even as renewed excitement flowered through her. It was impossible to want him again, so soon, and yet it was not. It was not impossible at all. She felt ripe and pleasured, but there was a tingling awareness beneath the surface of her skin, and when Henry drew one hand across her bare stomach in casual possession she felt her body tighten and sing again.

He lifted her to sit on the edge of the china cabinet, her skirts once more spread out about her. He brought her head down so that he could kiss her, long deep kisses that felt as though he was stealing her soul from her body. His hands moved over her, over her bare back, sweeping down to her waist and up to stroke the under-side of her breasts. Margery arched to his hands and his mouth, feeling the throb and pull of desire deep in her belly.

"So…" He bit down on one tight nipple, fierce and hot, licking and sucking on her until she gasped. "Will you marry me?"

Margery almost smiled. Thwarting him was becoming a positive pleasure.

"No," she said. She heard his breath hiss in. He bit down a little harder on her in response. Her body jerked upward. Hot pleasure unfurled inside her.

"Please reconsider." His tone was very polite even if his lips were a mere inch from her bare breast.

"I'm afraid I will not." To prove that she could not be dictated to she took his erection in her hand and heard his breath catch again. He was iron hard and smooth as she stroked and explored him. She watched as he closed his eyes. She heard him groan deep in his throat.

"Madam, I must insist—" He drew in a painful breath. "If you are to have me you must marry me. I will not be your lover."

Margery drew him closer between her spread thighs. She leaned forward so that her breasts brushed his chest. She planted a soft kiss on his lips. "Yes, you will," she whispered against them.

He snapped. He slid his hands under her buttocks, lifted her and plunged into her again, driving into her so fiercely that the entire cabinet rocked and shook beneath her. The china crashed and tumbled. It was fast and furious and mindless and so blissful that Margery wanted to scream with it. It snatched her breath and drove every last thought from her mind in a welter of urgent sensation. This time her climax built and rolled over her in slow, pounding waves that shook her whole body.

She clasped Henry so tightly he shouted out as he came in her and then Margery fell into the deepest pleasure, where her love and desire for him were so entangled she knew she would never be able to separate them again.

IT WAS SOME TIME LATER and Margery was in her bedchamber and Chessie was helping her to retrieve both her gown and her reputation. Margery had come round from the most explosive and soul-shaking experience of her life to find herself held safely in Henry's arms and Chessie knocking frantically at the door of the China Room with the news that her grandfather was asking for her. According to Chessie, if she was away any longer than another ten minutes the entire ton would start to put two and two together and make a very big sum indeed.

Henry had released her reluctantly. His cheek pressed to hers, his mouth against her hair, he had asked her if she had changed her mind. He had not said that he loved her. Margery, her heart breaking, had said that she had not. She would not marry him.

Chessie had given Henry one very hard stare and whisked her away from prying eyes. Some story had been put about that Margery had suffered a tear in her gown. Chessie had helped her tidy herself; she had retied her ribbons and smoothed her skirts, had looked her over and had expressed very dry approval for Henry's ability to make love to a woman without creasing her gown or disarranging her hair. Margery had blushed to her toes.

Margery looked herself over in the mirror. She doubted she would ever be able to look in a mirror again without seeing Henry making love to her, his hands dark against the paleness of her skin, his body sliding into hers. She felt hot and light-headed again, sated with physical pleasure, wanting nothing more than to sleep. At least she looked respectable again now, even if she felt anything but.

"I heard Henry ask you if you had changed your mind," Chessie said. She had been busy tidying up various pots and brushes on the dressing table that did not really need tidying, as though she needed the occupation. Her hands paused. Her blue eyes held a troubled expression. "Tell me to mind my own business if you wish. I am only anxious that you do not get yourself into a deal of trouble."

"He proposed to me," Margery said. "Again," she added scrupulously. "Several times."

"And what did you say?" Chessie asked.

"I told him I would not marry without love," Margery said.

"Oh, Margery," Chessie said. Margery was shocked to see that her blue eyes were full of tears. "I hope," Chessie said, "I truly hope that this has a happy ending for you but I fear it will not. Henry—" She hesitated, then sat down abruptly on the edge of the bed. "Henry was in love with someone when he was young," she said, her words tumbling out in a rush. "Her name was Isobel. I did not want to tell you because it was not my business and I hoped he would tell you himself, but…" She looked up and met Margery's eyes. "Henry was married at only nineteen. He was very much in love with his wife."

Margery felt an odd rushing sensation in her ears.

Henry had been in love? Henry had been married?

She grabbed at the upright post of the bed to steady herself. "What happened? Did she die?"

"Eventually," Chessie said dryly. "She had *affaires* all over Town. She shamed Henry by sleeping with his own father. In the end, Lord Templemore paid her to go away and she went abroad. She died a few years later, but only after she had dragged Henry's name and his honor through the gutter."

"Why didn't you tell me before?"

"I wanted to but I thought it was Henry's place to tell you himself. I'm sorry."

Margery's legs felt so shaky that she sat down next to Chessie on the fat purple coverlet. Henry had been in love. The words repeated over and over in her head. He had been married and he had never told her. No one had mentioned it to her. She thought about the coldness that had come into Henry's eyes when she had spoken of love, of the remoteness she had felt in him. Now she understood. Henry had cut himself off completely. He had not want to feel again.

"I wish he had told me," she said. "I wish he had explained." She was so candid herself that keeping such an enormous secret felt impossible and wrong. Yet, at the same time, she could blame Henry for nothing. His wife had taken all the love he had offered, and twisted and despoiled it beyond recognition.

Margery swallowed hard. She remembered wondering how Henry had felt as a small, solemn child in the huge edifice of Templemore. No siblings to show him love or bear him company in the way that she had

had Jem and Jed and Billy. Nothing but a cold, distant mother and an absent, libertine father.

She had misunderstood, she realized now. She had thought that Henry had never learned to love. She had accused him of being a stranger to love. But what had happened to him had been worse. Despite, or perhaps because of the example of his parents' marriage, despite the licentious ways of his father and his godfather, he had, with faith and courage, offered his love and his honor to this woman, Isobel. And she had destroyed them.

A small, hard knot tightened in Margery's throat. She felt so angry with the unknown woman who had shattered Henry's faith that she wanted to kill her, though she was prepared to admit that that might have been partly jealousy, as well. Or possibly a very great deal of jealousy.

"I hate her," she said viciously. "It is fortunate she is dead." She checked the clock and grabbed her little cream satin reticule. "We must go back to the ball. I know we must. I have been absent far too long. But Chessie—" She pressed her friend's hand. "Thank you for telling me."

Henry had gone when they reached the ballroom. Margery was relieved; it would have been impossible to dance with him again or make inconsequential chat in front of a crowd.

Chessie's revelation had shaken her badly. She was not naive enough to imagine she might teach Henry to love again. That was the sort of blind hope destined to end in tears. That was the sort of misery that had lain in store for her mother. What she had to decide now was whether Henry's offer of a marriage, based on mutual need and mutual desire, was sufficient when her stubborn heart argued for more.

CHAPTER NINETEEN

The Ten of Swords: Ruin

"You look blue-deviled."

Henry jumped as his cousin Garrick spoke in his ear. He had been watching Margery—it was becoming something of a dangerous habit—as she threaded her way through the guests at Lady Fowler's rout. It was another hot London night and another ton ballroom. As ever, Margery sparkled, a tiny, bright figure looking completely at ease in her new setting. As ever, she was under siege; a positive battalion of suitors pursued her around the room and he had to stand there and watch like a chaperon on a rout chair. Of course he felt blue-deviled.

"You've quarreled with the divine Lady Marguerite," Garrick said, guessing the cause of Henry's bad temper with disturbing accuracy.

"She asked me about Isobel," Henry admitted. "She wanted to know why I hadn't told her I had been married before."

"And you told her that it was because it was not important," Garrick hazarded.

Henry shrugged. "It isn't."

"I've said it before and I'll say it again," Garrick said. "You understand nothing about women, Henry."

"Evidently not," Henry agreed.

Bafflingly, Margery had rejected all his subsequent invitations. She had refused to drive with him again, she had turned down his offer to escort her to any number of concerts and exhibitions, and she had even declined his invitations to dance, brandishing an undeniably full card at him when he had challenged her. He had been reduced to standing on the sidelines and it was not a position he was accustomed to occupying.

He had been obliged to admit that his plan to seduce Margery into agreeing to be his wife had been badly flawed in any case. Instead of entrapping her, he had been the one who had been captured, dazed and disturbed by the fierceness of his response to her. The longer she thwarted him, the more acute became his need for her. But it was not a need that could be satisfied simply by taking her to his bed. He wanted more than that. Only marriage would suffice, and while Margery refused him he was obliged to watch other men court her, thwarted by a slip of a girl whose strength of will was as powerful as his own.

He leaned his shoulders back against the pillar and watched Margery as she danced a mazurka with Lord Donnington. Tall and clumsy as a young giraffe, the young peer was not the most elegant dancer. He had just stepped on Margery's hem, but she was smiling at him anyway.

There was warmth in her eyes and an irresistible lift to her lips and the candlelight burnished her hair to a glorious spun bronze and shadowed the vulnerable curve of the nape of her neck. She looked beautiful. Henry felt that beauty like a punch in the gut.

"I suppose you have heard that Lady Marguerite has had twenty offers of marriage?" Garrick said slyly.

"Make that twenty-one," Henry said, straightening up. "Or twenty-two, since she has turned me down twice."

Garrick grimaced. "Do you want to drown your sorrows?"

"Not particularly," Henry said, but he followed his cousin into the refreshment room. Garrick took two glasses of champagne from a passing footman and gestured Henry over to some quiet seats.

"If you want my advice—" Garrick began.

"I don't."

"She doesn't trust you," Garrick said, ignoring him. "Look at what happened to her mother."

Henry shook his head. "You've lost me."

"Try not to be so obtuse," Garrick begged. "Lady Rose fell in love and eloped with a downright scoundrel."

"I hope you are not implying there is any similarity between Antoine de Saint-Pierre and myself," Henry said, scowling. If Margery thought that he was like her ne'er-do-well father then she really did have a poor opinion of him. He hoped it was not so. Cursing, he ran a hand through his hair.

"Of course you're not like Saint-Pierre," Garrick said. "But there is a similarity between Lady Marguerite and her mother. Marguerite is in love with you, just as her mother was with Saint-Pierre. Saint-Pierre ruined her mother's life. So Lady Marguerite will never put herself in the position her mother was in and marry a man she cannot trust, a man who does not love her."

Knowing Margery's family history, Henry found it

puzzling that she was so set on marrying for love. He imagined it would be the last emotion Margery would trust, but then he realized that with her generosity of character it was not in her nature to withhold love. She gave it openly and unconditionally. And she would want the same in return, only trusting a man with her heart as well as her body if she believed he would love her, and only her, forever.

"How lovely Lady Marguerite looks tonight," Garrick said. "Donnington will be just the latest to fall. It's because she has—"

"Warmth," Henry said. His soul felt cold now that Margery had withdrawn her love from him. The sweetness and generosity in her had been the flame that had drawn him back to her, time and again. He had needed to capture and hold that warmth, and yet somehow it had slipped through his fingers, as elusive as water.

Through the open door of the refreshment room he could see Margery twirling her way through the waltz in the arms of Lord Plumley. The Templemore diamonds glittered at her throat. She looked beautiful and elegant and as though she had been born to grace every ballroom in the land. Henry shifted in his seat. He was not likely to forget just how beautiful Margery had looked stretched in half-naked abandon over the glass case of the China Room, those diamonds her only adornment. He loosened his neck cloth, which, like his trousers, felt intolerably tight. If he were never allowed to touch Margery again he would be fit for bedlam.

"She is beautiful and accomplished and courageous," Garrick continued. "I imagine you must feel very proud of her."

"I do, curse you," Henry ground out.

Garrick grinned. "Then you should ask yourself," he said gently, "just what is the difference between what you feel for Lady Marguerite—and love." He got to his feet and clapped Henry on the shoulder. "Good luck, old fellow. You were always so good at solving mathematical problems. A pity if the one calculation that really matters should evade you."

MARGERY SLEPT LATE the morning after Lady Fowler's rout and came downstairs to breakfast as the clock struck eleven. The morning newspapers were on the rosewood table in the hall waiting for Barnard to take them up to Lord Templemore. Her grandfather liked to take all the papers into the library after breakfast and read them at his leisure, everything from *The Times* to the *Gentleman's Athenian Mercury,* which he said gave a balanced impression of the news since they expressed such opposing views. Today it was the *Mercury* on the top of the pile on the silver tray. Margery squinted sideways at it in passing, her eye catching the gossip column of a person who rejoiced in the title of Lady Loveworn.

"Disappointing news for the many suitors of Lady M S-P," the piece began. "It seemed that nothing could topple the famous heiress from her place at the pinnacle of the ton, but now it appears that Lady M is not the innocent she seems. Hopeful swains should note that at least one lover has been before them in the lady's affections. Whether the determined hordes of bachelors can overlook this lapse in the interest of two-hundred-and-fifty-thousand pounds remains to be seen. We are sure there is some hardy soul out there who will regard a little shop soil as worth the price of a fortune."

The shock and understanding hit Margery with a

force that stole her breath. She sat down heavily on the second step of the stairs and tried to think, but all she could see was the print of the paper swimming before her eyes, the horrible innuendo that hid the terrifying truth.

Someone knew what had happened at Templemore. One of the servants must have seen her leaving Henry's chamber and now they had gone to the press with the story. Or perhaps someone knew that she and Henry had slipped away from the ball the previous week. Suddenly her chest felt tight with panic. She could not breathe. What had been secret and special to her alone was now exposed to the world. It had become squalid, picked over by the gossipmongers, discussed in the clubs, sordid and scandalous.

Not the innocent she seems… A little shop soil…

Margery realized that she was shaking and cold. Her whole body trembled. No one had seen her yet because she was hidden by the curve of the stair. Through the delicate wrought iron she could see the servants ferrying food into the dining room. There were voices within; evidently Chessie and Jem and perhaps even Lady Wardeaux and Lady Emily were already up and partaking of breakfast. Everything was running a little later today because they had all been out at the ball the previous night.

Margery tried to concentrate, but her thoughts were scattered and broken and she did not know what to do. It had never occurred to her that anyone would go to the papers with what they knew about her, but of course she was famous now, rich, eligible. Gossip about her would be in high demand. It had been so naive of her to imagine no one would know, and that if they did know, they would not speak.

She was ruined.

She grabbed the other papers from the pile. *The Times* did not deal in scandal, of course, but plenty of other papers did. The same story, implying that she had taken at least one lover, was in more than half of the other papers. There was even a suggestion that she had spread her favors and much else besides in Mrs. Tong's bawdy house before her elevation to the peerage. Each story was more distasteful than the last, as though the papers were trying to outdo each other. By the time she had scanned them all she felt sick.

Fear clawed at her stomach. Her grandfather. He could not see this, not after the tragedy of her mother. Such a heinous scandal might indeed kill Lord Templemore, and she had brought it on them all.

Bile rose in her throat. She felt so shamed. The malicious words cheapened what had happened with Henry. She could not bear it. Her love for him was exposed to everyone as no more than a lustful indulgence, a piece of gossip to be picked over and judged, as she would be, too. And tomorrow, no doubt, there would be more of the same and she was powerless to prevent it.

Her mind scrambled around like a mouse in a trap. By the time the story had run its course she would be branded a licentious whore and she would have ruined her grandfather's life as thoroughly as her mother had done.

A maid passed with a tray of food. The rich smell of kidneys and bacon made Margery's stomach heave and she pressed a hand to her mouth to hold back the nausea. She reached for the silver tray, scrabbling in sudden panic to steal the papers from the table before Barnard appeared to take them to her grandfather. It could only be a temporary delay. She knew that. Lord Templemore would hear the gossip soon enough, as would the rest of the world. But she did not want him to read it. The news had to come from her.

Her shaking fingers caught the edge of the tray and sent it tumbling onto the floor with a resounding crash. Barnard appeared from the breakfast room and behind him, Chessie and Jem. Margery saw with inexpressible relief that Lady Wardeaux was not present.

"Margery!" Chessie had run forward to catch her arm. "Whatever is the matter? You look dreadful—" Her voice faded away as Jem made a sudden movement. Looking at him Margery saw he had picked up the *Mercury* from the floor. All the color had drained from his face. He looked as bad as Margery felt.

"Moll?" he said incredulously. "Surely this is a pack of lies?" His voice was hoarse.

Chessie grabbed the paper out of his hands. Her horrified gaze came up to Margery's face and in their silence lay Jem's answer.

"The story is everywhere," Margery said. She scarcely recognized her own voice, it was so rough with anxiety. "Grandfather cannot see—"

"Wardeaux," Jem said viciously, crumpling the paper in his fists. "I'll kill him. God help me I will."

Margery drew a breath but Chessie, with the greatest presence of mind, grabbed Jem's arm and did not let go. "Please do not," she said calmly. "Margery would not like it."

Jem swung around on her. "Moll?" he said again.

"I love him," Margery said. She fought the tears that

filled her eyes. "It's not Henry's fault," she said. "He asked me to marry him and I refused."

Jem swore. "Why the hell—"

"Not now," Chessie interposed with the same steely calm and Jem stalked off, swearing under his breath.

Margery stumbled to her feet, grabbing the banister for support. "I have to go to grandfather and tell him at once," she said.

"No," Chessie said. "You have to go to Henry. This malicious tittle-tattle—" she tapped the papers disparagingly "—will already be all over Town. The only way to counter it is with the announcement of your betrothal. Then—" She squeezed Margery's hands. "Then you talk to your grandfather."

"Yes," Margery said. Her mind felt fuzzy and unfocussed. "Yes, of course. Thank you, Chessie."

Chessie gave her a brief, fierce hug. Margery could see she was very pale. "I'll come with you," she said.

"No," Margery said. "I'll go alone." She wanted no one with her when she went to Henry.

Chessie nodded but her eyes were still anxious. "If you are sure."

Once Margery was upstairs in her room, though, she found that she did not actually know what to do. She sat down on the bed. She stood up again. She walked to the window and looked outside. She did not seem to be able to focus on anything, neither the busy street, nor the carriages rattling past, nor the quiet green spaces of the park stretching away into the distance. Everything looked strange, too brightly colored and too distant.

She startled herself by giving a little sob. It felt as though there was a huge weight building in her chest and that any moment it would burst out and she would cry as though her heart would break. She had been so determined only to marry for love. Now she would be the one begging Henry to wed her out of duty. She grabbed her hat and spencer. The hat was yellow, frivolous and completely inappropriate. She did not care.

As she came down the stairs a second time she heard voices in the hall.

Henry.

He knew. He had come to her. She stopped on the landing, one hand on the banister, and looked down at him. He was waiting for her in the hall below, head tilted up to watch her, the sunlight from the fan window falling on his face. In that moment of stillness Margery noticed several small things about him. He had taken the time to dress immaculately because this would be his third marriage proposal to her, and despite the circumstances he wanted to do it properly. He had also stopped on his way to buy her a small bouquet of flowers. Behind him was rank upon rank of elaborate arrangements from the flower cart, but Henry had brought her two tiny sprays of pink roses, just like the ones he had given her on the night long ago before she had become Lady Marguerite.

For a second the tears stung Margery's eyes but she blinked them back. She saw that Henry had a copy of the *Mercury* in his hand and the breath caught in her throat, tight and painful. He threw it aside and came forward to take her hands as she reached the bottom step.

"I'm so sorry," she said brokenly. The grief was back, searing her chest with hot tears. "So sorry that this has happened."

Henry shook his head. "You are not to blame," he said fiercely. "It is my fault."

Chessie touched his arm. "You should be in private," she said, and Henry nodded. He took Margery gently by the hand and led her into the drawing room. It was so bright with sunlight that it hurt her eyes. She threw her hat and spencer down on a chair and turned back to him. She was so anxious that she could not wait.

"Will you marry me, please?" she burst out.

Henry's lips twitched into the smile she loved but his eyes were grave. "It would be my privilege," he said.

He said nothing of love, but Margery had not expected it. She trusted him. If, all her life, she felt the ache of loss in not having his love, she at least knew he was not like her father. He would never leave her. He would always stand by her side.

She smiled and he took her hands and drew her toward him and kissed her very gently. And so they were engaged.

CHAPTER TWENTY

*The Six of Cups: Memory. The answer to a question
lies in the past*

"MOLL!"

Margery had been shopping for bridal clothes in Oxford Street with Joanna Grant and Tess Rothbury, and
had just dropped the ladies back in Bedford Street when
she heard Jem hailing the carriage from the other side
of the road.

It was a beautiful July day. Traffic on the streets
was light. Members of the ton were starting to drift
away from London to their country estates to escape
the heat. Margery's wedding was planned for a week's
time, at Templemore, and she could not wait to return
to the country. Holding her head high and facing down
the gossip in the full storm of all the lurid newspaper
headlines had been one of the hardest things she had
ever done in her life.

It had been amusing to see Lady Wardeaux torn between gratification at the match she had wanted for so
long and outraged disapproval at the way Margery and
her son had behaved before they were engaged.

"Really, Henry, I do believe that you have a great
deal more of your papa in you than I had ever imagined," she had said, on seeing the lurid headlines in the

scandal sheets. "That sort of bad behavior comes from the Wardeaux side of the family."

Later, when Henry was absent, she had spoken to Margery.

"No lady would ever behave the way that you have done, Marguerite," she had said. "And if they had, they would not have been caught."

"So, my sin was to be found out rather than to sleep with Henry in the first place," Margery complained to Chessie later.

"Well, of course," Chessie said, smiling. "Ladies behave badly all the time, Margery, but as long as no one finds out, everyone can pretend they are not."

"I never was very good at pretending," Margery said gloomily.

Chessie, Lady Grant and Lady Rothbury had been at her side every moment of the scandal, forcing her to go out when she would rather have pulled the bedcovers over her head and hidden away, helping her through the disgrace that had stolen her fragile confidence and forced her even further into the glare of publicity.

"You should see what the papers used to write about me," Tess Rothbury had said one day when they were in Gunters taking hot chocolate together. "And only half of it was true. The other half I wish I had tried, but alas I never did."

Henry, too, had been stalwart in his support, always beside her. No one dared say a word when Henry was there. But it was her grandfather whom Margery most regretted hurting. Not once had Lord Templemore reproached her, but she felt guilty through and through.

"Moll!" Jem shouted again and Margery rapped on the roof for the carriage to stop. The groom let down the steps and Jem bounded in to throw himself down on the seat opposite her.

"Hell's bells," he said, eying the huge piles of shopping with disfavor. "How can one small bride require so many clothes?"

"I'm not sure," Margery confessed. Ladies Grant and Rothbury were truly terrifying once they hit the shops and she had come away with bandboxes piled high with an astonishing number of items. Some of the underwear and nightgowns had made her blush, lacy, transparent, barely there. She imagined Henry would appreciate them once they were safely wed and allowed to be alone together again. Now that they were formally engaged, she was strictly chaperoned to make sure there was no more scandal.

The carriage turned into Bedford Square. Some of the bandboxes started to tilt at a precarious angle and Margery put out a hand to steady them.

"I say, Moll." Jem leaned toward her. She could smell wine on his breath even though it was only the middle of the afternoon. "Could you lend me some cash? My pockets are to let."

"I don't have any cash," Margery said, dismayed. Over the past few weeks she had heard all manner of rumors about Jem's profligate spending. His gambling losses were particularly acute. Barnard had also confided in her that a number of small items of gold and silver had disappeared from Templemore House. Margery knew exactly where they had gone. She had put temptation in front of her brother and he had been unable to resist.

"I cannot give you any money, Jem," she said firmly.

"You know my fortune is all in trust. All I have is my allowance."

"You could ask your grandfather," Jem said. His mouth set in an obstinate line. "He'd pay up. I dropped two thousand pounds at faro last night and they are dunning me for payment. Tell him there'll be another scandal if he doesn't settle the bill." His gaze swept over the parcels and bandboxes. He scowled. "It's not fair, Moll."

"No, it isn't," Margery snapped. She was furious at his attempt to blackmail her into getting him some money. "Life isn't fair, Jem. How many times have you told me that in the past? That doesn't mean you should go around stealing just because you don't have everything you want."

Jem turned a dull brick-red. "Never thought you'd notice," he said. "I suppose it was that poxy butler. Might have known he would keep a list."

"Of course he does," Margery said. "It's his job. This has to stop, Jem." She leaned forward and put a hand on his arm. "I'm worried about you. The gambling and the drinking and all those women—"

"Devil a bit," Jem said. He broke into a grin though his eyes were cold. "Can't a fellow have a bit of fun?" He shrugged, the casual gesture full of bitterness. "Let's not talk about it anymore." He turned his face away and stared fixedly out of the window at the bustling streets.

"All right," Margery said. She felt miserable. She knew this was not the end. It could not be, not with Jem. She had known for years that he was weak in some ways. He could not resist the lure of money. She had chosen to ignore it because she liked him and because he had always been on her side. Until now.

There was a shout in the street outside and the car-

riage pulled to an abrupt halt. Margery and half the
bandboxes and parcels cascaded onto the floor. The lids
came off the boxes. Silks and laces spilled around her
in a sea of tumbling color. She sprawled on the floor
of the carriage with her trousseau frothing about her.

Jem was laughing. He leaned down, extending a
hand to help her. "Here you go," he said. "Take my
hand. We'd better get you home before anything else
happens."

Take my hand. We'd better get you home.

Margery froze, gooseflesh breathing along her skin.
With no warning and a terrifying and vivid suddenness,
the darkness in her memory lifted. She was four years
old again, and she was in a carriage, and the night was
black, and it was raining and the door of the coach was
swinging open and Jem was looking down on her and
extending a hand.

*Why, what have we here? Take my hand, sweetheart.
I'll take you home....*

She gave a gasp. For a moment, she thought she was
going mad. She could see her mother's body sprawled
on the seat and smell the gunpowder in the air. And
there was blood. Jem was smiling as he bent to pick up
little four-year-old Marguerite. His body was warm as
he held her close and she could smell his scent and see
the way his fair hair fell across his brow.

A dream. A nightmare.

Margery opened her mouth, but no words came.

Jem was still holding out a hand to her. She did not
move. She saw his expression change. Wariness came
into his blue eyes, and then sharp awareness.

"I knew you would remember one day," he said. He
spoke easily, conversationally, but the look in his eyes

was colder than a whetted knife. He stuffed his hands in his pockets and sat back. "I was afraid that you would remember one day."

Terror closed Margery's throat. She tried to find the words to deny it but already it was too late. She knew Jem had seen in her face that she knew the truth.

"It was you," she whispered. "You killed my mother."

Jem shrugged. "It was me," he said.

"Why?"

Jem laughed. The sound ripped the air. It was loud and incongruous. "For the money, of course," he said. "You know me, Moll. Why else?"

Then his hands were about her throat, tight as a vise. The blood roared in Margery's ears and she struggled and fought amid the cascading piles of bridal clothes, but it was no use. Jem was too strong. She felt consciousness slide away as the darkness came.

MARGERY WAS NOT SURE how long she was unconscious. She woke feeling sick, dizzy and disoriented. For a long moment she could not remember anything that had happened, then the images came rushing back, images of the carriage, of Jem, his hands about her neck. Her throat felt terrible, sore and bruised. Her entire body ached.

She opened her eyes and squinted at her surroundings. She was being dragged up a staircase like a bag of coal, her body bumping on every tread. There was no carpet on the steps and the wood was old and splintered, scraping the back of her legs, pulling on her hair. Jem was carrying her. She could hear him swearing as he heaved her upward. She allowed her head to slump forward onto her chest to give the impression that she was still dead to the world. The very last thing that she wanted was for Jem to realize that she had regained consciousness.

Jem pulled her around a turn of the stair. There was a scent in the air now. It was elusive, teasing Margery's nostrils, a heavy perfume, and out of place against a background of peeled walls and bare boards.

Light flared for a second and Margery screwed up her eyes against the brightness. Then it was gone. She felt herself lifted and tossed carelessly aside. She braced herself for a hard landing but instead rolled over in the yielding folds of a mattress that smelled old, of dust and damp. Somehow the reek of it filled her with desolation as though she were locked away forever in a room imbued with lost hopes and despair.

Sound faded. She was alone. She opened her eyes and blinked painfully. Everything seemed to hurt. Needles of light exploded in her head. Her throat was rough and dry. She could feel her stomach rising. She lay still, trying to quell both the sickness and the panic.

When she felt a little better she opened her eyes again and saw that the room she was in was small and lit by faint daylight from a dirty window far above her head. She could see a slice of rooftop, a chimney pot and a pale piece of blue sky, but that was all. She was in an attic, then, with a tiny dormer window and no way of climbing out. There was a door, though. She slid off the bed, being very careful to make no sound, and crept over to it, steadying herself against the wall as the dizziness threatened to engulf her.

She could hear voices. One was Jem. The other was familiar, too, a woman's voice, angry and vicious.

"Why would you bring her here, you fool, and in full daylight? I want no part in this."

Jem replied, too low for Margery to hear though she strained her ear against the panel of the door.

"Get rid of her!" The woman's voice again. "You know plenty of people who could tip her in the Thames, no questions asked. You could do it yourself. Just don't involve me!"

Again Jem's voice, louder this time, rising with anger. "You'll do as I ask, you old bitch, or I'll drag you into this so deep you'll drown. Who do you think finds you the best girls for your filthy trade and makes sure they stay in line? Who pays for the roof over your head?" His voice quieted again. "All I'm asking is that you keep her here while I go and rattle the old man's cage for some money."

"Then you'll give me my cut, too!"

Margery pressed a hand hard against her mouth to smother her sickness and fear. She recognized the voice now, and the elusive smell of perfume. The woman was Mrs. Tong and this was the Temple of Venus.

Jem and Mrs. Tong were in business together. She felt sickened. Jem as pimp to the girls and financier to Mrs. Tong. It was the violent underside to the trade that she had always tried to ignore.

Horror and cold fear rolled over Margery, setting her teeth chattering. In her heart of hearts she had always known that Jem was in bad company. He had run wild even in his teens. He could only have been fifteen when he had stopped her mother's carriage in the robbery that had gone so dreadfully wrong. And now he planned to blackmail her grandfather into paying for her.

She had loved Jem the best of all her brothers. He

had protected her and watched over her and fought her
battles for her, and all the time he had been the one who
knew the bitter truth of her identity and her mother's
death. She wondered if he had protected her out of guilt
for taking her mother's life. She realized she would
probably never know.

She remembered everything about the night she had
disappeared. She could see it running out like a silken
thread through her memory, unrolling in all its horror.
Her parents had quarreled and her mother had bundled
her back into the carriage. They had driven off through
the night, the London streets giving way to the dark
countryside. All the while her mother had cried, and
Margery had sat still and frozen in a corner, shrinking
as small as she could to escape the misery she could
feel but not understand.

She saw it in images and emotions, not as one con-
tinuous memory. There was the sudden shift and sway
of the carriage as it had come to a halt, the sound of
a shot and the blast of cold air as the door had swung
open. Her mother was screaming, then nothing, nothing but blackness and the cold and Jem scooping her up
and taking her away to his home where there had been
warmth and candlelight. There had been food, too—a
rough broth Margery could remember even now. She
had felt kindness—Mrs. Mallon hugging her tight and
saying she had always wanted a daughter....

She was left with an overwhelming feeling of loneliness. She raised a hand to her face and felt it wet with
tears again.

The rest were memories from a new and different
life, and now she wondered if the shock of the experience as a small child had wiped the entire episode from

her mind until she had seen Mr. Churchward and started the painful process of memory.

She frowned. There was one small piece of memory missing, a shadowy figure who had also been there that night, standing by the carriage in a waft of veils, a clatter of bracelets and the scent of lily of the valley. Margery shuddered, blinked. She saw the face of Lady Emily Templemore.

Lady Emily. It seemed impossible, mad. Yet she was certain that Lady Emily had been involved. She thought of the accidents at Templemore and Lady Emily's repeated questions to her from the very first day.

My, what a striking resemblance you bear to your late grandmama...not your mama, she was tall. Do you recall anything about her?

Lady Emily must have been terrified that she would remember what had happened. Every day she must have been afraid. Margery rubbed her temples. They ached fiercely. The only thing that made no sense was why Lady Emily would have wanted her mother dead. Emily had been illegitimate at birth and could never have inherited Templemore.

The voices had faded now. There was a silence. Margery waited, listened. Then she put out a hand, groped for the doorknob and turned it stealthily.

The door was locked. She felt her hopes sink. She sat back against the wall, curling her legs up, resting her head against the flaking plaster of the wall. The scent of dampness and decay was in her nostrils now. She felt cold.

After a little while she stirred herself and scrubbed the tears from her cheeks. A tiny flicker of rebellion kindled in her and grew stronger. She was not going to sit around here waiting for Jem to dispose of her in a sack in the Thames. He thought he had won. She was going to show him he had not. She thought of Henry, too, and felt possessed by a fierce, bright determination. Henry would never let Jem's blackmail succeed. He would do everything he could to find her. She felt it, felt such faith and love in him, as strong and powerful as anything she had felt in her life before. She knew without a shadow of doubt that it would be enough to bring him to her through the dark.

"THIS IS VERY BAD," Mr. Churchward said. His hand shook slightly as he read the ransom note. "Very bad indeed."

No one was inclined to contradict him. The atmosphere in the drawing room of Templemore House was bleak. No one believed that Jem Mallon would release Margery alive even if the earl did as requested and paid the seventy thousand pounds that Jem was demanding.

It was night, full dark. The curtains were drawn and the candles lit. Around the table sat Henry, Mr. Churchward, the Earl of Templemore, Garrick Farne, Alex Grant and Owen Rothbury who, as soon as they had received Henry's note, had come to offer their services in the search for Margery.

The first indication that anything was wrong had been the return that afternoon of the carriage with the groom and coachman badly beaten. They had told Henry that they had been bringing Margery home from Bedford Square when they had stopped to pick up Jem Mallon. He had directed the coach away from Grosvenor Street toward the river on some errand but once they were trapped down a narrow back street with no escape they had been toppled from the carriage, clubbed viciously and sent back, reeling and shaken. Of Margery there was no sign.

Henry knew he would never forget how he had felt then, no matter how long he lived. Something had fractured inside him. Obligation and duty fell aside leaving his emotions painfully and dangerously exposed, as they had been the night at Templemore when Margery had run from him.

Then, he had refused to confront his demons. He had turned away from love when Margery had offered it to him. He had not even acknowledged in his own mind that he had loved her on that hot and passionate night when she had given him her body and her soul.

Instead, he had dismissed what he felt as need, as lust and passion, and he had run from love because he did not dare open himself to hurt as fearlessly as Margery had done.

It was late to realize his mistake, but he was not prepared to accept that it was too late. He would find Margery and he would tell her he loved her.

Henry had gone out then, down to the river where the carriage had been ambushed, trying to pick up news, any news, of what might have happened to Margery and where Jem might have taken her.

Farne and Rothbury and Grant had scoured the town all afternoon and evening for a word, for a whisper of Margery's whereabouts, but there had been none. Henry refused to give up hope, because to do so would be to abandon Margery and that was impossible, unimaginable, but as time slipped by and there was no word, he felt the fear for her wedge itself in his blood.

They had called Churchward in to find out if they

could draw on his extensive investigations into Jem Mallon's business in case it offered any clues. It read like a list of all the most criminal and disreputable enterprises in London: illegal clubs, drinking dens and brothels, shops dealing in stolen goods, gangs running extortion rackets and all manner of other lawbreaking.

"I did try to warn everyone at the time," Churchward had said unhappily.

Then the ransom note had arrived, demanding the money and threatening to kill Margery if Lord Templemore refused to pay or anyone tried to find her. Shockingly, Lady Emily Templemore had gone into hysterics then, screaming that it was all her fault, that she had never wanted Margery dead, only for her to go away before she remembered everything. Lady Emily had sobbed as she confessed to paying Jem to kidnap Rose Saint-Pierre twenty years before.

"I didn't want him to kill her," she cried, a sodden hiccupping mass of grief. "I told him I just wanted her to go away, far away, somewhere I would never see her again. It was for Antoine." She had clutched at Henry's sleeve with desperate fingers. "I loved him. We would meet sometimes at the Temple of Venus.... I was so afraid he would take Rose back and I would lose him." Her hand fell. "I only wanted her to go away," she said tonelessly. "She had everything I wanted. It was not fair...."

Henry had seen Lord Templemore shrink in on himself as he realized the extent of his half sister's guilt and the wretched grief and misery that had driven her. The doctor had come to give Lady Emily a sedative and now she slept, Lady Wardeaux at her bedside, and the earl had downed a stiff brandy without a word, his knuckles white on the head of his cane, his face withered and drawn as he relived the loss of his daughter.

"I'll find Margery," Henry had said fiercely to the earl. "I swear it. I'll find her and bring her back to you."

He saw the fear in the earl's eyes then, and the knowledge they both shared, that Jem would never let Margery go.

"I'm going out again," Henry said. He caught sight of himself in the mirror, pale and drawn with exhaustion, filthy from the streets, haunted with fear for Margery. "I'll start checking the places on Churchward's list."

"I'll come with you," Garrick said at once. Alex and Owen stood up, too. They gulped down hot coffee and prepared to go out again into the night. Henry felt each second, each minute, stretching out unbearably. He felt exhausted, yet intolerably awake and on edge. He would not permit himself, even for a moment, to think that he might not see Margery again.

The street door opened suddenly and three ladies came in from the night, sparking with jewels, wrapped in silk.

"Joanna," Alex Grant said, pausing as he swung his great coat about his shoulders. "You should not be here."

"Nonsense, Alex," Lady Grant said robustly.

"Have you found Margery?" Tess Rothbury demanded.

"No," Owen said. "Not yet."

"In that case," Merryn Farne said, "you need our help."

"I really don't think—" Garrick began.

Merryn quelled him with a look. "Garrick, darling," she said, "you know that we all care about what happens to Margery. She has been so loyal to us all in the past that we owe it to her now. Let us help you."

"All right," Henry said. He was willing to accept any help if it meant that they found Margery. "We're going to divide up all the places connected to Jem Mallon," he said, passing Joanna the list. Tess and Merryn crowded around, looking over her shoulder.

"It's a long shot," Henry said, "but it's the best we can do."

Tess was rapidly scanning the list. "This will take days," she murmured. "It covers every conceivable illegal activity in London."

"I know," Henry said. He felt his heart sink and forced himself not to lose hope. He took the list back and read it again. His mind felt fuzzy with tiredness. He felt as though he was missing something important, trying to make a link that was just beyond his reach.

Mallon is part owner of The Hoop and Grapes flash house, he read, in Mr. Churchward's neat hand. He could almost feel the lawyer's disapproval. *He also part funds the brothel at The Temple of Venus....*

"I know Mrs. Tong at the Temple of Venus," Tess said suddenly. "We go back many years. Even if she does not know where Margery is, she might be able to give us the name of someone who does, or tell us where to find Jem Mallon."

"She'd never help you," Henry said.

Tess smiled sweetly. "Oh, I think she will."

Garrick looked at Henry, who nodded.

"Let's go," he said.

CHAPTER TWENTY-ONE

The Chariot: Victory. The force of destiny

MARGERY SWIFTLY REALIZED that, as she could not get out the door, the only way was up through the skylight and out onto the roof. She did not like heights but that was irrelevant since it was a matter of life and death. She dragged the battered bed beneath the tiny attic window. The light was fading now and night was coming on. As it was high summer, she calculated that it must be almost eleven o'clock. If Jem was waiting until full dark to dispose of her, she did not have much time left.

By standing on the wooden rail at the base of the bed, Margery was able to reach up to a bar fixed to the ceiling beneath the window. Since this was a brothel she suspected that it had some sort of sexual purpose because there were chains hanging down from it.

She did not allow her mind to dwell on the use of either the bar or the chains and concentrated on them solely as a means of escape. She had spent many times as a child swinging on the ropes that her brothers had slung between the trees in the Wantage woods. Chains were no different.

Climbing in a muslin gown and slippers was, however, a lot less easy than it had been in the hand-me-down trews and boots she had worn as a child. Soon her slippers fell off and her skirts were in shreds but she reached the bar on the ceiling and pushed against the dirty skylight.

It did not budge. She pushed harder, clinging to the bar with one hand and pushing with the other, but she could get little purchase. The window squeaked and shifted but did not open. She knew she was going to have to break it.

Far below her—she risked a quick look down and felt a little queasy—a brass candlestick stood on the dresser. There was nothing for it. She shimmied down the chains again and they clanked softly together. She grabbed the candlestick and started back up again, the candlestick tucked into the waist of her gown. Suddenly, with no warning whatsoever, the chains started to uncoil. Her weight, small as it was, had obviously operated some sort of long-neglected mechanism and now it cranked into action. As Margery hung on for dear life, the chains unrolled and rattled down, faster and faster, depositing her painfully on the floor. She did not even have time to gather her breath before a hidden trapdoor opened and she fell straight through.

Gasping, the breath knocked out of her, she lay on the rug in the room below. There was light and sound. Someone was screaming. Margery opened her eyes and looked up at an enormous bed where one of Mrs. Tong's whores was peering around the large, naked shoulder of the man on top of her and shrieking fit to burst.

Margery scrambled to her feet. The screaming stopped.

"Oh, it's you, Margery," the redhead on the bed said. "Sorry, didn't recognize you for a moment."

The fat peer hauled himself off the girl like a bad-tempered walrus. "You're putting me off my stroke," he said peevishly. "Have you come to join us?"

"I thank you, but no," Margery said, averting her eyes. "I'm so sorry to disturb you, Miss Kitty. Please excuse me." She edged toward the door.

"Got any of those marzipan cakes?" Kitty called as the man climbed back on top of her.

"Not tonight!" Margery shouted. She grabbed a thick braided whip off the dresser—the perfect weapon—and slipped out the door.

From the landing it sounded as though all hell was breaking out in the hall below. Margery leaned over the banisters and her knees weakened with relief at what she saw. She had planned to sneak out by the servants' entrance, but she had wondered how she might get past Mrs. Tong's burly doormen if they were in the hall.

Now she saw that the problem was solved. In the center of the tiled hall of the brothel stood Tess Rothbury. She was facing Mrs. Tong and holding a tiny silver pistol in her hand. On one side of her was Joanna Grant and on the other was Merryn Farne. At the door a mill was in full swing. Henry had already laid out one of the doormen with a blow that had him reeling across the floor. Garrick Farne was dealing with a second. A third stood irresolute looking from Henry to the pistol in Alex Grant's hand. Henry turned to him.

"Try," he invited.

For one long moment Margery allowed herself simply to look at Henry. His usually immaculate clothes were disheveled, as though he had thrown them on in a hurry. His chin was dark with stubble and his face gray with fatigue. He looked like a man on a mission, one who would let nothing stand in his way. Margery could feel the driving tension in him and the absolute determination. She drank it in and she loved him for it.

At the sound of the fight in the hall below, all the doors along the landing had flown open and now customers and girls in various states of undress had shot out to see what was going on. Peers whom Margery recognized were hastily pulling on their breeches.

"Good evening, your grace," Margery said cheerfully as the Duke of Cumnor hurried past, dragging on his jacket in such a rush that he had both arms down one sleeve.

"Your servant, Lady Marguerite," the duke puffed. "Must be going! If my mama were to hear about this there would be hell to pay."

"I'll have the fair-haired one at the back," Miss Kitty said, craning over Margery's shoulder to look at Owen Rothbury. "He looks luscious."

"I'd rather have the tall, dark and handsome one," Miss Martha said, with a voluptuous shiver, gazing at Henry. "He's gorgeous and he knows how to fight dirty."

"They're taken, girls," Margery said.

Mrs. Tong, seeing her henchmen fall, seemed inclined to turn tail and run, but Joanna and Merryn between them had grabbed her before she could flee. Tess was speaking in cut-glass tones that carried up to the landing above.

"Mrs. Tong," she said, "please do make this easy for yourself. We believe that Lady Marguerite Saint-Pierre is here, held under duress. We have come to take her back."

Mrs. Tong had turned pale under her paint. She gave Tess a sickly smile. "Why, you're a one, aren't you, madam," she said archly. "Bursting in here, causing a mill! I don't know anything about this Lady Marguerite—"

Margery heard Henry swear but Tess simply looked at Mrs. Tong for a full thirty seconds before she said, "Shall we start again, Mrs. Tong? Think hard now, before you refuse to help. If you do not release Lady Marguerite immediately we will search the entire brothel until we find her, and then we will turn you over to the authorities for your part in kidnap and abduction. I really do not think you would want that—would you?"

"My, she's a cool one," Miss Kitty whispered in Margery's ear.

"I know," Margery said. "I want to be like her when I grow up."

She was about to step forward and reveal herself when the brothel door burst open and Jem came in with a couple of men a few steps behind him. Immediately the tableau in the hall shifted. One of the men went down to a punishing right hook from Owen Rothbury. The other turned tail and ran. Henry drew himself up and looked at Jem.

"You *bastard*," he said.

Jem had a knife. Margery saw the glint of it in the candlelight.

"Henry!" she yelled.

Both Henry and Jem looked up instinctively. Quick as a flash, Margery picked up one of Mrs. Tong's priapic marble statues and dropped it over the balcony. It fell like a stone and caught Jem by the shoulder, knocking him to the floor then shattering into a dozen pieces. Henry pounced on Jem, kicking the knife away and dragging him to his feet, but only so he could knock him down again.

"Take him away," he said to Garrick and Alex. "Just get him out of my sight before I kill him."

Margery ran to the top of the staircase. The last time she had descended it, she had been a lady's maid and she had crept down to find Henry waiting for her in the hall below. Now she walked down the center of the red carpet, in her bare feet and ripped muslin dress, with the whip in one hand, the candlestick in the other and Mrs. Tong's girls trailing her like bawdy bridesmaids.

Suddenly she realized that it did not matter who she was, Margery Mallon or Lady Marguerite Saint-Pierre; to Mrs. Tong's girls she had always been the maid who had brought them delicious marzipan treats. To Joanna and Tess, and the other scandalous ladies she had worked for, she had been a loyal friend and far more than a servant, and now they had repaid that loyalty by coming for her when she needed them.

"Thank you for the rescue party," she said, a little breathlessly as she reached the bottom step. "I do appreciate it very much."

Mrs. Tong's face had convulsed with fury. "How the devil did you get out?"

"I swung on the manacles in the ceiling and fell through the trapdoor into Miss Kitty's chamber," Margery said serenely. She heard Owen Rothbury give a splutter of laughter.

"Tess evidently taught you well," he said.

Then Henry was there, striding through the crowd, dragging her into his arms. Henry as Margery had never seen him before, cool reserve shattered, his eyes blazing dark, shaking as he pulled her to him and kissed her in front of everyone.

"I thought I had lost you," he said against her hair, and his voice was so hoarse she barely recognized it. "Margery…" He kissed her again, with raw desperation and need. Margery could feel him shaking, pouring out all that he felt, the yearning and the promise.

"I love you," he said, when he released her. "I love you so much."

"Oh!" Margery said. Her heart felt as though it was going to burst with happiness. "Henry. I have so wanted to hear you say that."

She returned his kiss in full measure before she drew back and cupped his cheek in one loving hand. She saw his eyes close at her touch and heard him sigh.

"We have an audience," she whispered.

Henry smiled down into her eyes. "I don't mind," he said. His voice was rough with emotion. "I want everyone to know I love you. It's about time I admitted it."

And he kissed her again.

HENRY STOOD ON THE TERRACE below Margery's bedroom window at Templemore House. Light was starting to filter across the eastern sky in radiant pink and blue. It was going to be another beautiful summer day.

Henry had not slept. They had taken Margery back to Templemore House where she had thrown herself into her grandfather's arms and cried and clung to him, and Lord Templemore had looked close to tears himself. He had shaken Henry's hand with speechless gratitude and then given Henry a fierce hug, too, while Lady Wardeaux clucked with shock.

"Hugging!" she complained. "Such bad ton!"

"It's a special occasion," Henry said.

There had been no opportunity for Henry and Margery to speak, because Chessie and Lady Wardeaux had carried Margery off to have a bath and sleep. Eventually the uproar in the house had subsided. Barnard had shepherded the servants off to their beds and Lord Templemore had retired.

Henry was pouring himself a brandy in the library when he heard Margery's voice calling to him from outside.

He walked out onto the terrace and looked up. Margery was leaning over her balcony, small and ethereal in a transparent white nightgown, her long golden-brown hair tumbled about her shoulders.

"At last!" she said. "I thought you would never hear me." She smiled. "Are you coming up?"

"Certainly not," Henry said, trying to drag his gaze away from the nightgown and the way that the candlelight from the room behind illuminated it in the most intriguing places. "You should be resting. You have had an ordeal."

"I know," Margery said. "That is why I simply cannot be left alone." She leaned over a little farther. The nightgown slid from one round shoulder and dipped to reveal the hollow between her breasts. Henry swallowed hard.

"Please, Henry," Margery said. "You would not want me to be frightened."

"Minx," Henry said. He eyed the ivy that cascaded down the wall. He had not climbed it for about twenty years and he had been a great deal lighter then. He set his foot to the first thick branch. The entire structure shivered.

"Did I ever tell you that I am scared of heights?" he asked grimly, gritting his teeth and pushing away thoughts of falling and being found sprawled on the terrace with several broken bones.

"I am sure you can do it for me," Margery said, leaning over farther so that the fine lace of the nightgown pulled tightly across her breasts and almost caused him to lose his footing completely.

"Thank goodness," she added, as he reached the stone balcony and hauled himself over, breathing hard. "I have been so lonely and afraid here on my own."

She put her arms about him and pressed close, so that Henry could feel every soft curve of her squashed against him.

He could also smell brandy. He caught her by the upper arms and held her away from him. "You're foxed."

Margery beamed at him. Her gray eyes were slumberous. She felt deliciously warm and yielding beneath his hands.

"They gave me brandy," she said. "Chessie gave me some and then your mother gave me some and then Edith brought me some more..." The other shoulder of her nightgown slid down and her head drooped a little like a cut flower. "I do confess to feeling a little sleepy," she confided. "Perhaps you could put me to bed now."

Put me to bed. Dear God. If ever a man was offered the precise opportunity he craved...

Henry scooped Margery up in his arms and carried her back inside her bedroom, sliding her beneath the turned-back bedclothes and pulling them up respectably all the way to her neck. There was no possible way, he told himself severely, that he was going to make love to a woman who was half-drunk and half-asleep, who had suffered a terrifying ordeal and needed to rest. Despite the tormented ache of his body, which was almost enough to drive him to perdition, he would act the gentleman and leave her to sleep. He turned away and tiptoed toward the door.

"Henry." Margery's voice stopped him when he was halfway across the room. "Please don't leave me. I don't want to be alone."

She sat up. The nightgown, so pale and virginal, slid innocently down the slopes of her breasts to leave one pink nipple partially exposed through the lace. Henry almost groaned.

"Margery," he said. "I really should go—"

She held out a hand to him. "You would not, I hope, reject a request from a lady," she said. She patted the bed beside her. "All I want you to do is hold me so that I feel safe."

Expressed like that, it would have been churlish of him to refuse. Or so Henry told himself later. He went back to the bed and took off his jacket and boots, very conscious of Margery's bright gaze watching him. He was about to lie down beside her when she put out an imperious hand.

"You cannot go to bed with your clothes on," she said. "Everyone knows that."

She was definitely foxed. Henry sighed. He stripped off his cravat and shirt. The breeches, he was determined, would stay on despite the fact they currently felt several sizes too small.

He slid into bed beside her. She immediately rolled into the curve of his arm, made a very happy sound and fell asleep. Henry felt awed and full of wonder, as though someone had given him a very precious gift.

It felt almost too much, as though he did not deserve it, as though something would snatch such happiness away from him.

He smoothed his hand down Margery's back, gently caressing the flare of her waist and the curve of her buttock. It was to soothe her, he promised himself. There was nothing sexual about it. He would not take advantage of an unconscious woman. Margery made another sleepy, happy sound and wriggled against him, so Henry stroked her again, and then again. This time the sound she made in response was definitely more sensual than sleepy. Henry licked her bare shoulder, letting his teeth graze her collarbone. Margery rolled back, away from him, eyes closed, a little smile on her lips. With one sinuous wiggle she shed the nightgown and lay naked and quite abandoned, her body open to him in flagrant invitation.

Henry struggled with his conscience for all of a minute then he bent his head to her breasts, teasing their peaks, kissing a path across the delicious swell of her stomach, dipping his tongue in her navel. Her legs parted invitingly, she arched in demand, but instead of obliging her, he rolled her over onto her front.

She gave a little squeak of surprise and then a sigh as he straddled her, brushed her hair over her left shoulder and started to kiss his way down her spine, his tongue flicking over her ribs, leaving not an inch of her skin untouched. She was shivering now, little delighted quivers that raised the goose bumps on her skin.

Henry bit down gently on the swell of her buttock and with great deliberation let his tongue dip into the tantalizing gap at the top of her thighs. This time she moaned and jerked beneath him, trying to turn over to face him again. He allowed her to roll over then slid his hand between her thighs to find the soft, damp core of her. He gave her one sly stroke. Her body jerked against his fingers, begging for more. He made her wait then did it again, each slide of his hand driving her higher, closer to completion.

Her hair was a mass of tumbled brown silk, her face stung pink with arousal, her lips parted. Her eyes were still closed and her lashes spiky against her cheeks. Henry watched her entire body tremble for him.

She opened her eyes. "Please, Henry," she said. Her voice was barely a whisper and her gaze was unfocused, lost. "Please."

Henry felt lost, too, utterly adrift with unfamiliar emotion. She looked so tempting and abandoned. He felt awed simply to touch her. She was all gentleness and vulnerability, strength and sweetness.

"Please," she begged again.

Henry pushed her thighs apart and placed his mouth against the hot center of her. She came at once, grabbing a pillow to smother her screams, biting on it as he held her down by the hips and licked her until she shattered again and again, arching under his hands. Her body convulsed with heat and pleasure until finally she lay tumbled in uninhibited bliss, and her gasps for breath were the only sound in the quiet room.

Henry watched her as she returned to consciousness, watched the flutter of her lashes and the slow, satiated movements of her body. He felt as though he would never tire of watching her, which was wonderful because he would have an entire lifetime to enjoy with her. He truly was the most fortunate man in the world.

Eventually she propped herself up on her elbows and

looked at him through half-closed eyes that glittered a deep, sensual gray.

"How glad I am," she said, a little smile curving her lips, "that you decided to stay with me." She glanced down. Her eyes widened to their farthest extent.

"Oh, my goodness," she said faintly.

Henry was sporting an enormous erection. It was not that he had not noticed, simply that somewhere along the way, arousing Margery had become more important than seeking his own pleasure.

Margery shifted, drawing him to her, their kiss a mixture of tenderness and desire. Henry slid into her slick body and felt her sigh with renewed delight. He took it as slowly as he could, drawing nearly out of her, surging back within, keeping the rhythm as slow and steady as he could.

The clasp of her body and the caress of her hands were almost too much for him, and when she came again, the vortex of pleasure became so intense it was almost pain and he emptied himself within her in the most explosive climax of his life.

He drew Margery close, holding her as though he would never let her go. She opened her eyes. They were as bright as stars. Her lips curved into the most perfect smile.

"I love you so much, Henry," she said, pressing a soft kiss to his lips. "So very much."

The pang of emotion that hit Henry then almost felled him. He thought of the cold expanse of his past, and the risk he had taken on love when he had been young, and how empty and shallow that feeling had been compared to the strength of his emotions now.

"I'm sorry it took me so long to recognize how much

I love you," he said, his voice ragged. "I'm not good at this. I don't like losing control."

He felt the laughter ripple through her. "I had noticed."

"But I'll do it for you," Henry said. "I will love you and cherish you and lay my heart beneath your feet—"

She stopped him with another kiss. "You already have done," she said dreamily.

Without her, he was not whole. She knew that without words. Her arms tightened about him and the world felt a sweet peaceful place again. The last of his barriers fell. She was his, his anchor, the still center he needed. He whispered again that he loved her. It was getting easier to say the words. In time he suspected he might even grow to like it.

"I want to tell you about Isobel," he said.

Margery opened her eyes wide. "Thank you, but I don't want to talk about her now," she said.

Well, perhaps not. In time, Henry thought, he would tell her everything, everything of his youthful infatuation and the way that Isobel had ripped apart his love and his faith, and the darkness that had followed. And he would tell her how she had brought back the light.

But now Margery was touching him with tender little strokes over his shoulders and his back and his hips, and he discovered that he did not want to talk either. Her small hands roamed in very interested exploration and in a while Henry felt himself grow hard again and he groaned as he slid inside her, to worship her with fierce caresses and endless words of love.

Margery gave herself with a generosity that awed him completely. And there in her tangled sheets they held one another, united in bliss and peace.

"So you'll be marrying me for love," Henry said later, Margery in his arms, her head pillowed on his chest.

She tilted her head and smiled at him. "I will," she said. "Oh, yes, I will." Her smile became more dazzling still. "And just so that you are aware, I do not expect you to give up your work simply because you are marrying the richest heiress in the kingdom."

Henry laughed. He rolled her beneath him and held her there, pinned against him, every one of her delectable curves pressed against him.

"What if I do not want to work?"

"You must," Margery said. She drew his head down to kiss him. "The Duke of Wellington says that you are the best engineer he ever knew," she whispered. "He threatened to have you court martialed if you give up your post at the Board of Ordnance."

Much later, as he slid toward sleep, Henry remembered that he had to leave. Morning was only a few hours away and the maid could not find him here, still less his mother. He tried to get up but Margery reached out and clung to him and she was so warm and so giving that he allowed her to draw him back into her arms.

The next thing he knew it was morning and Edith was screaming and had dropped Margery's hot chocolate on the floor because somehow the covers had rolled back and he and Margery were lying there in complete abandon, naked as when they had been born.

Margery was complaining at the noise and saying that she had a headache and what had happened because she could remember nothing at all after Edith had given her brandy the previous night. For a dreadful moment

Henry had thought it was true, then he saw Margery was laughing at him, and felt a huge rush of relief.

Chessie was standing at the bottom of the bed, trying to keep her face straight while his mother picked his clothes up and threw them at him. Lady Wardeaux said that she had been wrong, he was not as bad as his father, he was much, much worse.

EPILOGUE

The Sun: Happiness and joy

EVERYONE AGREED THAT IT was a lovely wedding.

Lady Wardeaux occupied the front row of the groom's side of the church supported by her nephew the Duke of Farne, with his duchess. The Earl of Templemore gave the bride away. Alex Grant and Owen Rothbury were groomsmen. Lady Grant and Lady Rothbury were matrons of honor. The *on dit* was that Tess Rothbury was increasing, and she did indeed look radiantly happy.

Lord Stephen Kestrel escorted Lady Francesca Alton and took advantage of the occasion to ask her brother, Sir James Devlin, for Chessie's hand in marriage. Chessie and Lady Devlin cried all over each other because they were so happy. The arrival at the last minute of the groom's cousin Ethan Ryder and his wife, Lottie, was the cause for yet more celebration, and when all Mrs. Tong's girls trooped into the pews at the back looking like a flight of gaudy butterflies, the congregation was complete.

The only sorrow was that Lady Emily Templemore had not recovered her health and it seemed she might never do so. There was also the delicate fact that the bride's adoptive brother was on trial for murder, but no one allowed that to spoil the day.

At the end of the service Henry picked his mother up and spun her around and kissed her. Lady Wardeaux had declared herself scandalized, but Margery had seen tears in her eyes and thought she had almost smiled. Perhaps, Margery thought, Lady Wardeaux would one day discover that it was safe to laugh; one's face would not crack.

The wedding breakfast was lavish. Margery had made the wedding cake herself. Mrs. Tong's girls made short work of it.

"You always were a dab hand with the confectionery, Margery," Miss Kitty said. "Don't suppose you'll be able to do that now you're a lady, though."

"I'm thinking of opening my own shop," Margery said. "There's no point in being an heiress if you can't do what you want."

The whole of Templemore was lit up that night in a party for their guests, family and friends. Blazing torches lit the drive. A thousand candles illuminated the mirrored ballroom. The house had come alive. Margery, in a pale green gown and the Templemore emeralds, waited for Henry to lead her down to dance at their wedding.

He came into her dressing room, very stern and handsome in his evening clothes with a battered red velvet case in his hand. He looked at her, looked at the emeralds and smiled.

"You know how much I love you in those jewels," he said, "but I have something here you might prefer."

He held out the case to her. Margery slipped the catch. Inside, nestling on its bed of red velvet, was her golden locket. It was open. The miniatures had been cleaned and they glowed in exquisite color, her mother and her father, so haughty, so handsome, so much a pair in many ways, even if they could not be happy together.

Margery smiled radiantly at her husband. "Thank you," she whispered as she reached up to kiss him. Henry had known, she thought. He had known how much it meant to her to reclaim her past before she could step into her future. No matter who her parents were, no matter what they had done, she needed them in order to feel whole.

Henry unfastened the emeralds. Margery felt his hands shaking a little as his fingers brushed her nape. She bent her head as he placed the locket about her neck and then it was nestling warm and golden between her breasts, against her heart.

"For a little while," she said, "when I first came to Templemore, I did not know who I was, who I had become. I felt as though I was no longer Margery Mallon but I did not know how to be Marguerite Saint-Pierre."

Henry wrapped his arms about her. His warmth cradled her close.

"And now?" His breath stirred her hair.

"Now," Margery said, "I have come home."

* * * * *

An imaginative and spellbinding new tale from
New York Times bestselling author

BERTRICE SMALL

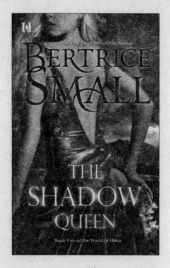

THE
SHADOW
QUEEN

Available wherever books are sold.

"Small's newest novel is a sexily fantastical romp."
—*Publishers Weekly* on *The Sorceress of Belmair*

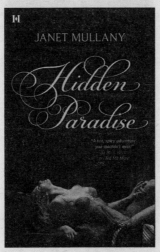

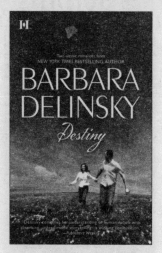

REQUEST YOUR FREE BOOKS!

2 FREE NOVELS
FROM THE ROMANCE COLLECTION
PLUS 2 FREE GIFTS!

YES! Please send me 2 FREE novels from the Romance Collection and my 2 FREE gifts (gifts are worth about $10). After receiving them, if I don't wish to receive any more books, I can return the shipping statement marked "cancel." If I don't cancel, I will receive 4 brand-new novels every month and be billed just $5.99 per book in the U.S. or $6.49 per book in Canada. That's a saving of at least 25% off the cover price. It's quite a bargain! Shipping and handling is just 50¢ per book in the U.S. and 75¢ per book in Canada.* I understand that accepting the 2 free books and gifts places me under no obligation to buy anything. I can always return a shipment and cancel at any time. Even if I never buy another book, the two free books and gifts are mine to keep forever.

194/394 MDN FELQ

Name	(PLEASE PRINT)

Address	Apt. #

City	State/Prov.	Zip/Postal Code

Signature (if under 18, a parent or guardian must sign)

Mail to the **Reader Service**:
IN U.S.A.: P.O. Box 1867, Buffalo, NY 14240-1867
IN CANADA: P.O. Box 609, Fort Erie, Ontario L2A 5X3

Not valid for current subscribers to the Romance Collection
or the Romance/Suspense Collection.

**Want to try two free books from another line?
Call 1-800-873-8635 or visit www.ReaderService.com.**

* Terms and prices subject to change without notice. Prices do not include applicable taxes. Sales tax applicable in N.Y. Canadian residents will be charged applicable taxes. Offer not valid in Quebec. This offer is limited to one order per household. All orders subject to credit approval. Credit or debit balances in a customer's account(s) may be offset by any other outstanding balance owed by or to the customer. Please allow 4 to 6 weeks for delivery. Offer available while quantities last.

Your Privacy—The Reader Service is committed to protecting your privacy. Our Privacy Policy is available online at www.ReaderService.com or upon request from the Reader Service.

We make a portion of our mailing list available to reputable third parties that offer products we believe may interest you. If you prefer that we not exchange your name with third parties, or if you wish to clarify or modify your communication preferences, please visit us at www.ReaderService.com/consumerschoice or write to us at Reader Service Preference Service, P.O. Box 9062, Buffalo, NY 14269. Include your complete name and address.

ROM11

#1 *NEW YORK TIMES* BESTSELLING AUTHOR

DEBBIE MACOMBER

A Friend or Two

Elizabeth Wainwright, an East Coast heiress in disguise, takes a job waitressing at a Fisherman's Wharf café, eager to live a simpler life. One day handsome and charismatic Andrew Breed walks in. He says he's a longshoreman, but things don't quite add up. Is Elizabeth falling in love with someone who's pretending to be something other than he claims? Is Andrew?

No Competition

Local architect Shayne Reynolds is an art collector, but when it comes to Carrie Lockett, he's as interested in the artist as he is in her work. The talented and reclusive Carrie, however, rejects his overtures, but she won't tell him why...even though he knows she returns his feelings.

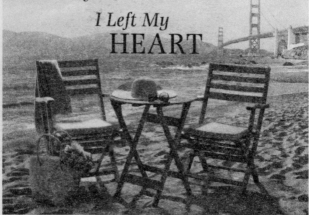

I Left My
HEART

Available wherever books are sold.

www.Harlequin.com

MDM1357

NICOLA CORNICK

77590	DESIRED	___ $7.99 U.S.	___ $9.99 CAN.
77583	NOTORIOUS	___ $7.99 U.S.	___ $9.99 CAN.
77488	MISTRESS BY MIDNIGHT	___ $7.99 U.S.	___ $9.99 CAN.
77487	ONE WICKED SIN	___ $7.99 U.S.	___ $9.99 CAN.
77440	WHISPER OF SCANDAL	___ $7.99 U.S.	___ $9.99 CAN.
77395	THE UNDOING OF A LADY	___ $7.99 U.S.	___ $8.99 CAN.
77389	THE SCANDALS OF AN INNOCENT	___ $7.99 U.S.	___ $8.99 CAN.
77377	THE CONFESSIONS OF A DUCHESS	___ $7.99 U.S.	___ $8.99 CAN.

(limited quantities available)

TOTAL AMOUNT
POSTAGE & HANDLIN
($1.00 FOR 1 BOOK,
APPLICABLE TAXES*
TOTAL PAYABLE
        (check or

To order, complete thi   money
order for the total abo   **e U.S.:**
3010 Walden Avenu   -9077;
In Canada: P.O. Bo

Name: _____
Address: _____
State/Prov.: _____
Account Number (if applicable): _____

075 CSAS

*New York residents remit applicable sales taxes.
*Canadian residents remit applicable GST and provincial taxes.